Helen MacINNES

AGENT IN PLACE

TITAN BOOKS

Agent in Place
Print edition ISBN: 9781781163351
E-book edition ISBN: 97817811643032

Published by Titan Books
A division of Titan Publishing Group Ltd
144 Southwark Street, London SE1 0UP

First edition: May 2013
10 9 8 7 6 5 4 3 2 1

A CIP catalogue record for this title is available from the British Library.

Printed and bound in Great Britain by CPI Group Ltd.

Did you enjoy this book?
We love to hear from our readers. Please email us at:
readerfeedback@titanemail.com or write to us at the above address.

To receive advance information, news, competitions, and exclusive offers
online, please sign up for the Titan newsletter on our website.

www.titanbooks.com

To Ian Douglas Highet and Eliot Chace Highet,
with all my love
Helen MacInnes

If hopes were dupes, fears may be liars

ARTHUR HUGH CLOUGH

1

The message had come at eight o'clock that morning as he was
swallowing a first cup of black coffee to clear his head and
open his eyes. But before he could cross over the short stretch
of floor between him and the telephone, the ringing stopped.
He started back to the kitchen, had barely reached its door
before he halted abruptly. The telephone rang again. Twice.
And stopped ringing. He glanced at the kitchen clock. He
would have one minute exactly before the third call. Now fully
alert, he pulled the pan of bacon and eggs away from the heat,
did not even waste another moment to turn off the electric
stove, moved at double time back into the living-room, reached
the telephone on his desk, sat down with a pencil in his hand
and a scrap of paper before him, and was ready. The message
would be in code and he had better make sure of each digit. It
had been a long long time since he had been summoned in this
way. An emergency? He controlled his excitement, smothered

all his wondering. Punctual to the second, the telephone rang again. Quickly he picked up the receiver. "Hello," he said— slow, casual, indifferent.

"Hello, hello, hello there." Two small coughs, a clearing of the throat.

He knew the voice at once. Nine years since he had last heard it, but its pattern was definite: deep, full-chested, slightly husky, the kind of voice that might break into an aria from *Prince Igor* or *Boris Godounov* with each of its notes almost a chord in itself. Mischa? Yes, Mischa. Even the initial greeting was his own sign-in phrase. Nine years since last heard, but still completely Mischa, down to the two coughs and the throat-clearing.

"Yorktown Cleaners?" Mischa was saying. "Please have my blue suit ready for delivery to 10 Old Park Place by six o'clock this evening. Receipt number is 69105A. And my name—" Slowing up of this last phrase gave the cue for a cut-in.

"Sorry—you've got the wrong number."

"Wrong number?" High indignation. "The receipt is here in my hand. 69105A."

"Wrong telephone number." Heavy patience.

"What?" The tone was now aggressive, almost accusing. Very true to life was Mischa. "Are you sure?"

"Yes!" The one-word answer was enough to let Mischa know that his prize protégé Alexis had got the message.

"Let me check—" There was a brief pause while a dogged disbeliever riffled through a couple of pages against the background noise of muted street traffic. Then Mischa spoke again from his public telephone booth, this time with sharp annoyance, "Okay, okay." Angrily, he banged down the receiver for an added touch of humour. He had always prided himself on his keen perception of Americans' behaviour patterns.

For a moment, there was complete silence in the little apartment. Mischa, Mischa... Eleven years since he first started training me, Alexis was thinking, and nine years since I last saw him. He was a major then—Major Vladimir Konov. What now? A full-fledged colonel in the KGB? Even higher? With another name too, no doubt: several other names, possibly, in that long and hidden career. And here I am, still using the cover-name Mischa gave me, still stuck in the role he assigned me in Washington. But, as Mischa used to misquote with a sardonic smile, "They also serve who only sit and wait."

Alexis recovered from his delayed shock as he noticed the sunlight shafting its way into his room from a break in the row of small Georgetown houses across the narrow street. The morning had begun; a heavy day lay ahead. He moved quickly now, preparing himself for it.

From the bookcase wall he picked out the second volume of Spengler's *Untergang des Abendlandes*—the German text scared off Alexis's American friends: they preferred it translated into *The Decline of the West*, even if the change into English lost the full meaning of the title. It ought to have been *The Decline and Fall of the West*, which might have made them think harder into the meaning of the book. With Spengler in one hand and his precious slip of paper in the other, Alexis left the sun-streaked living-room for the colder light of his dismal little kitchen. He was still wearing pyjamas and foulard dressing-gown, but even if cold clear November skies were outside the high window, he felt hot with mounting excitement. He pushed aside orange-juice and coffee-cup, tossed the *Washington Post* on to a counter-top, turned off the electric stove, and sat down at the small table crushed into one corner where no prying neighbours' eyes could see him, even if their kitchens practically rubbed sinks with his.

Now, he thought, opening the Spengler and searching for a loose sheet of paper inserted in its second chapter (*Origin and Landscape: Group of Higher Cultures*), now for Mischa's message. He had understood most of it, even at nine years' distance, but he had to be absolutely accurate. He found the loose sheet, covered with his own compressed shorthand, giving him the key to the quick scrawls he had made on the scrap of paper from his desk. He began decoding. It was all very simple—Mischa's way of thumbing his nose at the elaborate cleverness of the Americans, with their reliance on computers and technology. (Nothing, Mischa used to say and obviously still did, nothing is going to replace the well-trained agent, well-placed, well-directed. That the man had to be bright and dedicated was something that Mischa made quite sure of, before any time was wasted in training.)

Simple, Alexis thought again as he looked at the message, but effective in all its sweet innocence. "Yorktown" was New York, of course. The "blue suit" was Alexis in person. "10" meant nothing—a number that was used for padding. "Old Park Place" obviously meant the old meeting-place in the Park in New York—Central Park, as the receipt number "69105A" indicated: cancel the 10, leaving 69 for Sixty-ninth Street, 5A for Fifth Avenue.

The delivery time of the blue suit, "six o'clock" this evening, meant six hours minus one hour and twenty minutes.

So there I'll be, thought Alexis, strolling by the old rendezvous just inside Central Park at twenty minutes of five this evening.

He burned the scrap of notes, replaced the sheet of paper in its nesting place, and put Spengler carefully back on the shelf. Only after that did he reheat the coffee, gulp down the orange-juice, look at the still-life of congealed bacon and eggs with a shudder, and empty the greasy half-cooked mess into the garbage-can. He would tidy up on Monday—the worst thing on this job was the chores you had to do yourself: dangerous to hand out duplicate keys to anyone coming in to scrub and dust. When things got beyond him in this small apartment, he'd call for untalkative Beulah, flat feet and arthritis, too stupid to question why he asked here to clean on a day he worked at home. Now he had better shave, shower and dress. And then do some telephoning of his own: to Sandra here in Washington, begging off her swinging party tonight; to Katie in New York, letting her know that he'd be spending the week-end again at her place. And he had better take the first Metroliner possible. Or the shuttle flight? In any case, he must make sure that he would reach New York with plenty of time to spare before the meeting with Mischa.

As he came out of the shower, he was smiling broadly at a sudden memory. Imagine, he thought, just imagine Mischa remembering that old fixation of mine on a blue suit, my idea of bourgeois respectability for my grand entry into the capitalist world. I was given it, too: an ill-fitting jacket of hard serge, turning purple with age, threads whitening at the seams, the seat of the pants glossed like a mirror, a rent here, some mud there; a very convincing picture of the refugee who had managed at last to outwit the Berlin Wall. (Mischa's sense of humour, a scarce commodity in his line of business, was as strong as his cold assessment of Western minds: the pathetic image always works, he had said.) And now I have $22,000 a year and a job in Washington, and a three-room apartment one flight up in a Georgetown house, and a closet packed with clothes. Eight suits hanging there, but not a blue one among them. He laughed, shook his head, and began planning his day in New York."

He arrived at Penn Station with almost three hours to spare, a time to lose himself in city crowds once he had dropped his small bag at Katie's East Side apartment. That was easily done; Katie's place had a self-service apartment and no doorman, and he had the keys to let him into both the entrance-hall and her fifth-floor apartment. It was a fairly old building as New York went, and modest in size—ten floors, with only space enough for two apartments on each of them. The tenants paid no attention to anyone, strangers all, intent on their own troubles and pleasures. They never even noticed him on his frequent week-end visits, probably assumed he was a tenant himself. But best of all was the location of the apartment-house between two busy avenues, one travelling north, the other south, buses and plenty of taxis.

Katie herself was a gem. Made to order, and no pun intended. She was out now, as he had expected: a restless type, devoted to causes and demonstrations. She had left a note for him in her pretty-girl scrawl. *Chuck tried to reach you in Washington. Call him any time after five. Don't forget party at Bo's tonight. You are re-invited. See you here at seven? Kate.* Bo Browning's party...well, that was something better avoided. Danger for him there, in all that glib talk from eager Marxists who hadn't even read *Das Kapital* all the way through. It was hard to keep himself from proving how little they knew, or how much he could teach them.

But Chuck—now that was something else again. There was urgency in his message. Could Chuck really be delivering? Last week-end he had been arguing himself into and out of a final decision. Better not count on anything, Alexis warned himself, and tried to repress a surge of hope, a flush of triumph. But his sudden euphoria stayed with him as he set off for Fifth Avenue and an hour or so in the Metropolitan Museum of Art.

By four o'clock he began to worry about his timing, and came hurrying away from the Greek gods' department, down the Museum's giant flight of steps, his arm signalling to a loitering taxi. It would take him south, well past Sixty-ninth Street, all the way to the Central Park Zoo. He would use that entrance, wander around the zoo itself to put in fifteen minutes (he was going to be too early for Mischa after all). Now he was thinking only of the meeting ahead of him. The initial excitement was gone, replaced by nervousness, even a touch of fear. It was a special encounter, no doubt about that: there was something vital at stake. Had he made some error, was his judgment being distrusted? Had his growing boredom with those quiet nine years shown in his steady reports? But they were good reports, succinct, exact, giving the foibles and weaknesses of the hundreds of acquaintances and friends he had made in government and newspaper circles. As a member of Representative Pickering's personal staff, with nine years of promotions all the way from secretarial adviser to office-manager controlling an office swollen to forty-seven employees, and now to the top job of communications director, he had contacts in every major office in government. He was invited around, kept an ear open for all rumours and indiscreet talk. There was plenty of that in Washington, some of it so careless that it baffled him. Americans *were* smart—a considerable enemy and one that posed a constant danger—that was what had been dinned into him in his long months of training; but after nine years in Washington, he had his doubts. What made clever Americans so damned stupid once they got into places of power?

The fifteen minutes were up, leaving him seven to walk northward through the Park to its Sixty-ninth Street area. Had he cut the time too short, after all? He increased his pace as he left the desolate zoo with its empty cages—animals were now kept mostly inside—and its trees bare-branched with first frosts. The Saturday crowd was leaving too, moving away from the gathering shadows. So he wasn't noticeable. And he hadn't been followed. He never was. But he was suddenly surprised out of his self-preoccupation by the dimming sky. The bright clear blue of the afternoon had faded. It would soon be dusk. The street lights were already on; so were the lamps posted along the paths, little bursts of brightness surrounded by darkening meadows, by bushes and trees that formed black blots over falling and rising ground. Fifth Avenue lay to his right beyond the wall that edged the Park. Traffic was brisk, audible but not visible; only the high-rising apartment buildings, lining the other side of the avenue, could be seen. Their windows—expensive curtains undrawn, shades left unpulled—were ablaze with light. What was this about an energy crisis?

Strange, he thought as he came through a small underpass, how isolated this park can make you feel; almost as if you were on a lonely country road. The crowd had thinned, easing off in other directions. He was alone, and approaching a second underpass as the path sloped downward, edging away from the Fifth Avenue wall. Now it was almost dusk, the sky washed into the colour of faded ink tinged with a band of apricot above the far-off black silhouettes of Central Park West.

The underpass looked as grim as a tunnel—a short one, fortunately. Near its entrance, on the small hillside of bushes and rocks that lay on his right, he saw a group of four men. No, just boys: two leaning against a crag, nonchalant, thin; two squatting on the slope of grass, knees up to their black chins: all of them watching. He noticed the sneakers on their feet. Keep walking and get ready to sprint, he told himself. And then his fear doubled as he heard lightly-running footsteps behind him. He swung round to face the new threat. But it was only a couple of joggers, dressed in track suits, having their evening run. "Hi!" he said in relief as the joggers neared him rapidly.

"Hi!" one said, pink-faced and frowning. He glanced at the hill. Both he and his friend slowed their pace but didn't stop. "Like to join us?" the other one asked, thin-faced and smiling.

And he did, breaking into their rhythm as he unbuttoned his topcoat, jogging in unison. Through the underpass, then up the path as it rose in a long steady stretch. "Race you to the top," the thin-faced man said. But up there, where the outcrop of Manhattan rocks rose into a cluster of crags, he would be almost in sight of the Sixty-ninth Street entrance. Now was the time to break off, although he could have given them a good run for their money.

He smiled, pretended to have lost his wind, stopped half-way up the path, gave them a wave of thanks. With an answering wave they left him, and without a word increased their pace to a steady run. Amazing how quickly they could streak up that long stretch of hill; but they had earned this demonstration of their superiority, and he was too thankful to begrudge them their small triumph. He was willing to bet, though, that once they were out of sight, they'd slacken their pace back to a very easy jog. What were they, he wondered—a lawyer, an accountant? Illustrators or advertising men? They looked the type, lived near by, and exercised in the evening before they went home to their double vodka Martinis.

He finished the climb at a brisk pace. Far behind him, the four thin loose-limbed figures had come through the underpass and halted, as if admitting that even their sneakers couldn't catch up on the distance between him and them. Ahead of him, there were a man walking two large dogs; another jogger; and the small flagpole that marked the convergence of four paths— the one he was following, the one that continued to the north, the one that led west across rolling meadows, the one that came in from the Sixty-ninth Street entrance. Thanks to his run, he was arriving in good time after all, with one minute to spare. He was a little too warm, a little dishevelled, but outwardly calm, and ready to face Mischa. He straightened his tie, smoothed his hair, decided to button his topcoat even if it was stifling him.

He might not have appeared so calm if he could have heard his lawyer-accountant-illustrator-advertising types. Once they had passed the flagpole on its little island of grass, they had dropped behind some bushes to cool off. It had been a hard pull up that hill.

"Strange guy. What the hell does he think he's doing, walking alone at this time of day?" The red face faded back to its natural pink.

"Stranger in town."

"Well dressed. In good training, I thought. Better than he pretended."

"Wouldn't have had much chance against four, though. What now, Jim? Continue patrol, or double back? See what that wolf-pack is up to?"

"Looking for some other lone idiot," Jim said.

"Don't complain. Think of the nice open-air job they give us."

Jim stood up, flexed his legs. "On your feet, Burt. Better finish our rounds. Seems quiet enough here." There were three other joggers—bona fide ones, these—plodding in from the west towards Sixty-ninth Street and home; a man walking two Great Danes; a tattered drunk slumped on the cold hard grass, clutching the usual brown paper bag; two sauntering women, with peroxide curls, tight coats over short skirts (chilly work, thought Jim, on a cool November night), high heels, swinging handbags. "Nothing but honest citizens," Jim said with a grin. The wolf-pack had vanished, prowling for better prospects.

"Here's another idiot," said Burt in disgust as he and Jim resumed their patrol northward. The lone figure walking towards them, down the path that led from the Seventy-second Street entrance, was heavily dressed and solidly built, but he moved nimbly, swinging his cane, his snap-brim tilted to one side. He paid no attention to them, apparently more interested in the Fifth Avenue skyline, so that the droop of his hat and the turned head gave only a limited view of his profile. He seemed confident enough. "At least he carries a hefty stick. He'll be out of the park in no time, anyway."

"If he doesn't go winging his way down to the zoo," Jim said. He frowned, suddenly veered away to his left, halting briefly by a tree, just far enough to give him a view of the flagpole where the four paths met. Almost at once he came streaking back, the grass silencing his running-shoes, the grey of his tracksuit blending into the spreading shadows. "He won't be alone," he reported as he rejoined Burt. "So he'll be safe enough." Two idiots were safer than one.

"So that's their hang-up, is it? We'll leave them to the Vice boys. They'll be around soon." Dusk would end in another half-hour, and darkness would be complete. The two men jogged on in silence, steps in unison, rhythm steady, eyes alert.

2

They arrived at the flagpole almost simultaneously. "Well timed," said Mischa and nodded his welcome. There was no handclasp, no outward sign of recognition. "You look well. Bourgeois life agrees with you. Shall we walk a little?" His eyes had already swept over the drunk lolling on the grass near the Sixty-ninth Street entrance. He glanced back, for a second look at the two women with the over-made-up faces and ridiculous clothes, who were now sitting on a bench beside the lamp-post. One saw him, rose expectantly, adjusted her hair. Mischa turned away, now sizing up a group of five people—young, thin, long-haired, two of them possibly girls, all wearing tight jeans and faded army jackets—who had come pouring in from Fifth Avenue. But they saw no one, heard nothing; they headed purposefully for the near-by clusters of rocks and crags and their own private spot. Mischa's eyes continued their assessment and chose the empty path that led westward across the park. His cane gestured. "Less interruption here, I think. And if no one is already occupying those trees just ahead, we should have a nice place to talk."

And a good view of anyone approaching, Alexis thought as they reached two trees, just off the road, and stepped close to them. The bushes around them had been cleared, so even a rear attack could be seen in time. Suddenly he realised that Mischa wasn't even thinking about an ambush by muggers at four forty-five in the evening—he probably assumed that ten o'clock or midnight were the criminal hours. All Mischa's caution was being directed against his old adversaries. "Central Park has changed a lot since you were last here," Alexis said tactfully. This was a hell of a place to have a meeting, but how was he to suggest that? "In summer, of course, it's different. More normal people around. Concerts, plays—"

"A lot has changed," Mischa cut him off. "But not in our work." His face broke into a wide grin, showing a splendid set of teeth. His clever grey eyes crinkled as he studied the younger man, his hat thumbed back to show a wide brow and a bristle of greying hair. With rounded chin and snub nose, he had looked nine years ago—although it would be scarcely diplomatic now to mention the name of a non-person—very much like a younger version of Nikita Khrushchev. But nine years ago Mischa had had slight gaps between his front teeth. The grin vanished. "There is no détente in Intelligence. And don't you ever forget that." A forefinger jabbed against Alexis's chest to emphasise the last five words. Then a strong hand slapped three affectionate blows on Alexis's shoulders, and the voice was back to normal. "You look like an American, you talk like an American, but you must never think like an

American." The smile was in place again.

Mischa broke into Russian, perhaps to speak faster and make sure of his meaning. "You've done very well. I congratulate you. I take it, by the way you walked up so confidently to meet me, that no one was following you?"

The small reprimand had been administered deftly. In that, Mischa hadn't changed at all. But in other ways, yes. Mischa's old sense of humour, for instance. Tonight he was grimly serious even when he smiled. He's a worried man, thought Alexis. "No, no one tailed me." Alexis's lips were tight. "But what about you?" He nodded to a solitary figure, husky and fairly tall, who had walked along the path on the heels of two men with a Doberman, and now was retracing his steps. Again he didn't glance in their direction, just kept walking at a steady pace.

"You are nervous tonight, Alexis. Why? That is only my driver. Did you expect me to cope with New York traffic on a Saturday night? Relax, relax. He will patrol this area very efficiently."

"Then you are expecting some interest—" Alexis began.

"Hardly. I am not here yet."

Alexis stared.

"Officially I arrive next Tuesday, attached to a visiting delegation concerned with agricultural problems. We shall be in Washington for ten days. You are bound to hear of us, probably even meet us at one of those parties you attend so zealously. Of course I shall have more hair, and it will be darker."

"I won't flicker an eyelash." As I might have done, Alexis admitted to himself: you did not live in a Moscow apartment for six months, completely isolated from other trainees, with only Mischa as your visitor and tutor, and not recognise him when you met him face to face in some Senator's house. But Mischa had not slipped into America ahead of his delegation, and planned a secret meeting in Central Park, merely to warn Alexis about a Washington encounter. What was so important that it could bring them together like this? "So now you are an expert on food-grains," Alexis probed.

"Now, now," Mischa chided. "You may have been one of my best pupils, but you don't have to try my own tricks on me." He was amused. Briefly. "I've been following your progress. I have seen your reports, those that are of special interest. You have not mentioned Thomas Kelso in the last three months. No progress there? What about his brother, Charles Kelso—you are still his friend?"

"Yes."

"Then why?"

"Because Chuck Kelso now lives in New York. Tom Kelso lives mostly in Washington."

"But Charles Kelso did introduce you to his brother?"

"Yes."

"Four years ago?"

"Yes."

"And you have not established yourself with Thomas Kelso by this time?"

"I tried several visits on my own after Chuck left Washington. Polite reception. No more. I was just another friend of his brother—Chuck is ten years younger than Tom, and that makes a big difference in America."

"Ridiculous. They are brothers. They were very close. That is why we instructed you to renew your friendship with Charles

Kelso when you and he met again in Washington. Five years ago, wasn't that?"

"Almost five."

"And two years ago, when it was reported that Thomas Kelso needed a research assistant, you were instructed to suggest—in a friendly meeting—that you would be interested in that position. Your reaction to that order was negative. Why?"

"It was an impossible suggestion. Too dangerous. At present I am making $22,000 a year. Did you want me to drop $14,000 and rouse suspicions?"

"Was $8,000 a year all he could afford?" Mischa was disbelieving. "But he must make—"

"Not all Americans are millionaires," said Alexis. "Isn't that what you used to impress on me? Sure, Kelso is one of the best— and best-paid—reporters on international politics. He picks up some extra money from articles and lectures, plus travel expenses when he has an assignment abroad. But he lives on the income he earns. That is what keeps him a busy man, I suppose."

"An influential man," Mischa said softly. "What about that book he has been writing for the last two years?"

"Geopolitics. Deals with the conflict between the Soviet Union and China."

"That much, we also know," Mischa said in sharp annoyance. "Is that all you have learned about it?"

"It is all anyone has learned in Washington. Do you think he wants his ideas stolen?"

"You had better try again with Mr. Thomas Kelso, and keep on trying."

"But what has this to do with your work in Directorate S?" That was the section of the First Chief Directorate that dealt in Illegals—agents with assumed identities sent to live abroad.

There was a moment of silence. It was impossible to see Mischa's expression clearly now. Night had come, black and bleak. Alexis could feel the angry stare that was directed at him through the darkness, and regretted his temerity. He repressed a shiver, turned up his coat-collar. Then Mischa said, "The brash American," and even laughed. He added, "It has to do with my present work, very much so." He relented still further, and a touch of humour entered his voice. "Let us say that I am interested in influencing people who influence people."

So Mischa had moved over to the First Chief Directorate's Department A: Disinformation. Alexis was appropriately impressed, but he kept silent. He had already said too much. If Mischa wasn't his friend, he might have been yanked out of Washington and sent to the Canal Zone or Alaska.

"So," said Mischa, "you will persevere with Tom Kelso. He is important because of his job and the friends he makes through it—in Paris, Rome, London—and, of course, in the North Atlantic Treaty Organisation. They trust him there in NATO. He hears a great deal."

Alexis nodded.

"About NATO..." Mischa was too casual, almost forgetful about what he had intended to say. "Oh yes," he remembered; "you sent us a piece of information a few days ago about that top-security memorandum they passed to the Pentagon. You said it was now being studied at Shandon House." He was being routinely curious, it seemed, his voice conversational.

"It is being analysed and evaluated. A double check on the Pentagon's own evaluation."

"What is the real function of this Shandon House? Oh,

we know it is a collection of brains working with computers; but—super-secret? Capable of being trusted with such a memorandum?"

"It is trusted. Everyone has top clearance. Security is tight."

"Ah, patriots all. Yet you said that it might be possible to breach that security. How? When?" The tone was still conversational.

"Soon. Perhaps even—" Alexis restrained himself. Better not be too confident. Better not be too precise. Then if the project turned sour, he wouldn't be blamed for promising too much and achieving too little. "I have no guarantee. But there is a possibility," he said more guardedly.

"When will you know more than that?"

"Perhaps later tonight."

"Tonight!" Mischa exploded. "I *knew* you had something. I knew it by the way you worded your message!"

So it was his information on the NATO Memorandum that had brought Mischa chasing over to New York. He had read Alexis's message last Tuesday or Wednesday. By Saturday he was here. In person. Was the memorandum so important as that?

"You are set to act?" Mischa demanded. "What is your plan?"

"I have three possible variants. It depends. But I'll deliver."

"You are using microfilm, of course? The memorandum is in three parts—over forty pages, I hear. You will need time."

Another hazard, thought Alexis. "I'll make time."

"And when you deliver, do *not* employ your usual method."

"No?" Alexis was puzzled. It was a set procedure. Any photographs he had taken, like his own reports in code, were passed to his weekly contact in Washington. The contact delivered them to Control, who in turn handed them over to the Residency. From there they were speeded to the Centre in Moscow. There had never been any slip-up. His contact had a gift for choosing casual encounters, all very natural.

"No! You will make the delivery to Oleg. He will alert you by telephone, and contact you some place of his own choosing. On Monday."

"But I may not have the microfilm by Monday. It may be the following week-end before—"

"Then you deliver it to Oleg on the following week-end," Mischa said impatiently. "You won't have any chance to get the NATO Memorandum after that. It returns to the Pentagon, we hear, for finalised recommendations to the National Security Council. Before then, we want the particulars of that document. So press your advantage with Shandon House. You do your job, and Oleg will do his."

"Oleg—how will I be able to identify him?" Surely not by a lot of mumbo-jumbo, Alexis thought in dismay: recognition signals wasted time, added to the tension. He had always felt safer in knowing his contact by sight, although there his interest stopped and he neither knew nor cared who the man was. The contact followed the same rules. To him, Alexis was a telephone number and a face.

Mischa raised his cane, pointed to their watchdog, who had stationed himself at a discreet distance.

"He isn't near any lamp-post," Alexis objected.

"You will see his face quite clearly as we pass him. Shall we go?" Mischa tilted his hat back in place. "We separate before we approach the flagpole area. I shall leave by way of the zoo. You head for the Seventy-second Street exit. Oleg takes Sixty-ninth Street—his car is parked there. He will drive down Fifth

Avenue, and pick me up at the zoo. Simple and safe. It will raise no eyebrows. You agree?" Mischa moved away from the trees.

Alexis, with a quick glance over his shoulder—he had thought he saw two lurking shadows in the rough background—stepped on to the path. Mischa noticed. "Scared of the dark?" he asked with a laugh. "At half-past five in the evening? Alexis, Alexis…" He shook his head. They walked in silence towards the waiting man.

As they passed close to him, he was lighting a cigarette. The lighter didn't flare. It glowed, with enough power to let Oleg's face be clearly seen. The glow ended abruptly. The cigarette remained unlit.

"You'll remember him?" Mischa asked.

"Yes. But could he see me clearly enough?"

"He has examined close-up photographs of your face. No trouble in quick identification. That's what you like, isn't it? I agree. No doubt, no uncertainties." Behind them Oleg followed discreetly.

Some fifty yards away from the flagpole, Mischa said, "Now we leave each other. Take a warm handshake for granted." This time the smile was genuine. "I shall hear from you soon?" It was more of a command than a question.

"Soon." No other answer was possible. He had forgotten how inexorable and demanding Mischa could be.

Mischa nodded and left. Soon he had drawn well ahead. Alexis slowed his pace slightly, letting the distance between them increase. Oleg passed him, intent on reaching the car he had parked near by, possibly on Sixty-ninth Street itself. It was west-bound, of course: just the added touch to Mischa's careful arrangements.

Alexis watched Mischa as he took the southward path at the flagpole. For a few moments a near-by lamp-post welcomed him into its wide circle of white light, showed clearly his solid figure and brisk stride against the background of massive rocks that filled this corner of the park. Then he was gone, swinging down towards the zoo.

Oleg was now well beyond the flagpole and heading for Fifth Avenue. Alexis noted for future reference the way he moved, the set of his shoulders, his height and breadth; the way he turned his head to look at the drunk, now sitting with his head between his knees. A dog-walker, enmeshed in a tangle of leashes, merited only a brief glance. One of the prostitutes still loitering under a lamp-post received no attention at all: virtuous fellow, this Oleg.

So now, thought Alexis with a smile when he reached the flagpole, it's my turn to branch off. Two steps, and he stopped abruptly as he heard a shout. One shout. He looked round at the path to the zoo.

Someone rushed past him—the prostitute, fumbling in her handbag, kicking off her high-heeled shoes with a curse, running swiftly, gun drawn. It's a man, Alexis realised: a policeman. Almost simultaneously, the drunk had moved, racing around the crags, pulling a revolver out from his brown-paper bag as he cut a quick corner to the zoo path. Alexis stood still. His brain seemed frozen, his legs paralysed. He looked helplessly at the dog-walker, but that young man was already yanking his charges towards the safety of Fifth Avenue.

Keep clear of the police, Alexis warned himself, don't get involved. But that had been Mischa's voice. Of that he was almost certain.

He began to follow the direction the two undercover men had taken. Again he stopped. From here he could see a man left lying on the ground, and three or four thin shadows scattering away from him as the policemen closed in. The one dressed as a woman knelt beside the inert figure—was he dead, or dying, or able to get up with some help? The other was giving chase to the nearest boy—the rest were vanishing into the darkness in all directions. Then he noticed the hat and the cane—pathetic little personal objects dropped near the body.

The policeman beside Mischa looked towards Alexis. "Hey, you there—give us a hand!"

Alexis turned, and ran.

He came on to Fifth Avenue, collected his wits while he stood listening to the hiss of wheels as the cars and taxis sped past. The traffic signal changed, and he snapped back into life. He crossed quickly, and entered Sixty-ninth Street. Kerbs were lined with cars, the sidewalks quiet, with only a few people hurrying along. Where was Oleg? He couldn't have gone far: there hadn't been time enough for that. Alexis's desperation grew, he was almost into a second attack of panic. Then, just ahead of him, not far along the block, he saw broad shoulders and a dark head moving out into the street to walk round the front of a car and unlock it. He broke into a run. Oleg looked up, alert and tense: a look of total amazement spread over his face. He entered his side of the car, and opened the other door for Alexis.

"And what is this?" Oleg began angrily.

"Mischa was attacked. In the Park. Not far down the path. Police are with him—undercover police. They'll send for more police, an ambulance. Get over there! Quick! See what's happening, see where they will take him. Find out the hospital. Quick!"

"Why didn't *you*—"

"Because they've seen me with him. The undercover man who was in woman's clothes saw us both together when we met."

"But—"

"There's the first police car." The siren was sounding some distance to the east, but it was drawing nearer. "Quick!" Alexis said for the third time, still more urgently. And left the car. He walked over to Madison. He did not look round.

Now it was up to Oleg. And Oleg (thought Alexis) is aware of that. He must know a good deal more than either Mischa or he pretended: being shown photographs of me, for instance, and given other particulars too—which proves he had access to my files? If he did, he's aware that I am just an agent in place, a mole that stays underground and works out of sight. My God, I was nearly surfaced tonight. So let Oleg attend to the problem of Mischa. He would have contacts in New York. He would know how to handle this. And above all, Alexis told himself, I have my own job to do. With Mischa or without Mischa, I still have an assignment to complete. I'll send the microfilm by the usual route, if Oleg does not contact me in Washington. This is no time to delay. If I get the information I'm after, I'm damned if I'm going to sit on it. You win no promotions that way.

He hailed a taxi to take him a short distance up Madison. From there he walked the block to Park Avenue and took a second cab. This carried him down to Fifty-third Street. There, among the tall office buildings and the Saturday-evening strollers, he walked another block to find a taxi to take him over to Second Avenue and up to Sixty-sixth Street. A circular tour, but a safety measure. He had heard of agents who had travelled for two hours on various subways, just to make sure.

It was a quarter past six when he reached the entrance of Katie's building. He did not get off the elevator at her floor, but at the one above. For a moment he stood in the small hallway thinking—as he always did—what a stroke of genius it had been to find an apartment for Chuck Kelso right in this apartment-house.

Then he pressed the bell. He was no longer Alexis. Now he was Nealey, Heinrich Nealey—Rick to his friends—an odd mixture of a name, but genuine enough, a real live American with legitimate papers to back that up.

3

The journey from Shandon House in New Jersey to Charles Kelso's apartment in New York took about an hour and ten minutes. It was easy—first a country road to lead through rolling meadows and apple-orchards on to the fast Jersey Turnpike lined with factories, and then under the Hudson, in a stream of speeding cars, straight into Manhattan. So Kelso had chosen to make the trip twice daily, preferring to live in the city rather than become a part of the Shandon enclave in the Jersey hill-and-tree country. Like the younger members on the Institute's staff, he preferred a change in friends: he saw enough of his colleagues by day, he didn't need them as social companions at night or on week-ends. As for the long-time inhabitants of the various estates that spread around Shandon's own two thousand acres, they kept to themselves as they had been doing for the last forty years. If they ever did mention the collection of experts who had invaded their retreat, it was simply to call them "The Brains."

So too the village of Appleton, five miles away from Shandon—it had been there for almost three hundred years and considered everyone arriving later than 1900 as foreigners, acceptable if they provided jobs and much-needed cash (cider and hand-turned table-legs had been floundering long before the present inflation started growing). On that point, the Brains were found wanting. They had their own staff of maintenance men and guards to look after Shandon House. Even the kitchen had special help. Four acres around the place had been walled off—oh, it didn't look too bad, there were small shrubs to soften it up—but the main entrance now had high iron gates kept locked, and big dogs, and all the rest of that nonsense. And those Brains who lived outside the walls in renovated barns, or farmhouses turned into cottages, might be pleasant and polite when they visited Appleton's general store: but they didn't need much household help and they never gave large parties, not even for the government big shots who came visiting from Washington.

The village agreed with the landed gentry that old Simon Shandon had really lost his mind (and it must have been good at one time: a $300,000,000 fortune testified to that) when he willed his New Jersey estate, complete with enormous endowment, to house this collection of mystery men and women. Institute for Analysis and Evaluation of Strategic Studies: that's what Simon Shandon had got for all that money. And even if the outside of the house had been preserved—a rambling mansion with over forty rooms, some of them vast—the interior had been chopped up. Rumour also said there was a computer installed in the ballroom. The villagers tried some computing themselves on the costs, shook their heads in defeat, and found it all as meaningless as the Institute's title. Strategic Studies—what did that mean? Well, who cared? After twelve years of speculation, their curiosity gave way to acceptance. So when Charles Kelso, taking the quickest route back to the city, drove through the village on a bright Saturday afternoon when sensible folks were out hunting in the woods or riding across their meadows, no one gave his red Mustang more than a cursory glance. Those fellows up there at Shandon House came and went at all times: elastic hours and no trade unions. And here was this one, as usual forsaking good country air for smog and sirens.

But it was not the usual Saturday afternoon for Kelso. True, he had some work to catch up with; true, he sometimes did spend part of the week-end finishing an urgent job, so that the guard at the gatehouse hadn't seen anything strange when he had checked in that morning. And he was not alone. The computer boys were on to some new assignment, and there were five other research fellows scattered around, including Farkus and Thibault from his own department. But they didn't spend much time on one another, not even bothering to meet in the dining-hall for lunch, too busy in their own offices for anything except a sandwich at their desks. They hadn't even coincided in the filing-room at the end of the day's stint. It was empty when Kelso arrived to leave a folder in the cabinet where work-in-progress was filed if it was considered important enough.

Maclehose, on duty as security officer of the day, let him into the room through its heavy steel door—he always felt he was walking into a giant safe, a bank vault with cabinets instead of safe-deposit boxes around its walls. Maclehose gave him the right key for Cabinet D and stood chatting about his family—

he hoped he'd get away from here by four o'clock, his son's seventh birthday; pity he hadn't been able to take today off the chain instead of Sunday.

"Then who's on duty tomorrow?"

"Barney, if he gets over the grippe." Maclehose wasn't optimistic. "He's running a temperature of a hundred and two, so I may have to sub for him. Thank God no one—so far—is talking about working here this Sunday."

"I may have to come in and finish this job."

"Pity you didn't keep it in your drawer upstairs." Maclehose could see his Sunday being ruined, all on account of one over-dutiful guy. That was the trouble with the young ones: they thought every doodle on their think-pads was worthy of being guarded in Fort Knox. "Then we could have locked up tight. Is that stuff so important?" He gestured to the folder in Kelso's hand.

Kelso laughed and began to unlock Cabinet D. He was slow, hesitating. Once its door was open, he would find two vertical tiers of drawers, three to each side. Five had the names of each member of his department, all working on particular problems connected with defence. The sixth drawer, on the bottom row of the right-hand tier, was simply marked *Pending*. And there the NATO Memorandum had come to rest. For the past three weeks it had been dissected, computerised, studied, analysed. Now, in an ordinary folder, once more a recognisable document, it waited for the analyses to be evaluated, the total assessment made, and the last judgment rendered in the shape of a Shandon Report which would accompany it back to Washington.

"Having trouble with that lock?" Maclehose asked, about to come forward and help.

"No. Just turned the key the wrong way."

And at that moment the telephone rang on Maclehose's desk in the outer office.

It was almost as though the moment had been presented to him. As Maclehose vanished, Kelso swung the cabinet door wide open. He pulled out the *Pending* drawer, exchanged the NATO folder for his own, closed the drawer, shut the door. He was about to slip the memorandum inside his jacket when Maclehose ended the brief call and came hurrying back.

He stared at the folder in Kelso's hand. "Taking your time? Come on, let's hurry this up. Everyone is packing it in—just got the signal—no more visitors today."

"How about Farkus and Thibault? They were working on some pretty important stuff."

"They were down here half an hour ago. Come on, get this damned cabinet open and—"

Kelso locked it, handed the keys over with a grin. "You changed my mind for me."

"Look—I wasn't trying to—"

Sure you were, thought Kelso, but he only tucked the folder under his arm. "It isn't really so important as all that. I'll lock it up in my desk. Baxter will see no one gets into my office." Baxter was the guard who would be on corridor patrol tomorrow. "Have a good birthday party—how many kids are coming?"

"Fifteen of them," said Maclehose gloomily. The door to the filing-room clanged, was locked securely. Its key, along with the one for filing-cabinet Defence, was dropped into the desk drawer beside those for the other departments— Oceanic Development, Political Economy, Space Exploration,

Population, International Law, Food, Energy (Fusion), Energy (Solar), Ecology, Social Studies.

"Quite an invasion." Kelso watched Maclehose close the drawer, set its combination lock, and turned away before Maclehose noted his interest. "All seven-year-olds?"

"Good God," Maclehose said suddenly, "I almost forgot!" He frowned down at a memo sheet lying among the clutter on his desk. "There would have been hell to pay."

What's wrong now? Kelso wondered in dismay, halting at the door. His hand tightened on the folder, his throat went dry. Some new security regulation?

Maclehose read from the memo. "Don't forget to pick up four quarts of chocolate ice-cream on your way home."

"See you Monday if you survive," said Kelso cheerfully, and left.

Kelso drove through Appleton, hands tight on the wheel, face tense. His briefcase, picked up in his office, lay beside him with the NATO folder disguised inside it by this morning's *Times*. He had opened the briefcase for the obligatory halt at Shandon's gates, but the guard had contented himself with his usual cursory glance through the car's opened window. After four years of being checked in and out, inspection of Kelso had become routine. Routine made everything simple.

All too damned simple, Kelso thought now, turning the anger he felt for himself against Shandon's security. I should never have got away with it. But I did.

He had no sense of triumph. He was still incredulous. The moment had been presented to him, and he had taken it. From then on there had been no turning back. How could he have done it? he wondered again, anger turning to disgust. All those lies in word and action, the kind of behaviour he had always condemned. And yet it had all come so naturally to him. That was what really scared him.

No turning back? He slowed up, drew the car to the side of the narrow road, sat there staring at his briefcase. Now was the time, if ever. He could say he had forgotten something in his office: he could slip downstairs to the filing-room—Maclehose would have left by now. He had the combination of the key drawer—127 forward, back 35—and the rest would be simple. Simple: that damned word again.

And yet, he thought, I had to do it. There was an obligation, a need. I've felt it for the last three weeks, ever since I worked over the first section of the Memorandum along with Farkus and Thibault. Yes, we all agreed that the first section should have been published for everyone to read. Now. Not in ten, twenty, even fifty years, lost in the Highly Classified files until some bureaucrat got round to releasing it.

The other two sections—or parts—of the NATO Memorandum were in a different category. From what he had heard they *were* top secret. Definitely unpublishable. Unhappily, he glanced again at the briefcase. He wished to God they were back again in the *Pending* drawer. But he had had only a few moments, less than a full minute, not time enough to separate them from Part I of the Memorandum and leave them in safety. All or nothing: that had been the choice. So he had taken the complete Memorandum. The public had the need to know—wasn't that the current phrase, highly acceptable after the secrecies of Watergate? Yes, he agreed. There was a need to know, there was a moral obligation to publish and jolt the American people into the realities of today.

He drove on, still fretting about means and ends. His conduct had been wrong, his purpose right. If he weren't so sure about that...but he was. After three miserable weeks of debating and arguing with himself, he was sure about that. He was sure.

He was late. First, there was a delay on the New Jersey Turnpike, dusk turning to night as he waited in a line of cars. A truck had jack-knifed earlier that afternoon, spilling its oranges across the road, and it was slow going, bumper to bumper, over the mess of marmalade. Next, there was a bottle-neck in Saturday traffic on the Upper East Side of Manhattan—huge caterpillars, two cranes, bulldozers, debris trucks, even a powerhouse, were all left edging a new giant excavation until Monday morning. If there was a depression just around the turn, these hard-hats didn't know it. And then, last nuisance of all, with night already here, he found all the parking spaces on his own street tightly occupied. He had to leave his car three blocks away and walk to Sixty-sixth Street, gripping his briefcase as though it contained the treasure of Sierra Madre. Yes, he was late. Rick had probably called him at five exactly; Rick seemed to have a clock planted like a pacemaker in his chest. It was now ten minutes of six.

"One hell of a day," he said aloud to his empty apartment. Switching on some lights, he placed the briefcase on his desk near the window and looked for any messages that Mattie, his part-time help, might have taken for him this morning. There was one. From his brother's wife, Dorothea. He stared at it aghast. Mattie had written out the message carefully, although the hotel's name had baffled her. "Staying this week-end at the Algonekin. Can you make dinner tonight at seven thiry?" God, he thought angrily, of all the nights for Tom and Thea to be in town! And then he began to remember: Tom was on his way to Paris on one of his assignments, and Thea was here for a day or two in New York. But surely they hadn't told him it was *this* week-end? Or had he forgotten all about it? His sense of guilt deepened.

He left the desk, with the typewriter-table angled to one side of it, navigated around a sectional couch and two armless chairs in the central area of the room, skirted a dining section, reached the small pantry where he stored his liquor, and poured himself a generous Scotch. Of all the nights for Tom to be here, he kept thinking. He dropped into a chair, propped feet on an ottoman, began trying several excuses for size. None seemed to fit. Best call Tom and say that he just couldn't make it. Not this time, old buddy. Sorry, really sorry. See you on your way back to Washington. No, no...that was too damned cold.

He sighed and finished his drink, but he didn't move over to the telephone. He went into the bathroom and washed up. He went into the bedroom and got rid of his jacket and tie. He put on some discs on his record-player. And when he did at last go to the desk, it was to open the briefcase. Plenty of time to get in touch with Tom—it was barely six-fifteen. Yes, plenty of time to find some explanation that would skirt the truth ("Sorry, Tom. I forgot all about it.") and yet not raise one of Dorothea's beautiful eyebrows.

The doorbell rang. Rick?

4

It was Rick. "Sorry I couldn't 'phone. Spent the last hour getting here from La Guardia. Traffic was all fouled up. He was at ease as he always was, a handsome man of thirty-three, blond and grey-eyed (he had that colouring from his German mother); but at this moment his face looked drawn.

It's the harsh light in this hall: I'll have to change the bulb, thought Kelso. He caught sight of himself in the mirror, and he looked worse than Rick—everything intensified. His dark hair and brown eyes were too black, his skin too pale, the cheekbones and nose and chin had become prominent, his face haggard. "What we both need is a drink," he said, dropped Rick's coat on a chair and led the way into the room.

"Nothing, thanks." Rick's glance roved around, settling briefly on the desk and the open briefcase. He restrained himself in time, didn't make one move towards it. Instead, he watched Chuck pour himself a drink. "You look wrung-out. A bad day?"

"Hard on the nerves."

"What happened?"

"I took the damned thing." Chuck lowered the volume of *Daphnis and Chloe*.

"You've got it?"

"Yes. It's in the briefcase."

"All of it?"

Chuck nodded. There was no other way.

"You aren't thinking of typing out the whole thing?"

"Not bloody likely. Part I is all we need. What about a reporter? You said several would jump at the chance to use it. Have you contacted any?"

"Yes. There's one on the *Times* who is interested."

"How much did you tell him?"

"Only that there might be something important for him to report in a week or two. Top-secret material, but no breach of national security if it were published. He sensed something big. Investigative reporting—that's got the appeal, all right."

"But why the *Times*?" Chuck objected. "That's Tom's paper."

"What does it matter? He's stationed in Washington—has never been near Shandon House. Besides, you aren't using your name, are you?"

"I don't want it used." Chuck insisted on that.

"Too bad, in a way. Think of all the lectures you'd be invited to give." Rick's smile widened. "The college circuit would really—"

"I want no publicity whatsoever. None. This is not an ego trip."

"I know, I know. Just joking."

"Does your reporter know that he can't use my name?"

"I didn't even mention it to him. I just spoke of Shandon House."

Chuck frowned. "Did you have to bring that in?"

"Yes. He knows who I am and what I do; in fact, he knows me quite well. But that wouldn't be enough to take to his editor and get the go-ahead to use the material. Shandon House carries real clout. Not to worry, Chuck. He isn't talking to anyone until I hand him a copy of the NATO Memorandum, Part I. Do you think he wants this story filched away from him?"

"Name?"

"Holzheimer. Martin Holzheimer. You've seen his byline, haven't you?"

Chuck tried to remember, then shrugged his shoulders. If Holzheimer had a byline, he was good. And Rick was an experienced judge: he met a lot of young journalists in his job as communications director for publicity-hound Pickering. Communications director. What titles these Congressmen could dream up for their swollen staffs! "How old is he?"

"Old enough. Twenty-nine. On his way up. Besides, the useful thing is that he lives in Manhattan, so I can get hold of him easily."

"When?"

"Why not tonight?" Rick crossed over to the windows and pulled down the shades. "By the way, once you finish the typing, would you pick up Katie at Bo Browning's party? She's expecting me, but I have to meet Holzheimer." He adjusted one shade to his liking. All I need is some time to myself, he was thinking as he moved over to the desk. "Now, let's see how much work we have to do. How many pages?"

"Just a moment—I'd better call Tom first."

Rick stared. "Are you crazy, Chuck?"

"He's in New York, wants to see me for dinner."

"Oh." There was a brief pause. "Why not go? I can start the typing, and you finish it when you get back."

"No."

Rick tried a smile. "Then may I at least read the memorandum? Just to get an idea of what we are into?"

"Sure. I didn't want you typing anything—you've been dragged into this business far enough."

"No worry about that. Holzheimer won't use my name or mention it to anyone. You and I are confidential sources. Privileged information."

"So is Shandon House," said Chuck firmly. "That name is strictly for his eyes alone. And for his editor's."

"Oh, come on, Chuck—"

"No. Its name does not get into print."

"I wonder if he'll agree to—"

"He'd better. Or else, no Memorandum. Besides, he will be reporting that it came from NATO. That's enough."

Rick nodded. "I suppose he will do some digging, check around, and find any possible leak in Washington—from State or the Pentagon—that would link Shandon House with the NATO Memorandum. That should convince him he is dealing with authentic material."

"I hope to God no one starts leaking too much."

"Beyond admitting that the Memorandum is now at Shandon? That's about all anyone does know. Except the top brass." If none of Mischa's agents in Washington—he must have one or two planted in both the Pentagon and State—had been able to get close to the NATO material, then no Washington informant was able to leak anything of value. "It's a well-kept secret. That will whet Holzheimer's appetite."

"Didn't he want to know *why* I was passing on this information to him?" I'd be curious about that myself, thought Chuck.

"Yes. And I told him the bare truth. You're a man who believes in détente and wants to see it work. The NATO Memorandum shows very clearly that détente is under attack. You thought the American public ought to know. And be warned." Rick studied Chuck's face. "Right?"

Chuck nodded. He was over at the desk now, taking out the Memorandum from the covering newspaper. Then he began removing Parts II and III, loosening them carefully from the close staples that bound the pages together. It would be a slow job.

"Have you read all the material?" Rick asked.

"Just glanced at the second and third sections. I wasn't working on them."

"What's so important about them? Part I—you told me last week—is a statement about the threats against détente. But what follows?"

"Part II gives facts and figures about NATO's defence capability and dispositions, along with facts and figures about the Warsaw Treaty Organisation's accretion in strength. Part III gives the sources of all information presented in the preceding sections, to back up their credibility."

"Sources?" That could mean intelligence agents as well as reports from military attachés. Intelligence agents—wasn't that what Mischa was interested in? "Don't tell me they were *named*?" Rick looked shocked.

"Of course not. Kept anonymous. Just identified by location."

By location. But possibly identifiable by the quality of their reports. Any good KGB analyst could place them by their area of interest and their selected targets. Mischa's department would know just where to look for them, might be able to confirm a suspicion and make identification. No wonder Mischa had been so eager to get his hands on the NATO Memorandum. "I suppose," Rick said, "that that much had to be disclosed, to make their reports acceptable on this side of the Atlantic. I've often wondered how any intelligence agent ever gets believed if he stays completely unidentified. A weird kind of life. Did you ever regret refusing it when you had that chance with Military Intelligence in Germany?"

"Not my line. Codes and cyphers weren't either. I soon backed out of them: remember?" Chuck had removed all the staples without breaking one. He put them carefully into an ashtray for later use in re-assembly. He gathered Parts II and III together, slipped them into the desk drawer, and locked it.

Rick lifted Part I. "Yes, you backed out of codes all right—into a job at the Pentagon." He laughed and began to flip over the loose pages.

"Go on, say it. I backed out of the Pentagon, too."

"No, you didn't. You jumped up the ladder and caught the Shandon rung." Rick was taking the pages more slowly, frowning in concentration.

"And there I am. Stuck." The chief of his department was only three years older than Chuck's thirty-two.

"Not you." Rick waved him into silence, seemed intent on reading. But he did not have to go beyond the first four pages to realise this was dynamite, and not the kind he had expected. He had assumed—and he cursed his stupidity—that this NATO statement on détente would aim some sharp criticism against the West. And it did. Danger lay in blind acceptance of détente as the magic word. Danger also lay in its complete rejection by prejudiced cold-warriors. NATO's advice lay between these extremes: détente was good—as far as it went; it merited support—but only with a clear understanding of its limitations. Without that, public opinion in the West could be exploited and splintered, weakening NATO's defence capabilities at a time when the Warsaw Pact countries' armed strength had increased to a point of superiority in many areas. (This sharp reminder was a natural lead-in to a plea for continuing American military strength in Europe. Depleted numbers of tanks and planes, as a result of Mid-East requirements, must be replaced. Any decrease in Western defence would only lessen the West's bargaining power.)

But that was not all of NATO's unpleasant warning. To bolster its thesis, it included a careful study of the Soviet interpretation of détente: military and economic agreements could be signed, but that in no way precluded Soviet interest in exploring the weaknesses of the West and pouring acid into open wounds. The old methods of cold war—open or threatened confrontation, brutal tactics such as the Berlin blockade—were now out of date. The new strategy of détente was "the conquest of the system," a phrase much used by German Communists. By this was meant the destruction of political democracy in the West, by *covert* attacks on its constitutional foundations and by the discrediting of fundamental political and social ideals. For this purpose, Disinformation (Dept. A of the First Chief Directorate, Committee for State Security) had become increasingly important in Soviet planning.

Disinformation. Mischa's department. What would he have to say about these details on the recent successful take-over of the Free University in West Berlin, for instance? His agents and their methods clearly described? Rick drew a deep breath to steady himself, then went on with what he had been discussing. "You'll be at the top of the ladder in ten years—Director of the Institute by Tom's age. How does that grab you? Better than being a foreign correspondent." He placed some of the pages on the desk, squared them off neatly. He pursed his lips.

"What's the verdict so far?" Chuck was eager to know.

"Packs a hefty punch. But—don't you think?—it might be considered a low blow against Kissinger and Ford?"

Chuck stared at him. "I told you what it was about, didn't I? What made you change around?"

"I haven't. I still think it ought to be published. Perhaps a little later. Not at this moment. Ford is in Vladivostok right now."

"All the more reason—"

"Why don't we wait until after Kissinger attends the NATO meeting on December twelfth in Brussels? That's not too far off." And, Rick thought, that would give me time to squelch Holzheimer's interest.

"And that is exactly why we are going ahead as planned. We'll make sure that the Brussels meeting is going to listen to NATO's assessment of détente, and talk about it openly. It isn't just the American public that needs a jolt. There's far too much secrecy about things that should be out in the open. How can people decide, if they get no choice? They've got to know the alternatives..."

"Okay, okay. It was just a suggestion. You've convinced me that it wasn't a good one."

"You know your trouble, Rick? You're too damned conservative."

"You know both our troubles? We need some food. I've had nothing to speak of since breakfast. And you? I bet you didn't eat much lunch. What's in the refrigerator?"

"You can fix us a sandwich while I'm typing."

"Right. But first let me finish reading. I could use that drink now. A dry Martini?"

"Coming up." Chuck left for the pantry.

Rick moved quickly. He dropped the sheets of paper on the desk, turned towards the typewriter, and lifted off its cover. Then he selected the A key, raised its type-bar, and bent it. He did the same with the S key next to it. That should be enough, he decided as he pushed the type-bars back in place as far as they would go. He slipped the cover over the machine and wiped his fingers clean of ink before picking up the memorandum again. By the time Chuck returned, he was sitting at the desk, a study in complete concentration. He finished the last page and placed it with the others.

"Well?" Chuck asked.

"It's good. Someone worked hard over all that. NATO Intelligence, I suppose?"

"It's something like our own work at Shandon. A matter of analysing facts, and evaluating, and wrapping it all up with judicial opinion. Prognosis is always the hardest part, and yet it's the most necessary. Here's your Martini—dry enough? I'm out of onions and olives. Like some lemon-peel?"

"No, this is fine. Just fine."

Chuck looked at the clock on the desk, checked his watch. "I'd better give Tom a call before I set to work." He was suddenly worried. "Hope I have enough carbon paper. I'll need a copy for myself—just to make sure that the *Times* prints all I give them." He went to the typing table and pulled out its drawer. "Enough," he said as he checked the box of carbons. "But there's no extra ribbon."

"Now you're starting to fuss over details." Any old excuse, thought Rick, to postpone the call to Tom. Has there been some brotherly quarrel?

But Chuck was pulling off the typewriter cover and inserting a sheet of paper into the roller. "Just testing the ribbon. If it's weak, you'll have to borrow a spare from Katie. No type-writer-supply shop is open at this hour on a Saturday night."

"Tom will be waiting—"

"Time enough yet." Chuck began typing, and stopped. He tried again. "Damnation."

"Something wrong?"

"Two keys stuck. They're out of kilter." He tried to straighten their type-bars, and then looked up at Rick in complete dismay. "No go," he said. "What the hell do I do now? And who—"

"Mattie? She has a strong dusting arm."

"She wouldn't touch the type-bars."

"She could have dropped something on them by accident."

"A load of bricks?" Chuck asked bitterly.

"Or she backed her two hundred pounds into the table and sent the machine flying."

"What the hell do I do?" Chuck said again. "Try Katie, will you? She'll lend us her typewriter." Katie had an old and hefty machine, a period piece that amused her, along with her stand-up telephones and big-horn phonograph.

"It's on the blink. It would chew up every ribbon you had."

Chuck stood very still. Then his face cleared, and he reached for the telephone book. "Algonquin, Algonquin..." His finger ran down the A section. "Here we are." He put through the call. "Tom? I just got in and found Dorothea's message. Look— I'm sorry: I have a load of work to do here. Can't manage dinner. But could I drop down to the Algonquin right now? Have a quick drink with you?... And say, could I borrow your portable?... I'll return it tomorrow without fail... Yes, I know you need it. I'll have it back long before you take off for Paris. Okay? See you in twenty minutes or so."

Chuck dropped the receiver, and was off to the bedroom for jacket and tie. He made a whirlwind exit, calling over his shoulder, "Back in an hour."

So I lost that round, Rick thought: he will have his typewriter, and a completed script by ten or eleven tonight. But I've been given the time and opportunity I need. Better than I planned. So take it. He began clearing the desk, moving the section of the memorandum he had been reading out of his way. One hour, probably more. He would aim at forty minutes, and be on the safe side.

He produced a small bunch of keys and selected the skeleton one—that was all he needed for this simple lock. Deftly he manipulated it, pulled the desk drawer open, and lifted out the two top-security parts of the NATO Memorandum. He only glanced at the number of pages, wasted no time in reading them, although he had a strong temptation to examine Part III. He adjusted the strong desk-lamp to the correct angle. Then he took out a small matchbox-size camera from his inside pocket, and placed the first page in position under the circle of light. He began photographing.

The whole job was completed—the sheets all back in order and replaced in the drawer exactly as he had found them—within thirty-five minutes. The precious film was left in the camera: he would extract it when there was less chance of any mishap—his hands felt tired, his eyes strained. The inside pocket of his jacket, fastened with a small zipper, would be safe enough.

Now he could put the desk back in shape again. The pages of Part I were neatly placed, ready for Chuck's use. He would make some sandwiches, get coffee percolating, and show some signs of a well-spent hour.

Lose one round, win another, he told himself, as he searched for his glass—he had laid it quietly aside on one of the small tables, unwilling to risk Chuck's potent mix while he still had problems to work out. The Martini wasn't worth drinking now. He carried it into the kitchen, emptied it down the sink, and poured himself a double vodka. He had earned it.

5

Tom Kelso got back to the hotel at ten past six, after a day divided between meetings—one with an editorial staff-member at the *Times,* to discuss the shape of his visit to France; another with a television reporter who had just ended a three-year assignment there; a third with an attaché on leave from the Embassy in Paris—and found Dorothea, clad in a black chiffon negligee and a white felt hat. She was seated before her dressing-table mirror, studying a profile view of the upturn-and-dip of the hat's wide brim. She turned to welcome him, as he came through the sitting-room and halted at the bedroom door, and gave him a smile that would lift any tired man's heart. "What do you think?" she asked him.

"A lot of things." He lifted the hat from her head, tossed it on to a chair. And I've only got fifteen minutes to shower and change, and order drinks from the bar, he thought in sudden frustration.

"Don't you like it?"

"It gets in the way." He bent down and planted a kiss on top of her soft smooth hair. She raised her face, still flushed and pink from her perfumed hot bath, to offer him a proper kiss on her lips. She smelled delicious, damn it. "I'll take a two-minute shower. Would you get out my blue shirt and red tie, honey?" He was on his way to the bathroom, pulling off his clothes as he went. "And you'd better start dressing, Thea."

"But Chuck won't be here till seven thiry. There's plenty of time."

"Not as much as you think. Tony Lawton is coming up for a drink. Brad Gillon, too."

"When?" she called in alarm, rising from the dressing-table and going into quick motion. First the shirt and tie. Tom was already in the shower, her question drowned out in a flood of water. She began pulling on panty-hose and bra. Gillon she knew well, an old friend of Tom's, once attached to the State Department but now out of Washington and into New York publishing. Tony Lawton? She started creaming and powdering. Yes, she remembered, she had met him once before—on a quick Washington visit—English—lived in London when he wasn't travelling around—another of Tom's friends from abroad. Some eyebrow-pencil, lipstick, hair combed into place. She was almost ready for her little black dress, in fashion again like the hat she had bought on impulse at the end of a hard day's shopping. Saturday wasn't her choice, exactly, to find Christmas presents, but that was the way Tom's schedule had been arranged, and so—she shrugged her shoulders. Tom was out of the bathroom, rubbing his hair dry. "When are they due?" she asked, dress in hand.

"At six thiry, dammit."

"Oh, heavens!" She began stepping into her dress.

"It's always the way—" He stopped combing his hair. "I'm getting an awful lot of grey at the sides," he said worriedly, looking into the mirror.

"It suits you, darling." She took a minute off dressing, and studied him. At forty-two, he was a healthy specimen: muscles firm, waistline still trim (he brooded about it, kept swearing off second helpings and desserts, but that was a vanity he shared with a million other men), dark hair plentiful even if greying at the temples, dark eyes watching her with a smile as he studied her in turn.

"Come on, blondie," he said, "get that dress on, however much it spoils the view. Old Brad would lose the sight of his good eye if he were to see you like that."

"Oh, Tom!" Her even eyebrows were raised, black eyelashes flickered, pink lips parted into a gentle protest.

"Yes, it's always the way," Tom said again, pulling on his own clothes. He had been delighted today when Tony Lawton had called him at the office, suggesting a drink this evening— and would Tom invite Brad Gillon, too? "Why didn't I say seven o'clock?"

"Because Chuck is coming at seven thiry. You'd never have time for any of that old-boys-together talk."

"Better order the drinks," Tom reminded himself, moving quickly to the telephone.

"How did your day go?"

"Not too bad." Tom waited for bar-service to answer, speculating again why Lawton had been so eager to arrange a meeting here this evening with Gillon, rather than going straight to Gillon himself. Tony's wiles always amused Tom: they gave him good copy too, although they weren't always immediately publishable. "Not too bad at all. I was well briefed. I'll know where to start digging for information in Paris, get the French points-of-view about the Brussels meeting next month. They've got a kind of—" He broke off to tell bar-service that he needed Scotch, bourbon, spring water, soda and plenty of ice. Pronto.

"A kind of what?" Dorothea asked as he left the 'phone.

"We-are-with-you-but-not-of-you complex. Tricky to evaluate. It could mean more than we think, or less than we hope." The French, dissociated since de Gaulle from NATO's military problems, would attend only the diplomatic and economic sessions of the Brussels meeting, but they still held definite opinions about European defence.

"So," she said slowly, "you'll be covering the NATO meeting on December twelfth." She was still hoping that he wouldn't have to return so soon to Europe. With this Paris visit, he would miss Thanksgiving at home. He might miss Christmas with his trip to Brussels. "It's all definite?"

"Definite," he said, and hoped there would be no more argument about that. "I'll be back before Christmas. All the NATO meetings will be over well before then."

But, she wondered, will your business be over, my sweet? Emergencies could stretch an assignment, as she well knew. She ought to be grateful, she reflected, that Tom wasn't staying on for extra weeks in Paris while he waited for the Brussels meetings to begin—a lot of men would have done just that.

"You look like a girl who needs help with a zipper," said Tom, and fixed her dress. "Perfect," he decided, swinging her round to look at the total effect, and it was no diplomatic lie. He kissed her gently.

"So are you. I like that dark red tie."

"Matches my eyes," he told her, and let her go, to hurry into the sitting-room as a waiter arrived with the tray of drinks. He heard her laugh. But his eyes were tired, he had to admit. As well as listening today, there had been a lot of reading and note-taking; and a head now filled with a collection of odd facts that kept swimming around. All he wanted was a relaxed evening, a pleasant dinner, and early to bed with his beautiful blonde. "Any message from Chuck?" he called to her.

"Not so far." Dorothea was selecting the right earrings. Tom's voice had sharpened. She could imagine the frown on his face. "Chuck will be here. Even if he didn't get my message, he'll turn up."

And there came the old twinge of guilt, whenever she mentioned Chuck: her fault, probably, that he had drifted away from Tom in these last five years. Before her day, they had enjoyed a fairly comfortable set-up from Chuck's point of view. Until she had entered the scene. Then, he had left Washington behind him for a job at Shandon House and a life of his own in New York.

About time, too, she had believed: Chuck, except for college and army service, had been on Tom's back since he was eight and Tom eighteen. At that ripe age, Tom had become father and mother combined, and found a cub-reporter's job to pay the bills (their parents' life insurance could scarcely meet the rent of the New York apartment). As soon as Chuck was safely into college, Tom seized the chance to be a war correspondent in Korea. With that over, he was back at the dutiful-brother bit, seeing Chuck through a youthful and disastrous marriage, remaining a bachelor himself—partly because he was into international politics and the new excitement of travel, partly because there was his move to Washington, but mostly because being a bachelor had become a habit hard to break. (After all, if the boy of eighteen was loaded down with family responsibilities, the man he became had already had enough of them for a while.)

And then Tom and she had met.

In a television studio. (She was arranging interviews on the Bud Wells Talk Talk Talk Show, and Tom was one of the victims that day.) Ten minutes, no more than that, ten minutes together, and there it was, bingo. "The hard-case bachelor of thirty-seven, the career girl of twenty-six—goodbye to all set plans and determined ideas; hello to a future of whatever it took to make it work."

She smiled at the memory, and carefully fastened her earrings into place. They dangled brightly. The rope of mock pearls was discarded. Enough was enough. Looking critically at her image in the mirror, she wondered what kind of woman Chuck had imagined for a suitable sister-in-law: plump and speechless, or grey-haired and motherly? He resented her; she could feel it, although he hid it well. Just as she resented the way Tom still worried about him. But one rule she had made right from the beginning: never criticise Chuck, that delightful, brilliant, and forgetful young man. Why didn't he call? Tom hadn't seen him in almost two months. And it hurt Tom: of course it must.

Dorothea went into the sitting-room. "You know, darling, he may never have got my message."

"Chuck? You worry too much, my pet." Tom's voice was carefully casual.

Do I? she wondered. Then she smiled in relief as the telephone rang. But it wasn't Chuck. It was the desk-clerk announcing Mr. Bradford Gillon.

Brad connected in her mind with another thought. "He *is* going to publish your book, isn't he?"

"Hasn't backed out so far."

"If only you could get some time to yourself and finish it. Just six months—"

"Would you settle for three?" He was laughing at the surprise he had given her. "Meant to keep the news for dinner, but you really coax things out of a man. You'd be a good reporter."

"Oh, Tom—did the *Times* tell you today, actually promise—?"

"They'll consider a three months' leave." He caught her, held her close. "But that will depend on how the world news breaks," he added to keep their excitement in check.

"Oh, Tom—" she said again, her arms flung around his shoulders. "I've got plans too. I'm taking a year off. Oh, I know, I may never get that job back again, but—"

"A year?" He looked at her quickly.

"Two, if necessary. There's more to life than having my name painted on my office door. Besides, I saw Dr. Travis first thing this morning. She says I'm in great shape now. No further risks. She sounded definite about that. Everything's fine. All systems go."

"Thea—"

A quiet knock sounded on the door. Tom released her and went to answer it. "Hello, Brad. Isn't Tony coming?"

"Sure. I saw him circling around the lobby." Brad's usually serious face was showing definite amusement. "He'll be arriving by himself any minute."

"By the stairs?" Tom asked with a grin. He left the door ajar.

Brad was now wholly absorbed with Dorothea. "You look wonderful." He gave her a brotherly hug and a warm kiss on the cheek.

"So do you." A little heavy, perhaps, but he was a tall big-boned man, so he carried his weight well. Strong features, hawk nose, heavy eyebrows, almost sombre in repose. White hair waving back from a large brow—plenty of brains inside that massive head. Gentle eyes, blue and quietly observant. "How is Mona?" Dorothea asked, minding her manners.

"Just recovering from her third attack of 'flu this fall."

"It's a hint to make you take her to Florida sunshine for ten days."

"Wish I could. Haven't had a week off the chain since last Christmas."

Recently he had been in France and Germany, Dorothea remembered, to discover some new authors and round up a belated manuscript or two. (Brad had reverted to his early interest in French and German literature—he had a degree from Harvard, way back in the early 1940s—which provided a pleasant niche for him in the publishing field.) "Why not take Mona with you on your next trip abroad?"

"Children," said Brad briefly. As a man of fifty-two who had married young, he now had all the problems of two divorced daughters and four grandchildren. "Why people can't stay married!" He shook his head. It seemed to him that after bringing up two strong-minded females, it was a bit much to have their offspring dumped on Mona. "Never own a house with five bedrooms," he said. "Should have got rid of it years ago."

"Well," said Tom, pouring bourbon for Brad and Scotch for

Thea and himself, "when home becomes unbearable there's always the office."

"Is Brad long-suffering, again?" Tony Lawton asked, as he stepped into the room and closed the door firmly. His voice and smile were amiable, and they all responded with a laugh, even a small one from Brad, who knew his own weaknesses better than most men. "Don't you believe him. He's addicted to work. Take that away, and he'd really be miserable."

"Overwork was never your complaint, Tony," Brad reminded him. But the indirect compliment pleased him.

"Wouldn't dream of allowing it to interfere with my pleasures. Yes, I'll have bourbon, Tom. And how are you, old boy? Mrs. Kelso—" Tony turned all his easy charm on her, and it was considerable—"how very nice it is to see you again. Or don't you remember me?"

He wasn't a particularly memorable man: nondescript features; brownish hair; grey eyes level with hers; no more than five foot seven. Age? Late thirties, early forties? His voice was attractive. He was dressed in grey, the suit well cut; his tie was subdued, his shoes gleaming. Clothes definitely made the man in this case, Dorothea decided: without that cut of suit and those polished shoes, she never would have identified him so quickly. Unless, of course, he retained that warm smile and gentle humour in his talk. "I remember," she said. "The wine-merchant who likes to drink bourbon and branch-water."

"Split personality," Tony agreed, and didn't even flinch at "wine-merchant." He rather liked that description of his wine-shipping firm, headquarters in London, branches all around the world.

"It's safer drinking bourbon than Bordeaux nowadays,"

Brad suggested, and that launched Tony into a hilarious version of the "Winegate" scandal in France. He had just come from there, seemingly. He does get around, thought Dorothea, and sat quietly watching the three men absorbed in one another. The talk was veering from French wine to French politics, then over to Algiers (wine as the lead-in to politics again) and next to Italy (Chianti troubles and—yes, there it was once more—political problems). It wasn't that the men had forgotten about her: there were smiles in her direction to keep her in touch, as it were. And she was fascinated. Free-flowing conversation like this seemed to bring out each man's character. Tom was the journalist, pouncing on a statement, questioning. Brad still retained much of his reserved and thoughtful State Department manner—everything weighed, and often found wanting. And Tony, eyes now alert and interested, tongue quick and explicit, must be a most capable business-man. In some ways, a strange trio; but friends, most definitely. She had a sudden vision of getting all three of them on to the Bud Wells talk show—they'd take it over. That would really freeze Bud's platitudes into astonished silence. She laughed. They stopped discussing Yugoslavia after Tito's death, and looked at her in surprise.

The telephone rang. Saved by the bell, she thought as Tom went to answer the call and attention switched away from her. Gentlemen don't listen to other gentlemen's phone-calls, she reminded herself, amused now by the low-voiced conversation that Brad and Tony had begun. But I'm no gentleman. It was Chuck on the 'phone. She could tell from Tom's face as he listened. Her heart sank.

Tom stopped beside her chair. "He forgot all about this evening," he said quietly, and managed a smile.

"Did he actually say—" she began, indignation showing in spite of all her resolutions.

"No, no. Pressure of work. He's dropping in here for a quick drink. Needs to borrow my typewriter."

"I'll get it ready for him." The portable's travelling-case was in the bedroom closet with Tom's bags. She left Tom explaining his brother's visit, and when she came back they were on the topic of Shandon House—old Simon's brainchild, Tony called it. Simon Shandon would have been astonished to see how big it had become.

"Not in numbers," said Brad. "They've held that down. But in impact—yes. Your brother must be a whiz-kid, Tom, to get in there."

"He's got most of the family brains."

Not true, not true, Dorothea thought in quick defence; but she let Tom have his moment of modesty. Damn it all, why did he always downgrade himself with Chuck? A long-standing habit, meant to encourage the young and bolster their confidence?

"What is Shandon going to do with its new property?" Tony asked. "Expand into Europe?"

I'm at sea again, thought Dorothea: what new property?

Brad noted her expression, began to explain. Simon Shandon's widow had never liked New Jersey, never even liked living in America. She preferred their villa on the Riviera. So, under the terms of old Simon's will, that was what she had been left—the villa, and a yearly allowance for the extent of her lifetime. When she died—no children, no near relatives to complicate Simon's wishes—the Riviera estate would become the property of Shandon House. She had obliged them by dying three weeks ago at the age of ninety-two, still fuming against her husband's will and all the wealth he had invested in New Jersey.

"Probably that's why she stayed alive so long—out of sheer pique," Tony said. "So now Shandon has a place near Menton. How very snazzy! Will it be a Rest and Recreation centre for tired intellects?"

"They could treat it in the way Harvard dealt with the Berenson villa near Florence," said Brad.

"A sort of Shandon-By-The-Sea?"

"Without computers. Just a gathering of brains, American and European, setting themselves problems to solve. A series of evening seminars after a day of solitary meditation." Brad's smile widened.

Tony said, "Each man with a private office and his feet up on his desk, thinking great thoughts as he stares out at the blue Mediterranean? It's a marvellous racket, this Institute business. Cosy little set-up, and tax-free."

"They do justify their existence," Tom reminded him.

"Every now and again. But—" Tony sighed—"it can be a dangerous situation, too. Get it under political control, and where will we all be? Listening to advice that will leave us more bewildered than ever." He smiled for Dorothea. "I bewilder very easily," he told her. She wondered about that.

The telephone rang—the desk in the lobby announcing Chuck's arrival. Dorothea packed the portable typewriter into its case. Tom had already opened the door and was waiting in the corridor, no doubt to tip Chuck off about the guests inside.

Chuck entered, his arm round Tom's shoulder. "Really sorry," he was explaining, "but I've got a rush job to finish. You know what deadlines are like, Tom." He relaxed as he saw that everyone—even Thea, or rather Dorothea: Thea was Tom's privilege, she insisted on that—accepted his explanation. He looked tired enough, God knew. And it was a relief to find others here: he could beg off staying for a twenty-minute chat. With this group there would be no chance for a *tête-à-tête* with Tom. He gave Dorothea a brief kiss on her cheek and one of his best smiles. A polite nod to the Englishman, a small word or two to Brad Gillon whom he remembered from Washington days, and he had the typewriter in his hand and an apology on his lips. "No, I won't sit down—I might not get up again for another hour. Besides, I have a feeling that I'm interrupting a good party. When do you get back from Paris, Tom?" He was already moving to the door.

"Sunday. A week from tomorrow."

"I'll see you then. Come and stay at my place—I've a couch that makes into a fairly good bed."

"I may do that."

"Wonderful!"

Dorothea said, "By the way, Chuck, you'd better clean the type. Some letters are a little blurred with ink and gunk. I meant to do that yesterday, but—"

"It works, doesn't it? Which is more than can be said for my machine. Thanks, Tom. Thanks a million. And I'll have it back tomorrow morning. Okay? I'll drop it off on my way to Shandon."

"Sunday on the job?" Tom asked. "You really are in a bind."

"It happens, every now and again."

"Doesn't it, though?" Brad agreed. "Bye, Chuck." Goodbyes from Tom and Dorothea, too. Tony Lawton smiled and nodded. The door closed and Chuck was on his way.

Throughout the brief visit, Tony had said nothing at all. His interest in Chuck had been politely disguised. "Now," he said, as he stopped examining his drink, "So that is one of Shandon's bright young men."

"Never met anyone from there before?" Brad asked. "If you like, I'll introduce you to Paul Krantz, the director. He's an old friend of—"

"A waste of his time. And of mine: Shandon isn't laying down a cellar of French wines, is it?"

"Hardly," said Tom. "At lunch, I hear, they are more apt to grab a ham on rye with a gallon of coffee."

"Then I'll stick to our customers in Washington. That," he said to Dorothea, "is where I am bound now. You'd be surprised how many embassy cellars need replenishing."

"I'll take the hint and replenish *you*." Tom reached for their glasses. And there's a gentle hint for Tony, he thought. "And then Thea and I are leaving for dinner. That mention of ham and rye made me remember my own lunch today."

"Go right ahead," Tony said easily. "I'd like to stay for a few moments with Brad, and dig into that memory of his. Nice to have a friend who goes back a long way."

Tom stared at him, said briskly, "Come on, Thea, we'll leave them to it. Get your wrap. We'll eat downstairs, make it an early evening." He looked pointedly at Tony, as Dorothea left for the bedroom to collect scarf and bag.

"We'll be away from here long before that," Tony promised. "Where are you staying in Brussels? The old hangout? I'll look you up if I'm around."

As he would be. "Do that," Tom said. "And don't make all your nice little news items off the record. Give me something I can write up. Here's the key to this room. Lock up tightly, will you?"

"That's Brad's department."

"Oh, I forgot, he's the one who will be dropping it at the desk. Exits must match entrances."

"Always kidding," Tony smiled blandly.

Brad laid the key well in view beside his drink. "We'll talk about the book when next we meet," he said apologetically. "How is it coming?" His rule with authors was never to press them, never harry or hurry.

"Needs some spare time, but I think I may get that."

"Oh?" Brad probed gently.

"I'll stop in to see you at the office, on my way to Brussels. I'll explain then. Okay?"

"Very much so."

Dorothea returned, her bewilderment growing as she was led in Tom's firm grip out of the room, her little goodbye speeches cut down to a bright smile. At a safe distance along the empty corridor, she let her feelings explode. "And what on earth is going on?"

"Nothing."

"Nothing?"

He calmed her with a kiss on her cheek. "They needed a place to meet. Why not in our room?"

She dropped her voice to a whisper. "What are they plotting?"

"It's no conspiracy against the United States, if that's what is worrying you," he said with a grin. "It's just some information that Tony wants from Brad."

There was no one in the elevator. Dorothea said, "But Brad isn't with Intelligence, is he?"

"Definitely not." No more. Brad had resigned from that

kind of work almost twelve years ago.

"But Tony is, isn't he?"

"Now, what gave you that idea?"

"Just a feeling, somehow. You know, I only remembered him tonight by his clothes. And I thought, what if Tony was dressed as a stevedore and I bumped into him on the docks—"

"*That's* a wild notion!" It amused Tom.

"Or, if he was dressed as a pilot and I saw him on board a flight to Detroit—"

"If my aunt had whiskers, she'd be my uncle."

"Some women do have whiskers," Dorothea reminded him coldly. "All I'm trying to say is that Tony's the kind of man I'd hardly remember unless I could place him by his clothes."

"Not very flattering to Tony, are you? I don't think he'd be too amused to hear all that. In fact—" Tom was suddenly serious—"I think we should drop the whole subject right now and enjoy our dinner."

He steered her through the lobby into the dining-room. He wasn't too worried. In five years of living together Thea had never repeated a confidence he had given her. Discreet. No gossiper. That was Thea. But he didn't like the little frown shading her bright blue eyes. "We'll talk later," he promised.

"It's just that I'm so sick of the word Intelligence," she began.

"Later," he said firmly. "Now, smile for the *maître d'*, and get us a good table."

"And you'll really answer all my questions?"

"Do my best. I'm no oracle, darling, just a newspaperman who is very very hungry."

She smiled then, for him entirely. They got a good table in any case.

* * *

In the sitting-room Brad Gillon had been listening intently to Tony. No more jokes, no more flights of fancy.

"Come on, Brad, dig into that memory bank. You must have heard of Konov in your OSS days. That time you raced into the ruins of Hitler's Chancellery neck and neck with Soviet Intelligence. Konov was with their team."

"The one that went through a mess of Hitler's private papers, trying to find some evidence that Churchill had been conspiring with him to attack Russia?"

"They wanted to believe it too," Tony said, shaking his head.

"A Soviet Intelligence officer's dream of glory? *Alone I found it.*"

"But there was nothing to find. If only Konov had been in Disinformation at that time, he would have invented a document then and there. Thank God he wasn't. He is now." Tony paused. "During the fifties and sixties, Konov worked in their Department for Illegals. Does that catch your memory? A lot of intelligence reports must have passed over your desk in that period."

"I left State by 1962," Brad reminded him. "But just around then—yes, I begin to remember Konov." His voice quickened. "There was that episode in Ottawa—left in a hurry just before the Canadians could arrest him. He was in the US too, I recall. A busy little beaver."

"North America was his field. Still is."

"Then why is NATO worrying about him—or don't you think our intelligence agencies can cope?" Brad asked with a wry smile.

"*If* they'd start co-operating with each other again—" Tony suggested but refrained from a sharp criticism of Hoover in the late sixties—"or with us. But that happy state got cut off abruptly. It's the root reason for all their present troubles, isn't it?"

"Could be." Thank God, I'm out of all that, thought Brad; but he couldn't bury his memories, or the latest headlines either. "I'm afraid for my country, Tony. These are bad days."

"Head-rolling time," Tony agreed. "I must say—when you Americans start swinging, you use a hatchet. Couldn't a neat scalpel and some precision surgery do the job?"

"You get no big headlines with a scalpel."

There was a brief silence.

"Look—I didn't bring you here to depress you," Tony said briskly. He rose and freshened their drinks. "All I want is a little help from you on the problem of Vladimir Konov."

"How?" Brad was wary.

"Konov is arriving here on Tuesday. He's with a grain-buying team meeting your agricultural experts in Washington."

That was a shock. "Cool customer, isn't he? After his exit from Canada—what is he doing here, d'you think? Gathering background for future Disinformation use?"

"He'll sound out those who are soft and those who are tough, and no doubt he'll go to work on the easy marks, and arrange some future approaches through his Illegals—they were his speciality during the sixties. He provided them with American passports and life-histories—sometimes belonging to real Americans, remember?"

Brad nodded.

"But Konov has another reason for coming here, just at this

time. A reason he has been trying to keep to himself. So we've heard, from one of our agents in Moscow."

"NATO Intelligence has an agent in place? Close enough to Konov to know his plans? Pretty good. In fact, damned good."

"So far, yes. He and Konov are in the same Department of Disinformation. He's actually senior to Konov, but they are rivals for the next big promotion. Tricky."

"That's one of your better understatements."

"So here's the set-up. Konov has suspicions—they are his meat and drink. Konov has ambitions. Konov is out gunning for our agent. And he will succeed if he can get his hands on a NATO memorandum that was sent to Washington. He knows it exists, but hasn't the particulars so far. And that's what he needs, to be right on target—a piece of evidence that would disclose our agent. Several others, too, but our man in Moscow would be the first casualty."

"What evidence? Surely NATO didn't mention names?"

"No, no. The evidence would be in the kind of specialised information that was sent to NATO. Konov could track the source down. At least, that's what our agent feels. He's jittery. No doubt about that. We had word from him yesterday."

"So you took the night flight out of Brussels," Brad said thoughtfully. "Washington next?"

Tony nodded. "I'm on convoy duty—making sure the NATO Memorandum gets safely back to Brussels, once the Pentagon releases it to me."

"But what help do you need from me?" Brad's sombre face was perplexed.

"Just sound the tocsin. Warn any of your old friends at State that Konov is in town. They'll get in touch with the Justice

Department and see that the message gets through to the right investigative agencies."

"What about your own CIA contacts in Washington?"

"Paralysed at the moment. You've been reading the papers, haven't you? How do you expect them to act—boldly, effectively?" Tony's face was grim. "This is important, Brad. One good man's life is at stake; and eight others too. And NATO *is* America's business. Without it, you'd really go bust in Western Europe."

"The FBI have a lot on Konov—they must have."

"We hope," Tony said, a trifle bitterly.

"You have no friends there?"

"Once upon a time. They resigned in Hoover's latter-day period of sainthood. All communications with European Intelligence cut off. No more quiet interchange of information. Let's wait until the dam breaks, and then we can all rush together. Hands across the sea, tra la la!"

Brad finished his drink. "I'll see what I can do."

6

Chuck rattled off a short line of connected dashes to mark the end of the text. The typewriter sounded triumphant, but he had no sense of exultation. No excitement: not even relief that the job was over. He pulled the last page out of the machine, separated it from its carbon copy.

"Twenty minutes past ten," Rick said. "Not bad at all." He placed the carbon copy with the others, studied the page for any errors. "Clean. Except for these damn letters." The *m* and *n* were ink-blocked, the *t* thickened. "Pity you didn't have any type-cleaner around. Still, it's legible. Quite professional. I'd hire you as a secretary any day."

Chuck said nothing at all. He gathered up the NATO Memorandum, Part I, and opened his desk drawer. Carefully, he placed all three parts together, and began fastening them into one complete document.

Rick spoke again. "Can't I have a look at the two last sections?"

Chuck went on with his job, finished it, and replaced the NATO folder in the drawer. "I'd rather we didn't handle it any more than necessary."

And Rick, who had been congratulating himself on his display of complete innocence in that last question, looked suddenly startled. I didn't wear gloves, he remembered, and his face went rigid.

"You'd better 'phone Holzheimer."

Rick tried to recall whether he had really grasped the sheets of the Memorandum between thumb and forefinger: he had lifted them gingerly by the tips of his fingers, but there had been speed and pressure. No, he decided, he hadn't left any identifiable traces of his work. But he ought to have gone downstairs to Katie and got the gloves he kept there: then he would have made sure that there were no fingerprints. He was almost certain now: what he was really nervous about was the expression on Mischa's face if he ever heard of this carelessness. Mischa...

"Holzheimer," Chuck repeated sharply. "You said he would be waiting until ten thirty. It's almost that now."

Rick nodded and reached for the telephone. And there went a perfectly natural excuse, he thought as he concealed his annoyance. Ten thirty had been a time that he had pulled out of the air: he hadn't expected Chuck to finish the typing job until eleven o'clock at the earliest. Too late, he would have explained, to get in touch tonight; better leave it till tomorrow. And tomorrow could have another tomorrow...any pretence to let him delay and postpone and delay. But now he could feel Chuck's eye on his fingers as he dialled the number, so he kept it accurate. When he got through, there was enough background noise in the news-room to give him a second chance at an excuse. "No go. I don't think he's at his desk. Gone home, perhaps. Or out on the town. There's so much damned racket—"

"But someone answered you—"

"Sure. And left the 'phone off the hook."

"Keep trying."

"It's the wrong time to call him. Obviously."

Chuck reached out and seized the receiver as Rick was about to replace it.

"What the hell—" Rick began.

"We'll wait this out." And simultaneously, a voice was saying angrily into Chuck's ear, "Who's this? Do you want to talk with me—or not?"

"Martin Holzheimer?"

"Speaking."

"Here's Nealey. Hold the line." Chuck handed the receiver back to Rick. "Tell him you'll meet him in Katie's apartment, as soon after eleven o'clock as possible."

"What?"

"Downstairs. Apartment 5-A."

"But—"

"Tell him."

Rick did all that. He ended his call, and smothered his anger as he turned to face Chuck. "Just what do you think you are doing? This was my end of the business—to meet him some place where it would be safe and quiet—"

"Katie's apartment will be very quiet. She's out until dawn, isn't she?"

"But why *her* place?"

"Because it's handy. I'll be there, too."

Rick was nettled. "I thought you were going to keep clear of—"

"I want to see this man, get a kind of feeling about him," Chuck said.

"Totally irrational behaviour."

"Possibly. Just following my instincts, I guess. I'm going to make quite sure that he won't publish the name of Shandon House."

"And what about you?" Rick asked.

"You can introduce me as the man who has access to Shandon House. That's all. We'll keep the Kelso name out of it."

Rick shook his head. "So that's why you chose to bring him to Katie's apartment? He will see her name on the door-plate. Not yours. And you can slip down—"

"Okay, okay. Let's get ready. Lock up tight. Check the windows, will you, Rick?"

As he spoke, Chuck pulled the couch well to one side, and turned back the rug that lay underneath. Next, he was over at the desk again, lifting the folder with the precious memorandum. He laid it under the rug, which he then smoothed into place. Satisfied with the look of it, he began heaving the couch into its original position. "That should do. I won't be gone for any length of time, but I don't trust that desk lock; any nitwit could force it open. Windows okay? Put four records on the player. Leave a couple of lights on." Chuck picked up Holzheimer's copy of Part I to carry inside his jacket. His duplicate copy was shoved inside a magazine, a folded newspaper flung carelessly on top.

"See this?" he asked as he opened the front door. "It's said to be burglar-proof."

Rick stared at the new lock on the door. "When did you have that put in?"

"A couple of days ago. The old one was too easy."

And so, thought Rick, if I had slipped downstairs for a pair of gloves, I'd have been locked out. My key for this door would have been useless. He began to laugh.

"It's no joke," Chuck said. "That damned lock set me back thirty-six dollars."

So it's this way, Rick was arguing with Mischa (or with Oleg, if it came to that): we got the second and third parts. Wasn't that worth the disclosures in the first part? And Mischa (or Oleg) would have to agree. Neither of them would pin a medal on him, but they couldn't say he had botched the assignment either. He looked at Chuck as they reached Katie's door. "You really are full of surprises," he said, and shook his head.

"As soon as you identify me to Holzheimer as his source—"

"I still can't imagine why you are taking the risk of letting him see you."

"Insurance."

"Against what?"

"Against a delay in publication. He'll carry more weight with his editor if he can say he has actually met me. And also—" Chuck paused.

Rick braced himself. He had underestimated Chuck tonight. "Also what?"

"I'll be able to identify him again, if necessary."

"Suspicious, aren't you?" Rick unlocked Katie's door and they stepped into the disordered hall.

"Yes," Chuck said frankly. "That's the hell of this kind of business," he added with distaste. "You have to think twice about every move you make, judge it from all angles." There was another pause. "I wish to God I had never—" He broke off.

"Backing out?" Rick concealed a rising hope.

"No." Chuck looked straight ahead, and was depressed by the view. The living-room was dark except for one light somewhere round the corner but he could feel, if not see, the combined clutter of objects inside. It was one unholy mess, he thought: no expense spared on the furnishings and pictures, and yet everything—like Katie's own styles of dressing (they varied each month according to whim)—looked as though it came from some attic or flea-market. "How can you stand this?"

"Stand what?" asked Katie's voice. Rick and Chuck looked at each other, stepped into the living-room and got a full view of the dining alcove at its lighted end Rising from its marble-topped table were four startled people: Katie, dressed in her current style of satin blouse, turquoise jewellery and Indian headband; a squat blond man, with shaggy hair and full beard, his eyes glaring at the two intruders; a tall thin black man with a rounded Afro and large dark glasses; a woman with Alice-in-Wonderland hair, sweeping its long locks round a middle-aged face, and a good pair of breasts (but beginning to sag) showing bra-less under a tight cotton shirt, pulled over patched blue jeans.

"Pigs," the woman said, gathering up a map and some scraps of paper from the table, her head knocking lightly against the shade of the overhead Tiffany lamp to send it swinging. The men's faces went blank and watchful. Katie was trying to laugh. "They're all right," she kept saying. "Just friends."

"Get them out!" said the woman. The two men, impassive, sullen, kept staring.

Rick recovered. "Katie, why the hell aren't you at Bo Browning's?"

"What the frigging hell are you doing here?" Katie replied in her Philadelphia Main-line accent.

"We're raiding your refrigerator for a late supper," Rick told her, moving towards the kitchen. "And then I was going to pick you up at Bo's party. That was our arrangement, wasn't it?"

"It was not," Katie flashed back. Normally she was an extremely pretty girl, dark-haired and slender, with a face that smiled gently. At this moment she looked almost ugly with fear, her large blue eyes watching her companions' faces, her mouth taut with anxiety.

The tall thin man moved first, straight for the hall, measuring Chuck as he passed him with bitter contempt. The middle-aged woman followed, silent now and angry as she stuffed the map and the scraps of paper into her large shoulder-bag. So did the short bearded man, his face averted, his hands tucked into the pockets of an old army jacket. Katie paused only to snatch up the woman's cardigan and her own coat. "I'll get them to leave—" she was pleading as she ran after them—"Don't go."

"Come on!" the woman told her. "Or stay behind with your pet pigs." Permanently, the angry eyes seemed to say. Katie didn't even hesitate. She closed the front door behind her, leaving Chuck to stare at its elaborately painted panels.

In the living-room, his amazement grew. Rick was selecting two books and some small personal objects, throwing them into his bag on top of clothing and shaving-kit. He moved briskly, checking the overpiled bookcase again, then the bathroom shelves. "That's it," he said, closing the bag.

"You're leaving?"

"As soon as you meet Holzheimer."

"Why? If ever there was a time to stay and argue Katie out of all this—" Chuck looked over at the table where four heads had huddled in a tight little conspiracy. "I mean, she's way into something that's too deep for her."

"That's obvious. Too deep for any of us." Rick was hearing an early-warning signal from Mischa: in America, you'll make friends with all kinds of people—conservatives, liberals, even Marxists. But stick to the ideologues; avoid the anarchist groups, the activists. Even if they are far to the left, they can't be trusted. They need a tight control, and you haven't got the capacity to do that: you can't supply them with money or weapons or training. You have no hold over them. Therefore, for you and your work, they are dangerous. They will involve you in trouble you can't handle. Keep clear of them and attract no suspicion.

Rick locked his bag.

"She needs someone," Chuck insisted.

Rick carried his bag into the hall, placed his coat and scarf on top of it.

Getting ready for a quick exit, Chuck thought. "Why don't you call her father, at least?"

Rick looked at his watch. "Almost eleven o'clock." He sat down to wait for Holzheimer. Mischa, he was thinking again, where was Mischa now? And how was he? Any use telephoning the nearest police-station, keeping everything anonymous, just an inquiry about a missing friend?

"Why not call her father? Or someone? She has a sister—"

"Married to a State Department man. And one brother who is a Wall Street banker, and an uncle who owns a newspaper chain. What do you think they could do? Argue. How far has that ever got them with Katie?"

"Well, they were just letting her have her little games. No one took her seriously. You didn't, did you? You never knew she was in so deep. It must be recent, though. Wouldn't you say?" Chuck looked over at the marble-topped table, and remembered the hard sullen glares from three pairs of cold eyes. "Rick, you can't just leave her to those people. She'll—"

"She's a spoiled brat."

"She always was. That didn't keep you from shacking up with her for two years. Look—if you don't stay around to persuade her out of this mess, I will."

"Will you? Then you are a god-damned fool." More of a fool than I had even guessed, Rick thought. "Those who want to dig their own graves, supply the measurements."

"An old East German saying?" Chuck gibed angrily. It was the first time he had ever referred to Rick's childhood. And then he felt a twinge of remorse: it had been no fault of a six-year-old, Brooklyn born, that he had been taken by his German mother to visit her parents in Leipzig once the war was over. No fault of his, either, that the two of them had been kept there until eleven years ago, when Anna Nealey had died and Rick had at last been able to escape to the West.

"No." Rick was smiling, unperturbed. Just one of Mischa's little bits of peasant wisdom, he recalled. He kept on smiling, said nothing more. The door-bell rang and ended the slight impasse. "I'll introduce you as Jerry, and then I'll slip away. No need to stay," he told Chuck as he rose to let in their visitor. "Shall I switch on some more lights?"

"No." Chuck pushed Katie and her friends out of his mind. "Ready," he said.

* * *

The meeting in the semi-dark room was brief. Martin Holzheimer was a tall lank man who curled up in his armchair like a question-mark. Let's change that attitude to an exclamation-point, Chuck decided, once his own curiosity was satisfied—Holzheimer's never would be unless he had a three-day session of probing—and reached inside his jacket for the document. "Okay," he said, "here it is." He laid Part I of the NATO Memorandum on the free corner of a coffee-table laden with bric-à-brac.

"Just like that?" Holzheimer asked. "No further stipulations?" His legs had stretched straight.

"You've agreed to everything I've asked."

Holzheimer was on his feet, reaching for the document. "As of this moment, you are privileged information. Turn on a light, will you, and let me have a look at this."

"Read it at your desk." Chuck was already in the hall, opening the front door. He came back into the room. "Just close the door behind you," he said. "Good night, Mr. Holzheimer."

Holzheimer looked at him with a suspicion of a smile. "Where can I reach you, Jerry? Here?"

"No."

"I thought not," Holzheimer said. Jerry's clothes didn't match this weird world around him. "Then where?"

"I'll call you. Every second day, until your story is published. How's that?"

"Not good, but not bad either." There was nothing to be gained by staying. It could be counter-productive, in fact. Holzheimer could sense when a man was obdurate. This one was granite. "Good luck," he said, and then wondered why that phrase had slipped out instead of "Good night."

"And to you." Chuck turned away. He heard Holzheimer pull the door shut. He checked the lock. And waited. Five minutes later he was back in his own small apartment. After Katie's, it seemed spacious. And safe. The folder under the couch and rug was safe too.

He sank into a chair and relaxed completely for the first time that day. He was too exhausted to go to bed. No sense of excitement, no feeling of a major victory. He couldn't even tell if the whole damn thing had been worth it. Then a strange thought came to him as he glanced round the room—would he ever see Rick here again? Possibly not. Rick was running scared tonight, no doubt worried about what Representative Pickering would have to say if he ever found out about his bright-eyed aide's liaison with a pretty little activist in New York. That was why Rick had cut off Katie with a karate-chop. Would he do the same to me, Chuck wondered, if and when necessary? It was a disturbing idea, so he turned away from it. Tomorrow, he preferred to think, Rick would be laughing at his attack of panic, and probably telephoning Katie, too. God, what a mess some people made of their lives. Chuck thought of Katie: all the advantages in the world, yet searching for more, and more. Strange restless ambition that drove some people. What was it that brother Tom used to say? People's lives are shaped by the choices they make. That was Tom, all right, trusting in each person's capacity to think and decide for himself. But what about people like Katie, all emotion and no forethought? If there was a wrong choice, pretty prattling Katie would take it.

Suddenly he went tense. What about my choice today? The

right one, he told himself again, and dropped that subject. He had plenty of other things to keep his mind occupied: a typewriter to be returned; a Sunday visit to Shandon House; the memorandum to be safely filed in the security room. Yes, an early start. He rose briskly and went to bed, plunging almost at once into a sleep untroubled by doubts.

As for Rick, he had no easy night. There was no late train, no late flight to Washington. He found a room at the Statler Hilton, just across the avenue from Penn Station, for an early departure tomorrow. The sooner he was out of Fun City the better. And what could he do about Mischa? Nothing, he told himself for the hundredth time. That was Oleg's problem. Or was it, entirely? As Alexis, Rick would have to make his weekly report on Monday. His Washington contact would call him without fail. And he would have to give an account of his meeting with Mischa. If he kept quiet about that, there could be harsh questions from the Centre in Moscow. It would be a different matter if Mischa were well and functioning: then the meeting need never be mentioned. But now? How would Oleg handle it? What would be his story? Rick had no way of knowing until Oleg met him in Washington. And would he?

No, the best thing was to make his usual report, stating he had been called to New York by Mischa. They had met in Central Park. The NATO Memorandum had been discussed, and subsequently secured. Mischa had been attacked after they left each other. Alexis had warned Oleg. He knew nothing more.

And then, he thought in alarm, in an emergency like this I must report immediately—not wait until Monday. I'll have to call my contact tomorrow in Washington. I'll have to give him a message to pass on to Control, then to the Resident. And let's hope that the microfilm I have secured will stop all questions. But what would Oleg have to say to that? He was to get the film from me—so Mischa ordered. Well, let the Centre settle it: Oleg may be the one to be disciplined—and Mischa, too. After all, my first loyalty is to Moscow, not to Mischa.

But there was enough of the old loyalty to Mischa to drive him downstairs into the lobby. (He needed cigarettes anyway, he told himself.) At one of the public telephones he put in a call to the Nineteenth Precinct of the New York police department. It was in Sixty-seventh Street—he had passed it often enough—and surely it would deal with any mugging around Sixty-ninth Street area. A woman answered and passed him over to an officer at the desk.

Rick's voice was polite and anxious. "My cousin went out for a walk on Fifth Avenue this evening and hasn't returned. I'm worried. Perhaps he was assaulted—have you any reports about a mugging? Somewhere near Sixty-ninth Street? That's where he lives."

"No, sir. No report of any assault in that area, as yet."

"Not as yet? But this was at half-past five!"

"Where was your cousin taking his walk, sir?"

"He probably went into the Park."

"In that case, try the Central Park Precinct."

"But don't you know—"

"They deal with anything that happens *inside* the Park," the officer said patiently. "We deal with *outside* the Park. You could also try Missing—" He stared at the receiver that had suddenly gone dead in his hand. He said to the sergeant, "It's always the same. Someone goes out for a walk and doesn't get back when he's expected, and his relatives start thinking he's been assaulted. What a town!" Then he added, "But how did he know the time when his cousin could have been mugged?"

It was a question, half-amusing, half-puzzling, that made him call the Central Park Precinct some ten minutes later. "Did you hear from the joker who knew what time his cousin got mugged in the Park?... Yeah, five thirty. That's what he said... Sixty-ninth Street entrance? Hey, he knew the place too. Somewhere near Sixty-ninth Street, he said... Yeah, sounded like a fairly young fellow. American? Sure. He was American, all right. Okay, okay. Just thought I'd let you know."

"What's going on?" the desk sergeant asked.

"Central Park Precinct has a John Doe problem. Unidentified victim of assault in Lenox Hill Hospital. But as soon as this cousin got the info, he hung up. Didn't say he'd come round to identify, dodged giving his own name."

"Could be he was in a hurry."

"Too much of a hurry, if you ask me."

The desk at the Nineteenth Precinct went back to its other problems. But its 'phone call hadn't been pointless. The sergeant at the Central Park Precinct was making a note of it: any small piece of information about the unidentified victim now in Lenox Hill was worth adding to the bits and pieces of strange little items that—so far—constituted the file on this John Doe.

Rick returned to his room. Yes, the telephone calls had been well worth his while. Now he knew where Mischa was—Lenox Hill, the nearest hospital to the scene of the mugging—and that

Mischa had carried no identification on him. These were two facts which would look good in his report tomorrow: he had done all he could. Oleg could have done no better.

He went to bed, only to lie staring at the ceiling. In all, he managed three hours of sleep before he rose to leave for Washington.

7

Oleg, along with a drift of other curious spectators, had seen the ambulance arrive and noted the name of Lenox Hill Hospital. The next thing was to find out its address. He did that from a directory in a 'phone booth. And then what? His English was good; he could pass for the John Browning of Montreal that his passport and driver's licence said he was. Which papers, if any, had Mischa been carrying? Canadian, or American? Or none at all? (That would be best under the present circumstances.) A complete mess, Oleg decided, anger growing out of his fears. That son of a bitch Alexis, running scared, leaving everything to be cleaned up behind him.

Oleg chewed over his ideas along with a hamburger at a Madison Avenue quick-service counter. He had several options, but calling the Soviet Mission to the United Nations was not one of them. Mischa had outstepped his authority this time. Unless his own assignment that had brought him secretly to

New York was fulfilled—and its results worth the risks taken—Mischa was in trouble. And so was Oleg. All for the purpose of nailing down a high-placed traitor. Exemplary, if their plan had worked: praise and promotion. But now? It would still have to work, even with this unforeseen accident. Or else...

So, first, he would have to get Mischa out of hospital before any identification became possible. Maintenance of security (and that was Oleg's own particular field in the Executive Action branch of Disinformation) was now the primary consideration.

From the Madison Avenue coffee-shop he made his way on foot towards the Lenox Hill district. What with the surfeit of automobiles parked along the streets that crossed the various avenues, he had decided to leave his Chevrolet exactly where it was, on Sixty-ninth. Once he had scouted the hospital area, he would know whether it was easier to use a taxi rather than his rented car for Mischa's removal. And how was that to be effected? By open legitimate means—such as a friend of the family come to take an injured man home? Or (if that was impossible) by a careful survey of the position of Mischa's hospital room, and later, with outside help, a well-planned abduction? That would take time, and there was danger in any delay, even if there was no fear of Mischa talking. Mischa would plead amnesia if he couldn't get away with feigning unconsciousness.

Oleg walked six blocks up Park Avenue, noting its spaciousness and its high-rising apartment houses. Against the cool blackness of night, lights seemed intensified. And there were too many of them: windows glowed with life, high overhead street-lamps cast no shadows, traffic signals—stationed along the three-mile stretch of broad pavement—

sparkled bright red or green at every corner. Above all, it was too quiet for his taste; there were some pedestrians, some taxis and cars, but not enough movement to make sure of an absolutely unnoticed departure from the hospital. (There were doormen, for instance, inside every well-lighted lobby he passed.) No, Park Avenue wasn't suitable. Madison, to the west, had been a busier place—although its small expensive shops, that reminded him of the Faubourg St Honoré, were all closed and tightly shuttered with heavy iron grilles. He cut over to Lexington Avenue, a block away to the east, and decided it was his best bet. It had a life of its own—nothing blatant, a district of neighbourhood stores, overhead apartments, cafés and bars and small restaurants. Taxis and buses, too. Enough animation for his purpose.

He was a stranger in this upper east-side district. His last assignment in New York had taught him a lot about the west of Manhattan, from Ninetieth Street right down to Chelsea. He knew his way around Greenwich Village.

Off Manhattan, he could even find his way around parts of Brooklyn, which was no mean feat. And in Queens there was the safe-house where he and Mischa had intended to spend tonight. With this experience behind him he had been considered an expert on New York by Mischa: one of the reasons why he had been approached for this current assignment. Again he cursed Alexis who (from the files on his activities) spent many a week-end in this section of the city. Alexis could, at the very least, have given him a number to call; could have waited by its telephone for further instructions; could have helped in several small ways without endangering his own security.

Oleg left the bright bustle of Lexington, walked back to

Park Avenue to approach the hospital, logically, from the front. The layout was simple. The building, high-storeyed, occupied a whole block on the Avenue, and stretched along the two side-streets—Seventy-sixth and Seventy-seventh—as far as Lexington Avenue. But the first difficulty in his plan of escape quickly became apparent: a huge project of construction work was going on, a new corner-wing was being added, the building's height increased, and the entrance from Park was blocked by high wooden hoardings and heavy equipment stretching round to Seventy-sixth Street—and there, the door was closed for the night. This narrowed his search to Seventy-seventh Street itself, a quiet thoroughfare, occupied on its north side by some apartment buildings, two houses, and a Christian Science church to challenge the doctors across the road in direct confrontation.

He walked past the hospital's main entrance, with glass walls and wide windows giving him a clear view of the brightly lit hall and a large desk. A busy place, complete (and this aroused a sardonic smile) with a gift shop just inside its door. One policeman outside—no, a hospital guard in dark blue uniform, who was having a sneak smoke on an eight-inch cigar. America, he thought contemptuously, his confidence growing. Beyond this there was another entrance, smaller and more business-like. EMERGENCY was the sign overhead; and, adjoining it, a shuttered garage marked AMBULANCE.

So that is the target, he thought. But he walked on, and soon reached Lexington again. Too early to make his move. Besides, he wanted to find out more about this whole area.

It was a clear night, a dark sky reflecting the city's glow: fine November weather meant no rush on taxis. He would hail one without much delay when it was necessary. There were plenty of them here, all cruising south, Lexington's one-way direction. And enough people on foot, dressed very much in the style he and Mischa had chosen for themselves. Prosperous bourgeois, with only a few long-haired types in jeans and leather jackets, and some weirdos dolled up with heavy platform shoes and other whimsies. A variety of facial characteristics, he noted: many central Europeans, judging from the small Hungarian, Czech, and German restaurants; Chinese too, and Cuban, Greek, Italian eating-places. And Irish saloons, of course. The usual New York hodge-podge, he decided. Easy to pass unnoticed in this racial mix.

He dropped into a café and had a cup of coffee with a sandwich, sat smoking his way through several cigarettes as he arranged a flexible plan in his mind. He would have to play it all very loose, perhaps improvise as he went along.

By half-past ten, he had explored enough, and turned back to Seventy-seventh Street. The hospital ambulance was coming out of the garage. Some new casualty, he thought, and perhaps an opportune moment to begin his inquiries in EMERGENCY. He drew a deep breath, and entered a brightly-lit hall: small, square, unfurnished. The short stretch of wall to his left was occupied by a glass-enclosed counter, revealing an office behind it where several people milled around. Opposite this, to his right, was the wide entrance to a room edged with plastic chairs, where waiting relatives sat in solemn silence. Facing him was a blank wall with a closed door and a clearly printed warning that it was for patients' use only. That was all: a bare no-nonsense place where he felt dangerously noticeable. Mischa's departure, unless it were authorised, would be impossible to arrange through this boxed-in trap. How much easier it would have been in the large hall inside the main entrance, with its moving currents of people, its busy desk, its lack of curious eyes.

He was being watched right now. A young black woman was already at the counter, sliding one of its windows open. In the office behind her there were three other women and two men, busy people, but interested in him, even momentarily. He decided on his best line of approach. He was a worried and bewildered stranger from Canada, searching for an old friend who had failed to keep an appointment tonight. But what name would be used for Mischa—the one on his Canadian or his American passport? Or had Mischa not been carrying passport or papers? So Oleg sounded harassed and vague.

"The police sent me here," he began. "They say there was an attack on a man in the Sixty-ninth Street area of Central Park, this evening. He may be my friend—I am searching for him."

The girl looked at him, no expression on her face, no reaction visible.

"The police said the man was brought here. About six o'clock," Oleg rushed on. "Would you please verify?"

The girl turned towards another clerk, called out, "About six o'clock. Central Park victim."

There was a quick check with some records. "Admitted at five fifty-eight," came the abrupt answer. Then someone else looked up to say, "Hey, wasn't that the guy with no identification on him?"

Oleg felt a jump of hope. Better than he had expected. He looked crestfallen. "There is nothing to identify him? Then how do I know whether he is my friend? And I'm the only one who knows he's missing. We were to meet this evening at six o'clock. I waited for over an hour. Then I kept phoning and—"

"You telephoned his family?"

Smart girl, he thought, in spite of her expressionless manner. "No. He lives alone. His wife lives on Long Island. In Patchogue. They are separated. I'll call her when I find out what has happened." Oleg raised his hands helplessly, let his voice trail off. "If I could see this man—" He paused, waiting for the right response. And he got it.

"Just a moment," the girl said, and went over to another section of desk, one that faced a broad interior corridor. She spoke to a nurse on duty there, who telephoned to some other part of the hospital. There was a brief explanation: we have a man down here who is inquiring... The rest was lost in the sudden flurry of activity as the ambulance returned. But the nurse had received an answer and the girl came hurrying back to Oleg.

"Yes," the girl said, "they want you to identify him. But you'll have to wait. Take a seat in there." She nodded towards the room opposite. Behind her the office had turned into a whirlpool of action.

"But why wait?"

"He isn't available right now."

"Why?"

"He is not available." That was all she had been told, seemingly.

"But I can't wait." He backed a couple of steps. "I must know. If this man is not my friend, I shall have to do a lot of searching tonight. I can't waste any time—they might keep me waiting for an hour. Even more." He half-turned and said angrily, "I'll come back tomorrow."

"Just one moment," she said again—a much-used phrase,

obviously. This time, after a glance at the hustle and bustle around her, she did the telephoning. "You can go up," she told Oleg. "You can't see him as yet. But you can give the police some particulars."

Police? He looked at her.

She didn't explain. She pointed to the closed door that led into the hospital. "Through there straight ahead. One flight up. The elevator is on the right. Near the end of the corridor."

"Police—is anything wrong?"

This amused her. "They always stay until identification has been made." Then her telephone rang and she was busy with some other inquiry.

Straight ahead, she had told him. Beyond the door he ignored the busy nurses' desk, the harshly-lit operating-room facing it, the large room on his right with several emergency beds separated by yellow curtains. It was all clean and bright and modern, with expertly-controlled pandemonium near the ambulance area far to his left. His pace quickened as he reached the end of the broad corridor, further progress barred by a door that must lead on to other stretches of this bewildering place. That might be useful, he thought, but he did not risk exploring it. Not at this moment. One flight up: that was where he was expected now. Police? He wondered again as he entered the elevator. And why was Mischa not kept downstairs in that room with the yellow curtains? In one way Oleg was pleased by this: privacy was better for his purposes. But in another way he found it somehow disquieting.

Yet, as he stepped off at the second floor and came down a corridor to reach the desk (it was all similar in set-up, he noted, to the first-floor area, except that here there seemed to be private rooms), his alarm about police vanished. There was only one officer in sight, and he was young. Inexperienced, Oleg thought with relief. So there were no suspicions brooding around Mischa. This was just standard procedure, as the girl downstairs had said.

As for the two nurses at the desk, one was middle-aged and pleasant-faced; the other young and pretty—at least the police officer seemed to think so. It was a relaxed picture, even if the light walls, bright lights, antiseptic smell all spelled hospital. Oleg felt his worry subside. "Is this where I have to identify a man?" he began, lowering his voice half-way through his question as he noticed the sign behind the desk: QUIET PLEASE. "Or am I on the wrong floor? This is EMERGENCY, isn't it?"

"Intensive care," the older nurse told him. "But we take the overflow from EMERGENCY when necessary. You've come to the right place."

Oleg's eyes followed her glance, to a closed door. "My friend is in there?"

"He is recovering from the anaesthetic."

"What happened to him?"

"A severe injury to the arm. But he is resting comfortably." She busied herself at the desk. The younger nurse, her smooth dark hair crowned by a saucy white cap that perched miraculously on top of her head, began to help her stack a pile of clothes into neat order. Mischa's clothes, Oleg saw.

He said, "Do these belong to the man in that room? If he turns out to be my friend, he'll need them. I am taking him home."

The senior nurse exchanged a glance with the policeman. "The wound required many stitches. The doctor will tell you when he can be—"

"But my friend would prefer to leave now. I know him well. He has a fear of hospitals."

"He has lost a great deal of blood. It would be dangerous to move him."

"I could hire an ambulance."

"He requires hospitalisation. His wound has to be dressed professionally. If he dislikes hospitals, there would be no point in moving him to another. Now, would there?" The tone was decided even if subdued, the argument over. She picked up a clipboard, consulted the instructions on it, and hurried off.

And I, thought Oleg, defeated myself in that interchange. Still, it is easier to extract a man from a sickbed in New York than it would be in Moscow. There, they really know how to be on guard. Here—one policeman, soft-spoken and hesitant, who is only now coming forward with a note-book and pencil in hand. He is about as urgent as if he were going to give me a traffic ticket.

The officer had completed his own quiet study of the stranger: just under six feet in height, husky, strong shoulders, dark brown hair worn short, eyes blue and deep set, features strong, manner argumentative. He spoke now, keeping his voice low-pitched. Pity he had to ask the questions right here. But where else? He must keep an eye on the door of that room. "Could you give me some particulars about your friend— height, weight, general description?"

"It's two years since I saw him last, in Montreal. You see, I am here on a short visit, just arrived this morning—"

"Height and weight, sir. Then we'll know if there is any reason for you to stay around."

Better keep the details accurate, thought Oleg, or else I'll be dismissed. "He is about five feet six inches tall. Weight—I'd say 180 pounds. At least, that's what it was when I—"

"Yes, sir. Hair? Eyes?"

"Grey eyes. Hair turning grey, worn long. Age—fifty-one."

"If he has had a haircut since you last saw him, he may be the right man," the officer observed. "You better wait and have a look at him. How did you learn he was in Lenox Hill Hospital?"

The surprise question fazed Oleg only for a few moments. He plunged into an amplification of the story he had told the girl downstairs. His friend, the tale now ran, had telephoned him at five o'clock, just before he set out for his usual evening stroll down through Central Park. They had arranged to meet on Fifth Avenue at Fifty-ninth Street and then have drinks and dinner together. His friend never arrived. "So I waited. For almost an hour. Then I telephoned his hotel. The clerk said he had left for the evening. I had dinner. Then I telephoned again. And again. He hadn't returned. I went out for a walk trying to think what I should do." Oleg paused. Better not mention any police-station—that could be too easily checked. "I saw a police car and asked them for help." The young nurse, he noticed, was enthralled by his story. She had finished her listing of Mischa's clothes, and was now listening wide-eyed. Encouraged, he went on, "They called in their precinct—"

"Which one was that?"

Oleg shook his head. "It's all very confusing to a stranger. Their precinct called some other police-station—one that had a record of—well," he demanded suddenly, "what record would it have? You know the procedure better than I do. Anyway, the patrol car directed me to this hospital—as a possibility." By now, he had memorised all the doors and exits that lay within sight. He might not need them. He would have another try at persuading the nurse. She couldn't stop him if he insisted on hiring an ambulance and taking his friend to a hospital in Patchogue. Ex-wife or not, she was the only family he had in this country. And so on and so forth.

The officer had listened patiently. "Yes, sir. Now I'd like to have some names."

"I am John Browning," Oleg volunteered, giving himself a moment to think up a name for Mischa. "I'm at the Hotel Toronto."

The senior nurse returned, frowned a little when she found them still talking at the desk.

The officer persisted, dropping his voice even more. "Your friend's name?"

"Robert Johnstone."

"Johnson?"

"No." Oleg spelled out the name, watched the slow pencil record it in the officer's book, and was ready for the next question when it came.

"His address?"

"Somewhere on East Seventy-second Street. He's been living there since he separated from his wife. That's all I know."

"You had his telephone number," the officer reminded him.

"Oh yes, he gave me it when he called, and I jotted it right down. I've got it right here—" He began searching his pockets, became frustrated. "Must have left it on the telephone-table in my room."

"We can get that later." The officer seemed amused by something else. "Johnstone," he said with a grin, looking at the young nurse. "A good old Russian name."

She reacted at once, large brown eyes widening with indignation. "But that man *is* Russian." Her tone was definite, her accent tinged with Spanish. "I know Russian when I hear it. I was in Havana in 1963." She flashed a glance at Oleg's startled face. The senior nurse shook her head over this display of Cuban temperament. The officer enjoyed it quite obviously.

Oleg had to be sure. "The man spoke Russian? My friend can speak French, of course. But Russian?" He looked at her in disbelief.

"Ask Dr. Bronsky," she told him sharply, quick to defend herself. "Dr. Bronsky knows Russian well. He was there when the man was fighting the anaesthesia. We *both* heard him."

"That's right, we've got it all down in Dr. Bronsky's statement," the officer said, trying now to calm the little storm he had helped to raise.

"Some patients do curse and swear when they are under an anaesthetic," the older nurse said. "I have heard some surprising things myself." Nothing to worry about, her crisp manner implied.

But Oleg had to know. "Perhaps my friend did learn some Russian in New York—enough for a cuss-word or two. That isn't so bad, is it?" he asked the girl.

"There was more than that. He cried out, began struggling and calling for his friend to help—"

"If we *must* talk here," the older nurse broke in, "then let us keep our voices as low as possible. Haven't you finished yet?" she demanded of the officer. I'm willing to co-operate, she thought, but really! This is a hospital, not a police-station.

"Almost," the officer told her. He had been watching Oleg. "Alexis," he said very quietly.

Oleg stared at him.

"Alexis," he repeated. "Does that mean anything to you, Mr. Browning?"

Oleg shook his head.

"His wife's name, perhaps?"

The Cuban nurse said quickly, "Alexis could be a man's name. Alexis and Oleg—he called on them both for help. And he cried out—"

"Yes," the officer cut her short, added placatingly, "It's all noted down, every word of it." He looked at Oleg again, sensing something he couldn't explain. And yet the man's face was expressionless, almost blank. "His wife?"

Oleg forced a smile. "His wife is called Wilma."

"Wilma Johnstone." It was written down. "Her address?"

"Patchogue in Long Island. She may now be using her maiden name. Konig, I think." Oleg could feel the cold sweat breaking over his brow.

"Do you have her full address so that we can notify her if necessary?"

But at that moment, Oleg was saved. The door to Mischa's room had opened, and all heads turned towards it.

Two men came out, both in ordinary civilian clothes. One carried a camera, the other a small hand-case. Behind them was a tall man dressed in white trousers and white tunic. A doctor?—No, an attendant, Oleg decided. After the two violent shocks that had almost paralysed him into this stiff and foolish smile, his brain was coming to life again. And the other two men? Detectives? The police officer seemed to know them, anyway. One of them was saying to him, "You can tell the lieutenant that we've finished here. Got a good set of prints.

They'll be on his desk tomorrow first thing."

Prints?

"Is he conscious yet?" the older nurse wanted to know.

"Sure, he's conscious," said the attendant. "And hating every minute of it. When they took his fingerprints, he—"

"Did he tell you his name was Johnstone?" Oleg burst out; and drew a censuring look from the nurse. "I'm sorry," he said, dropping his voice back to the proper level for a hospital corridor.

"He's telling nothing to nobody," the attendant said as he left. "Doesn't remember a thing about anything."

Oleg measured the distance to the room with its open door: twenty steps, perhaps less. Then his ear caught the Cuban's words to one of the detectives. "What do we do with these things?" He looked back at the desk where she had placed a cane, a pair of cuff-links and a cigarette-lighter. "We were told to keep them aside for you."

"Not for us. The lieutenant probably wants to have a look at them. He'll be here shortly."

The police officer couldn't resist saying, "Try the lighter, Ed."

The man with the camera picked it up gingerly. It was just the usual throw-away-when-finished lighter that had become popular in the last few years. This one was white in colour, like the one he had bought for his wife last week. He flicked it on. There was no flare from the flint. Instead, a strong light glowed through the white plastic, turning it transparent. "Well, what d'you know?" He laughed, shook his head, released his finger pressure, and let the glow disappear. "A flashlight."

"Useful for a keyhole in the dark," the older nurse said as she left for Mischa's room.

"Pretty strong for that," the policeman suggested. "It's got no brand name on it. No patent mark, either. That's what caught my eye. And then I couldn't see any butane inside. Empty. So I flicked it on."

"Real cute."

Not half as cute as the cuff-links, Oleg thought, as he watched the group gathered at the desk. It would take more than that young pig's curiosity to open them. But let someone with more experience get his hands on them, and the cuff-links would be quickly identified as a tool of espionage. He hesitated only for one moment. All his plans were abandoned. The situation had become impossible. He walked over to the door of Mischa's room, his hand searching deep in his pocket.

The nurse had checked the cords attached to the vein in Mischa's left arm. Now she was adjusting the bottle of glucose overhead. "Come in, come in," she said briskly.

The room was deeply shaded. Oleg said, "I can't quite see," and came nearer, drawing his hand out of his pocket. Mischa was lying very still, his eyes closed against the world.

The nurse went to the door to switch on the ceiling light. But before it blazed over the room, Oleg's hand had grasped Mischa's wrist and pressed. That was all. For a second, Mischa opened his eyes, almost smiled. He knows, thought Oleg, and took a step backward.

"That's better," said the nurse. "Now you can see him."

"Yes." Oleg's hand slipped deep into his coat pocket, and edged the small empty vial with its broken needle into its hiding-place. Then he couldn't speak. He stood there, looking down at Mischa as if he were a stranger.

"You don't know him?"

Oleg shook his head. He turned away abruptly, made for the door. The policeman was there. "Any identification?"

"None," said the nurse.

The officer closed his book and tucked it into his breast pocket. He said nothing at all.

She glanced back at the bed. "Sleeping peacefully. And about time, too."

She switched off the light, leaving only the small night-lamp gently glowing over the side table. The door she left ajar. She looked at the watch pinned to her stiff apron front. "The rush begins any time now. Saturday night, you know." It was a hint to the officer to go sit on a chair and stop upsetting her routine. Thank goodness, the two others had left. Really, as if she hadn't enough to do without all this interruption. What had been gained by it, anyway? A lot of notes in a police officer's little book, that were now useless.

Oleg had hesitated at the desk, as if he had lost his sense of direction. "What do I do now?" he asked her. He eyed the cuff-links.

"Try Missing Persons. The police will help you," she said not unkindly. Her voice sharpened. "Maria—put all that stuff on the desk out of sight until the lieutenant gets here. Safely, now!" She moved the cuff-links well aside from Oleg's hand. "You know," she told him to give him a little encouragement— he seemed so depressed, "you should be glad that the man is not your friend. He is in trouble." She tapped the cane. "Because of this. Carrying a concealed weapon."

"It didn't protect him much," the officer said. "That happens: your own weapon turned against you."

"That happens." Oleg nodded a good night to the nurses,

and started towards the elevator.

The officer came with him. "As we figure it," the young confident voice went on, "four perpetrators attacked and the victim drew the sword to scare them off. But there were three too many for him. One seized the sword and slashed him as he put up an arm to defend himself. Two officers were in the vicinity and intervened before he was killed. Yes, you can say he's a lucky man."

"You got the sword back, I noticed." Oleg's pace slowed almost to a halt.

"Thrown away as the perpetrator tried to evade arrest."

"But no wallet?"

"We have it. It wasn't lifted. Not enough time."

"And there wasn't even a credit card inside?"

"Just money. Plenty of that," the officer said briefly.

Yes, thought Oleg, almost a thousand dollars. Mischa had always put his trust in money. It was more reliable, he used to say, than any false documents.

What's his interest in these details? the officer speculated. First he was too impatient to wait, and now he's dawdling around.

"And not one label on his clothing?" Oleg asked.

"None. But we have the clothes. The lab can start work on them, if necessary. There's always a way. Good night, sir."

"Good night." Oleg stepped into the elevator.

"We'll let you know if we hear anything about Mr. Johnstone. The Hotel Toronto?"

The elevator door closed, leaving Oleg to his own thoughts.

* * *

Slowly, he walked back to his car on Sixty-ninth Street. There could have been no other solution. There was too much information packed inside Mischa's brain. Too many chances that he would be interrogated by experts. Too many question-marks around him, too much risk for all of us. "There's always a way," the young officer had said, a trite phrase, but one that Oleg had found to be true. Given the right men, properly trained, complete identification of Mischa could be made within a few days. There it was: no other solution possible. His pace quickened.

Reaching the car, he thought of Alexis as he stepped into the front seat. Alexis was now on record. So was the name of Oleg. And Alexis must have been seen tonight when he met Mischa. *Two officers were in the vicinity...* How many more? Had he himself been observed? Almost certainly. Yet no cause for alarm, he concluded as he eased the car towards Fifth Avenue—he had kept his distance from both Mischa and Alexis. But the sooner he left New York, the better. He gave up the idea of spending any time in Queens. Instead, he would drive to Trenton, where he knew the location of another safe-house. From there, too, he could send out the news of the assault on Colonel Vladimir Konov—place, time, and hospitalisation.

And his report would state, quite simply, that he had tried to save Colonel Konov and failed. Konov had died before he could be reached. Unidentified. The body would remain in the hospital morgue for three days: after that, it would be moved to the police morgue for one week. (This he knew from a previous incident, on his last visit to New York.) Therefore any plan to claim the body should be made as soon as possible, although he himself would advise against it. End of report.

8

Tom Kelso, with a successful visit to Paris behind him, arrived back in New York only one day late. Which was pretty good going, considering what he had packed into the preceding week: lunch with an editor of *Le Temps*; two interviews with foreign affairs experts (on the record); two sessions with other Quai d'Orsay men (off the record); a brief but important meeting with a cabinet minister; four encounters extending past midnight with journalists ranging from far-left to right-wing in their opinions; and a relaxed dinner with an old friend (Maurice Michel, once assigned to NATO, and now back at his desk job in Paris at the Quai d'Orsay), a purely personal evening which was passed amusingly, a welcome interlude in a week of hard business.

The twenty-four-hour postponement of Tom Kelso's return did mean that he couldn't take up Chuck's suggestion to spend Sunday night at East Sixty-sixth Street. But the invitation had been casual enough: Chuck had probably sensed that Tom would be heading home to Washington and Dorothea.

He delayed in New York just long enough to drop in at the *Times* and deliver his final article on Paris and its current attitudes to NATO. "Sorry about the typing," he told the copy-editor. "Finished the piece at two o'clock this morning."

"Seems okay."

"It gets messier towards the end. Three of the letters have started acting up. I cleaned them, but they keep gathering ink. The type-face is worn. Needs replacing, I guess."

"What have you got against a new typewriter?" the copy-editor hinted. Reporters' loyalty to their old machines always amused him: brought them luck, they thought, although they'd never admit it openly.

"I'm attached to this one. Easy action. Rattles off a fair copy in no time flat."

"This looks clear enough. I've seen worse. At least, you can spell."

Tom glanced at his watch. He had twenty-five minutes to board the Metroliner for Washington, and none to spare. He gave a casual wave and was on his way.

The editor began reading Kelso's copy with more concentration. Then, as he reached the third page, he stopped and frowned. I've seen worse, he repeated to himself; and I've also seen another just like it: these letters, *m* and *n*; that blocked *t*... Identical. He looked up, startled, but Kelso was already out of sight. "Who the hell does he think he's kidding?" he asked aloud. He signalled to the girl at the next desk. "Hey, Melissa, get me that copy we were working on yesterday. The Holzheimer story."

"Just his piece, or the attached memorandum?"

"The memorandum, dammit."

When it arrived at his desk, he needed only one glance.

"Well, what d'you know?" he said softly. He had never thought Kelso was one of the smart alecks, but this put him right at the top of the list. "That guy is full of surprises."

"What guy?" Melissa asked.

He didn't explain, just sat there grinning as the meaning behind Kelso's trick became quite clear to him. Then he rose and went to see if some of his friends had ten minutes to spare: this joke was too rich not to be shared around. It would cause some small earth-tremors, but Holzheimer would feel most of them. And serve him right, too cocky by far; all that contemptuous dismissal of the "oldies," all those paeans of praise for the "new" investigative reporting, hallelujah, amen. As if that concept of journalism had just been invented, and never practised for a hundred years or more before this latest crop of *Wunderkinder* made the newspaper scene. What had a good reporter ever been, except investigative?

Tom had a standard rule about his arrivals in Washington. He never wanted to be met at the airport. What he liked was to reach home and find a wife with arms outstretched, ready to meet his, as he dropped his bag and closed the door and shut the world away. Dorothea had her own rules: everything prepared to welcome the traveller—steak ready to broil when needed, flowers arranged, candles waiting to be lit on a supper-table for two, ice-bucket filled, Ravel or Debussy gently playing, bathroom tidied up from her own hasty dressing, a large towel folded near the shower; and her own appearance, from brushed hair and careful make-up right down to house-gown and pretty slippers, never betraying the mad rush around the apartment since she had got back from the office barely one hour ago.

Tonight had been more of a wild scramble than usual. She was fixing the earring in place, congratulating herself that she had possibly ten minutes to spare for a last check on things—when she heard the key in the lock, and Tom's voice. She came running, cheeks pink with haste, eyes dancing with amusement at her undignified scamper that suddenly changed into a more decorous approach. But it didn't last. Tom's arms swept her up as he kissed her, swinging her off her feet. One sandal was lost, an earring dropped, hair sent flying free. And "Oh, darling," was all she could say once his grip was loosened and some breath came back into her body.

He looked round the room, looked back to Dorothea. Nothing had changed: everything was just as he had been remembering it. Strange, he thought, that this is the one fear I take travelling with me: that some day I'll come back and find it all different, all lost. This is the only truly permanent thing in an impermanent world. He kissed her again, long and gently.

He had managed to catch some light sleep on the flight across the Atlantic, which kept him going until he reached home. But the preceding week had been a tight stretch of work, and Tom was tired, admitting it frankly. It was difficult to shake off the tyranny of hours: Paris time had been seven thirty when he rose Monday morning; and now, after he had showered and changed and had supper (but not steak tonight—a chicken sandwich and a drink were all he wanted), Paris time would be three fifteen A.M. Tuesday. The glamorous life of a travelling journalist, he told himself wryly. There was Thea, radiant, desirable, glowing with life and love; and here he was—adoring her, yet longing, as he thought of the big beautiful bed in the next room, for deep instant sleep between smooth cool sheets. But his willpower was adrift too: he seemed incapable of moving, of breaking away from this quiet happiness. He sat at the table, relaxed and content, finishing his last drink slowly, listening to Dorothea's soft low voice filled with interest as she questioned, watching the subtle changes in her expression and mood as he answered.

Now she was talking about her own week in Washington. Yes, she had burned all bridges, faced Bud Wells in his TV den. "Oh, of course there were all kinds of objections and counter-arguments. But I was firm; I really was, darling. That's the side of me you don't know."

"Don't I?"

"Anyway anyway anyway, I'm free as a bird from the first of January," she said lightly. "Have you heard any more about your own leave of absence?"

"Didn't have time to check."

"It will come through?" she asked anxiously.

"I suppose." Then he grinned and added, "Yes, it will come through, darling."

"Oh, Tom—stop teasing! Where shall we spend it? Not here. That telephone will never stop ringing, and you'll be yanked back to the office."

"That happens," he agreed.

"I've been making a list of places where we could find a small cottage. It keeps getting shorter as I cross them off, one by one. I'd like some spot where we don't have to dig ourselves out of the snow before we can collect the morning mail. No sleet or cold rain, either."

He said nothing, only watched her with growing amusement.

"You don't really want to go into the wilds of Vermont for the winter months, do you?"

He shook his head, smiling now. Thea's concern touched him. He knew what her own choice would be. "You'd like some sun and sand," he suggested.

"But the trouble with Florida or the Caribbean is that I can't see you beachcombing. All very well for a week, but for *three* months?"

"You don't finish writing a book by staring up at blue skies," he agreed.

"And then," she said, "you need a place where you can keep in touch with everything that's going on—newspapers sold at every street-corner, isn't that your idea of bliss? Book-stores, too. A museum, galleries, interesting little streets to wander around in—after all, you can't be glued to your desk for ever."

Again he shook his head, his smile broadening, letting her run on, keeping his own suggestions to the end.

"And what with the way you check and double-check, you'll need a reference library near by, won't you?"

"Or else ship three crates of books."

"Then I give up. There's no place that feels like a holiday and yet offers all that. We'll have to settle on some college town—oh Lord, I had *enough* of college towns when I was a faculty brat. Where else, then?" She was disconsolate. Perhaps they'd stay right here in Washington, after all. An end to all her dreaming of something different, something new. Vacations in the last five years had been few and interrupted: either her job or his was always tugging holidays apart. "All I wanted was some place where you could finish the last two chapters of your book as well as—" she paused—"oh, just being together. Or does one cancel the other?"

"Only if I get sidetracked."

"I won't—"

"You sidetrack me very easily."

"This time, I promise. Truly."

"Truly and seriously, I'll need six clear hours at the desk each day. And a couple more to rewrite what I put on paper the night before."

"I promise, darling," she repeated most solemnly. "I'll start a book of my own. *The Talkative Great*—all about the tongues swinging loose on TV interviews. Or I could call it *Strip-Tease In Words*. Or *The Day of the Exhibitionist*. Or *Leaking Secrets—Drip Drip Drip*."

"At least, you've got plenty of titles," he teased her. "No problem there."

"The only problem we have at this moment is—not how we'll spend these three months, but where."

"What about the south of France?"

She stared at him. "Don't joke."

"I'm dead serious," he assured her.

"But it's impossible—out of our reach, darling."

"Not as I see it."

"I had a look at our savings account last week," she told him. "We've got to put aside a large dollop for income tax in April. Remember, April is the cruellest month."

"And that leaves us about six thousand dollars flat."

"Which isn't so much, once you pay fares across the Atlantic and—"

"We make use of this apartment. I've found someone who wants it."

"A stranger—here? Can you trust him with your books and records and—"

"Not a stranger. Maurice Michel."

"Your Paris friend? The diplomat?"

"He and his wife are coming to Washington in February for a couple of months. So we've agreed to trade. We get three months in his place for his two months here. Fair enough."

"We're exchanging?" She was still astounded, scarcely believing.

"Why not? I had dinner with him last night. It's all settled. He has a cottage on the Riviera—nothing elaborate—his father once lived there, owned a small flower-nursery. It's simple and rustic."

"Running water?" she asked.

"I don't see Michel fetching a bucket from a well."

She began to laugh, remembering the immaculate Frenchman who had visited them here last year. And to think of all the lists she had made of possible places and expenses—and Tom had arranged everything. No fuss, no trouble. In one night. Over dinner in Paris. "Darling you are *wonderful*." She rose, came round the table to meet him with a tight hug and a wild kiss.

"And that's a pleasant idea to take to bed. Come on, Thea." He put out the candles, began switching off the lights, and checked the front door lock. "No, no," he said as he came back to the table and found her beginning to gather the supper dishes together. "Let's just relax tonight."

"I'm too excited to sleep." It was barely ten o'clock. Even if she had an office to remember each morning, her idea of bedtime was usually midnight or later. Days were always too short, somehow.

"I'll persuade you into it." Then he looked at her quickly. "What's wrong, Thea?" Her eyes were wide as she stood so very still, watching him. She was close to tears.

"Nothing's wrong. Everything's wonderful." Her voice trembled, and she tried to cover the surge of emotions with a little laugh. She failed quite happily, as he smoothed away the threat of tears with a kiss. "I love you love you love you."

He kissed her again. And again, straining her close to him, saying in a voice that was almost inaudible, "Never leave me, darling. Never leave me."

The morning came, bright and beautiful as far as he was concerned. Thea had let him sleep on for an extra hour—he had a dim memory of her, fully dressed, dropping a goodbye kiss on his cheek as she was about to take off for a nine o'clock appointment at her office. Complete metamorphosis, he thought now: the girl of last night, all floating chiffon and soft shoulders, teasing lips and hands, sweet seduction complete, had become the successful woman, neat in sweater and well-cut pants suit, attractive and competent, equalling the male competition in brains, surpassing it in looks and natural warmth. What poor man had a chance against all that? Fifty-fifty, Women's Lib insisted, and with every right on their side of the argument; but weren't they forgetting some natural advantages that tipped the scale? And long live those natural advantages, he thought, leaving the disordered bed as he recalled that he too was due at an office this morning. Nine thirty now, he noted: time to get a move on.

The supper table's remains had been cleared, his breakfast tray ready along with a note warning him that Martha came in to clean around eleven. He'd be well out of here before the vacuum-cleaner—one of his minor dislikes—started breaking up the peace of this apartment.

He scrambled some eggs, and had a leisurely breakfast, with four newspapers for company. Recession was deepening, inflation swelling, the Middle East seething as expected, Vietnam making its unhappy way back into the headlines, the CIA a cripple and perhaps to become a basket-case, terrorism in London, floods in Bangladesh, drought in Africa; and oil-spill over everything, from prices and veiled threats to bitter denunciations. By comparison with all this gloom, his own piece on current French reactions to NATO seemed almost reassuring although, when he turned it in yesterday, he had thought, Here goes another report to ruin a lot of breakfasts tomorrow. There was only one misprint in it—*fare* instead of *fire*—to wrinkle a few eyebrows. His lucky day, he thought: no transposed lines, no broken paragraphs.

On the page opposite his own by-line, was another column with Holzheimer's name heading it. So young Holzheimer was starting to dig into NATO too, was he? And with considerable help from someone: the full text of a NATO Memorandum "now under serious consideration in Washington" was printed along with Holzheimer's analysis and comments. There was no hint of the source for this piece of information, beyond the usual "official who preferred to remain anonymous, but who verified the authenticity of the document." Also, of course, "The Pentagon has not denied the existence of the memorandum" and "The State Department offered no comment in response to this reporter's repeated questions."

So there was another abominable leak, Tom Kelso thought: we are becoming a nation of blabbermouths. It wasn't only on harmless TV programmes that there were (in Thea's words) "Leaking Secrets—Drip Drip Drip."

He had heard of this memorandum—some evasive, upper echelon gossip had been seeping around for the past few weeks, but no one knew the details. (Maurice Michel, last night in Paris, had quizzed him about it. If the French hadn't been able to learn its particulars, then it was pretty secret stuff.) What was it all about, anyway? With professional interest as well as private misgivings, he began reading it carefully.

It was a warning bell, he decided when he finished its final paragraph: an attempt to shock the Americans into taking a closer look at détente and its actualities, at pitfalls ahead for unwary feet. It wouldn't make NATO more popular with several segments of the public, he decided, but when did Cassandra ever have an easy role? He'd question some of NATO's statements himself—there was no proof offered, for instance, of certain ominous trends, unless one allusion to certain facts and figures meant that there was some appendix, some other part of the memorandum perhaps, that had not been included in today's publication. But as it stood now, the document was simply an unpleasant shocker: not an actual breach in security, as far as he could see—except that some son of a bitch had taken it upon himself to make it public. He wasn't blaming Holzheimer: few journalists could resist a chance of a scoop. But the point was

simply this: NATO's opponents would use it to help weaken
the Western alliance still more. He could hear them even now.
"Scare tactics," the right-wingers would say, "to get more men
and money out of old Uncle Sam." Or, from the left, "shocking
belligerence...cold   warriors...imperialist   aggression." As
for Holzheimer himself, he carefully avoided giving his own
private judgment. (Perhaps he hadn't made up his mind. The
by-line was everything, was it?) He had contented himself with
heaving a brick through a plate-glass window: often tempting
enough, Tom admitted, but definitely resistible. Holzheimer
shared one belief with his unknown source—he mentioned it
twice so that no one would fail to understand his high motives.
The public has a right to know, he stated. And who would
quibble with that, when (apparently) no breach of real security
was involved?

Well, Tom decided as he got ready to leave the apartment,
I'll find out more about all this at the office. The first day back
at work was always a heavy one, with a pile of mail and a list
of possible news-items all waiting for his attention. He'd be
willing to bet that the first joking comment he got would be,
"Hey, Tom—do you see Holzheimer's out after your job?"

Is that what's really worrying me? he asked himself. No not
altogether... Yet why the hell can't I shake myself free of this
small depression? Last night, even early this morning, I was on
top of the world. Now—

No, he couldn't explain it. But his misgivings didn't vanish
either. It was a serious-faced man who strode into the office,
and once the greetings were over, the first joking comment was
made and he had won his private bet. There was an additional
remark, too, a question that he hadn't been prepared for. "What

was your idea in giving Holzheimer this break? Or didn't you want your own sources to dry up on you?"

Tom stared blankly. "I don't follow—"

"Come off it. They would freeze stiff if you'd given it your own by-line."

"That's a pretty sick joke."

A small stare back at him, a laugh and a shrug of the shoulders. "Okay, okay—if that's the way you want to play it."

Let's get to the bottom of this, Kelso told himself, and he telephoned his oldest friend at the *Times* in New York. The replies to his questions were meant to be soothing. Not to worry, just a rumour flying around, based on very little actually and the *Times* saw no cause for any alarm.

"What rumour?" Tom demanded. Everyone seemed to know what they were talking about, except himself.

"The typescript of the memorandum."

"What about it?"

"Your machine, Tom."

"*What?*"

"Yes. But even if you did copy the memorandum, what harm really? You didn't break any—"

"I didn't copy it. Never saw it—"

"And of course we wouldn't have published it if we felt there was the remotest chance of breaching the security of the United States."

"But I didn't—"

"Tom, listen to me! The less said about this, the better for you. We're trying to contain it within the paper, don't want it spread abroad. You could get hurt by it, Tom, if your NATO friends thought you had pulled this off. Actually, I think you were right to want to see the memorandum in print. Otherwise, we wouldn't have published it. So relax. We aren't criticising you, even if your method was slightly—well, odd. We'll stand by you, in any case. You know that, Tom."

Tom said slowly, "I repeat, I did not—"

"See you before you leave for Brussels on the tenth. We'll have all this under control by that time."

The telephone went dead, leaving Tom staring at the receiver with grim set eyes. And what would be the use of going to Brussels if this gossip was not only controlled but completely disproved? He had seen journalists' careers smashed by less than this. He was in deep trouble. And the hell of it was that he didn't know why. Not yet, he told himself in sudden cold anger; but he'd find out, that was one thing for damned sure.

9

Along with *The New York Times*, there had been a series of shocks delivered that morning.

First, there was Tony Lawton, who—within two minutes of reading the Holzheimer page—was calling the Pentagon.

The Pentagon, in turn, was telephoning Shandon House.

There the Director had left a ruined breakfast for an all-hell-breaking-loose session in the filing-room. The entire NATO Memorandum was there, he could report. Completely safe. Security had not been breached. Of course, he'd make further checks, find out more details about access to the memorandum at Shandon; of course, he understood the future implications for the Institute if the fault lay with it. And, testily, he added the suggestion that the Pentagon might start investigating its own security: it had had the memorandum in its possession before sending it to Shandon.

Washington then stepped in, quietly, to contact the *Times's*

New York office. There, questions were coldly received and answered. No source could be divulged. Surely it was understood, in this day and age, that there was freedom of speech guaranteed in the Constitution? The *Times* stood by its reporter, Martin Holzheimer. What was more, this morning's news had contained nothing to injure US security.

The office of the Secretary of Defence chose its own tactics. Again there was a long telephone call to the New York office of the *Times*, but now an attempt at conciliation: yes, yes, yes, total agreement that there was no breach of security in the publication of this part of the memorandum. And then, with everything flowing more smoothly, came a sudden stretch of white water: had Holzheimer known that there were two additional parts to the memorandum? Had he seen them? If so, security had not only been broken, but a highly dangerous situation created that could involve all members of NATO (and that, don't forget, meant the United States too).

The *Times* went back to square one. The second and third parts of the memorandum, if they existed, were not its concern. Mr. Holzheimer had neither seen nor heard of them. He refused to divulge his source of information on the first part of the memorandum, which was his constitutional right. Prior to publication there had been intensive study of the text of this section of the NATO Memorandum, as well as considerable investigation of the place from which it had originated. It was found (*a*) to be authentic, and (*b*) to contain no actual military information. In fact, its publication was a service rendered to the American people, who ought to know some of the vital opinions that were held in certain influential circles of Western Europe, opinions that might influence the possible future of the United States.

The impasse seemed complete.

It was then that Tony Lawton decided to make his own move. Frankly, today's little bombshell might be a fascinating debate for some people in New York or a red-faced embarrassment to others in Washington; but for a NATO Intelligence agent in Moscow (and for eight others scattered through Eastern Europe in sensitive assignments) there could be imminent arrest, interrogation, death.

You can't bloody well waste any more time, Lawton warned himself. Ninety minutes already wasted in well-meaning talk. Get hold of Brad Gillon.

He telephoned Brad at once, using his private number and avoiding the office switchboard. "Brad—I'm flying in to New York. I'll be there by two o'clock. Cancel the three-Martini lunch, and see me in your office."

"See you here?" Brad sounded startled.

"That's right. And if you haven't read your *Times* this morning—" A delicate pause.

Gillon reflected for a moment, and came up with the proper assumption. "I have. But what's the excitement? No infringement on security as far as I saw."

That's what *you* think, old boy. "No?" Tony asked blandly.

Gillon said, "Okay. Come to the twenty-second floor. I'll tell the receptionist that Mr. Cook is delivering his manuscript. She'll announce you at once."

"Two o'clock," Tony reaffirmed. That would give him time to drop in at Shandon for a quick check on his way to New York. Bless the Cessna that he could call upon in an emergency, making this hop-skip-and-jump journey plannable.

* * *

From its marble-coated walls to its array of high-speed elevators, the large and busy lobby of the building in which the publishing house of Frankel, Merritt and Gillon occupied three floors, was definitely impressive. Tony Lawton was both subdued and amused as he faced the young woman who sat on the other side of a vast gun-metal desk in the twenty-second floor's reception office. It was an interior room, small and antiseptic, with one giant abstract mural representing—? Tony had several interpretations, but repressed them as he looked at the virginal face of this latter-day Cerberus. "Mr. Cook," she repeated, voice frank mid-Western, dress chic Madison Avenue. Languidly, she picked up the telephone and announced him; but her eyes, outlined with heavy black fringes, took a visitor's measure as efficiently as any guard back at Shandon's main gate. "You can go in, Mr. Cook. That door—" she nodded to one of three. "I'm sorry Mr. Gillon's secretary is still out to lunch, but if you go straight through, you can't miss his office. It's the corner one—on your right."

Tony entered an enormous stretch of windowless space, divided by shoulder-high partitions to form a beehive of cubicles. Bright lights, the air conditioned to Alaskan temperatures, people beginning to gear up after lunch (mostly young women; only two men in sight), machines machines everywhere, a forest of them, ready to add and subtract, and type, and transpose, and copy, and possibly do your thinking for you. But "straight through" did bring him to a row of closed doors. The corner one, on his right, had Gillon's name in very small letters—typical of Brad, Tony thought with pleasure.

"How to deflate a male author," Tony said as he closed the door behind him. "By the time he reaches here, he's walking on his knees."

"Or demanding a flat twenty per cent royalty," Brad Gillon said with a shake of his head.

Tony gave him a warm handshake and the room a quick glance: a wooden desk piled with galley-proofs and manuscripts, jacket designs in the raw stage propped for consideration on a battered leather armchair, books climbing the walls wherever there wasn't a window. "Now I know I'm really in a publishing house," he said, as he cleared a small space on the desk, zipped open his briefcase and brought out a newspaper. "Ballast," he explained. "Tried to look like a pregnant writer. How am I doing?"

"Not bad at all," said Brad, eyeing Tony's tweed jacket, turtle neck, disarranged hair, and unpolished loafers. He himself was in shirt-sleeves, with a slight loosening at the broad knot of his restrained blue tie. "You do throw yourself into your role, Tony."

"I was a writer, once: mostly aspiring," Tony reminded him. He was already taking a chair to face Brad across the desk. And then, just as abruptly, voice and manner changed. "You still know some people over at the *Times*, don't you?"

Brad recovered from the direct approach, and made a guess at Tony's train of thought. "Don't ask me to try and persuade them—"

"To reveal the source of Holzheimer's little piece? Of course not. The idea never crossed my mind."

"Didn't it?" Brad's serious face was lightened by a wide smile.

"I simply want you to take a wise, reliable friend aside, and tell him what he should know."

"And that is?"

"The real reason behind all this fuss from Washington about the surfacing of the NATO Memorandum."

"I'd like to hear that myself."

"You shall, you shall. But first let me give you the background."

"Off the record?"

"For you and your wise, reliable friend—no. For others, yes."

"Good. If you want me to approach anyone about the NATO Memorandum, I've got to be able to tell him—"

"All the facts," Tony agreed. "Here they are. The memorandum consisted of three parts, all inter-related. The second and third parts were considered so important for future American policies, that the entire document was given top-secret rating and a transatlantic journey to Washington by courier. After being studied there, it was delivered—again by courier—to Shandon House. And, as at the Pentagon, only people with the highest security clearance were put to work on it."

"The Pentagon wanted a double check on its own long-range projections?"

"Perhaps to strengthen its own final report, which would be submitted to your policy-makers for their serious consideration." Tony shrugged. "But the point is this: no copies of the memorandum were ever made; all working notes were shredded and burned at the end of each day; there was constant supervision, even surveillance. Once the job of analysis and evaluation was over, the various parts of the memorandum were linked together again by heavy staples, placed in one folder, and filed securely away. That was ten days ago."

"Why the delay in returning it to Washington?"

"It was waiting for Shandon's own top-secret report to be completed. Tomorrow is the deadline on that."

"And they go back together to Washington?"

Tony nodded. "Standard operating procedure." He added, trying to control his annoyance and not succeeding, "But why the Pentagon ever sent it to Shandon in the first place—" He buttoned his lip.

"Supercaution. Understandable, if some of the contents of the memorandum might influence American policy. There has to be double and triple checking of the facts, Tony."

"I can see that," Tony said, but he was still depressed.

"You think the leak came from Shandon?"

"It's possible. That is what we are trying to nail down. I've been in Shandon's filing-room—a couple of hours ago, in fact. It's a bank vault. No outsider could get in there without dynamite. And no insider without supervision. So they say." Tony frowned, not so much at that problem as at the way he had sidetracked himself. Brad's questions had been good enough to let him stray. "The point I want to make is this: the memorandum, intact, is now filed in its correct folder at Shandon. So, if someone at Shandon did take it out, he must have separated the three parts, copied one of them to hand over to a reporter, and then put everything all back in place again. But here's the main question: what happened to the second and third parts while he was typing out the first?"

"Perhaps Part I was all that he took."

Tony shook his head. He wouldn't have the time needed to separate the three parts. Remember, he was in that filing-room *under supervision.* He might get a chance to snatch the NATO folder and put it under his jacket, but that would be all the time available to him—a minute or less. No, he took the whole bloody thing."

"You think he actually photographed the entire memorandum and sent it to Moscow?"

"The KGB wanted it. We know that."

"Ah—" said Brad, remembering his last meeting with Tony. "Vladimir Konov? Now I see what is really bugging you. Konov arrived last Tuesday in Washington, didn't he?"

"No, he did not," Tony said shortly. There had been some disturbing developments that he couldn't explain at this moment. Konov had not arrived with the agrarian experts in Washington last week. Instead, there had been a coded message for Tony, relayed via Brussels from NATO's man in the KGB. Warning: Konov has left the Soviet Union four days early, departure secret, destination New York. Possibly accompanied by Boris Gorsky, colonel, KGB, Executive Operations (Department V, Disinformation). "He was already in New York nine days ago."

"And when did the *Times* reporter hand in his material for publication?" Brad asked.

"A week ago, we were told."

Brad was now both worried and angry. "And you think the man who filched the NATO material might have handed it over to Konov?"

"Indirectly—yes. But directly? No, I don't think so. He's responsible for taking it out of deep security and making it accessible to others. That's all. Bloody fool. He's a thief, but he isn't the traitor."

"Why not?"

"If he had been one of Konov's agents, the first part of the memorandum would never have been supplied to any reporter. It contains some hard facts about Konov's department of Disinformation and its use of détente. *The conquest of the system*, remember?"

"That was only a small part of the published document. Most readers will concentrate on NATO's unwanted advice. I'm willing to bet that Konov's propaganda boys are going to play up that aspect: see how NATO is trying to influence the United States—another Vietnam being prepared—NATO still pushing the cold war."

"Et cetera, et cetera," Tony agreed. He lapsed into silence, kept staring out at the shapes of disguised water-towers on the roofs of the high-risers opposite. Blue sky, unclouded. Everything in sharp focus. He wished his thoughts were as clear as the picture through the window. He went back to the essential problem, arguing it aloud. "There *must* be one other man involved—one man, at least, who played traitor without any compunction. And the only way we can uncover him is to find the idiot who took the memorandum in the first place. Then we might learn a few leading facts—how did he protect it, did he let anyone else know about it? If so, who? And that's the fellow I'd really like to know about."

"But how do we discover your idiot? We can't get a definite name, that's for sure. Holzheimer will go to jail rather than tell. There was a case, last year—"

"I know. I read about it. We don't *ask* for a name, Brad. We find it out for ourselves." Tony was recovering from his depression. There was a sudden sparkle in his eyes at some amusing prospect.

"How?"

"You could have a short conversation with Holzheimer. He might be just enough shaken by all the fuss he has created to tell you the place where he met his informant.

"No, that wouldn't work—"

"Not even if his bosses wanted to know? They might, once they have a close look at the typescript of the memorandum—at your suggestion, of course. I'd like you to examine it. Carefully."

Brad frowned, puzzling out the reason for that. Yes, several details about that typed copy of the memorandum could be useful. "You want me to examine the brand of paper, the spacing, the margins—"

"Exactly."

"—and the type itself."

"That's hardly necessary."

"But to trace all those things will take time. It's the long way round to uncovering—Hey, what was that you said about the type?"

"It has already been identified. There's a whisper starting up—one of my Washington friends heard it this morning—that Tom Kelso must be the man responsible. He got the memorandum from one of his high-placed informants, possibly in Paris."

"Tom? I don't believe it." Brad was shocked.

"His typewriter did the copying."

"Impossible!"

"If it did, then someone borrowed it. That's the simple explanation. The gossips prefer a more cynical interpretation."

"Ridiculous," Brad exploded. "If Tom wanted that

memorandum published, he'd have done it under his own by-line."

"And lose future confidences from his Paris informant? Tom was safeguarding himself. So the rumour goes."

Brad rose abruptly, began pacing the room. For a few moments, there was only the sound of three sharp curses.

"I agree entirely." Tony waited for the storm to subside. "Why else did I ask you to look at the typescript?" He paused for emphasis. Then he said, "We all have our own way of arranging a typed page, don't we?"

Brad nodded. There could be small but definite differences, a matter of personal preference, of habit or training. "And so we get closer to finding Holzheimer's source," he said slowly. It was a start; small, but perhaps a lead.

"You clear Tom—and that would please the *Times*, wouldn't it? They might be more amenable to letting you talk with Holzheimer."

Brad almost smiled. Tony's old practice of the honest *quid pro quo* always amused him. Tony never expected to get something for nothing.

"So," Tony summed it up, "no name is requested or divulged. Holzheimer is kept happy and virtuous. Tom is exonerated. And I get a chance to start tracing the second man."

"You are really hipped on that second-man bit."

"I can smell him. There has to be someone on the sidelines— the direct connection with dear Comrade Konov."

"If," Brad said with heavy emphasis, "Konov did receive the memorandum."

"If," Tony echoed, offering no argument. Then he added, "But I'd prefer to start action on the problem now, and not wait until I heard some disastrous news from Moscow."

Your agent there? Brad wondered. He moved back to his desk and reached for the 'phone. "I'll get on to this, right away."

Tony picked up his briefcase and the newspaper. For a moment, he seemed about to leave. Then he changed his mind and walked over to the window. So far below him that he couldn't even see it, was Fifth Avenue. And in that direction to the north, lay Central Park. That's where it had happened, according to this newspaper, which he had folded back to the page with the police report, brief and simple but headlined in bold print.

Brad ended his call. "Okay. The first hurdle is taken. I'm now heading for the *Times* itself. I'll be leaving in ten minutes." Tony made up his mind and decided to risk his hunch. "Can you spare me two of them?"

"Something more for me to tell my—"

"No, no. Just your opinion on this." He handed his copy of the *News* over to Brad, and tapped the small paragraph with his finger. "What do you make of it?"

Brad began reading. "The *News* has a corner on crime stories in New York. This is just another case of a mugging in Central Park, the body still awaiting identification in the morgue." And then he looked up in surprise. "Carrying a sword-stick, and a lighter that could be used as a flashlight?"

"I wonder," Tony said thoughtfully. "I saw a couple of jokers keep a secret rendezvous in West Berlin last month. They used that kind of lighter for identification. They met casually at a dark street-corner. One needed a light for his cigarette. All he got was a brief flash. So he said he would use his own lighter, and flashed right back. It's a new gadget. Simple-minded, but quick and sure."

Brad glanced back at the newspaper. "This fellow was mugged over a week ago."

"On the Saturday when we met at the Algonquin. Interesting date, don't you think."

"There is only a bare description of him—about fifty years old, five foot six." Brad looked up sharply. "No mention of eye-colour. Or hair. Or build."

"Naturally. Do you expect the police to make it easy for anyone who'll try to make an identification?"

"No, it can't be," said Brad, staring at the newspaper.

"Probably not."

"A coincidence, that's all."

"I suppose so. I'd still like to see the police file on this case, though."

"Now look here, Tony—I don't know anyone in the Police Department," Brad said in alarm.

"All right, all right." Tony put the *News* back into his briefcase. He would just have to find a less easy solution to that problem. But he'd find it.

"It's a long shot."

"They are the interesting ones."

Brad said slowly, half persuaded in spite of good common sense, "I wouldn't mind seeing that police file myself."

"At this moment, you've got another job to do."

"That I have. But the hell of it is—even if you and I and my friends over at the *Times* know that piece of gossip is ridiculous—is Tom really cleared? Rumours in Washington have a way of seeping through all the cracks."

"It would take some publicity to kill this one dead. Perhaps an open admission from the man who started all this damage?"

"Publicity... No, I don't think that would be too popular with my friends." Brad paused, then added, "Have you any notion who that man might be?"

"Perhaps. And you?"

Brad said nothing at all, but his lips tightened.

Tony said, "I hope we are both wrong." They shook hands. "I'll call you. When and where?" He zipped up the briefcase and tucked the hat under his arm.

"I should be back here by half-past four. I'll be working late this evening. Until eight, possibly." Brad glanced at his watch. "Good God!" Quickly he reached for his jacket and adjusted the knot of his tie.

Tony left. The huge office was now a humming hive of machines and voices. Outside, at the reception desk, the girl interrupted a call at the switchboard to give him a bright smile and a parting wish. "Have a good day," she told him, and sped him happily on his way to the police morgue.

Entry to the morgue was not too complicated. Identification of the mystery corpse had obviously been given top priority. It was Konov. Definitely.

Tony stood looking down at Konov's waxen face.

"You know this man?"

"Perhaps."

"Perhaps?" Another kook, the attendant thought, as he stared at the visitor: he appeared normal enough, English voice, quiet manner, but definitely a kook.

"I'd like to see the detective in charge of this case."

That's a new line, the attendant thought, and ignored it.

"Do I have to go to the FBI?" Tony asked. That got a quick reaction from a couple of men in plain clothes who had drifted in to keep an ear open for any possible identification. "The detective in charge," Tony insisted as they accompanied him out. "And possibly an interesting exchange of vital information."

"You don't say!"

"I do indeed."

The two men eyed each other, then studied the Englishman. Their well-developed instincts gave them a final prod. "Follow us, sir," the senior man told him. "What did you say your name was?"

"Let's make this more private, shall we? Take me to your leader." His grin was infectious, and his accent slew them. They were glad to have an excuse to enjoy the small laugh that each had been repressing for the last full minute. Suddenly their smiles vanished, as Tony flipped open his Pentagon identification and held it briefly in clear view. "And if we must argue about this, first get me to your top brass. Let him check me out with Washington," he added very softly.

They were watching closely, still hesitant but no longer so doubtful. Exchanging a glance, they made a silent decision. "This way, sir," the senior detective said. Any bit of information about that stiff on the slab back there was worth a risk.

At five minutes to eight, Tony called Brad's office on its direct line. "Like to buy me some lunch?"

"Haven't you eaten—"

"Thought I'd visit the morgue on an empty stomach."

"You actually—"

"Yes, actually. Where do we meet?"

"Can't you talk now?"

"Too much to tell. What about your news?"

"Good, I think. Yes, on the whole, good. Are you near this office?"

"Around the corner."

"Then meet me at Nino's on West Forty-ninth Street. Italian food. Two stars. It's crowded, of course."

"How are the tables? Close-packed?" Tony asked doubtfully.

"That won't matter. The noise level is intense."

"Well—as long as we can get our heads close together—see you at the bar in ten minutes?"

It may have been the recession that was affecting people's willingness to spend, but Nino's had four tables empty. They chose a back-corner one, insulated from the service door by a thin row of plastic plants. "Fine," said Tony with approval.

He had a plate of minestrone, a little Bel Paese with Italian brown bread, a glass of white wine, and that was all. Brad, deep into his *calamares*, didn't question the choice. Tony wasn't living on food today.

"Yes, it was Konov all right, laid out like a mackerel on ice. And you know what? I felt sorry for him," Tony admitted. "Can you imagine that? I felt sorry." He studied the wall panel, across the room, of Vesuvius about to spew its ashes over Pompeii. "And then I kept wondering—why was the body left unclaimed? You've seen how the KGB takes care of its own. It always does."

Brad skewered a piece of white bread on his fork and

mopped up the excellent sauce. "Yes. Like inventing a wife and daughter and touching family letters for Colonel Abel. They even had the woman—he had never seen her in his life—meet him, all tears and embraces, at the exchange point in Berlin."

"Yes, I remember those letters. They seemed to be in every newspaper I picked up."

Brad nodded. "Wide coverage. Everyone loves a hard-boiled spy with a much-loved wife. It must have turned Abel's stomach, though. He was a cool professional." Abel had slipped into this country just after the war via Canada, and set himself up in the New York area at two separate addresses, with two different names and identities as Control for a communist spy ring.

"Abel was GRU, wasn't he? Still, the KGB usually looks after its men too. Why not in Konov's case?"

"Interesting question."

"I'm thinking about it." Tony poured himself a second glass of Valpolicella. "This is better," he said with slight surprise, "than the Montrachet I had in Washington last night." He studied the bottle with a touch of indignation.

"Something else to investigate?" Brad asked with a smile. He hadn't felt as good as this for a long long while. He thought of the novel, the newest output from France, waiting for him back on his desk. All very well, but— He sighed, watching Tony and remembering the days when.

"How did *your* investigation go?"

"At the *Times*? Couldn't have asked for a more attentive audience. Unpleasantly shocked, just as I had been. I saw the typescript. And also a couple of pages of Tom Kelso's last copy. Tom always uses plain inexpensive paper. The anonymous typescript had the best Basildon Bond. The left-hand margins were about the same width. But I noticed that Tom likes to get as much on a line as he possibly can, while the typescript finished each line neatly—no runovers on to the right-hand margin. And its end was marked by a series of dashes. Tom finishes off with three asterisks in a row. You were right, Tony. There were differences, small certainly, and not eye-catching unless you were on the lookout for them."

"Reassuring to everyone, I hope."

"They never really doubted Tom."

"Of course not. But a little proof is always comforting, even to non-doubters. Did you get to meet Holzheimer?"

"No need. He had already told his editor where he met his unidentifiable source."

"I hope to God it wasn't in a subway station or on a street corner. No lead there. Except that we'd know that we were dealing with a professional."

"We are dealing with an amateur. He arranged a meeting with Holzheimer in an apartment."

"Where?"

"In New York. Holzheimer hadn't given the full address."

"And is that all we get? A New York apartment?"

"I couldn't push too hard. Contraproductive. Everything is being treated very low key. No publicity, of course. The rumours will be scotched wherever they are met. And they'll die away—no real substance in them. Tom can handle the situation."

Tony said nothing. How did a reporter deal with a sudden lack of confidence in his discretion? There were no cagier informants than those in high government circles. Anything they leaked was off the record unless they wanted it to go public.

"Well," Brad said as he concentrated on lighting a cigar,

"is that all our news?" His gentle blue eyes, in such marked contrast with his hawk nose and strong mouth, were studying the younger man. He could sense something more, well hidden as it was behind Tony's quiet control. A pleasant face, conventionally good-looking with its even features and bland expression, quickly accepted by most people when Tony produced his charm, too often underestimated when he adopted his blank-innocence routine.

Tony smiled. "You haven't lost your touch, have you? No, that is not all our news. I saw the police file."

Brad's lips nearly lost their grip on the cigar. "And how did you manage that?"

"By a neat *quid pro quo*. I'll tell you who the dead man was, if—in return—you let me see the file."

"No, no, it took more than that."

"Well, I got one of my pals at the Pentagon to vouch for me. After that, there was no real difficulty."

"He must have packed a real punch."

"Heavyweight class, definitely. Besides, the police are now in a contest with the FBI to see who hits the bull's-eye first. I was delighted to give whatever help I could. After all, the police had done all the real work. The FBI were called in when no record of Konov's fingerprints were found in New York. But there was no record of them in Washington either."

"What about Konov's clothing—material, cut, place of origin?"

"The experts are working on that."

But it took time. And the results might be inconclusive, too. Konov had been a careful operator. "What did happen to Konov? Was he shot or stabbed?"

"Sliced deep." Tony paused. "Gruesome conversation for this kind of place," he added, glancing at the brightly-lit room: people eating and drinking and talking; waiters flashing around like so many humming-birds; no one loitering near by, no one interested in anyone but themselves, everyone having one hell of a good time. "Yes, I have to hand it to the New York cops. They really had gathered a lot of material, but none of it made any sensible pattern. That's why they allowed me to see the police reports, of course. They needed an identification to give them a steer in the right direction: not organised crime, not narcotics, just plain old-fashioned espionage. All they had was bits and pieces of information. Tantalising, when you don't know what is the *type* of jigsaw puzzle you have to fit together."

"Bits and pieces." These had always fascinated Brad. Puzzles had at one time been his speciality. "What, for instance?"

"For instance, two police joggers were trotting in their rounds in Central Park, and reported meeting a young man whom they escorted, for his safety, as far as the flagpole at Sixty-ninth Street. Where, as one of the undercover policemen further reported, he saw the young man meet the victim. An hour later the two were back at the flagpole, this time walking separately. There was a third man near them, at first seemingly unconnected with the other two, but observed again later, when he watched the ambulance leave. And one more thing— the young man who had been rescued by the joggers actually witnessed the mugging, but kept his distance. He ran off when a police officer called to him to lend a hand. Yes, your cops really do take notice."

"As a city taxpayer," Brad said, "I find that very comforting."

"The clincher is this," Tony went on. "The man who appeared

at the hospital to identify Konov—and he was the only one who did turn up there—seems to bear a decided resemblance to the man who watched the ambulance leave Central Park. A composite picture was made, you see."

"But why?"

"None of his story checked out."

"He saw Konov and disowned him? Then why did he go to the hospital—risk being seen?"

"A scouting expedition, perhaps." Tony's voice hardened. "After he left the hospital, about twenty minutes later, Konov was found dead. Heart-failure."

They were both silent. Tony was thinking now of a call for help, cried out in Russian. Alexis and Oleg. The two men in the Park? Two names to remember, at least. And that composite picture might be useful too. Alexis and Oleg...

Brad was saying, "Did you identify Konov by his real name?"

"By one of them." Tony smiled. "No lies, Brad. I kept my story most checkable."

"Thank God for that."

"Relax, old boy. I don't plan to get the law on my back!"

"You actually blew your cover?"

"As little as possible. After all, the Pentagon vouched for me. Probably stamped me top-secret. I wasn't asked to identify myself further."

"Dangerous. Going down to the morgue—"

"What isn't dangerous?" Tony asked lightly.

"It was probably being watched."

"Everyone was watching. Big strong detectives—"

"Damn it all, Tony, you know what I mean."

Yes, thought Tony, was Alexis or Oleg around, waiting to

see who was interested in Konov? "I know," he said abruptly.

"It was a risk." Brad was really worried. The brief mention of Konov's sudden death had sounded an alarm.

"Calculated, I assure you."

"When are you leaving for Europe?"

"Want to get rid of me?"

"You're too much on your own here." Too vulnerable, Brad thought: not enough back-up.

"Leaving on Friday."

"Don't try to solve all your problems before then. You may work them out more easily in Europe, anyway."

Yes, thought Tony, that was where the biggest problem was now rearing a very ugly head. Why had there been no more messages relayed from Moscow? By this time the NATO Memorandum must have arrived. By this time, too, the death of Konov must have been reported. So why the hell was there no message from Moscow? No call for an arranged escape? "Let's pay the bill and get out of here," he said, suddenly stifled by the laughter in the room.

10

Thirteen days had passed since Rick Nealey kept his appointment with Mischa. Almost two weeks of silence. Each morning, he would rise and go through the motions of making breakfast, an ear cocked—even when he was taking a quick shower—for the expected 'phone-call before he left the apartment. In the evenings, with all engagements cancelled, he waited once more. But the signal never came. Oleg made no attempt to get in touch with him. There were no Monday messages, either, from his usual contact, and when he tried to reach her (five times in all) there was no answer. All communications were cut off. He was isolated. Temporarily, of course. But why? Either there was an alert, a time for caution; or he was being disciplined. And again, why?

Not disciplined, surely. There was no cause for that. He had taken grave risks and acted promptly to procure the NATO Memorandum for Mischa. Any divergence from his instructions had been made necessary by the mugging incident in Central Park: he had delivered the microfilm on Sunday as soon as he returned to Washington, instead of waiting to hand it over to Oleg on Tuesday. Just as well that he had acted as he did. Otherwise he would still be sitting here, with the microfilm of the memorandum to worry him every waking hour. It was too big a responsibility, too dangerous, and far too urgent.

But how long would this isolation go on? he wondered as he cleared away breakfast and prepared to leave for the office. This was Friday, the sixth of December. He couldn't go on playing the hermit without arousing some suspicions in his friends. There was a limit to excuses about overwork or 'flu. Which reminded him that he would have to call Sandra and cancel their week-end in Maryland. As for Katie, in New York—no, he wouldn't be back there for a long long time. She'd get that message without being told. And Chuck—well, the less he saw of Chuck the better. In any case, Chuck's usefulness was over.

He was about to pick up the receiver and dial Sandra's number, when the telephone rang right under his hand. Startled, he almost answered at once. And then checked himself in time. Two rings; then silence. He waited. Again, there were two rings and a break-off. Now only one more minute... When the ring came again, he was ready with pencil and paper for the coded message that would come over the wire.

The voice was not his usual contact's. It was a man's. Oleg? He was almost sure of that, but he had to concentrate on the words. To his surprise, they weren't in code. They were disguised, of course, and sounded innocent enough to any curious ear. "I am sorry I could not keep our engagement last week. There was illness in the family, and a great deal of work to be done."

"Sorry about that." Yes, Alexis thought, that is Oleg's voice. "What about lunch?"

"Today's impossible. I have an important engagement—" The luncheon at the Statler, to be exact.

"I know."

So Oleg was probably in Washington. The luncheon had been well advertised locally. Four speakers (including Representative Walter Pickering, on the look-out for a cause to tide him over the next election) and eight hundred guests. Theme: Responsibility in the Media. But was Oleg actually going to be there too? *Lunch*, he had suggested. What was he pinpointing—time, or place? Or both? Alexis cleared his throat, gave a small cough to indicate that he was about to use code, and calculated quickly. He could slip away from the luncheon by ten past three. "Half-past four," he said. "I'll be free by that time."

"Why don't you telephone me as soon as you leave?"

"I'll do that."

"How is your cousin Kay?"

"She's fine."

"Just had her sixteenth birthday, I hear."

"Right."

"You can give me all the family news when I see you. Don't forget to telephone." Oleg rang off.

He's a bold type, thought Alexis; he didn't even follow my lead and go into code, except for some disguised words: "telephone" meant "contact;" Kay and her sixteenth birthday emphasised the Statler at K and the Sixteenth Street; and "family news"—if that meant a certain microfilm, then Oleg was going to be disappointed. His own fault, damn his eyes.

Now, let's see: I slip away from the luncheon towards its

end, and contact Oleg at ten past three. Where? In the lobby? He's brash enough for that. It will be crowded, of course. In any case, the contact will be visual. He leads, and I follow at a discreet distance. Or it may be the other way around: I may have difficulty in picking him quickly out of a mob of people—he may have changed the colour of his hair or added a moustache—but he will have no difficulty in identifying me. Yes, that is how I will play it. I'll leave the lobby, taking my time, giving him the chance to see me and follow. But a meeting in daylight? And a message sent with so little attention paid to code? Oleg's style is certainly different from Mischa's. He scares me, Alexis admitted.

He selected a subdued blue tie as suitable for a public appearance as Representative Pickering's aide. (The Congressman was the first speaker of the day, with his eye on the clock and his own private plans for that afternoon.) He surveyed the full effect—grey suit, pale blue shirt for possible television—and added a navy silk handkerchief to his breast pocket. Yes, Rick Nealey was a personable character, quiet, dependable; and a damned good speech-writer, too. What would huff-and-puff Pickering have done without him in these last nine years?

The hotel was large, its lobby a constant stirring of people: arrivals and departures, guests waiting around either for friends or for reservations, visitors drifting in and out of the restaurant and coffee-shop. A town within a town, thought Tony Lawton as he left the notice-board with its verification of various luncheons—a formal one big enough to need the ballroom, offering four speeches on Responsibility of the Media as special enticement; something smaller on the mezzanine for Environmental Science; a third room booked for the Fife and Drum Historical Society; a special meeting of Agrarian Economists. It made him feel inundated: facts and figures, statements, pleas, warnings, perorations were pouring out all over this building. Its thick-carpeted floors must be ankle-deep in eloquence and good will.

He went over to the newspaper-stand, a small shop in itself, and walked slowly along its rows of magazines, trying to decide which he would buy to keep him company on his way across the Atlantic. It was almost three o'clock, and he had a full hour to spend before he left. There was nothing to delay him here, now that the NATO Memorandum was being sent back—with some embarrassment—to Brussels. If Shandon House had been dilatory, Washington had been prompt. And serious attention had been given to the memorandum. When the NATO meetings started next week, there might be more consensus and less disagreement on future planning. So this week, bad as it had been, could have ended worse.

He was far from cheerful, though. From Brussels yesterday had come a brief but disturbing message: Palladin, the NATO agent, had left Moscow for a short vacation in Odessa. That was all. Was he playing it cool? Nothing he couldn't control? Or was it the beginning of flight, and the proof that the worst fears about the NATO Memorandum were realised—it had reached Moscow?

Grim thoughts for a bright talk-filled lobby... Tony forced them out of his mind, concentrated on buying his magazines—one on travel (the kind of travel he never had the time to do), another on food and wine, a third on foreign affairs (must keep up with what the great minds are prognosticating, he told himself). Two paperback novels completed his armoury against possible delays and certain boredom. And a couple of newspapers, of course. One of the headlines caught his eye—some young bombers blown up by their own concoctions—and he began reading as he walked slowly through the lobby, apparently purposeless.

There was a sudden thickening in the crowd around him. A stream of serious-faced men had drifted out of the elevators. The agrarians, Tony noted with satisfaction, including some of the Soviet delegation. He could place them all: ever since Konov had been scheduled to attend the Washington meetings along with his equally mysterious friends called Boris Gorsky, Tony had made a point of identifying each face with its announced name. Most of the Russian delegates were for real, the usual hard-headed farmer and business-man types now turned bureaucrats. Konov's absence had not been explained, either by a fabricated excuse of unexpected illness or by the announcement of his actual death. In fact, whatever name he might have used was no longer on the official list. He had become a non-person. As for Boris Gorsky, he could be any of three secretarial aides and translators, or even one of the two Russian journalists who had been touring the Mid-West with the delegation. Tomorrow was their departure date. The luncheon today was a cordial and sympathetic farewell.

Still absorbed by his newspaper, Tony took up his position behind a family group—mother and two children waiting for Dad to pay the bill—and let his eyes study the scene. Some of the agricultural experts were now debating a point: they had gathered in a tight knot in the centre of the lobby, voices firm but expressions friendly. The translator was busy. And who was he? He hadn't been around last week. Covertly, Tony studied the stranger. Powerful shoulders, about five foot eleven in height, dark hair liberally streaked with grey. Well, thought Tony, the hair-colour doesn't correspond to the New York Police report, complete with composite sketch, on the man who had visited Lenox Hill Hospital; but the height and build, the heavy dark overcoat, seem just about right. (Bless that young police officer who had noted so many details about the man who came to view Konov.) Now, if I could only see his face and his bone-structure—blue eyes, too—then I might have found Boris Gorsky... A long shot, of course. Still, who else but Gorsky would have gone to the hospital and talked his way into Konov's room? Who else? The two of them had arrived secretly in New York: that we do know. Both were coming to Washington, and then touring Chicago and the Middle West along with the agricultural experts. Cancel Konov. But that left Gorsky to fulfil their mission here. So he was probably still around. And what easier way to return to Moscow than accompanying the delegation home? No suspicions aroused, no need for any covert and complicated escape-route via Canada or Mexico.

And still the broad-shouldered man kept his back turned to Tony. A lot of talk going on, over there. Impatiently, Tony glanced at his watch. Seven minutes past three. Come on, he urged silently, turn around, let me see your face. From the direction of the ballroom, others were now emerging, no doubt slipping away before the last speech had ended—they had the slightly harried look of people who had to get back to their offices. A woman, young and smartly dressed and—even from

151

this distance—decidedly pretty, caught Tony's eye. Dorothea Kelso? Yes, it was Dorothea. She was now pausing at the cloakroom, speaking to a man who waited to retrieve his coat. A youngish man, Tony noted automatically: fair hair, pleasant face, excellent grey suit and blue shirt. A smart dresser. And with curt manners. He had made a quick goodbye to Dorothea and was already walking away from her. And that, Tony found, was astonishing. Particularly as the young man was now crossing the lobby at a most leisurely pace, even pausing half-way to pull on his topcoat and fold a blue scarf around his neck. He was looking around him, and yet giving the impression that nothing interested him. Which was less astonishing than leaving a very pretty woman so abruptly, but still—to Tony's expert eye—a little peculiar. He's looking for someone, Tony decided; I've seen that kind of frozen expression before.

Then Tony's senses sharpened even more. The fair-haired man was about to pass the group of agricultural experts. At last, they were showing signs of leave-taking. Tony's attention switched to the man with the grey-streaked hair. He was saying goodbye, speaking clearly and in English, thanking everyone, a neat little speech. Dorothea's friend, still adjusting the blue scarf at his neck, paused for a second as he glanced at the speaker. Had he recognised the voice? Tony wondered. Or perhaps it was a natural hesitation, a curiosity about all those foreigners blocking his path. At that moment the Russian ended his farewell, and, without waiting for the rest of his friends, walked with smart decisive steps towards the front entrance. He passed barely six feet away from Tony, who caught a glimpse of piercing blue eyes before he dodged behind the shelter of Mom's bouffant hair-do. And there was no doubt about the man's features. Strong: determined chin, high-bridged nose, broad brow. It was the composite sketch come to life.

Drawing a deep breath, Tony stepped away from his camouflage group (the two children were becoming impatient; poor Mom was losing her temper) and prepared to follow. It was an instinctive movement, and it brought him almost into collision with the young fair-haired man, no longer fussing with his scarf but leaving in a definite hurry. "Sorry," said Tony. The man barely nodded, turned his head away, continued on his set path to the main door.

Tony checked his step, and stood irresolute. Yes, it could be interesting to follow the possible Gorsky. But what was the use? This wasn't his territory, he was about to leave anyway, his job here was over. A telephone call to Brad Gillon should be enough. Brad would know where and how to drop this piece of information. For what it was worth, Tony added. Perhaps his own curiosity had led him into exaggerating the importance of this small discovery. Now, if he were only playing on his home ground, with plenty of back-up—yes, that would be another kind of game altogether. And yet, and yet... On impulse he began walking to the front door. Just ahead of him the fair-haired man with the blue scarf quickened his pace. Gorsky had already left.

Coming out into the broad busy street, Tony mixed with a small cluster of people waiting for taxis in front of the hotel entrance. He looked left along K Street and saw neither of the two men who had interested him. To his right was K's intersection with Sixteenth Street. And there, at least, was the younger man, waiting to cross—no, it seemed as if he hadn't quite made up his mind. Perhaps, thought Tony in quick dismay, he isn't following Gorsky at all, yet I'm damned sure I heard a voice-contact being made in the Statler lobby: Gorsky spoke, the younger man noticed him, and everything went according to schedule after that. Until now. Then suddenly, with a last glance around him, the man in the blue scarf crossed Sixteenth Street at a smart clip. Tony followed, trying not to hurry, and reached the other side as his quarry was half-way along to Seventeenth Street.

Careful, Tony warned himself. There weren't too many people around in this stretch of handsome buildings, and no shops to give him the excuse of window-gawking. But he didn't have far to travel. There, some distance ahead, was Gorsky, stepping smartly into a parked car. His young friend had marked the spot, and headed for it. As he reached it, he glanced back, but Tony had already stopped two passing girls to ask them the way to Lafayette Park. They were a pleasant and diverting screen, delighted to set him straight with wide smiles and repressed giggles—you go *down* Sixteenth Street, can't miss it. What he didn't miss was the open door of Gorsky's car, ready and waiting for the fair-haired man to slip out of sight. All very neat, thought Tony.

He said thank you to the two girls, and retraced his steps to Sixteenth Street, letting them draw well ahead so that they wouldn't notice he was losing his way again as he crossed over to the hotel.

Dorothea's attendance at the Media luncheon was one of Bud Wells's bright ideas: she had been seated between two prospects for his Sunday Special—interviews in depth, as Wells liked to subtitle it—so that she might gauge, between shrimp cocktail and tournedos and raspberry sherbet, the way they talked about what and where. The journalist on her right was easy in manner, with a wry humour about his recent assignment in Indonesia: he'd make an interesting guest on television. But the writer, expatriate by choice and now on a buy-my-new-book tour of his native land (it galled him, obviously that the country he continually criticised should make him the most money, although he concealed that with his usual deft barbs about the American scene), was in one of his spiritually constipated moods. Apart from initial remarks calculated to annoy the journalist, and a mild pass at Dorothea herself, he relapsed into heavy concentration on food and drink. A difficult guest, Dorothea decided, to be handled with metal gauntlets. Or a hatpin, she added to that, dodging a leg that slid over hers just as the fourth speech of the day began. She left with a smile and a whispered excuse for the journalist.

There were other early departures, so she wasn't alone in her long walk through the ballroom. Ahead of her was Rick Nealey, making his way carefully through the array of tables. Immediately she thought of Chuck, and wondered if Rick had any news of him.

She increased her pace and reached the cloakroom outside, only a few steps behind Rick. She hesitated but briefly. Her anger with Chuck was mixed with worry: his silence was incomprehensible. Tom hadn't heard one word from him all this hideous week. "Hello, Rick."

Startled, he swung round. His smile of recognition was slow in coming, almost nervous. "Hello there. Just dashing back to the office," he explained unnecessarily.

"How have you been?"

"Fine."

"And Chuck—how is he?"

"Chuck? I haven't seen him in ages."

"Oh, I thought you went to New York for week-ends."

"Haven't been able to get away for several weeks." Rick reached for his coat and scarf. "Nice seeing you." He gave a parting nod.

Dorothea didn't even have time to say her goodbye. He was off, heading for the lobby. How odd, she thought: scarcely the same man who used to visit us and stay and stay. Oh damn, why did I even bother to talk to him? The feeling of rebuff grew sharper. Angry with herself, with Rick, with Chuck, she turned towards the powder-room, there to comb her hair, and wash, and apply lipstick. In the mirror she was glad to see she looked normal and not someone infected with hideous leprosy. Lighting a cigarette, she allowed herself five minutes to let her emotions subside. Also, to let Rick Nealey be well out of sight before she braved the lobby again. She tried not to think of what Tom would say when he heard about her attempt to get news of Chuck. (She wouldn't mean to tell him, but it would slip out: it always did.) Tom was refusing to discuss Chuck at all. He was waiting—of that she was certain—for Chuck to call him. An explanation was more than due about that borrowed typewriter. But Tom wasn't making the first move. He was right, of course. How did you go to your brother and say, "You were responsible for breaking security, and you did it with my typewriter, you bastard"? No, you waited for your brother to come to you and admit what he had done. That was all Tom wanted: an honest admission. After that, there could be frank argument. And for my part, thought Dorothea, I'd tell Chuck to resign from Shandon House and find a job designing chairs and tables, something where his ideals wouldn't do any damage to other people's careers.

She had a second cigarette.

Then she went back to collect her coat, just ahead of the grand rush out of the ballroom. Still thinking about Chuck, still worrying about Tom, she paid scant attention to anyone in the lobby.

"Dorothea!" a voice said delightedly, and she turned to look. At first she scarcely recognised him, with his hair wind-blown and his tie carelessly knotted. He was wearing a tweed jacket and flannels today, and carrying a bundle of magazines and papers under one arm; he looked like a college professor rather than a wine-merchant. "Mrs. Kelso," Tony Lawton said, more restrained, "how very nice to see you." There was no doubt he meant it. "What about a cup of coffee with me?"

"I really have to get back to the office—"

"Ten minutes, twenty minutes?" He had a most disarming smile. "I'm just about to leave Washington. There's nothing more depressing than waiting around in a giant hotel by oneself."

"The café may be closed."

"Then we'll try the drug-store." He took her arm in a gentle but firm hold and steered her towards the café. "How is Tom?"

"He's in New York today."

He noticed the evasion. "It has been pretty rough on him." And will be rougher, he thought. "I visited Shandon a couple of days ago." She looked at him inquiringly. Her step no longer lagged. But he said nothing more until he had managed to persuade a waitress in the empty café that they only wanted two cups of Irish coffee and a quiet place to sit. He selected an unobtrusive corner, helped Dorothea slide her coat back from her shoulders, took a chair directly facing her, and studied the picture she made, blonde hair, blonde wool dress. "The colour of champagne," he said with approval. "You should always wear it."

Dorothea laughed, and surprised herself.

"Much better," he told her. "You had a bad day, I take it."

"And a very bad week. Does it show?"

"It did. I saw this beautiful creature walking across the lobby and said to myself, 'Tony, if ever a girl needed a cup of coffee with a slug of Irish whiskey topped with cream—' And here it is. To order." He gave the elderly waitress a warm smile of thanks. "Now, have a few sips, and I'll tell you about Shandon House."

"You saw Chuck?"

"Briefly. He was buried in work." A slight smile played around Tony's lips.

"He's the best excuse-manufacturer I know."

Tony nodded, his smile deepening, his eyes studying her with some surprise.

"I shouldn't have said that," she retracted quickly.

"Why not? It's the truth."

"Tom—" She paused and sighed, shrugged her shoulders.

And that tells the whole story, Tony thought. "Tom hasn't got in touch with Chuck? No, I don't suppose he could. Perhaps it's just as well. I tried. And got nowhere."

"Nowhere at all?"

"I talked about the NATO Memorandum—it's the main topic at Shandon these days. But Chuck is admitting nothing. He answered in generalities. The fellow responsible must have had very good reasons for doing what he did. It couldn't have been for money; and it certainly wasn't because of lack of patriotism. There were no traitors at Shandon. In fact, if this hypothetical fellow was keeping silent now, it was probably to protect Shandon and keep its good name untarnished by publicity."

"What?" She stared at him.

"Yes. There was no proof that the leak had come from Shandon. So why should this hypothetical fellow supply that proof?"

"And what about the typewriter—or didn't you mention it?"

"A mild suggestion: wasn't it a little odd, most peculiar indeed? But his reply was rather lofty. I shouldn't believe all the gossip I heard. The whole thing had been blown out of all proportion. Anyone could borrow a portable typewriter—slip into a hotel room and use it when the owner wasn't around. A couple of hours were all that was needed." And that, thought Tony, had been an interesting admission.

"Oh, come now—" Dorothea began.

"Besides, as Chuck pointed out, no one who knew Tom was going to believe any of that gossip. The whole idea was best treated with complete contempt. And silence."

"And Tom, meanwhile?"

"Tom could handle anything."

Dorothea stared out, through the wall of windows, at the open stretch of Sixteenth Street with its quiet houses and placid traffic. "And that is that," she said, trying to mask her anger and failing.

"The truth is," Tony said slowly, "Chuck is a very scared young man. He is suddenly faced with the unpleasant realisation that his whole career might be ruined. So he rationalises: and persuades himself he is right."

"And that will really break Tom. Far more than any gossip could do. Oh, Tony—"

"I know."

Here I am, thought Dorothea, discussing family with a man I once disliked. No, not exactly disliked; not exactly distrusted, either. A man I couldn't understand, perhaps a man whose job scared me. Too mysterious, too much out of my world. And yet now—"How do I tell Tom about this? He ought to know." She waited anxiously for his advice.

"Let Brad Gillon do it," Tony suggested. "He's coming to Washington this week-end, isn't he?"

Dorothea half-smiled. Tony was really a most perceptive character, she thought. "I just can't discuss it with Tom," she admitted. "I'm too impatient with Chuck. Prejudiced, perhaps. So I back away from any criticism. Family loyalty—" She shook her head. "I wish it weren't so one-sided, though. Doesn't Chuck realise what his actions have done to Tom? It *was* Chuck who copied the NATO Memorandum, wasn't it? You and Brad were there when he came to borrow Tom's typewriter. You both know and Tom knows and I know. And Chuck knows we know. Oh, how can he *not* come to Tom and admit it?"

"Because the natural reaction in most people who have made a big mistake is to cover up. It takes a very honest man, and there are damned few of them around, to admit an unpleasant truth. Not right off, at least."

"I hate to believe that."

"Why?"

"Because—because I want people to be honest."

"And all things bright and beautiful?"

"What makes you so cynical, Tony?" she asked softly. "Your job?"

His smile vanished. "Cynical? Realistic is a kinder word." Then, very quietly, he added, "What job?" His anger was sharp, even if concealed. "Has Tom been fantasising?"

He doesn't do that!"

"Not usually."

"I'm the one who thought you might be—well, attached to some kind of—" She hesitated and dodged. "Tom argued me out of it, told me to stop speculating about people. It's one of my bad habits. But, Tony, you really are a mystery man."

"Me?"

"Yes, poor little innocent you."

"What on earth gave you such a mad idea? Flattering, of course. I'd hate to be considered just a routine type."

"You'd never be that." This pleased him in spite of himself. Encouraged, Dorothea said, "And anything I've noticed about you is strictly for my eyes only. I don't chatter, Tony. Not about serious matters."

"And just what have you noticed?" He had decided to play this for laughs.

"Well...the way you met Brad in our room at the Algonquin."

"Old Brad rather likes that kind of mystery. Reminds him of the best years of his life."

"Yes," she agreed, and her eyes sparkled bright blue with amusement, "there's some truth in that."

"What else?" he asked lightly. How could he explain that he had been followed all the way from Brussels, kept under tight surveillance until he had managed to dodge it in New York? Even then, he had been forced to move with the greatest care. There had been no purpose in dragging either Brad or the Kelsos into any possible danger. Contact with them had, for their sakes, best been kept disguised. Now, of course, in this last week—since the memorandum had actually been filched—interest in him had dropped. It would be revived again, once he was identified as the man who had been so interested in viewing Konov's corpse. So far that had not happened. Either he had actually avoided being photographed as he came out of the morgue, or the KGB had been slow for once—it was possible that Konov's death had meant a lot of rearrangement in their priorities. At any rate, these recent days had been blissfully free of any surveillance.

Dorothea was saying nothing at all. The smile in her eyes spread to her lips.

He changed the subject by glancing at his watch. "I'm being picked up here by a friend at four o'clock. Before then I'd like to 'phone goodbye to Brad. Too bad I can't be here for this week-end, but I'll see Tom trailing Kissinger in Brussels next Thursday. He's still going there, isn't he?"

"Yes. Not very enthusiastically, though."

"A delicate situation," Tony agreed. He helped her with her coat. "By the way, wasn't it Basil Meade I saw you chatting with? I didn't know he was in town."

"Basil Meade?" She was puzzled.

"You met at the cloakroom—"

"Oh—that was Rick Nealey. He's one of Chuck's friends."

Tony left a good-sized tip and led her to the cashier's desk at the door. "From Shandon House?"

"No. He's communications aide or something to Representative Pickering."

Tony paid the check, and guided her into the lobby. "Does he still see Chuck?"

"At week-ends."

"You mean he goes to New York each week?"

"Yes. At least, I always thought he did. But he hasn't seen Chuck in ages—so he said."

"Does he stay with Chuck in New York?" Tony asked, his voice casual.

"He's at the same address, but in the apartment underneath. It belongs to his girl-friend." Dorothea frowned. "Perhaps he and Chuck have quarrelled." That might be the reason for Rick's embarrassment at meeting her. "But they always got along so well. It's really very odd. Oh, I'm sorry, Tony. This can't possibly interest you. I'm only trying to find some reason why Rick practically cut me dead. You saw it?"

"I saw it. And I thought he was a bloody idiot." That brought the smile back to her face. "How long have they been friends?"

"From away back. Ever since Germany."

"Old Army buddies?"

"Rick was a refugee, actually. From East Germany."

"With a name like Nealey? The Irish do get around."

"Rick was born in New York. His mother was German. The Nealeys were Brooklyn. His father was killed in the Pacific, and so Rick ended up in Dresden or Leipzig—some place like that."

"A beautiful sequitur. Clear as mud."

Dorothea laughed. "But perfectly normal. His mother wanted to see her own people as soon as the war ended."

"And once in, they couldn't get out?"

"Yes." She was studying him thoughtfully. "You seem to know his story."

"Just the pattern. It happened often enough. When did Rick escape from East Germany?" Tony's voice was conversational.

"As soon as his mother died. She became an invalid, you see, and Rick couldn't leave her there alone."

"Rick—short for Richard?" The question was casual.

"Heinrich." Then Dorothea challenged him, her eyes widening. "This really *does* interest you."

"I always like a sad romantic tale." He took her hand. He held it gently, his face suddenly serious. "Goodbye, Dorothea." And always my luck, he thought: the beautiful woman out of reach.

"Goodbye." Then, as their hands dropped, she said with undisguised amusement, "And who *is* Basil Meade?" She left before he could even think of an answer. He watched her as she walked towards the door and passed out of sight. He was smiling too.

He had six minutes for his call to Brad Gillon. He wasted no time on explanations. "Listen, Brad," he said as soon as he got through. "Remember the chap in the composite sketch I saw last Tuesday? He's here. In Washington—with the same delegation that our late unlamented friend should have been accompanying. Possibly leaving tomorrow. Today he has been meeting Rick Nealey, a friend of Chuck's and some kind of factotum to a Congressman—Pickering by name. Nealey visits New York at week-ends—apartment in same building as Chuck's. Got all that? Okay. I leave it in your hands. You have such interesting friends. Goodbye, old scout. Take care."

Tony left the public 'phone, gathered up his magazines and papers (now slightly crumpled), and was out at the front door as the small army car drove up. His luggage was already waiting for him at the airport, along with the NATO Memorandum under heavy guard. The stable door was securely locked, he thought.

"Had a pleasant lunch, sir?" the sergeant-driver asked civilly.

"Very pleasant."

"Nice hotel. You'd enjoy staying there some time. There's a lot going on in the evenings."

There's a lot going on any old time, thought Tony. Not a bad day after all.

11

Nothing had gone as he had planned. Rick Nealey's irritation increased. First, there had been the unexpected encounter with Dorothea Kelso, detaining him, wasting precious seconds when each one of his minutes had been carefully estimated. Next, Oleg had chosen to make contact by voice and lead the way out of the hotel. His own preconceived ideas of how to deal with a difficult meeting, far too dangerous for his taste, had been swept aside. And now here he was, as Alexis, following this madman along a public thoroughfare on a bright afternoon, neither the place nor the time appropriate, and far from his choosing. Insanity, he thought.

Grudgingly, he had to admit it was paying off. So far. The lobby was safely behind him, and no one was on his heels. To make sure of that, as he walked along K Street—keep nonchalant, no haste, let the space between Oleg and him widen—he took the usual precaution of dropping a book of matches, which gave him a quick glimpse of the Statler entrance as he bent to pick it up. He saw only a cluster of people outside its door waiting for taxis, no solitary figure, no head turned his way. At the corner of Sixteenth Street he hesitated, as if in doubt of his direction—a harmless excuse to look around him. At the Statler, there was still the cluster, and no one following him. Quickly he crossed Sixteenth Street and continued along K. Well ahead of him was Oleg, halting beside a parked car.

Irritation flared into alarmed anger. In broad daylight, for God's sake: Oleg stepping into a car as if he were an old-time Washington bureaucrat, not even glancing back. He's leaving that job for me, thought Alexis. Perversely, he didn't look over his shoulder until he had almost reached the car: only two women standing in front of the Fiji Legation, talking with a man—legs were all that was visible. Beyond that, a mother and small child; two priests on the other side of the street, some automobiles driving at a quick steady pace.

The car door was open. All he had to do was step in. Somehow the simplicity of it only angered him more, proving Oleg was right and himself over-worried and fearful.

"You weren't followed?" Oleg asked, as he eased the car out into the traffic.

"I could say no, and I could say yes."

"And what does that mean?" Oleg's mouth was tight.

"Anyone could be following us. Secretaries, priests—"

"And your own shadow."

There was a long silence. "Where are we going?" Alexis asked at last.

"Driving around, like good Americans."

"You take a lot of risks. That telephone call this morning—"

"Stop talking and let me pay attention. There are bigger risks in getting a traffic ticket than in walking out of a hotel." As Oleg spoke, his eyes kept watching the rear and side mirrors. "No one did follow you," he said at last. He was concentrating carefully now on the one-way streets, avoiding the busy circles or the underpasses and the giant avenues. It was as if he had memorised a certain number of blocks in this part of town and wasn't going to venture into strange territory. As it was, Alexis had to admit, Oleg was doing not at all badly for someone who didn't know Washington too well; and how typical of the man, to keep the wheel himself instead of asking him to drive. Within six minutes Oleg had found the parking spot he wanted, back once more on K Street, but this time further east, near the bus terminal for Dulles Airport. It was a busy section with plenty of movement. Their car, a rented Buick in unobtrusive brown, was not conspicuous; nor were they. Just two people waiting for friends to arrive from a flight to Washington.

But Alexis could not resist raising an eyebrow. It wasn't unnoticed. Oleg, switching off the ignition, said, "Less risk too, in not driving far afield. And to what purpose?"

True enough. The shorter the time they spent together, the safer. They had not been followed. No other car drew up within view. That was all that mattered. But Alexis was still nervous and unsettled. He searched for a cigarette.

"Ah, the microfilm. You had enough sense to bring it with—"

"I've already sent it to Moscow." Alexis lit the cigarette, only remembered then to offer his pack to Oleg. It was impatiently brushed aside.

"There has been no report of its arrival," Oleg said, eyes angry, face tense. "When did you send it?"

"As soon as I got back to Washington."

"You were instructed—"

"I know. Mischa told me to give it to you on the Tuesday. But that was before he was injured. Which changed everything."

"Who told you it changed anything?"

"You did not contact me. You could have been back in Moscow for all I knew." And if Oleg wasn't notified about the arrival there of the microfilm, Alexis thought, then he isn't as important as he thinks he is. Encouraged, Alexis said in a cool crisp voice, "The NATO Memorandum went by the usual channels. It is in Moscow now—has been for the last seven or eight days."

"Usual channels," Oleg repeated, his eyes narrowing. "Which means it reached the desk of the wrong man."

"Wrong? It would reach the usual office—"

"Where one man has sidetracked it, misfiled it, kept it hidden for as long as he dared." Oleg's cold anger mounted with his voice.

"But why?" Alexis was instantly alarmed.

"To let him make his escape. He is a traitor. And you gave him a week to perfect his plans. By this time he is well away from Moscow. And he's laughing at you, Alexis. You were too clever by far. You played right into his hands."

"I don't believe it," Alexis said, fighting back. "A traitor? In such an important job? He wouldn't have lasted one hour."

"He lasted twelve years."

Alexis stared, aghast. "If you knew he was an enemy agent, why didn't you—"

"Mischa had suspicions, that was all. The proof could be in the NATO Memorandum, Part III." Oleg's bitter face was accusing.

"Which you sent, so obligingly, so kindly, straight to him."

"His office always has received my reports. Mischa did not warn me, nor did you. I only followed—" Alexis broke off, his worry doubling as he saw a new and immediate danger. "All these years, he has known who I am."

"No. We are not as stupid as that. He only knows that there is an Alexis, established in Washington, who sends weekly reports."

"If he is as good an enemy agent as you say he is, he could analyse the material I sent him, and know what kind of job I have here, even trace—"

"At this moment, he is too busy saving his own skin. If he gets clear—*if* (and we'll see about that)—then he may start tracking you down." Oleg looked as though he might enjoy that idea. "In the long run you may have damaged yourself. And others too. Unless we find him."

"He is CIA?"

"No. He's an agent of NATO."

"The same thing."

"Only in our propaganda." And that, thought Oleg, is at least one recent success. The slogans and chants against the NATO—CIA combination were growing stronger each week in Europe. "It even impressed you," he said contemptuously. "You have become an American."

The sneer reminded Alexis of Mischa. He had said something like that too, but jokingly. And then Alexis wondered why Oleg had given no news of Mischa. "How is—" he began, and was cut off by Oleg's next question. It dealt with the problem of Chuck Kelso.

"I see no problem," said Alexis. "He is reliable."

"He may endanger you."

"I don't think so." But Alexis frowned.

"How did you procure the memorandum?"

Alexis told him, keeping it brief, and waited for a word of praise.

Instead, "Kelso may tell his brother that you were with him on that evening."

"Even so, would that matter?"

"The brother has several friends in NATO. That would matter."

"Intelligence officers?"

"They could be. And they would certainly be interested in anyone who handled the full text of the NATO Memorandum."

"Chuck doesn't know I touched it. He has no way of guessing."

"You had better find out. Exactly. What is he feeling? What is he thinking? Will he talk? Make your report next week."

"Too soon. I can't get away to New York until—"

"Next week. And direct it to me personally in Moscow. Make sure of that. It will be your last report for some time. Do nothing. Keep quiet. I shall let you know when you can be active again."

So he is giving the orders now, thought Alexis. "Where is Mischa?" he asked. Had Mischa been demoted, blamed perhaps for the escape of a traitor?

"Mischa is dead."

"Dead?" A moment of disbelief. "But how? Where?"

"In New York."

Mischa is dead. Oleg is in command. The shock died away. "But how?" Alexis repeated. Oleg kept silent. "The result of the mugging, I suppose."

"The result." Oleg drew out something from his pocket. Three small photographs. "Have you ever seen this man with Chuck Kelso? The one in the tweed jacket?"

Alexis studied the snapshots of three men. There was no clear view of the face above the tweed jacket. The man had his hand up, coughing, in one picture. In the second, he held a large handkerchief at his nose. In the third, his head was bent as he looked at the ground. "No," Alexis said slowly. "But these photographs don't help much. Who is he?"

"An expert," Oleg said.

"And the other two?" Their faces were clear enough.

"New York City detectives."

"Arresting the expert?" It was the kind of small joke that would have amused Mischa. Oleg said nothing. Reproved, Alexis became serious again. "Where were the pictures taken? That could be a clue."

Oleg came slowly back from his own far-ranging thoughts. Suspicions, always suspicions that couldn't be pinned down... Anthony Lawton, wine-merchant... Or NATO Intelligence officer? On a tip from an informant, he had been followed from Brussels to New York. (Possible close connection with memorandum, the informant had said.) In New York he vanished. Reappeared in Washington. Reported to have entered Shandon House this Tuesday, the morning of the newspaper publication of the first part of the memorandum. What reason for this visit—Chuck Kelso and NATO security? Or had it been merely wine-business? The only detail the report had given was that Lawton was casually dressed in tweed jacket and sweater. Tweed jacket...yet many people in New York dressed casually, even wildly. Oleg stared down at the elusive figure in the photographs. Yes, Lawton—if he were a NATO agent—would certainly have an interest in Mischa. But how had he found out Mischa was dead? Oleg slipped the snapshots back into his pocket. "They were taken at the morgue," he said.

Alexis looked uncomprehending. But there was no further explanation.

"I'll be waiting for your report on Kelso," Oleg said, and gestured to the door. "Give me five minutes before you take a cab." He started the engine. Alexis got out. The Buick edged into the traffic and was soon part of a steady stream of cars.

Alexis walked into the bus terminal. Five minutes, Oleg had said. Alexis wondered where he could find a drink, a stiff Scotch. And then, remembering that cold look on Oleg's face, he found a telephone-booth instead. *He would call Chuck now. At Shandon.* Catch him before he left for the day, keep the conversation generalised and innocuous, try to arrange a meeting, something. Something that would look adequate in his report to Oleg. Adequate? He would have to do better than that.

"Rick here," Alexis began.

Chuck sounded surprised, then diffident. No, he wasn't going to be in New York tomorrow. He had a pile of work to finish at Shandon. And Sunday too was impossible. Anything wrong?

"Of course not. Just thought I'd like to see you, chat about everything. What did you think of that item the *Times* published last Tuesday? About NATO. Caused quite a sensation."

"Yes," said Chuck. He didn't sound enthusiastic.

"I thought you'd have liked it. It sent me. It's good that we know what's really going on, isn't it?"

"Yes," Chuck said again.

"You seem—disappointed."

"Oh, it's just that—" Chuck hesitated. "I don't know whether it was worth printing that kind of thing. Who listens?"

"Plenty. Here are you and I discussing it, for instance. It really was an attention-getter."

"In the wrong direction."

"What do you mean?"

"People are more interested in how it came to be printed than in what it said. The message itself got lost."

"Far from it. It came over loud and clear. Say—aren't you feeling well? You sound as though you were coming down with grippe."

"That's all I need," Chuck said. "By the way, Katie is in real trouble."

"Katie?" Alexis braced himself.

"She was arrested last night."

Alexis was silent.

"Rick—are you still there?"

"Yes. Arrested for what? Hiding a marijuana joint in her pocket?"

"Arrested in a bomb-factory down in Greenwich Village. There was an explosion. Two of her friends were injured. Katie was found wandering in a daze."

"That's Katie all right."

"It's no joke, Rick."

"No joke," Alexis conceded.

"And Rick, I don't think we should talk, either of us, about—about that Saturday night."

"I agree. Button our lips."

"About Katie, I meant."

"And we'll say nothing. About anything. *Anything*," Alexis repeated with emphasis. "Got that?"

"I suppose you're right."

"I am. Katie has complicated everything in her own sweet way. You see that, don't you?"

"Yes," Chuck said reluctantly. "Yes, she certainly has," he added, and now he sounded definite.

"Signing off, Chuck. This call is ending and I've no more loose change. See you some time."

"Yes. Some time."

He wants to see me as little as I want to see him, Alexis thought as he went to find a cab. And now he is really worried about admitting he handed over a copy of the memorandum to that reporter—what's his name, Holzheimer?—in Katie's apartment. If he was on the point of breaking down and confessing to big brother Tom, Katie and her friends have taken care of that noble impulse. My report next week about Chuck Kelso will be simple: Chuck is depressed and worrying, but holding fast. (He has to, now. Unless he wants Holzheimer breathing down his neck with questions about his connection with a mad bomber.)

He found a cab, but he didn't take it to the garage where he had parked his car that day. Instead, he directed it over to the Mayflower, where he slipped into the bar for a much-needed drink. He didn't think he was being followed, but it was just as well not to have his movements traceable.

And what about you? he asked himself after a second drink. Your report next week will deal with Chuck. It will also have to pass on this newest information about Katie. How does it affect you? (Oleg knows you've been shacking up with her. It's on your file.) Lucky that you already stated you were going to keep clear of her: dangerous situation developing. So they can't blame you for being blind. But there's danger still around. Once the police start searching her apartment, inquiring about her associates—yes, that's something to be really concerned about. Katie won't talk. Not to the pigs. To her lawyer? Yes. He won't talk either. And yet something can slip out, some damned investigative reporter can start digging...

He finished his drink. In his report he would ask to be transferred from Washington, from the United States for that matter. Oleg wouldn't like that—all of Alexis's expensive training had been geared to let him mix freely among Americans. Okay. He had done that. Now it was time to move: he was bored with all-things-to-all-men Pickering, anyway. How the hell could he have put up with that shoulder-thumper for nine long years? Time to move on—where? There were places, plenty of places outside the good old US of A, where he could work with Americans. Be one of them. No training lost. That was it: a brilliant idea. He'd suggest it to Oleg, and let Oleg take it over as his own bright solution. Yes, that was it. Alexis paid and left. A brilliant idea.

And now he was out on Connecticut Avenue, dark with sudden night. He felt safer in its shroud. This was the way he and Oleg should have met. It would have given him more confidence, caught him less off balance. Or perhaps Oleg had been trying to dent his self-assurance. Had Oleg been testing him? An unpleasant meeting, certainly: everything tight and strained. Why? Wasn't Oleg sure of him?

He put that spiky question out of his mind by hailing a taxi and driving to the station. There he spent a couple of minutes buying a paper at the bookstall to see if anything had yet been printed about Katie; and, if so, how much. There was only a bare description of the explosion, no details about the girl. They would come later. Unless her family succeeded in clamping down on any information about her. They would certainly try. My unwitting allies, he thought, as he took another cab, this time to a street corner a block away from his garage. He'd be home by six, a normal enough routine. And now he'd no longer have to wait for any contact to telephone him. Lie low, stay inactive, Oleg had instructed him. So now he could call some of his friends, arrange some dates, enjoy himself. He might even go on that week-end with Sandra to Maryland. Why not?

His spirits lifted. White buildings, spacious and majestic, raised their lighted columns into the darkness. Trees and grass and stately monuments, broad avenues and streams of cars. Another working day was over. Speeches made, committees attended, letters dictated and signed; offices closing; and now the scurry through the giant mausoleum to neat houses in neat gardens where humans could come into their proper proportion again. Yes, he thought as he persuaded himself he would be glad to leave Washington, I have been too long here. It bathes you in dreams of glory, entices you with power and rewards, blinds you to the reality outside its magical radiance. These people, and he looked at the cars' lights sweeping steadily in front of him, are doomed.

For a moment he felt sorry for them, kindly and blundering as they were. And then he repressed his touch of emotion. Sympathy was treacherous, self-defeating. He had been Americanised, Oleg would say. Next time he heard that, he would have a reply ready for Oleg: "Just part of my job." Or would he ever meet Oleg again? I hope not, he admitted to himself.

12

And there she was, in view, exactly on time, sitting at a small table near the window of the café, smooth dark head bent over the *International Herald Tribune*, one hand holding a cigarette, the other about to raise her cup of mid-morning coffee to her lips. She was frowning either in complete concentration on the paper's English, or in bewilderment over some of the news.

Tony Lawton stepped out of the cool breeze that blew along Menton's waterfront, entered the café, looked for a vacant table, and chose one a short distance from the girl. She didn't look up. They had worked together often enough in the past, so that old routines came back quite naturally. He slipped off his leather jacket as he ordered his coffee, and prepared to settle down for a pleasant half-hour like the other Riviera visitors scattered around the room... Naturally, he glanced around him. Naturally, he became aware of the girl. He gave an obvious second-glance, a double-take, and looked both astounded and delighted.

"Nicole!" he said, rising and coming over to where she sat.

Nicole's dark brown eyes stared up at him, at first blankly, and then with astonishment. Pink lips parted in a real smile. "But how extraordinary! What are you doing here?" She spoke in slightly accented English, with emphasis on the "r's" as any Frenchwoman would.

Now don't overdo it, darling, Tony admonished her silently. "I'm on holiday—supposed to be sailing along the blue Mediterranean with a couple of friends." He signalled to his waitress to bring the coffee to this table. "May I?" he asked Nicole as he took the chair opposite her.

"Sailing? What happened to that idea?"

"The engine. It began hiccupping just as we rounded Cap Martin yesterday, so we made for the nearest port, and here we are."

"Your friends?"

"They are still over at the harbour, trying to fix what has gone wrong. They know boats. Frankly, I don't. We had hoped to leave today, but the experts aren't sure about that. I think if we make it out of Menton by tomorrow, we'll be lucky."

"Tomorrow is Saturday," she reminded him. "The week-end is taken seriously here. If your experts aren't already at work, you'll be ashore until Monday at least. Why don't you use the sails? You have sails, I suppose."

"We've already had a taste of a south-easter off Cannes. Thank you, but I'm no enthusiast about sails when the blowing gets rough. But what about you, Nicole? On holiday, too?"

"I live here."

"You do? So you have deserted Paris?"

"I prefer the weather in Menton. Besides, I have a job.

I'm secretary—really a research-assistant—to a writer: an American. W. B. Marriot. You must have heard of him."

"You know me. I never open a book unless it's to sign a cheque." Tony drank the last of his coffee and lifted the two tabs which had been tactfully tucked under a saucer. Prepare to move out, was his unspoken suggestion. "And what is your Mr. Marriot working on now? Or perhaps he is just enjoying a happy life like a thousand other writers and artists on the French Riviera."

"Côte d'Azur," Nicole corrected in liquid French. "Actually, Mr. Marriot is writing a script for a movie about the Americans who landed in Menton and joined up with the French Resistance."

"Way back then?"

"Well, if Dunkirk and Normandy are worth a war movie, so is the Côte d'Azur. In fact, it was a marvellous operation." She had to laugh at her own enthusiasm.

"So you are now an expert on World War II," he teased her. He studied the tabs as an added prod: establishing your cover was all very well—and necessary—but it was time for more serious talk.

Nicole got his message, and began folding up the *Tribune* to slip it into her large leather bag.

"And this is your day off?" he went on. "My luck has turned. Let's have lunch together."

"It isn't my day off. I came in to collect the mail and buy some typewriter ribbon."

"So I see."

"But I always come here for a cup of coffee when I'm shopping in town," she protested. "I've stayed too long today. Your fault, Tony. I must go."

"What about dinner tonight?"

She had risen, picking up her cardigan—a bulky thing of giant stitches, the newest chic this spring—and smiled her goodbye to the couple, man and wife, who stood behind the counter. They wished her a warm good-day. The waitress echoed it, politely ignoring the five francs that Tony had dropped beside the tabs on the saucer. Even allowing for the fifteen per cent tip already added to the bill, the prices came high these days. "I'm sorry," Nicole was saying. "If only I had known you were in Menton, I could have rearranged this evening."

She began walking to the door, followed by several appraising glances from various tables. She was a fragile-looking girl, small-boned, who could carry the latest fad in fashion: a casual shirt topped by a heavy sweater, covered by an outsize cardigan above a wide skirt, its mid-calf hemline flaring over her long dark-red leather boots. Yes, thought Tony, as he jammed one arm into his jacket and hurried after her, she was very good in every way: a natural part of the prevalent scene. And all her words, chosen carefully, had told any listening ears (possibly innocent in their curiosity, but always interested: a part of the nothing-much-to-do holiday feeling when the weather, if sunny and bright, was still too cool for the beaches) only what the local people already knew and could verify if questioned.

"Well," he said as he reached the heavy glass door in time to push it open for her, "perhaps you could rearrange something tomorrow?"

"If you are still here," Nicole said over her shoulder.

Standing on the scrimped sidewalk, jammed tight with rows of empty tables and chairs hopefully set out with bright-patterned table-cloths fluttering in the breeze and hanging on by a miracle, Tony Lawton only paused to zip up his jacket and say, "I'll walk you wherever you are going."

"To the market. I parked my car not far from there. It's a small red Opel, second-hand, just the right price for a secretary's salary."

"Which direction? East?"

"Yes. Towards the port."

Couldn't be better, he thought. The street, fronting the Mediterranean, was a one-sided affair, with a continuous row of small cafés and bars crowding the sidewalk. On its opposite side there was a promenade edging the shore, only a few strollers now taking the salt air along the wide curve of Menton's west bay. The port and the market were some distance ahead. Nicole and he would have ample time to talk without any danger of being overheard. And on the promenade they'd be protected, by the constant rush of cars along the narrow street, from any observant eyes across the way in one of the interminable cafés. "Let's walk by the sea," he said, catching her arm, choosing a moment when the cars and taxis slackened their pace. They ran, hand in hand. She was laughing as if he had just made one of his better jokes, and he was smiling: two carefree and happy people, not a thing in the world for them to worry about.

"Well arranged," he told her when they reached the promenade. He squeezed her hand affectionately as he released his grip. A few couples, women with children, retired people having their morning constitutional, resident English still clinging to their favourite Riviera town in spite of inflation, several visiting foreigners. Not too many at this time of year—today was the last day of February—but enough. In summer this promenade would be pure jammed-up hell. What vacation place wasn't, nowadays? "Couldn't be better."

Nicole's face, always pale-skinned even in deep-tanning weather, flushed slightly with his compliment. He gave them rarely. "I was worried," she admitted, "that my description of the café hadn't been clear enough to let you find it easily." Now her English was both fluent and perfect, although a Londoner might have quibbled at a touch of American in an occasional phrase. But she had spent four years in New York as well as ten in England. Her French was authentic: she had been born in Paris and lived there for the first fifteen years of her life. Her Russian was better than adequate: her grandparents had come from Moscow, settled in France as Czarist exiles in 1912 and rejected Lenin in 1917 as no solution for any true liberal. Her father was Swiss, and internationally minded. She believed fervently in the necessary survival of the West. And with equal sincerity she saw NATO as its main defence.

"No problem," Tony assured her. "That yellow-striped awning over the pink and green tablecloths would have been hard to miss."

"When you called me this morning, I just couldn't think of any other place where you could find me quite naturally. Was it all right?"

"It was your usual morning routine, wasn't it?"

"Yes."

"Then it was best to stay with it and raise no questions." She relaxed then. So now he could get down to business. "And how is our friend?"

The sudden change in Tony's voice caught her by surprise. "He is well."

"No new developments?"

"None. He really has recovered. He feels safe here."

"Has he remembered any further details to pass on to you?"

"No. And I don't imagine there is anything to add. He was thoroughly debriefed in Genoa."

Tony nodded. Genoa was where Palladin had stopped running. He had insisted that the NATO team of debriefing experts come to him. He wasn't going anywhere near Paris or Brussels, or even into Switzerland—all too obvious, all dangerous. He was ill, exhausted, and had come far enough by difficult routes. He had had enough of travel and tension: from Moscow to Odessa, to Istanbul where he made contact with a NATO agent. From Istanbul, his journey had been arranged for him, step by step—to the island of Lesbos by fishing-boat and then on a mail-boat to the Piraeus, with a quick change to a decrepit freighter bound for Brindisi near the heel of Italy. Italians had smuggled him by truck westwards to Reggio, and then north to Naples: another freighter—this time bound for Genoa; and there, in a safe-house, he decided to call a halt for three weeks. He had won that battle of wills. The specialists slipped into Genoa one by one, in order to gather all the information that was still so fresh in his mind. And he had won the second battle too: Menton, just across the French-Italian border, was where he had decided to start his new life.

"And he really is safe," Nicole went on, "as safe as a man like him can expect to be." Palladin had been one of the most important NATO agents in Moscow, a top-ranking KGB official. "He has changed his appearance, of course. He will really astound you when you see him." Then, as Tony still kept silent, she said, "You do want to see him, don't you?"

"I wish I could. But I think not. Your report will be enough."

"But—"

"It isn't necessary. Let's keep his visitors to a minimum." Especially the ones who might be traced, at some time, in some way, to NATO Intelligence. Nicole, of course, had been chosen for this assignment because her cover was secure and her connection with NATO unsuspected. W. B. Marriot ("Bill" to his friends) was also unknown to Soviet agents; and his household help, Bernard and Brigitte—a reliable couple from Switzerland, where Bill had supposedly spent the winter—were an efficient part of the team. Palladin completed the W.B. Marriot ménage as chauffeur—his own choice of occupation for his new identity as a French-Italian from Nice, name of Jean Parracini. (Bill carried his arm until recently in a sling, and leaned on a cane when he walked—a skiing accident last winter, the story went. It was obvious to everyone that he needed a driver.)

"But we've made arrangements to take care of any special visitors. They'll bow in as Bill's associates from the movie world—dropping in to see him for consultations on his new film-script. So, if you want to come up to the villa, it would be safe enough. Look—" she searched in her bag and found a small tourist folder with a map of Menton—"I've marked our house, very lightly. It's a difficult place for strangers to find."

He knew where it was—high on the eastern side of the town, where houses and gardens were scattered around on a steep hill-slope. But he took the folder without comment and slipped it into his pocket. "And you've noticed no unusual interest in you or Bill?"

"Just ordinary French curiosity—no more. It dropped away within two weeks."

"And no interest in Brigitte or Bernard—or the chauffeur?"

She shook her head. "We've been accepted as part of the local scene."

"And Brigitte and Bernard don't know Jean Parracini's real identity? Or any of his past history?"

"Nothing. He insisted on that right from the beginning. And the set-up *is* working. He is very pleased about that."

"I bet he is. He wrote most of the scenario, didn't he?" Palladin had insisted on that too, including exchanging his original role as W.B. Marriot the writer, for Bill's part as Jean Parracini the chauffeur. Tony could see the reason behind Palladin's change—any interest in the household would be focused on the writer. A chauffeur wouldn't arouse much local speculation or gossip.

"And you still don't like it." She shook her head, half-amused by Tony's excessive concern.

"There isn't enough protection for him. It's too open, too simple. And why did he choose Menton?"

"He says simplicity is his greatest protection. No one will expect him to be living in a busy little resort town with so many approaches."

"Far too many. It's impossible to watch them all." Tony glanced at the small port ahead of them, with its moles and jetties and anchorage for fishing vessels and pleasure-boats. And beyond that crowded harbour, lying at the far eastern end of Menton under the shadow of a giant wall of red cliffs that marked the French-Italian frontier, was a new large marina, filled with yachts and cruisers. The land view was equally disturbing. There was this shore road, linking all the towns along the whole stretch of the French Riviera. And there was the old Corniche, and the new Corniche topping it, each twisting its tricky way along steep hillsides above the coast. And then there was the Marseilles—Genoa expressway, that had been completed three years ago straight across the mountain slopes, way high up there, supported on tall cement legs as it crossed ravines and deep glens, as direct and fantastic as any Roman aqueduct. They all had their own tunnels, too, to let them stream through the red cliffs, *Les Rochers Rouges*, and pour right into Italy. Even the damned railway-line, thought Tony, had its tunnel. "Just too many quick ins and outs," he said to Menton. "And too many bloody foreigners wandering around." He glowered briefly at two innocuous visitors from West Germany.

"But that also works for Palla—" She caught herself in time. "For him," she ended weakly.

"If he wants to make a quick break for it—yes."

"That isn't what he's planning."

"He's a great planner, isn't he?"

"Wouldn't you be, if you had spent the last twelve years—"

"Yes," Tony said quickly, and silenced her. For twelve years, Palladin had worked right under the sharp eyes of men like Vladimir Konov. With each passing day, he must have wondered at his success in skirting detection, prepared himself for sudden disaster. When it came, he was ready. He had been lucky, luckier than Konov stretched out on a slab in a New York morgue, but he had made his luck. With some help from us, thought Tony, he had made it. But no amount of help could take away full credit from Palladin for brains and guts.

"You don't trust his judgment?"

"It's Menton that is worrying me," Tony admitted frankly. "I just wish he hadn't been so determined about it. That's all."

"But no one, no one, would expect him to come to a small resort town, so open and innocent. The opposition will expect us to send him to a country of our choice—and one where he can speak English. It's his best foreign language. He knows it well. Also some German, some Italian."

"What about French?" Tony asked quickly.

"He has been learning French. And fast. He spends every free hour on it. Talking records, books, papers, TV, and conversations with me."

Tony stared at her. "So he comes to live in France because he doesn't know French? Does he think the opposition will look in every other direction because of *that*?" And the opposition was not just the KGB alone, enormous as that intelligence force was. It had control over the intelligence services of the Soviets' allies. They'd all swing into action.

"Yes," said Nicole quite simply. "He believes that the opposition will search in the English-speaking countries. They'll expect him to be hidden in a large city like London or Liverpool or Toronto or Glasgow—some place where crowds would make him feel safe. And if that fails, they'll try the opposite extreme—look for a remote Canadian farm, a lonely ranch in the United States."

Tony's pace slowed. They would soon reach the end of the promenade. Near the harbour area a lot of construction work was in progress: men and machines, digging and filling, and bottling up traffic. This was already complicated by the density of people attracted to the market; they cluttered its sidewalks, moved in and out of its giant entrances and gave—from this short distance away—a good imitation of bees swarming around their honeycombs. They were even spreading across the final stretch of promenade itself. Soon no more serious talk would be possible. He halted, looked out at the Mediterranean admiringly. "Okay," he said, as if his doubts about Menton had been cleared away. He came in on them from another angle. "Does our friend have much to say about Shandon House?"

Nicole had been startled, but she kept her eyes fixed on a view of blue sky, blue sea. "At first, yes. Now, very little." She drew the cardigan's collar more closely across her throat. "His anger doesn't show any more. And he had every right to be bitter about Shandon's criminal stupidity. They let someone steal their NATO Memorandum right out of their top-secret files, and it ended up in Moscow. Jean lost two of his Moscow contacts through that piece of idiocy. Arrested in December, executed four weeks ago. Did you know?"

"I heard."

For a long moment, they were silent.

Then she said, "We have been reading in the local newspapers about a villa owned by Shandon, right here in Menton. The same Shandon—as in New Jersey?"

"The same. They inherited the villa last year."

"Another think-tank?"

"Mostly a talk-pool—on a very deep level, of course." His smile had returned. Somehow the idea of Shandon owning a villa on the Riviera appealed to his sense of comedy. Although there were now other villas strung along the Côte d'Azur, quiet retreats in vast gardens, taken over by Institutes of This and That for the Betterment of Thee and Me. Shandon, situated in the wealthy enclave on Cap Martin, was only following a very pleasant pattern. "And what else do the papers report about it?"

"Not much. It's all played down. Does that mean Shandon Villa is a hush-hush operation?"

"Officially, no. The aim is 'free discussion by delegates from various countries on topics of general concern.' So they say. But—" Tony paused—"I shouldn't be surprised if there are some private exchanges between delegates, which deal with very sensitive material indeed. Have you noticed that people just can't keep their lips buttoned when they want to assert themselves? Or win an argument? Or when they are feeling relaxed—sun and sea and flowers and palm-trees and no journalists around to print off-the-record talk?"

"Surely Shandon wouldn't bug its own guests?"

"Not Shandon itself."

She didn't quite follow. "They've been discreet enough about their guest-list for the first seminar. Even the local newspapers weren't given the names. Security precaution, I suppose."

"No names at all?"

"Only those of the permanent staff in a kind of Welcome-To-Menton paragraph. The director is an American, of course. Now, what's he called?" Her brow wrinkled.

"Maclehose. Security officer of the day when the NATO Memorandum was taken out of Shandon House."

"Oh no!"

"Oh yes."

"Do they never learn?"

"No blame could be pinned on Maclehose. Unthinkable. He's a stalwart fellow. His wife and children will *love* living in Menton." Tony's sarcasm ended. "But, secretly, he did embarrass them: so the easiest solution was to kick him sideways across the Atlantic. It's a cushy job. With some prestige, too. His guests will be cabinet level." Then Tony asked the question that worried him most. "What is Jean Parracini's reaction to Shandon-by-the-Sea?"

"None."

"He reads the local papers—part of his French lessons, aren't they? Didn't the mention of Maclehose raise any comment?"

"Maclehose was just a name. Jean didn't recognise it."

"He must have. He saw my report on Shandon."

"You gave it to him?" She couldn't believe it.

"Not my idea. Someone in Genoa thought he deserved to know how his cover had been blown—he kept asking about that. Naturally enough. And we owe him a great deal." Tony shrugged. "But not to the point of letting him carry a grudge. In our business, there's no room for a personal vendetta."

"Surely he wouldn't—"

"You know him better than I do."

"He isn't a maniac. He has a cool detached mind. He wouldn't do anything wild and endanger us all."

"I hope not." Tony was remembering the description of Palladin's sudden rage in Genoa when he had read the report on Shandon. By all accounts, it had been a painful and terrifying scene. "Let's head for the market," he said abruptly, and turned away from the laughing sea, little white teeth gleaming in the curving lips of each small wave.

Nicole shivered. "I feel frozen," she said. But it wasn't altogether the cool breeze that had caused this momentary chill. She stepped out smartly, her wide skirt swinging around her red leather boots, her dark hair blowing loose in the wind.

"By the way," he said in his most casual manner as they waited to cross the street, "does the name of Rick Nealey ring a bell?"

"Nealey," she repeated, frowning. "I've seen it." The frown deepened; and then disappeared. "Yes. He's on the new Shandon staff, isn't he?"

"Executive assistant to Maclehose."

She stared at Tony's expressionless face. "Another name in your report?" she asked, her voice almost inaudible.

"You may be frozen, but your brain is still cooking," he said and won a small but delighted smile.

And then it vanished just as quickly. Jean, she was thinking, must have recognised Nealey's name in the newspapers. And yet there had been no comment at all. None. And none about Maclehose. None at all... As though he had no interest in them whatsoever. Not natural behaviour, she told herself. A danger signal? But Tony's hand was on her arm, guiding her, giving her some comfort. "When do you leave?" she asked in mid-street.

"The boat is going to take some time to fix." He had seen to that, with a neatly applied hammer. "Georges and Emil will come on shore, take rooms in the Old Town. I'll wander around."

"Will you come up to the villa? Bill would like to see you."

"Georges will be in touch with him," he had time to say before they reached the sidewalk.

"We could use some extra help," she admitted. "We now have two problems." The first was to keep Jean Parracini safe from the KGB. The second—to keep Jean Parracini safe from himself.

"At least two," said Tony, thinking of Rick Nealey, and stopped at a mass of flowers for sale. Tables, set up roughly outside the market, were covered with them. "Buy some carnations." They were the only flowers, apart from roses, that he recognised.

He waited for Nicole to choose, heard her discussing prices with one of the ruddy-faced women behind the flower display. But his thoughts were still with Nealey: sudden resignation in late December from his job as Representative W.C. Pickering's aide (nicely explained, of course, no hard feelings), and a quick exit from Washington in early January; nothing against him in FBI files; unknown to CIA's informants in East Germany (but they'd keep digging); papers in order, according to US Army who had employed him as civilian-interpreter—1963–1965— after his escape to West Germany; 1941 birth-certificate (Brooklyn); total acceptance by grandmother Nealey, sole surviving relative but since deceased, on his return to USA. (A newspaper account of that happy reunion seemed to think it perfectly normal that an eighty-four-year-old woman should recognise a grandson she hadn't seen for twenty-seven years.) Blank-Wall Nealey: all Tony had got was one large headache from butting his head against it. You didn't have the evidence, not a shred of hard proof, he told himself. So how did you expect the Americans to act, especially when they were all walking on eggs these days? Nealey's apartment *and* his office, too, would have needed to be bugged. Just try that on for size in a newspaper headline.

"Aren't they divine?" Nicole asked, thrusting a bunch of red and pink carnations under his nose. "They grow all over the hillsides around here, in plastic-covered greenhouses. Imagine the work!" She dropped her voice. "Do we drift apart now?"

"Too open. Let's get under cover."

The market was a huge cavern of a building, filled with stalls, rows and rows of them, piled with all varieties of produce. And the crowd was large enough to please him: his leave-taking of Nicole could pass ignored in this mass of people, buying, selling, or simply strolling among the good things to eat. "No one in this part of France will ever starve," Tony said. "Almost tempts me to take up cooking." Half the shoppers, he noted, were men. "Admirable place." And he wasn't only referring to its gastronomical delights. He relaxed, felt secure.

Nicole touched his arm. He looked at her sharply as she drew him behind a poultry stall, with ducks and geese and chickens swinging from overhead hooks. It was the first time, he thought, that he had used a screen of plucked hens to dodge behind. "Jean," she said quietly. "He's over there, next to the sacks of onions."

"What the bloody hell does he think he's doing?"

"I don't know." Her eyes were troubled. "He does go out on errands, of course. A chauffeur doesn't sit in a house all day."

There were several people, a mixed group, crowded near that stall. "I don't see him," Tony said.

She laughed, then. "I told you he had done wonders with his appearance. He's the man in the dark suit. Why don't you come and meet him—hear his French accent, too?"

Tony studied the man. No resemblance. Palladin's hair had been blond, thin on top and straight, above a cheerful round face and pale complexion. He had been a permanent wearer of glasses, and definitely corpulent. Jean Parracini had dark brown hair, thick and wavy. His tanned face was haggard and furrowed, the cheeks fallen, the eyes (with no glasses) deep-set and shadowed. He had grown a moustache, dyed it black. And he must have lost about forty pounds in weight. Even his height, the usual giveaway, seemed to have increased slightly with the way he now held his shoulders. New posture and thick-soled shoes, judicious use of subtle make-up, an expensive hair-piece fitted securely over a head shaved bald, and—above all—a crash diet: these were the complete transformers. "Contact lenses, too," Tony murmured. He was fascinated. But Jean wasn't walking around picking up any purchases. Jean was waiting. Even when he moved on a few steps, seemingly engrossed with onions and the neighbouring potatoes, he was waiting. "He may be looking for you. Did you tell him you were going to buy some artichokes?"

"No. I left as soon as you called me this morning on Bill's private line."

"Would Bill tell him you had gone into town?"

"Possibly. But not to meet you." Of that she was sure. "Perhaps he came here to buy something Brigitte had forgotten to order."

"He's pressing his luck too hard."

"I'll go over and join him," Nicole decided. "Ease him out of here." But Jean was already leaving.

Tony's eyes still stayed on the dark suit, watched it move slowly towards another entrance.

"That leads into the town itself. He has probably parked Bill's car—"

"What make?"

"A Mercedes, black, four-door, Nice registration."

Jean had almost disappeared behind the fruit stalls. "Think I'd like to get a closer look. See if that disguise is as good face-on as it is at a distance."

"Meet him? I thought you were avoiding—"

"He won't know me." A one-way mirror in a small Genoese room, old dodge, had made sure of that. "I hope," Tony added along with a goodbye smile. "Go buy your artichokes, my pet. And tell Bill what I told you. All of it." He drifted away, seemingly in an aimless wandering between the rows of stalls. He too was heading definitely for the market's town-side entrance.

Once he was far enough away from Nicole, who was now absorbed in the price of poultry, his pace could quicken. But he had delayed too long, and Jean Parracini was no longer visible. Lost between the fruit and the cheeses, Tony thought, and swore silently.

He came out into the sunshine, wondering which direction to take. He noticed a parked black car, near by. But it was a Citroën, newest model, with a swoop of bonnet to give it a sporting air. The man who was dumping his packages on to the back seat before he stepped in to take the wheel was obviously alone. He wore a suit and tie, too; but he was not Jean Parracini. He was Rick Nealey.

Slowly, Tony lit a cigarette. The Citroën went slowly into the traffic. And from some distance behind it, a black Mercedes left its parking-place. It increased speed as much as it dared in the busy street, and then—as it came nicely up behind the Citroën—slackened its pace to keep a decent following distance.

We have a maniac on our hands, thought Tony, and crushed his barely-smoked cigarette under his heel. Better warn Nicole at once; explain Rick Nealey just enough to let her know how deeply Parracini was endangering himself. This was no ordinary American he was following. Nealey could outfox even a Palladin, when he was blinded by bitter rage. And

Nealey wouldn't be here alone. He must have some back-up, a contact... "Hell, bloody hell," Tony said softly, and turned to re-enter the market.

He stopped abruptly, almost bumping into a woman carrying a wicker basket filled with a morning's shopping.

"Tony!" Dorothea Kelso said.

13

Typed, retyped, torn up. The discarded pages filled the wastebasket. A typical morning's work, thought Tom Kelso, and pushed his chair away from his desk. Maurice Michel's desk, to be exact, in Maurice Michel's library, no longer looking the neatly-ordered place where a diplomat had worked. Tom's notes and maps were scattered everywhere; even the small room's name (a little too grand for ten feet square, walls lined with bookshelves that encased door and window too) had been changed to "study"—his own quiet corner, far removed from living-room and kitchen. Much good its peace had done him. Thea and he had been here since the beginning of January, and the last two chapters of his book refused to shape up. Tomorrow was the first of March, the last month here before their return to Washington. Return to what?

Every aspect of his work now seemed to have become uncertain. Who the hell will want to read this book anyway? he asked himself angrily. Who in the United States worried about long-term policy and what they would have to cope with, ten years from now? Short-term, that's us—jumping from one crisis to another. "We'll cross that bridge when we come to it"—and that we will, even if the bridge blows under our feet and we have to swim for it.

Thoroughly despondent, restless, he rose and made his way through the silent house to the pantry where the Michels had installed a little bar. He'd better bootleg a drink or two before Thea got back from the market in Menton.

She wasn't saying anything about his change in habits, but she must have noticed. She was too smart a girl not to be aware of them, and too sensitive not to feel the perpetual state of worry and dejection that had seized him, away back in December, after his return from the NATO meeting in Brussels.

It hadn't been a complete failure for him—real friends at Casteau rallied round and talked with him as they had always talked, but few of them could hand out vital information. And the others, important sources for sensitive material in the past, had become tight-lipped, even evasive. He had never thought he was a particularly prideful man, but the snubs struck deep. And the results, in his reports back to the *Times*, were clearly seen—by himself, at least. The journalist was the first to know he was slipping, next his editors; and then the public. End of a career. Any newsman was only as good as his sources. ("Like a policeman?" Thea had asked when he discussed this problem with her. "They need informants too. Don't they?" He had laughed and agreed, but wondered how journalists' high-placed sources would react if they were called informants. "Let's say," he had answered, "that Watergate would never have been explained if there hadn't been leaks of information.")

He poured the second drink, another double, and wandered back through the living-room, a room he usually found cheerful and pleasant. Solange Michel had taken great care with the colours and chintzes. ("*Toile*!" Thea had corrected him. "Chintz my eye.") And Maurice had made sure that his wife hadn't sacrificed the old fireplace and the beamed ceiling in her splurge on remodelling an old house. The Michels had spent money, time, and energy on fixing up their place in Roquebrune; but Tom wondered how long it would take them to sell it, once they came back to see the huge condominiums that were being built further up the hillside behind them. Nothing, he thought, nothing ever remains perfect. In deepening gloom, he went out on to the terrace.

The trouble—or rather today's trouble—was the telephone call that morning. From Chuck. At the airport in Nice.

The first time I've heard from him... Tom tried to stop brooding about Chuck, and stared down at the olive-trees in front of the house. Condominium builders hadn't yet got their hands on that long stretch of descending terraces, but no doubt they would. And they'd be eyeing that nice piece of real estate lying far below the olive-trees, a cape that pointed its long finger into the Mediterranean, a promontory of very private land occupied by expensive villas and perfect gardens. Cap Martin wouldn't listen to the jingle of big promoters' coins. It could buy and sell them with cash still left in the till. It probably wasn't even aware of the glass and concrete spreading over the Roquebrune hills above it: a density of trees, a richness of foliage, covered and protected and hid it completely.

That was where Chuck was spending the next few days. At

Shandon Villa. Transportation from Nice? That was taken care of—Nealey had met him at the plane. No, he couldn't make it for lunch. Catching up on his sleep, he had said: he never could handle overnight flights. After that, he had some business to attend to. He would drop in to see Dorothea and Tom this evening. Sixish. Okay?

The first time since November—and all I got was a drop-in promise. Not, "Tom, I wanted to see you." Not, "Tom, I have a lot to talk over with you." Not, "Tom, let's have a quiet evening together, and get a lot of things straight." Just—sixish.

Tom finished his drink at a gulp, wondered about another, decided not. His career might be slithering downhill, his book might be choking itself to death, but he still had Thea. And this, he knew, as he looked at his glass, was no way to keep her. He knew it, and yet he kept slipping away from his resolution. How else did you blot out the feeling of failure?

He had made a real effort to stop thinking about Chuck; and Shandon; and the memorandum; and that god-damned Olivetti. (He wasn't using it any more.) He wouldn't even discuss these subjects with Thea. But the subconscious was a real devil, eating away at him. No matter how determinedly he dropped the hurts and disappointments out of his conscious mind, they only sank below the surface; and lay there.

So now Chuck was here, and perhaps ready to talk... There had been a slightly too jocular manner in that 'phone-call. Is that what we are going to have—an hour of chit-chat and sweet evasions? God damn it—Tom nearly walked back into the house to pour himself a third drink. At least he had started counting: a step in the right direction. But this meeting with Chuck— He dropped all speculation, tried to let his emotions subside and his mind stop questioning, and concentrated on the far stretch of coastline. It was a continuous sweep of cliffs and bays, with a backscreen of mountains whose rocky spurs ran out into the sea and sheltered the indentations of beaches. To the west, he could see the bold plunge of Monaco's headland. Then came the bay, where Monte Carlo had tucked itself into one corner, curving eastward to the green-covered promontory of Cap Martin lying below him. In jutted the shoreline again, to form the wide bay where Menton lay with its Old Town built high above the port. And beyond that, the bay curved further inland before it came sweeping out again to the red cliffs, a mountain wall of sheer rock that formed a most definite frontier. Next stop—Italy, and the Riviera dei Fiori, and a distant view of Bordighera. And then nothing but a horizon where blue sky met blue sea. Florida, he thought, had started with several strikes against it when it set out to bat against the Côte d'Azur.

Nerves calmed, mind more at rest, he turned away. That view was better medicine, he admitted frankly, than the empty glass in his hand. Keep remembering that, he told himself. He set the glass down on the table at the side of the terrace, a private corner shielded by lemon-trees, and began walking down the rough driveway that led, from the east side of the house, to the Roquebrune road.

Thea was late. Menton, adjoining Roquebrune (or was it the other way round? One moment you were driving in Menton; next block you were in Roquebrune), was only a couple of miles from here. It was just like her to go dashing off to the market, to buy extra food—and no doubt some special items that their tight budget didn't usually allow. (Money was another of his hidden worries: it melted, like first snowflakes on a city sidewalk, in this spreading inflation.) "Chuck may stay for dinner," she had said when the 'phone call from Nice was over. Tactfully, and again true to Thea, she hadn't said what was really on her mind—and on my mind too, thought Tom: why the hell doesn't Chuck stay here with us? We've got two unused bedrooms, damn them.

Back to Chuck again, are we?

He quickened his pace, putting distance between himself and the silent house and a desk littered with discarded manuscript. I've become too critical, too hesitant about my own work, he thought now. I'm not fit company for Thea these days. The only time we are really happy, and not often enough either, is in that big beautiful bedroom upstairs. Solange—so she had told them proudly—had furnished it after the style of the Byblos Hotel over at St Tropez: white carpet everywhere, white plaster walls cleverly finished to look as if they were carpeted too; outsize bed, practically floor-level, covered with a white fur rug. "A love-nest at first sight," said Thea, setting them both laughing. Well, if we can both laugh together and love together, there is hope for us. Without that, we'd have started drifting apart in these last months. It could yet happen, his common sense warned him. If he didn't get a better grip on himself—I'll get over this, he told himself. I must. I don't need a sense of guilt to add to my problems.

The last stretch of driveway ran through the old Michel flower-nursery, still functioning, now owned and worked by honest Auguste and his stalwart Albertine, who came up the hill to oblige once a week with a thorough housecleaning, or, for a special evening, to cook. There had been too few of those.

Not fair to Thea—I'll have to take some days off, drive her around, visit the hill towns, explore. We'll do that next week. The hell with my work, it's getting nowhere as it is. I've got to do some rethinking of the last chapter, organise its material better, reshape and—or should I just throw the whole thing out and start over again? Remake it, fresh and alive?

He passed the rows of flower-beds, some bright with bloom, the rest promising flowers next month, and halted at the clump of mimosa by the gate. He could see no sign of their car—a small Fiat they had rented—in the rush of traffic to and from lower Roquebrune. The road was narrow, twisting up the hill, built in the days when people walked or used real horse power. His worries sharpened as he watched the stream of cars and trucks and buses. Where was Thea anyway? he wondered irritably. What had delayed her so long in Menton? She was usually back by noon. And it was certainly noon—the nursery was deserted, all hands now engaged in their mid-day meal.

And there she was at last, safely returning. The accident he had begun to fear hadn't taken place. But it nearly did, at this very moment, as Dorothea took a wild chance to make a left turn across the path of the descending traffic.

"For God's sake, Thea!" he yelled as she stopped inside the gate and waited for him.

"I didn't even chip a tail-light," she told him cheerfully. "Jump in. I'll give you a lift to the house if you'll trust my driving. And there's nothing wrong with it either," she reminded him. Hadn't he noticed? If she had pulled up and waited to make the turn, the car behind her could have rear-ended the Fiat? He is too much on edge these days, she thought unhappily. And all her excitement about her meeting with Tony Lawton drained away. Silently, she made room for him on the seat beside her.

"You're late." He picked up the sheaf of papers and magazines she had bought in Menton: the *Herald Tribune* and *Le Monde* from Paris, the *Observer* and *Economist* and *Guardian* from London, the current *Time* and *Newsweek*. "What about the *New York Times*?"

"It's later than I am." Besides, it always arrived four days old. Another day wouldn't hurt. "Headlines are hideous, aren't they?"

His eyes scanned them. "Yes," he said briefly. That's where I should be, he thought: right back where the wires are bringing in all the latest alarums and excursions, the stuff that journalists' dreams are made of.

"I picked up the mail on my way into Menton. You'll find it in my handbag."

"More bills?"

"A letter from Brad Gillon." She brought the car to a very smooth halt beside the row of orange-trees near the back door.

Tom searched in her purse and found the envelope. It had been opened. He looked at her.

"It's addressed to me as well as you." Dorothea's lips tightened. "Oh, really, Tom—do I *ever* open your mail?"

"What's he saying? Telling you to keep after me about the book?"

"He isn't badgering you about anything. He had a meeting with Chuck. Brad took him to lunch at the Century. There was a lot of serious talk."

Tom said nothing. The serious talk should have been between Chuck and me, he thought bitterly. He was about to slip the letter unread into his pocket—he'd have a drink first and feel more able to deal with it—when the stamp on the envelope caught his eye. "Just look at that postmark, will you? February fourteenth! Two weeks on the way!" he said in disgust. "And by air mail, too."

"Normal delivery nowadays." Dorothea thought of her own postcards to Washington that had taken four weeks. "Better read the letter, Tom." It was important. Doubly so because its arrival was so late.

Tom stuck the letter into a pocket. "It's all old news by this time." And he had a feeling he didn't want to hear it.

"It's still urgent enough." She glanced at his face, saw worry increasing. So she made an effort to lighten her voice, and her manner, and the news. "He had planned to come and see us last week, after some publishers' meeting in Paris. But Mona was in Acapulco and guess what she did? She developed pneumonia. In Acapulco—I ask you! So Brad had to cancel Europe and fly down to bring her home."

"Stop circling, Thea. You're getting into a constant habit of doing just that recently. You can give me the bad news."

Can I? she wondered. If I circle around it you are the one who evades it. She drew a deep breath. "He must see us, Brad says. And so he is arriving in Nice on March eighth, straight from New York."

"But that's next week-end."

"Yes. Before he goes on to Paris. He wants to talk with you."

"So we are getting top priority." He didn't like that idea either. "What's his problem? Is it the book? Or—" he forced himself to say it—"about Chuck?"

"About Chuck." She reached over, kissed him on the cheek. "I'm sorry I was late, darling. But I met—"

He silenced her with a kiss on her lips. "I'm sorry I was so damned sharp-set. It's just that—" He hesitated, fell silent.

"You are worrying far too much these days," she told him gently. "I was barely thirty minutes late. And you can blame twenty of those on Tony. We bumped into each other just outside the market."

"Tony? Tony Lawton's in town?"

"Come on, darling. Let's get this basket of food into the kitchen, or the Brie will be melting over the lamb chops."

"What's he doing here?"

"On holiday. Sailing. The boat needed emergency repairs, so it's stuck in Menton for today. I invited him to come back here with me for lunch, but he had some 'phone calls to make. So I asked him to come up this evening and have a drink." She was already heading for the back door, carrying the smaller packages. Tom gathered papers and basket, and followed her into the kitchen.

"When?" His voice was sharp.

"Oh, around five."

"But Chuck will be—"

"Chuck will be late." He had a habit of lateness whenever something unpleasant was on the horizon, and this meeting with Tom wasn't going to be easy for either of them. "And before you meet him, Tony wants to have a word with you. Sort of background information, I think. Necessary, Tony said. Otherwise, you'd—"

"I don't need advice on how to handle my own brother."

"Oh, Tom! Tony's only trying to—"

"What the hell does he think he's doing, sticking his nose into—"

"Read Brad's letter." Abruptly, she turned away and began unpacking the basket: cheeses and meat into the refrigerator; fruit and vegetables to be washed and dried. Tom turned on his heel, walked into the pantry, but the letter was now in his hand. She found she was waiting, tense and nervous, for his footsteps to stop at the bar, and chided herself for even listening. But there was no sound of a bottle set down on the tiled counter, or of ice dropped into a glass. He must be reading, not pouring another drink. Not yet, at least. She faced the window, tears in her eyes as she stared out blindly at five little orange-trees trying to screen the torn-up land farther up the hillside.

Then Tom was beside her, one hand slipping around her waist, the other holding Brad's letter. "He's so damned diplomatic. As far as I can make out, he had something important to tell Chuck at that lunch. And Chuck didn't like it." He frowned at a closely-written page, trying to read between the lines. "I wish he had been more explicit. I suppose he couldn't be—not old Brad, at least."

"He was giving Chuck some off-the-record information. So he said."

Tom liked the look of the whole matter less and less. "Brad wouldn't entrust it to a letter," he agreed, "or to a 'phone call." His frown deepened and he looked once more at the paragraph dealing with Chuck. Brad's script was as discreet as Brad himself.

...And so I tried some frank talk with your brother. He didn't believe me, not then. But I think I've jolted him enough to start him thinking about the net result of his actions last November. Some of it can be told now, off the record. (I had to take this chance with Chuck; and he will be the last person to want it publicised. It goes far beyond personal matters.) We parted coldly, yet I still have hopes that my news will have some effect on him. He has some extra worries, too— new developments which must trouble him: Katie Collier has jumped bail, leaving her family to forfeit a hundred thousand dollars; and Martin Holzheimer has stumbled on a story that seemingly convinced him to get in touch with the police. So my guess would be that Chuck is a deeply worried young man, and more than a little scared by the way things are turning out, although—so far—he is persuading himself that he can cope. I gave him your address and telephone number, by the way; and I shouldn't be surprised if you have a letter from him, as the first sign that my words had some effect. I hope I didn't overstep our friendship, Tom, in trying to handle this tricky situation. But I knew the facts, and I was on the scene. That's my excuse, anyway.

Tom slipped the letter back into his pocket, and loosened his hold on her waist. "I'd better cable Brad at once—let him know we did get the letter. He's probably been worrying for the past week why he had no answer from us." Tom thought over that, and impatience returned. "Why the devil didn't he call and ask if his letter had reached us? That wouldn't have broken security."

"And risk having his ears pinned back for interfering?" More nervous than she let herself appear, she glanced at Tom. "I'm just following your advice, my love. I've stopped circling."

"Does Brad think I'm so damned touchy as all that? And you know me better than to even think I'd—" He checked his rising temper. "I'm sorry, Thea. Sorry." He took her in his arms, felt her stiff spine begin to relax. "I know, I know. I've had my moods recently. They're over. All over. Believe me. I can't afford them now. I've got more to worry about than myself." He kissed her, hugged her close, kissed her again. Now her body felt soft and warm, supple against his.

She said, "I've been difficult too. I—"

He silenced her with another kiss before he let her go. "I'd better start sending that cable. Or perhaps I'll risk a telephone call."

"It's seven in the morning in New York."

"All the better. I'll get him before he leaves for the office." Tom halted half-way across the kitchen. "Who is Katie Collier?"

"Oh, that's the girl who nearly got blown up with her friends when their bomb-factory exploded."

December headlines, he remembered then. "But what has that got to do with Chuck?"

Dorothea could only shake her head.

"And what's this flap about Holzheimer? There's no reason why he shouldn't be in touch with the police—he's a reporter. And a good one."

Dorothea was less generous. The man who started all our troubles, she thought. She said, "Couldn't he at least have told you where he got that copy of the memorandum? After all, you're fourth estate, too."

"I didn't ask him. Because I knew. Because I didn't want to hear." He began walking to the pantry door, stopped there, said, "He got the memorandum from Chuck."

At last, she thought, at last he has actually said it out loud. She heard his footsteps go briskly past the bar towards the telephone. Relief surged over her. His mood had indeed changed. Permanently? Certainly for this afternoon, making

Tony welcome—like old times. And thank God for that.

She began pulling leaves of lettuce into small pieces for a *Salade Niçoise*. Radishes to be sliced. Chop up some of that red thing that looked like a blood-soaked cabbage. (She never ate it, was that why she could never remember its name?) Anchovies. Small black olives. Pieces of tuna. Croutons, garlic flavoured. Hard-boiled eggs—"Damn and blast," she said aloud. She had totally forgotten them this morning. Okay, okay. Almost *Salade Niçoise* but not quite. Blame it on a telephone call from Chuck.

But at least he had telephoned. Give him credit for that first gesture. He had sounded normal enough. Perhaps Brad had exaggerated the trouble around him. And yet, if the situation wasn't as bad as Brad had seen it, why had Tony changed his own plans so suddenly when she mentioned Chuck's call from Nice? Yes, that was when Tony had dropped all interest in the busy street outside the market, even in the pretty girl (well worth admiring, conceded Dorothea) who was passing by with her long wide skirt swinging over dark red boots, and had shifted his entire attention to Dorothea.

"Chuck?" Tony had asked. "In Nice?"

"He must be in Menton right now. Rick Nealey met him at the airport."

Tony whistled softly; an eyebrow went up.

"I agree. A little unexpected, isn't it?"

"Frankly, I'd have bet on a letter. That's always easier than direct confrontation. Is he staying long?"

"I shouldn't think so. He's at Shandon Villa, and there won't be much room for him when it starts filling up next week."

"Why stay at Shandon at all?"

"Oh—some business, he said. But he does want to see Tom.

211

At least he invited himself for a drink this evening."

"Shandon... I'd have thought Tom would have advised him against that."

"But why?"

He stared at her for a moment, openly puzzled. "Let's walk a little—to your car? You lead the way and I'll carry this." He took the basket over one arm and began steering her through the mid-day crowd. "Now tell me what Brad had to say last week-end—didn't Tom believe him?"

"Brad never got here. Mona fell ill. He hopes to see us next week-end."

Tony's lips tightened. He walked in silence for several paces. "When do you expect Chuck for that drink?"

"At six."

"I'd like to have a word with Tom before then."

"Come up and have lunch."

"Wish I could, but I've some heavy telephoning to do." He plunged into a quick explanation about the boat, engine failure, two of his sailing chums now working on it down at the harbour and waiting for his return with some supplies.

"You have a busy day ahead of you. Come and have lunch tomorrow. Bring your friends too."

"How about five this evening?" Tony asked. "All right with you?"

"Can you manage it without too much trouble?"

"I'll make sure I manage it."

"And stay to dinner?"

"Better not. I'll disappear before Chuck arrives. Strangers, keep out. Isn't that what Tom would say? How is he, how's the book, how are *you*?"

"Worried," she said frankly. "Your news for Tom—unpleasant, isn't it?"

"But necessary. Believe me. Someone has got to give him the details, provide some argument-power when he is dealing with Chuck." He had noted the disbelief in her eyes. "Tom," he said gently, "is accustomed to dealing with facts. He would want to know the situation. Wouldn't he?"

"Once—yes." Her voice was unsteady. "But now—"

"Once and always," Tony insisted. "He can take it."

And then Tony made one of his conversational leaps into the charm of southern French towns, red-tiled roofs rippling, light walls and brightly-painted shutters, flowers and palm-trees popping up all over, nineteenth-century hodge-podging with the twentieth, and wouldn't it be wonderful if you could have tourist money without the tourists? But why this good bourgeois street, along which they had walked, was named in honour of the naughty president Félix Faure, he would never understand.

By the time they reached the car Dorothea had even begun to smile again. He stowed away the basket, glanced over at the heap of newspapers and magazines lying beside the driver's seat as he opened the car door for her. He misses nothing, she had thought, not even the way I looked when I spoke about Tom.

Then, as she was about to enter the car, she turned to give him a quick light hug and a kiss on his cheek. "Thank you, Tony."

"Not at all. Delighted to carry baskets for pretty girls, any day."

"I wish I had dark red boots too."

That had startled him. Briefly. "You are a proper caution, you are. See you at five, love."

14

"Some heavy telephoning," Tony had said—a truthful excuse—as he backed away from Dorothea's lunch invitation... But now, first of all, he had some heavy thinking to do. And quickly.

He watched her grey Fiat safely on its way, and then began walking back to the market district. Slow steps, racing thoughts. Two problems now: Jean Parracini's safety—the damned fool must be restrained somehow; Chuck Kelso at Shandon Villa. Why couldn't that self-assured idiot have stayed with his brother? Here on business, was he? What kind of business? Chuck was a young man who surrounded himself with question-marks, Tony thought as he found a small café where he could have a ham-and-crusted-roll sandwich—a difficult feat in a country devoted to *table d'hôte* menus.

Twenty minutes later he was out in the streets again, plans made, searching for a safe telephone. (The café's 'phone had been the free-to-all-ears type.) Streets were almost empty, shops closed, restaurants crowded, in deference to the mid-day ritual of eating. The main post office, large and capacious, usually packed but possibly half-empty at this time of day, was his best bet. Its telephone booths, nicely tucked into one corner of its ground floor, had doors to ensure reasonable privacy. And he had a sufficient supply of the mandatory *jetons* in his pocket—in France, where coins for public telephones were distrusted, he always made sure of that.

He put in his first call—to Bill and Nicole, up in their hill house in the Garavan district. (Thank God, he thought, that Jean Parracini's hiding place, on the other side of town from Cap Martin, was so far from Shandon Villa.)

"Keep a better eye on Jean," he began, wasting no time.

"But he's safely back. He's eating dinner now," Bill said.

"Where?"

"In the kitchen with Bernard—as usual. Everything normal. Don't sweat."

"When did he return?"

Bill consulted with Nicole, who took over the receiver. "He arrived only eight minutes after I did," Nicole said. "I was here by quarter past twelve."

"That's odd." Impossible, in fact.

"Why?"

"When I last saw him, he was tailing Rick Nealey from the market. And that was at five minutes to twelve."

"Then he couldn't have followed for very long. Perhaps it was a coincidence—he just seemed to be—"

"It was a tail." That silenced Nicole. "Who does Parracini think he is? The Invisible Man? He is taking too many chances." Curious, thought Tony: he hadn't had time to tail Nealey all the way to Cap Martin—so why had he followed at all? Or hadn't Nealey returned to Shandon Villa? Stopped a few blocks from the market area? And Jean, curiosity or ego satisfied, had headed home? A puzzle… "Let it go meanwhile. Keep him under wraps this afternoon. Don't lose sight of him."

"Even when he's resting in his own quarters?"

"Where are they?"

"Above the garage, of course."

"Separated from the house?"

"Yes."

"Put Bill back on the 'phone—Bill, move Jean over to the main house—put him up in one of your spare rooms. For his own security."

"He will refuse. He likes his privacy. And the only room available is right next door to Brigitte and Bernard."

"Who's in charge, anyway? You and Nicole better start sweating along with me. Now—here's some other business. I want you to 'phone Shandon Villa, see if Charles Kelso is around. Have a good story ready if he is there to take your call: you've just heard that his brother, an old friend, is staying in Menton—can Chuck give you his address? Then I want Nicole to call Shandon—yes, she's to 'phone too. She will ask for Rick Nealey, try to find out if he's there. She can be a reporter from Nice, wanting an interview. I'll call you back in twenty minutes, get your answers."

"Planning a visit to Shandon?"

He's too damned smart, Tony thought irritably. He didn't answer the question, said, "And now hear this. I'm sending out for reinforcements. And I want you to accept their invitation to take you and Jean sailing tomorrow."

Bill said, "What if he refuses to go with them?"

"They'll be senior men, they'll pull rank. Besides, it is a matter of security. He'll listen. Explain to him that they want to clarify some of his earlier information. What better place than a boat?"

"We're using the *Sea Breeze*? I thought you had engine trouble."

"Not so much as all that. We'll be ready by the time the reinforcements fly into Nice tomorrow morning."

"Serious problems?" Bill was really listening now.

"When weren't they?"

"Sounds like an alert," Bill said reflectively.

Tony hung up, checked his watch with the post office clock. He had used up several *jetons*, and his next call was to Paris. But all he'd have to do, when he did make sure of the right connection, would be to identify himself by his code name (Uncle Arthur) and leave a message with significant phrases for further relay. "Weather deteriorating, heavy winds possible. Advise dual repairs, best available, at dockside by eleven A.M. tomorrow." They'd know where the *Sea Breeze* was moored, its exact location in the harbour—all that had been reported on arrival yesterday evening.

And let's hope, he thought, once the brief talk with Paris was over, that the best they have available for this repair-job will be a couple of men senior enough to keep Jean Parracini in place. Bloody nuisance: protecting an ally could be more difficult, and definitely less rewarding, than tracking down a hidden enemy.

His third call was to Georges, in the room he had rented at the seaside edge of the Old Town. (Excellent position, right across from the harbour, with a view of the *Sea Breeze* neat in a

217

row of small boats, large boats, old boats, spanking-new boats; short masts, long masts, or none at all.) "Cancel your visit to Bill," he told Georges. "And Emil is still working on repairs? Fine. Get in touch with him. Everything has to be ready by eleven tomorrow morning. And he is to lay in supplies for five people—better make it enough for three days—perhaps more. Did you rent that Citroën? Oh, a Renault, cream-coloured, two-door. Okay. Pick me up near my hotel at two thirty. And wear a collar and tie—and a jacket. We're turning respectable."

Back now to Bill on his hill. Four minutes later than arranged, dammit. Would Bill notice? Of course he did.

"Four minutes late," he said in mock surprise. "Run into trouble?"

"Napped too long. Forgot to set the alarm clock."

Bill laughed. "I believe you. Okay, listen to this: Charles Kelso lunched at the villa with the Director and his family, but he seems to have gone out. The girl at the 'phone didn't know where. Couldn't care less, if you ask me. There was a lot of banging in the background. I joked about it. Seems there are a lot of workmen still around, trying to get everything finished for next week's grand opening. And here is Nicole to add her little piece."

Nicole said, "Rick Nealey hasn't been around since he delivered Chuck at the villa this morning. He had to dash off to Eze and La Turbie—making arrangements for next week's guests. He should be back around five or six this evening."

"Good. Now, how's Jean our intractable friend? Sulking in his tent like Achilles?"

"He balked at first, but now he's packing his things to move over to the main house. Regrets his good TV in the chauffeur's quarters, though. His new room isn't set up for television."

"Has he a telephone there?"

"No."

"But there was a telephone in the old room?" There would have to be one linking the main house and its garage.

"Of course." Nicole sounded puzzled. "Two, actually."

"An outside line as well?" Somehow, a disturbing thought.

"It came with the place."

"And no one thought of having it disconnected."

"Why should we? He'd avoid using it, wouldn't he? He's more security-minded than—" She paused, realising her tactlessness.

"Than I am?" Tony suggested. "Okay, okay. Glad all is under control at your end. One thing you can do for me, Nicole— scout around the harbour near the *Petit Port* this afternoon. *Not* the new marina in Garavan—the old one. And mark where the *Sea Breeze* is berthed. She's lying just under the big mole—you can stroll right along it, many people do. Got that? About the middle of that row of boats. She's a cabin sloop, a one-master: porpoise bow, inboard engine." But although she might look slow, she could make ten knots, and there was space enough for six people, even if slightly cramped.

"*D'accord.*"

"Put Bill back on."

Bill spoke at once. "Here."

"Get Parracini down to the *Sea Breeze* tomorrow at eleven A.M. On the dot. Can you manage that?"

"Yes. I've already told him that he will have two NATO visitors."

"His reaction?"

"Just what you'd expect. Thinks their visit here could be dangerous for all."

"Tell him that's why you've decided, as a security precaution, to make arrangements for him to meet the visitors elsewhere."

"Will do. But aren't we going to a lot of extra trouble—"

"Yes." Indeed we are, thought Tony. "But it's a safety measure. And keep him happily occupied at the house for the rest of the day."

"He has already arranged with Bernard and Brigitte to take in a movie tonight. It's one they all want to see."

"Where?"

"At the Casino."

"*Where?*"

"The movie house is part of the building."

There was a deep silence.

"I'll tell him that idea is out," Bill said. "It won't make anything easier for tomorrow morning, though."

"What showing of the movie? Early or late?"

"There's only one show. This is off season. Eight thiry, I think."

Tony calculated quickly. "Let him keep his engagement tonight, and have him in a good mood for tomorrow. How did he get away with arranging a visit to the movies, anyway?"

"Said it looked unnatural if he stayed cooped up here all the time like a prisoner. Some people might start wondering."

"I see. He has got his confidence back, has he?"

"Well, it's true enough: if a fish doesn't want to be noticeable, it had better learn to swim with the school."

Seems to me, thought Tony, that I've heard that dictum before. "His phrase, or yours?"

"His. And a good one. Don't you think?"

"Yes." Now, where did I hear it? Tony wondered. He glanced at his watch. It was one thirty-five. "See you tomorrow, dockside. You can throw away your crutch. Use a cane and limp slightly."

"I'm going for a sail, too?"

"You know how to handle a boat. It looks better—chauffeur goes along to help you board. Right?"

"And you?"

"Vaguely in the background. If you need to contact me before then, leave a message with Georges. He has rigged up an answering device on his 'phone. You have his number? And you won't see him this afternoon. He's needed elsewhere." Tony rang off.

He took a taxi to his hotel, one of the new ones on the *Quai Laurenti* that stretched east along the waterfront from the Old Town and its port. He had registered there that morning, left his bag. He'd change into something more in keeping with a visit to Shandon Villa—tweed jacket and flannels. He could risk bumping into Chuck Kelso; the important thing was to keep out of Rick Nealey's way. Meanwhile.

And his ostensible reason for the visit?

He had found a good one before he had left the hotel and was strolling towards Georges and the waiting Renault. Certainly, over the 'phone, it had impressed Maclehose enough to let him extend a welcome for a brief tour of Shandon Villa. He couldn't very well snub a visitor who brought direct greetings from the Director of the Shandon Institute in New Jersey: Paul Krantz's name packed a punch even at this distance. Hadn't Krantz given his own guided tour to Tony, on that unpleasant morning back in November when the memorandum crisis was in full flap? "Of course," Maclehose had said, "I remember you. Drop out here any time. This afternoon? If you could make it early—I'll be here to show you around. And how is Paul?"

"Couldn't be better. I'll be with you before three."

"Good enough."

"Oh, just one thing—what's the quickest road to take through Cap Martin to reach Shandon?"

Maclehose gave him the directions—much needed, he told Tony with a laugh—and the call ended amicably.

Now, as Tony stepped into the Renault, he could say, "All set. We'll head for Cap Martin. And stop at the Casino on the way. I've a brief visit to make there."

And Georges, tall, thin, dark-haired, a thirty-year-old Frenchman, carefully selected for this assignment in Menton— he knew this area well from family vacations as a boy—said in his usual offhand way, "Don't expect much action there until the evening. At this time of year, you'll probably find the Casino closed for the afternoon."

"All the better to let me see the layout clearly."

"Planning a night on the town?" Georges's sharp brown eyes looked both interested and amused. "You won't find it pulsing like Monte Carlo's Casino."

"Where the busloads start arriving in the morning?" Tony's smile was wide, his spirits rising. All arrangements made, nothing forgotten.

Georges smiled too. "And I thought this trip was going to be all dull work." He approved of the change. His manner was deceptively mild, cloaking his natural exuberance. Like Tony and Emil and Bill and Nicole, he wasn't in this profession for money. He had brains, a contempt for danger, and deep convictions. He had lively curiosity, too. It surfaced now. "Any excitement this morning?" he couldn't resist asking.

And Tony, sketching in the details, put him neatly into the recent picture. Enough of it, anyway, to let him know what was on the agenda, and why. (Later, Georges would fill in Emil, who was now superintending the repairs to the boat's engine.) There were moments, Tony believed, when a need-to-know was the best safeguard for concerted action. He enjoyed team-work (strange as that would seem to some people who thought of him as a loner) and based it on his old *quid pro quo* maxim. You got good co-operation if you gave it. To those you could trust, of course. And Georges, with whom he had worked for the last seven years, was a man who was dependable. Even to the way he now drew up the car a short distance from the Casino's entrance—not too far to walk, not too near to be noticeable.

The entrance steps faced a square, complete with flowers, palm-trees, and a small taxi-rank. (Tony noted it for future use. There weren't many taxi-stands around this town.) Inside, a small vestibule and more steps and no one to stop him. He found himself in a totally deserted hall, spacious, light—the wall directly opposite the vestibule's steps was of glass—giving a view of terrace and large pool, and beyond that, a glimpse of the front street where Nicole and he had walked along the promenade. There were two wings to the hall; the left one consisted of the *Salle Privée*—well marked, well screened from curious eyes—but a thin young man, dark-suited, pale-faced, appeared out of nowhere at the sound of Tony's footsteps, and politely barred him from pushing open its curtained door. Near by was a large and empty dining-room, handily adjoining that side of the pool's terrace; and across from it, close to the vestibule steps, was a pleasant (and equally empty) bar. The main hall itself had two large green-covered tables, where play would be less private and certainly easier on the budget. Beyond them, occupying the right wing of the building, there actually was a movie theatre.

That was all he needed to see. He headed back for the vestibule, nodding his thanks to the dark-suited young man still guarding the other end of the hall, and came out on to the busy street. He was thinking automatically that there must be other ways in and out of the building. The movie theatre must have at least one emergency exit: even two? The pool, with its garden and colonnades along the waterfront view, had possibly an entrance of its own. The dining-room? After all, it was a public place, this municipal Casino—except for those who enjoyed high stakes in a *salle* kept *très privée*.

"Quiet as the tomb," he told Georges. And about as cold. Some summer sun was needed to heat that high-ceilinged hall. "Only one character bobbed up, near the *Salle Privée* door. What did he think I was going to do, anyway? Jiggle the wheel? Place marked cards in the shoe?"

"You don't gamble, do you?"

"What do you think we are doing right now?" And the stakes couldn't be higher.

As Georges drove past the wooded gardens, past glimpses of large houses surrounded by flowering trees beyond impressive gates, he said, "I think this address you've given me lies on one of the private roads. In that case, we'll be stopped. Only residents' cars and their friends' cars and taxis can get through. Everyone else—well, drive around some other road if you must, but keep out of this one."

"Taxis allowed?"

"It's a local rule. There's logic to it, I suppose. People in taxis are usually going to a definite address."

"We are too."

"I hope your Mr. Maclehose told the guards you were expected."

"Guards? We aren't visiting the Elysée Palace."

"Not really guards. More like—well, guardians."

They turned out to be a fresh-faced woman in a cotton dress and cardigan, and her elderly husband with a cloth cap almost as old as he was. They looked like small stall-holders, down in the market-place, ready to sell Tony a dozen oranges. But they took their job seriously, checked the name of Lawton on their list (Maclehose had remembered) and—with a nod from the man and a smile from the woman—let the car proceed.

Georges took it easily, for the road was narrow and twisting. "I know what you're thinking," he told Tony. "They couldn't fight off more than their shadows. They might not stop a jewel thief, but they could certainly identify him to the police."

"The strangest Keep Out notice I've ever seen." But Georges was right: no stranger could come wandering round here unescorted. Jean Parracini, if he were tempted to seek payment for the damage done to him and his friends by Shandon (justice, he would call it), would find a direct approach impossible. "Wonder if Shandon Villa has a beach, a landing-place for small craft?"

Georges stared at him, and then went back to keeping count

of the houses. "That's the second on the left. And Shandon's the fifth?"

Tony nodded. The villas were generously spaced, securely separated from one another by walls and hedges, scarcely visible behind the screens of shrubs and trees that decorated smooth lawns. "And here we are, gates wide open. Shandon Villa doesn't subscribe to the closed-door theory, I see."

"But they have two muscular gardeners working close to the driveway," Georges pointed out with amusement.

They studied the villa before them. It was a massive assertion of an architect's dream of Italy with Spanish memories creeping in. The gardens, even from a view mostly blocked by pink stucco, were lush and extensive. "A touch of Eden. All right, Georges. Let's find the snake."

The door to the villa was impressive: two tall bronze panels, one of them ajar, both of them encrusted with decorative scenes depicting myths and men. "A slight echo of Florence?" murmured the irreverent Tony, not quite sure whether to let the massive doorknocker clatter down on Aphrodite's backside as she received the apple from Paris, or to heave the door fully open and enter. "If the Duchess of Shandon couldn't have Ghiberti, she hired his great-great-great-great-grandson." He compromised by both knocking and pushing. "A fake," he added sadly as the panel swung back easily: wood covered with copper. "Now what?" A broad hall stretched before them, running through the villa until it ended in a wall of glass. Sunlight and a terrace lay out there, making an inviting vista from this dark threshold.

Beside them a door opened, and Maclehose came bouncing out from his office, his hands outstretched in a slightly effusive, if belated, welcome. "Come in, come in—just finishing off some dictation." His face was tanned and healthy, his large and cumbersome body several pounds heavier, his smile beaming, his eyes wary but clearing, as Tony conveyed warm greetings from Paul Krantz. Delighted to see Tony again, delighted to meet his friend.

"Georges Despinard," Tony explained, "a journalist from Paris. He is writing a series of articles for *La Vie Nouvelle* about social changes in the Côte d'Azur. Naturally he is very much interested in Shandon Villa. We were lunching together, and when he heard I was coming here—"

"Of course, of course. Delighted," Maclehose said for the third time. "Yes, we are changing things," he told Georges. "But for the better—I hope."

He's nervous, Tony thought: under all that exuberance is uncertainty. He's wondering if I'll mention that unpleasant morning back at Shandon Institute, when heavy flak was flying around and unhappy Maclehose was dodging the fallout. I'll do him a real favour: I won't even breathe a reference to the NATO Memorandum.

"Let me show you around," Maclehose was saying, leading the way past the open door of his office—really an anteroom tucked near the front entrance—where his secretary was pretending to be unaware of the two visitors. A handsome redhead, Tony noted: tight sweater, slender legs, face pretty but expressionless. Maclehose waved a hand to her. "Find that guest-list for the first seminar, Anne-Marie. Bring it to me." He went on his way, hurrying along the hall, gesturing to right and left as he identified the rooms. "That's the library—I'm afraid I must leave in twenty minutes—the dining-room is over there—but as I explained to you on the 'phone, I have engagements for this afternoon—and here's the main sitting-room, must have some place where our guests can relax between serious business—this place is a madhouse today, last-minute checks on electrical work—" he nodded to two men who were carrying their toolboxes down a broad staircase. "Bedroom up there, of course—ten of them, not counting the quarters for my Executive Assistant, he has his office and bedroom in the corner suite, he's constantly on the job, I tell him he even sleeps with his problems—and next door to him, two very sizeable rooms which we've turned into group-discussion areas. Now, down here, we have the main seminar room—it was a large drawing-room at one time, and across the way—the terrace room just beside this door of course." He swept them through the large glass panels that slid apart at their approach, and brought them out on to a terrace over-looking a series of descending gardens that stretched to the sea.

"Remarkable," said Tony, thinking of the Executive Assistant's suite. "And your quarters, where are they?"

"Oh, we thought it better to keep the family at some distance from our distinguished visitors. So Mattie and I have set up house in the cottage over there; you can't see it because of the acacias. Very comfortable—seven rooms—Simon Shandon used to live in it when his wife had her friends to stay here." Maclehose looked around. "Beautiful, isn't it?"

"Remarkable," Tony said again. So the Director has only a small office in the main building, and placed right at the front door as if he were the concierge. Doesn't he realise he is giving up his power-base? Distinguished visitors were going to see much more of his Executive Assistant than of the Director. Cosy chats and late-night conversations would not be shared with Maclehose. And at dinner, who would be the host? Seldom Maclehose, I'm willing to bet: he can't leave Mattie and the children night after night, can he? Not his style. A nice good-hearted family man, as virtuous and well-meaning as they come. "An ideal place. Don't you think so, Georges?"

Georges reacted out of shock: what wealth could build, when it set its mind upon it, always stunned him for a few initial moments. "Extraordinary!" Georges lapsed into French and let off a run of sentences.

Maclehose looked embarrassed, covered his perplexity with a wide grin.

"My friend is saying that you have done an outstanding job of transforming this place," Tony obliged. "He is deeply impressed. And so am I." Tony's eyes were now on the gardens, green terraces with bright beds, edged by shrubs and groupings of trees. "Georges would also like to stroll among your flowers. He is interested in gardens too. In fact, he was a landscape-architect before becoming a writer."

"By all means. Tell Monsieur—" Maclehose was uncertain of the name—"tell your friend to go down to the pool—it's just above the beach—we've had some workmen fixing the lights there—underwater illumination." He glanced markedly at his watch. "I'd like to spend the next five minutes showing you the guest-list for our first seminar." He looked around for Anne-Marie, but she wasn't in sight.

"See you back here in five minutes," Tony called after Georges. And don't forget a visit to the beach.

"I envy you your French," Maclehose admitted. "They speak so quickly—that's my trouble. A pity my Executive Assistant can't be here to meet you. He's an expert linguist. But he had some final arrangements to make for our guests next week—up at Eze—they'd enjoy lunch up there—a very fine restaurant."

"That's a pleasant idea: relaxation for tired minds."

Maclehose laughed. "All part of public relations. That's my Executive Assistant's main job, but he really can turn his hand to anything, don't know what I would have done without him. He took charge of the alterations, found a reliable contractor with a team of first-rate men—carpenters, painters, electricians— and the work was completed yesterday—except for a few corrections. And all in less than eight weeks, imagine!"

"And who's that? The contractor himself?" Tony asked as a quietly-dressed man came climbing up from one of the lower terraces along with an obvious workman.

"No. I think that's the inspector, who is checking our wiring system. We had a certain amount of trouble with it."

"He looks satisfied now," said Tony. "All must be well. Your Executive Assistant will be relieved."

"Nealey? Yes, indeed. He had to call in two other electricians to get the final adjustments made."

"And the contractor himself didn't blow a fuse?" And what about his team of first-rate workmen?

"Oh, Nealey added a bonus—the work was finished in time, except for a few modifications we wanted to make. The contractor has nothing to complain about."

We wanted to make? Tony let that go, although it was tempting to hint that a bonus might be construed as bribery. But he resisted putting at least one warning fly into Maclehose's too trustful ear, his full attention now on the man who called himself an inspector.

The man drew near, the workman a step behind him. And suddenly Tony was on the alert, memory stirring, another scene floating up to the surface of his mind. Washington. The Statler Hotel. A group of Soviet agricultural specialists. An interpreter, who left, and was followed...and Rick Nealey slipping into the car where the man waited. A man in his early forties; five feet ten or eleven; broad-shouldered, strong build. The dark hair was no longer streaked with grey; the placid face was now tanned. The eyes were the same, blue, cold, and confident. Boris Gorsky.

He passed close enough to make Tony (now admiring the profusion of the nearby flower-beds) feel a touch of cold sweat at the nape of his neck. Boris Gorsky, good God... Yes, Gorsky himself, as cool as when he had walked into Lenox Hospital, and couldn't identify his old comrade Vladimir Konov. "These huge pink and purple patches, what are they?" Tony asked.

"Cyclamen," Maclehose told him. "Certainly," he was replying to the inspector's query, "go right upstairs. I'm sure you'll find it's all in order now."

The two men reached the house as the redhead at last stepped on to the terrace.

"Cyclamen? Massed close like that?" Tony shook his head in wonder, and managed a glimpse of the redhead's brief hesitation, a momentary question on her pretty face and a small smile on her lips, as she glanced at Gorsky. Then she came forward to Maclehose, a sheet of paper in her hand, her face once more expressionless. She isn't as dumb as she looks, thought Tony; she knows Gorsky. He looked at Maclehose, standing proudly on his beautiful terrace, in front of his beautiful house, above his beautiful gardens, and he fell silent.

Maclehose took the list with a warm smile of dismissal for Anne-Marie, and began explaining the importance of the names it contained. The subject they would discuss was of paramount importance to the allies of the United States: *The Weakness of Super-Strength*. "A good title, don't you think?"

"Applicable only to the United States?"

"For this seminar, yes. Later we'll examine Russia's response to challenge."

"Responses," Tony corrected gently. "And when will that be?"

"Oh—some time, I hope, this summer. It's a matter of getting the right specialists together."

"And there are more of them on America's weaknesses than on Russia's?" Tony asked blandly. Then, glancing at his watch, he exclaimed, "Our time is almost up. Disappointing. I did want to hear about the rest of your staff too. Surely you can't run a place as important as this, only with Nealey."

"Oh, he will have an assistant. Besides that, there are two seminar aides, three translators, four secretaries."

"A neat progression."

Maclehose laughed. His anxiety about this visit from Krantz's friend had left him. The report back to New Jersey would be positive.

"Will they live on the premises, too?" Tony asked. "A bit crowded."

"I agree. There's no room—domestic staff and storage take our top floor. They'll stay in town."

"And go home early?" Tony was smiling. "Very nice work, if you can get it."

"No, no. They'll work a full day. They start on Monday—no need to have them around with all the hammering and sawing going on." Maclehose looked at his watch and tried not to frown.

"We are detaining you, I'm afraid. Why don't we say goodbye now, and I can find Georges—"

"Would you?" Maclehose's hand was out.

"There he is at last," said Tony, looking down over the garden. Georges had been running, and now—as he saw them standing on the high terrace—halted abruptly, signalled urgently. He called out something unintelligible, ending with a shout of "*Vite! Vite!*"

At the first signal, Tony had already begun moving and was ten paces ahead of the startled Maclehose. Georges, turning on his heel, raced back the way he had come. A gardener lifted his head from setting out masses of begonias in a lower-terrace bed, rose from his knees as he saw the running men, and, trowel still in his hand, followed Georges. Someone else—a workman in dungarees—emerged from some trees to stand bewildered at this madness. He let Tony and Maclehose pass him before he too started downhill. There was a shout from the gardener, now hidden on the last terrace by a hedge of trimmed shrubs. Another yell from him—a warning? An answering shout from Georges.

Behind Tony, Maclehose called out, "They're at the swimming-pool. My God—the children—" And he put on a desperate burst of speed that brought him slithering over the steep slope of grass to end up crashing against the hedge. He tried to see over the top of the clipped yews, but they were chin-height, and dense. "Oh, my God!" he said again, and he followed Tony down the short flight of steps to the last terrace.

Then his fears calmed as he caught sight of the pool.

It was only half-full of water, probably had been emptied that morning for work on the under-surface lights—some heavy wires still snaked over the terrace as evidence that the electricians had been busy there, perhaps still were. At the shallow end, floating face-down with arms stiffly spread, was a man. He was fully clothed, tweed jacket and all, except for his shoes. They lay haphazardly, scattered below the body, on the pale blue floor of the pool.

The gardener, in a mixture of Provençal and French, was shouting at everyone. Georges translated as best he could. "He says the water's dangerous—he was warned to stay away from this terrace—work was going on here."

Tony stared down at the pool. The back of the dead man's head, dark hair, was all he could see. Sharply, he glanced at Maclehose who stood there, absolutely speechless, his eyes bulging in a face whose tan had faded to a pale yellow. Then, as a woman appeared on the far side of the terrace, Maclehose came to life. "Get back, Mattie, get back there! For God's sake don't step on those wires. Keep off the wet paving! Get back!"

Mattie stood still, incredulous. "Chuck Kelso," she said slowly. "It's Chuck!"

"I know, I know," Maclehose shouted angrily. "Get back to the house, Mattie! Keep the children away from here."

"The children—but they're safe at the garage. We were all waiting for you, and I came down to see what was delaying—"

"Get someone else to drive you into town."

Unbelievable, thought Tony. Here we all are standing in the exact same spot where we stopped short on this terrace as if we were in a bloody minefield, a man is telling his wife he can't drive her into town, and there's a corpse floating in the water beside us. And as background to all this, a three-way argument was going on between the gardener and Georges and the workman. The gardener said there were live wires all around; the electrician said the current was shut off—no one, but no one, would work at the pool with the current still on; and Georges was trying to get an answer to a sensible question. "Where is the main switch?" he kept asking. "Where?"

Tony walked over to the gardener, took the trowel from his hand, threw it into the pool. It broke the surface without a flare or a sizzle, and sank. "Let's get the body out of there," Tony said, and looked round for a rake.

15

"We'll stop here for a few moments," Tony said, breaking their long silence, as they reached the Roquebrune road. Georges nodded, found a parking space near a group of small shops, and turned off the Renault's engine.

Neither had spoken since they left Shandon Villa. The police were still there, questioning the electrician, all interest now focused on what power near the pool area had been turned off, what turned on, when and why. The pool itself was safe enough, all work there completed. Only one section, controlling the lights that would illuminate the trees at one side of the pool, was still under repair. The power-switch controlling that small area was still active. A regrettable oversight, a case of human failure; judgment against which the unfortunate electrician kept protesting. (The power had been off today on all areas of the pool and its surroundings. No, he hadn't seen this done: he had just assumed it to be so. As for the other electricians, they'd be back tomorrow to clear up the mess they had left: his job was to check the lights on the upper terraces, and that's where he had been working, hadn't heard or seen anything.)

Yes, everyone had been thoroughly baffled. And Maclehose gave the verdict that possibly would stand. "An accident, a terrible accident," he kept repeating. It seemed a plausible explanation: the trees at the dangerous corner of the terrace screened the small pavilion where Maclehose had installed his visitor. "Official guests at the villa, our own friends in the pavilion near the pool—Mattie fixed up the upper floor nicely for them, just no room over at our place. Poor Kelso, he was the first to use our guest-house. Arrived this morning, was only going to stay here overnight. Tomorrow he'd be on his way to Gstaad—always takes a winter vacation—two weeks, he said. Suicide? Ridiculous. He wasn't depressed. Preoccupied, perhaps. Certainly, he was in a serious mood at lunchtime, seemed ten years older than I remembered him. Just wouldn't let us plan his afternoon. He said he was going to wait for Rick Nealey's return. And after that he was going to see his brother. His brother— good God, Lawton, what do we do about his brother?"

And Tony said, "You let him know."

"Yes. Yes. I'd better call him right away. You are leaving?"

"The police have our names and addresses. They'll know where they can reach us." Which was true enough. And if the police wanted to check further than Tony's hotel or the *Sea Breeze*, they'd end up at a wine-shipper's office in London and a journalist's desk in Paris.

"I don't think they'll trouble you," said Maclehose. And I hope, his anxious eyes were praying, they won't trouble Shandon Villa either. "No publicity about this," he added, glancing at Georges. "The less the better, don't you agree?"

"I agree."

"Accidents will happen," Maclehose said miserably. He sighed a deep sigh as he shook their hands, and went back to staring at the figure, covered now by a blanket, as if he could by sheer will-power bid the stretcher-bearers move it out of sight, out of his life.

Tony turned abruptly away, said nothing more. He began climbing up through the gardens, with Georges hurrying to catch up.

"Accident?" Georges wondered aloud. "Perhaps it was. When I passed across that terrace on my way to the beach, there was nothing to see. No one, nothing. Just a pool that was half-full of water. And five minutes later, there he was—Kelso."

"And a few minutes before that two men had come up from that terrace."

"Two men? But I saw nobody—or were they inside the pavilion—?"

"Where else?"

Then Georges remembered Tony's brief visit to the upper floor of the pavilion in search of a blanket to cover Kelso's body. "What did you find there?"

"A bed where a man had been lying. Tie and sweater on one of those valet-stands. Keys and wallet on a dresser. Jacket certainly off—who sleeps in a jacket? Shoes probably off, too. They managed to get the jacket back on him, hadn't time for the shoes—you had given them a scare, walking down towards the beach—so they heaved him into the pool and the shoes after him; turned on the power to look as if he had stumbled over a live wire and been jerked into the water by the shock."

"How was he killed? There was no sign of a wound."

"An injection, possibly: enough to knock him out and let the pool do the rest."

"Expert."

"They should be. I recognised one of them. Boris Gorsky."

"Gorsky is here?" Georges was dumbfounded. My God, he thought, Nealey has some real support: he must be of major importance. He glanced back over the placid gardens. None of the stress and strain down at the pool was either audible or visible from this upper terrace. Sheltered by hedge and trees, it was all peace and tranquillity.

In silence, they entered the house and passed through the hall. A policeman was taking statements from two electricians. But there was no sign of Gorsky. "Expert," Georges had murmured again. Tony's only comment had been a tightening of his lips.

And then, on the Roquebrune road, as Georges switched off the ignition and sat back to wait for further instructions, his eyes on the traffic, his thoughts on Boris Gorsky, Tony startled him by saying vehemently, "Jean Parracini—that's our best bet. Our only one, now."

Georges, his mind still circulating around the pool, the body, the guest pavilion, looked blankly at Tony.

"He must have something tucked away in a corner of his memory that could help us. Just one small lead, that's all we want to find Rick Nealey's true identity. God damn it, Parracini must have tried to uncover that. His chief Washington source— surely it was something he would try to ferret out."

"He did name Alexis as his chief source in Washington," Georges volunteered.

Tony brushed that aside. "No big deal. We had guessed that.

239

But who *is* Alexis?—Rick Nealey?" Tony paused for emphasis. "And who is the man who calls himself Nealey?"

"And what happened in East Germany to the real Heinrich Nealey?" Georges asked softly. Silenced, as Chuck Kelso had been silenced?

But Tony was following his own train of thought. "You worked with Gerard, when he was in charge of Parracini's debriefing in Genoa. Did you talk with Parracini himself?"

"No. Never met him. My job was background research on all the reports Parracini—as Palladin—had sent us from Moscow. The idea was that I might find certain pieces of information in them that needed more clarification or expansion. Gerard questioned him about than. Results were satisfactory."

"With occasional blackouts?"

"What did you expect? Palladin's reports from Moscow covered twelve years."

"How many altogether?"

"Just over a hundred—only about nine or ten each year. He was a very careful operator. Didn't send them regularly, and never from the same location twice running. A broken pattern like that makes it more difficult to recall every small detail stretching over twelve years."

"I know, I know." Tony was irritated. Not with Georges. With Gerard. "He didn't press Parracini hard enough."

"Gerard? He did shoot off the names you had suggested. Alexis. Oleg. Heinrich Nealey."

"And no impact on Parracini?"

"None. Except for an educated guess about Alexis, someone with important contacts and friends in Washington; someone who could supply all varieties of information, from facts and figures to scurrilous gossip. So he could be a political journalist on an important newspaper, or a television reporter, or a columnist. Not a young man—too judicious, too experienced— possibly in his forties or even fifties, judging by the age-groups with which he mixed."

"An educated guess," Tony echoed in disgust. "Was that the most that Gerard could get out of Parracini?"

"It doesn't sound much like Rick Nealey," Georges admitted. "Could it be that there's another agent—"

"There were only two of them in Central Park with Vladimir Konov on the night he was mugged."

He's really stuck with his theory that Alexis must be Nealey's code name, Georges thought, and Parracini's analysis doesn't back it up. "Take it easy, Tony."

"Two of them. Alexis and Oleg," insisted Tony, exasperated with everyone, himself included. "One was security; the other was Konov's Washington agent. Which name fits Nealey?"

"Are you certain he was in Central Park that night?"

"The New York police have a description that matches Nealey exactly. Also a composite picture of the other man. He is a ringer for Gorsky."

"Ah," said Georges, "I didn't know that."

You might, thought Tony, have assumed that I did know. Or were you actually thinking I was just frothing at the mouth? He glanced at his watch. Surely Maclehose had called Tom Kelso by this time. "All right, Georges—let's get cracking. Up the hill until you see, on the left-hand side, a nursery marked MICHEL. There used to be yellow mimosa trees to mark the spot. Drop me just inside the gate."

Georges switched on the ignition, released the brake, kept

his eye on the traffic and waited for the first safe chance to join the procession of cars. "We really may trigger some new detail in Parracini's memory tomorrow. He's had time to rest and think. And remember."

"He'd better."

"That was a devilish journey he had. He almost lost his life in an Aegean north-easter—the fishing-boat that was taking him from Istanbul to Lesbos nearly foundered. Most of their gear went overboard, and two of their men."

"I know, I know." Tony restrained himself, tried to smile. "I'm short on patience today. But we haven't much time. Shandon Villa is a perfect set-up for Nealey's kind of work." Nealey could gather all kinds of information, some hard intelligence, some dealing with the personal quirks and indiscreet remarks of prominent men. The Disinformation boys in Moscow would have a propaganda bonanza. They'd take the facts and twist and magnify and drop them into a willing journalist's ear for his next exposé of Western chicanery. It was all too simple nowadays to drive a wedge between democratic friends and allies: they were in a self-destructive syndrome, always willing to believe the worst about themselves and the best about their enemies. "Yes," he said as Georges at last joined the stream of traffic, "it's a perfect set-up."

"And Nealey won't be working alone. We'll have a nest of agents—"

"That we will."

"Who's directing them? Gorsky?"

"Could be. He's senior enough." Or perhaps he was only acting as protector-in-chief.

"He doesn't hesitate, does he, when he thinks security is

threatened? Could Chuck Kelso really have been such a hazard to them?"

"You saw the action they took." Which only proved, in its desperate haste, that Rick Nealey was an agent of prime importance. "One more thing: memorise this telephone number in New York." Slowly Tony repeated Brad Gillon's private number. "Call it immediately. Speak only with Bradford Gillon, tell him the message is from me. Give him the news about Chuck Kelso. Advise him to warn Martin Holzheimer to keep his mouth shut and get an assignment in Alaska."

"Alaska?"

"Don't be so damned literal, Georges. *Any* place that's out of sight, out of mind. We've got to keep at least one witness alive. I don't want any more convenient accidents on my conscience."

The yellow mimosa shimmered in the sunlight, air-spun gold, as heart-lifting as a host of daffodils. Georges was signalling for a left turn into the gate, and Tony's hand was already gripping the release knob on the door beside him. He wasn't a man of protracted goodbyes, thought Georges with amusement.

But Tony had some afterthought. As the car drew up under the powdery blossom of the mimosa trees, he sat very still. "What are Parracini's plans?"

"Plans?"

"His future? There must have been some discussion about that."

"Oh, he will keep a low profile in Menton for the next few months. And once it's safe enough he can move into a new job. With us."

"With NATO Intelligence? What branch?"

"Gerard could use him in his department."

"Gerard's idea, or Parracini's?"

"Does that matter? It was a natural, whoever thought of it. Of course Parracini will keep his cover as chauffeur." Georges studied Tony's frown and tried a small joke. "Bill and Nicole will give him excellent references." But Tony wasn't in a mood to smile and make one of his usual quips. He's exhausted, thought Georges. He doesn't need this visit to Tom Kelso. He needs a couple of hours' rest; an evening to relax, enjoy himself. Tomorrow will be a heavy day.

Tony said, "Like to join me this evening for a drink in the bar at the Casino?"

"Shall I be literal about that?" The word still stung. "Or do we just keep an eye on each other?"

"A very close eye. And ear. Eight o'clock. Okay?" Tony stepped out of the car and began walking uphill towards the house high above the olive-trees.

Georges noted the slow footsteps, the slightly bowed head. He could have ditched going up there, Georges thought, as he reversed and turned to point the Renault in the right direction for the drive down to Menton. Damned if I wouldn't have telephoned my sympathy and condolence, and let it go at that.

From the olive-trees came a persistent sound, a light and steady tapping of wood on wood. Tony halted to look. The house was only fifty yards away, and perhaps he wanted any excuse to delay the first meeting with Tom and Dorothea. If I hadn't promised her, he thought, I'd never have faced the next half-hour. What good would it do, anyway? I can't tell them what I know or fear, can't drag them into this bloody bloody mess.

It's safer for them, for everyone, if they just stay out and accept what will be reported as a tragic accident. Tom is too intelligent not to ask questions: that will be my worst problem. And Dorothea—God, I wish she hadn't so much quick intuition. Not now, at least.

The constant sound of the small firm blows didn't miss a beat. He could see, far below this driveway, a white cloth spread under a tree, and, perched on its gnarled branches, two men with long canes. What the devil were they doing?

"Tony!" Thea called, and she came hurrying down to meet him in spite of high-heeled sandals. She had dressed up for this afternoon—a white frock whose pleats floated around her as she moved, some thin soft material that was as fluid as the swirl of a *chiton* on a Greek vase. "Tony, are we glad to see you!" she cried, happy and breathless, her smile radiant. "You're early, and that's sheer luck. Come on, come on." She caught his hand, urging him forward.

They don't know. Tony halted, looking away from her. They don't know. He stared down at the olive-trees. What now? Blurt everything out, or wait till I get them both together? That was the thing about news: if it were good, you'd tell it and repeat it and go over it a third time willingly; when it was bad, you only wanted to say it once, briefly, and then wish you hadn't been forced to do even that. "What's going on down there?"

"They are tapping the olives. They sit up in a tree and beat it gently, and the ripe olives fall to the ground." She looked at him curiously. "Does the sound annoy you? Tom said it was getting on his nerves. So we'll probably avoid the terrace and sit indoors— too bad on such a heavenly day. Come on, slow coach!" She pulled his arm gently, and started him towards the house.

"Where's Tom?"

"Oh, the telephone rang just as we were coming down to meet you. He went back to take the call."

He checked the time on his watch. Ten minutes to five.

"You're early and Chuck is late. But that's all to the good—Tom has some questions he needs answered before he sees Chuck."

"Dorothea—"

"Just like Chuck," she was saying; "he decided he couldn't wait till six o'clock, so he 'phoned—"

"When?"

"After lunch. Around two, I think."

"What did he say?" The fool, Tony raged secretly, he actually called them from Shandon Villa; and told them—how much?

Dorothea's smile had vanished. "He was going to give Rick Nealey exactly until four o'clock. If Nealey was still avoiding him by that time, he was coming up here. By half-past four. He said he had a tremendous problem and would Tom help him solve it? Tom had friends who worked in Intelligence—or even Brad Gillon—people who could act, take the right measures. What measures, Tony?"

They had reached the terrace, and Tony stood there silent, his face averted, his whole interest seemingly on the view of coastline that spread before them.

"Tony—what is wrong? Oh, I know Chuck must have had a bad quarrel with Rick. But why?"

"Didn't he tell you?" And I hope to God the answer is no, thought Tony. Let the pros deal with Nealey, not the amateurs. "Hints, mostly—but they were strong enough."

"What kind of hints?"

"About Rick Nealey. Chuck's anger was all directed against him. What could have happened between those two? They were so close." She drew a deep breath. "But out of bad news there comes some good. Chuck's call ended abruptly—he was using the telephone in Maclehose's office—his own was out of order. But as he signed off, he sounded less worried, even relieved. When Tom promised to help in any way he could, Chuck said, 'I've been a god-damned idiot. I know that now. And I'm sorry, Tom. I'm sorry.' Which, you know, was a considerable admission: I've never heard Chuck say sorry like that, meaning it, truly meaning it. For once, he wasn't going through his usual routine—all charm and little substance. He was really contrite." She studied Tony's impassive face. "But that *is* good news," she insisted. "Tom needed it. Oh, he's worried about Chuck—yes. But contact between them is re-established. And that counts, you know. Tom—" She broke off, unwilling to admit just how difficult those last months had been. And then, still watching Tony's face, she asked quietly, "Is Chuck's news as bad as that?" Her eyes widened, pleading with him for the truth.

There was no evading the directness of her gaze. "It was bad enough. And now it's worse—the worst possible kind of news for you and Tom. I didn't want to break it to you, not alone. Better that you and Tom should hear it together. But possibly he already knows—if the telephone call was from Shandon Villa. Chuck has met with an accident. A fatal accident."

For a moment, Dorothea stood rigid. Then she turned and ran into the house. Its silence paralysed Tony. The Shandon call must be long over. And Tom? Tony slumped into a chair, lit a cigarette, listened to the insistent tapping on the olive-trees below.

I handled that badly, he thought. But how could news about

death ever be handled well? And now Tom would come out here, start asking questions once the first shock had worn off. (And, as a seasoned reporter, he was adept at questioning.) I'll tell him everything that's possible to be told. No mention of Palladin's escape, or that he's still alive as Jean Parracini. Enough to let Tom know that the NATO Memorandum had been lifted from his brother's New York apartment and ended up in the hands of the KGB in Moscow; that Nealey seems to have been the only man who had access to Chuck's apartment on that Saturday night. Yes, we'll have to talk about Nealey—Chuck made sure of that. But I'll keep silent about Mischa and Alexis and Oleg, and not only for security reasons. A matter of safety, Tom's and Dorothea's.

Chuck was true to the last: lost in his self-centred world, righteous anger at being duped, hints blurted out about the source of his problem, sharing trouble when it overwhelmed him. Involving others, endangering them?—No, Chuck hadn't thought of that. Or he would never have unburdened himself in a telephone call. From Maclehose's office. Where a red-headed secretary had monitored every word. Why, oh why, couldn't Chuck have stayed in New York, made contact with Brad again once the truth began to get through to him? Perhaps he still couldn't believe he had been duped until he had a chance to confront Nealey and demand an explanation. Whatever Nealey had told him, on that ride from the airport this morning, hadn't worked. And Nealey knew it.

Tony lit a second cigarette, and then threw it away. If Brad hadn't pushed Chuck into facing unpleasant realities—and that was my doing: I suggested Brad see Chuck, lay the facts on the table (two men executed, several still under rigorous questioning, others scattered and hunted)—yes, if I hadn't urged Brad to talk frankly, pierce through Chuck's rationalisations with some truth, Chuck would probably be alive today. Skiing merrily in Gstaad, no thought of Nealey or Shandon Villa in his head, all things right with his own world; and who worried about what happened to other men in other places? Especially when they were espionage freaks, spooks wandering in a maze of threat and danger—their own choice, wasn't it? Probably their own creation, too. They did it for kicks or the money, everyone knew that. (Read your friendly local newspapers.) Saving the West? Me included? That's a big laugh. All part of their own hothouse fantasies. Who's threatening me—little men in black pyjamas? Look, get rid of the ego-trippers, the paranoiacs. Then we can all make nice profits and get promotion and enjoy our skiing (or bowling or golf or fishing) and our suntanning (or dining or wining or women) and live in a better, still better and better, world without end amen.

Tony lit a third cigarette. It tasted worse than the others.

Yes, Chuck would have been alive if I hadn't wakened him to the truth. (He awoke. That's something. Millions wouldn't have.) He'd be safely far away, in happy Switzerland. And when I visited Shandon Villa today, Nealey would have been on hand to give me a guided tour, all wreathed in smiles and innocence. But Boris Gorsky would not have been there. Not visible, certainly.

And so I'd have learned nothing, and known less.

Not that I know too much. But now I make that knowledge count. This I owe to Chuck Kelso.

Behind him he heard Tom's footsteps on the terrace. He rose and faced him.

16

Sunset had come, a blaze of vermilion and gold dissolving into an amethyst sky. The olive-trees, twisted ghosts rising out of deepening shadows, rested in peace. Down on Cap Martin, the heavy foliage became a massive block of blackness against a sea of faded ink. The air had turned shrewd and cool, but the two men still talked and walked on the terrace. Dorothea, chilled perhaps as much by Tony's information as by the evening breeze, had long since retreated into the warmth of the Michels' living-room.

Tom's manner was quiet, dangerously quiet. From the first moment he had come out on to the terrace, he had been in taut control of himself. His first words to Tony were cold, totally unemotional. "How did you learn about Chuck's death?"

"I was visiting Shandon Villa."

"You saw what happened?"

"No one did."

"Tell me what you can. Exactly."

And Tony had done just that.

Then came the questions. And answers. And long pauses. And more questions. And now, with the sun already set, colour and warmth drained from the land, Tom halted his steady pace and stared out at the bleak scene.

"And who," he asked at last, "is to deal with Nealey?"

"We will."

"How? You haven't had much success in these last months."

"There wasn't enough hard evidence to support official action. No witnesses to back up some of the statements in my report on Nealey."

Grimly Tom said, "And you've lost your best witness now. Holzheimer, if you could get him to tell what he knows, could only testify that Nealey approached him, put him in touch with my brother, was present when the first part of the memorandum was handed over... Where did that happen?"

"Holzheimer supplied his editor with the address—the apartment below Chuck's. Nealey spent the week-ends there. But that's still not enough evidence." Then, as Tom's face twisted with sudden emotion, Tony said, "We have one possible lead." And Parracini had better come through, he thought. "I can't tell you any more than that. Not now, Tom. There's no need to know. And it's much better not to."

"I'm going down to Shandon Villa tomorrow, look around, question Maclehose."

"You'll get no information—"

"I'll pick up some details. That's my job, Tony. And I don't expect much from Maclehose. He didn't even telephone me this evening. Bugged out."

"Then who—"

"Nealey. All-purpose Nealey. Yes, that little bastard called me himself to tell me that my brother was dead."

"Good God."

"I let him talk. You know what I think? He was trying to find out how much I had learned from Chuck. He even brought up the subject of the quarrel they had this morning. About a girl—Katie, he called her—all a misunderstanding. So Nealey blamed himself for not having cancelled his engagements today and stayed with Chuck, explained more, made him understand the truth of the matter." Tom stuck a clenched fist against the palm of his hand as his anger broke loose. "*His* phrase. The truth of the matter."

"And what did you say?"

"Is that important?" Tom asked bitterly.

"It could be."

"I said, 'You son of a bitch.' And I hung up."

Tony was silent. Nealey had caught Tom at an agonising moment when all defences were down.

"You think that wasn't too smart of me," Tom said, suddenly truculent. "But that is what Nealey is. He's one—"

"I know, I know. I agree completely. I'd probably have called him worse."

"Not you. You wouldn't have given him a hook on to which he could latch his suspicions. Sure, he now probably thinks I know too much. So let's see what he will try with that."

"Stop goading him, Tom."

"How else do you trap him into a false move?"

"Don't you try it."

"That's right," Tom said, "leave it to the professionals. And what use have they been so far?"

Tony's fatigue suddenly caught up with him. His voice sharpened. "Ask that question of your own people. Who has been building up public opinion against your professionals? Nothing but denunciations, imputations, revelations, recriminations—how the hell do they manage to work at all?" He turned away. "I have to get back into town. I'd better call a taxi." He headed for the living-room. At the French windows, he paused. "I'm sorry, Tom. Forget what I said."

Tom didn't answer, didn't even look round. He stood staring out at the lights circling the bay, hearing nothing, seeing nothing.

Tony found the telephone easily enough. It stood on the same old, rickety, eighteenth-century table he remembered from his week spent as a guest here. Solange had put him to work—she believed in keeping her visitors busy. These wall panels, on the other side of the room, testified to that. He had painted them and Michel had added the finishing touch by smearing them with a dirty rag. Antiquing, Solange had called the process.

"You know," said Dorothea as she appeared quietly beside him and noticed his interest in the panelled wall, "Solange did that. She's really very clever about such things."

"Indeed, she is." He opened the telephone directory, and actually smiled. There was relief, too, to see that Dorothea was avoiding an emotional scene. "That's sensible," he observed of her change of clothes: the thin dress had been replaced by a heavy sweater and tweed pants.

"I was frozen." She studied his face. "I've made some coffee. Boiling hot. Sandwiches, too. I think you need both."

It was twenty to seven, he noted in dismay. The half-hour planned for his visit had stretched considerably. "I'd like that. I'll have some coffee while I wait for a taxi."

"No need to call a cab. We'll drive you down to Menton."

"Wouldn't hear of it." He glanced back at the terrace.

"Tom often stays out there by himself. Don't worry. Please don't. And, Tony, don't let his words disturb you. He didn't mean them. He—he often has these moods."

Tony concentrated on dialling. "Tom's had too rough a day to drive anywhere tonight."

"He's going down to Menton anyway."

"Why?"

"To see the police. They 'phoned him just after Rick Nealey's call."

"Time enough to talk with them tomorrow. They'll know more by—" He broke off as he made the connection with the taxi-stand near the Casino. (A cab for seven thiry without fail, at the gate of the Michel Nursery, Roquebrune. Night rates, of course, and a hefty tip, if punctual.)

"That's what the police suggested. But Tom wouldn't wait. He's a man who needs action." She hesitated. "These last months have been difficult for him."

And for you? Tony wondered. He remembered his first glimpse of her today, down at the market. An unhappy girl, he had thought. "Let's have that cup of coffee." Possibly a sandwich too, just to please her. Besides, she was right: he needed it.

"Rick Nealey—" she began, as they sat down at the kitchen table, and then fell silent.

Tony braced himself. More questions, more answers. The only way to handle them was to plunge right in, keep everything brief and restrained, and—above all—generalised. "He's been working in Washington for the last nine years."

"As an enemy agent?"

So she had either heard talk from the terrace, or added up her own suspicions to score a solid guess. He shrugged a reply.

"And never discovered?" That horrified her.

"He's good at his job."

"Good? How can you say that? He's a monster."

"To us, yes—he's one of the bad guys. To the opposition he's the hero, and we are the villains. It just depends on what side you stand."

"But you can't approve of what he has done."

"No. If I did, I wouldn't be interested in him."

"Were you following him on the day we met in the Statler lobby?"

"Frankly, until I saw him there, I didn't even know the fellow. It was you who told me who he was, remember?"

"But you *were* interested. Immediately." She looked at him angrily. "Why didn't you tell the CIA?"

"And have them up before another investigatory committee for more interference in domestic affairs?"

"Then the FBI—"

"From that day at the Statler until he left Washington, Nealey kept his head down. No peculiar 'phone calls, no contacts with anyone doubtful: just an innocent citizen going about his own business."

Her anger faded, leaving only bewilderment. "How can these things happen? The cold war is over."

"A matter of terminology. You can call boiled cabbage a *pourri* of roses, but it still smells and tastes like cabbage.

There's too much rhetoric, too little thought nowadays—much of our own fault: we keep accepting words and ignoring acts."

"You don't."

"Which makes me a very bad buy indeed. And, it hurts me to say, not just to the other side," he reminded her.

"Yes," she admitted. "Once, I thought you were—were—"

"An anachronism? A bit of a fake? Like that antiqued panelling, cheap pine pretending to be weathered oak?"

"Not a fake," she said quickly. "Never that. I just thought you were wrong, all wrong—a waste of a good brain."

"I'm a pretty good wine-taster. Doesn't that justify my existence?"

"Oh, Tony!" She almost smiled, checked herself and frowned. Tears were not far away.

In alarm, Tony said, "I didn't mean to—"

"You didn't. It's just me... I feel—I feel terrible. About Chuck. I always found something to criticise in him—oh, not openly. But I had a lot of hard thoughts, especially when Tom kept excusing—" She shook her head. "Chuck didn't like me very much either. I wish now it hadn't been that way. And I'll always keep thinking that I—"

"No, you won't keep thinking about that," he told her. "Everyone feels guilt when sudden death comes to someone close to them. There's always remorse as well as regret. The last tribute. But no brooding, Dorothea: you aren't the morbid type. And how much would that help Tom? What guilt is he feeling right now, do you think?" He rose from the table. "Restrain Tom, will you? Don't let him do anything on impulse. That's usually disastrous." He raised her hand and kissed it. Just as abruptly, he left.

He took the exit through the living-room's French windows. The terrace was in darkness. Tom called to him. "Hey—wait there, Tony! I'll run you down to Menton." Voice normal, friendly. Tony halted in relief. Tom's arm went round his shoulders. "Why don't you stay and have some supper?"

"Wish I could. But I have promises to keep. Besides, I'm bulging with sandwiches and coffee. You could use some yourself."

"Let me give you a lift."

"Thanks, Tom. But the taxi will arrive any minute now. I'm meeting it at the gate." Tony began walking towards the driveway with Tom at his side, relaxed and friendly.

"No direct connection with this house?" Tom asked, making the right assumption.

He has recovered, Tony thought: he's using his brains instead of his emotions. "Better not, don't you think?"

"Anyone been following you?"

"Hope not."

"How many of them are there, I wonder?"

He has recovered too damn well, thought Tony.

Tom went on, "Who arranged the accident? Not Rick Nealey. He must have had help."

"They're around. And all the more reason for you to watch your step, old boy. Keep Dorothea safe, will you?" He grasped Tom's hand. "Take care. Both of you."

"I'll walk you to the gate."

"Not even that," said Tony. A final handshake, a grip that reassured both of them, and Tony was off.

Where is he bound for? Tom wondered as he turned back to the house. *Promises to keep*. Business or pleasure? No, not pleasure: not tonight. Business that dealt with Nealey? That was

HELEN MacINNES

Tony's main preoccupation now. *We have a possible lead*. His words. Was that what he was searching out? A possible lead…

Tom burst into the kitchen. "Look, Thea," he said, "I think I'll go down to Menton right away. Get it over with."

"But—"

"I don't feel like eating. I may as well learn what the police have to say." He put his arms around her, kissed her anxious face. "Lock up after me. Thoroughly. And go upstairs. It's cosier there. You'll be all right, won't you?"

"Yes, of course," she said in some surprise.

"I'll be as quick as I can."

"Must you, at all? Tonight?"

"Yes." He left as quickly as he had entered.

Obediently she locked the kitchen door, the front entrance, and the French windows. In the study she searched for a book to take to bed. Nothing in English, all in French. The television was black-and-white, a discussion from Paris with solemn novelists disagreeing at great length. French intellectuals talked in paragraphs, not in sentences. She picked up *Time* and *Newsweek*, switched off most of the lights, leaving just enough to welcome Tom back.

Then, with a last look at the lonely rooms, at the empty terrace, she broke into tears. I wish I were home, I wish I were home.

Down by the gate, headlights swooped into the driveway and stopped, their beam casting a wide arc around the flower-beds as the taxi turned to face the road again. One moment more, and it began moving out.

Tom was already in the Fiat, its engine running. Smoothly he

258

started downhill. He knew what Tony would say. Or perhaps he would be so tightlipped with anger that the words would choke in his throat. But this, thought Tom, is when I must take some action of my own. I will not be stuck on that terrace, knowing little, doing less.

Once past the gate, he abandoned caution until he picked up the rear lights of the taxi. Then he kept an even speed at a safe distance. From the front road along Menton's west bay, the taxi made a left turn and cut up into town. Not far. It dropped Tony just short of the English Church, at the corner of the square—if that's what you could call it: really an open stretch of central flower-beds bordered by two avenues, a pleasant prospect for the Casino's entrance.

Tom found a spot to park, and took it. What now? His first impulses were draining low; he felt both foolish and uncertain. But he got out of the car—he wouldn't have far to walk from here to the *Commissariat de Police* in any event—and began strolling towards the church.

Menton, in the off season, was an empty place by night. There were few people around at ten minutes of eight, as if everything had closed up tight for dinner. Tony could be easily seen in the well-lit streets. Which means that I can be easily seen too, Tom reminded himself. As a small protection he hunched up his coat-collar—he needed that too, in the cool wind blowing up from the sea—and stared into a shop window. As he risked another look, he saw Tony cross the street, start up some steps, and disappear.

The Casino? It couldn't be. Tom followed, his mind incredulous. But yes, it was the Casino. First, there was the shock of disbelief; next, a sense of frustration. Damned if I'm going in there, he told himself, his face grim as he turned the corner at the church, and strode past the taxi-rank, the stretches of flower-beds and palm-trees. So he had come chasing into Menton after Tony, and got nowhere. At the last moment, he had balked. Totally irrational behaviour. But he had been in no mood to step into a world of fun and games. His emotions were too raw, unpredictable. Better get them under control and his mind working again—this was no way to enter a police-station.

Half-way up the avenue, he halted and looked back at the Casino. Even if he had put his own feelings aside, entered there, what good would he have done? What purpose served? He would have been too noticeable—the Casino trade hadn't begun as yet. This wasn't Monte Carlo with all its slot-machines, Las Vegas style, packing in the bus-loads of people from early afternoon until dawn. No, he realised now, I'd have accomplished nothing at all, only caused unnecessary complications. Tony wasn't here for amusement: Tony was strictly business tonight. And he had no part in it.

For a moment even now, something of the old urge to know, to help, to do, reawakened in Tom. He hesitated. Cursed his feeling of uselessness. Turned away. Walked on.

The *Commissariat* lay a short stretch to his right, somewhere off these avenues. Few people around here: everyone enjoying their *bonne petite soupe*. The idea of eating still nauseated him— it was something else than hunger that gnawed at his guts. He had judged his direction and distance accurately, at least: the police-station was just where it should be. It was functioning, too: a visitor was leaving. The figure, clearly seen under the brilliance of the street lights, was familiar. Automatically Tom ducked behind a row of parked automobiles, the new-style barricades of every western city. He hoped he looked part of a logical explanation: a man, with head and shoulders bent, about to unlock his car door. For the figure, young, well-dressed, fair-haired, now hurrying across the broad street, was Rick Nealey.

Tom kept motionless, attracted no nervous eye. Nealey had reached a black Citroën, new model—and waited for a man to leave an automobile parked just a few yards ahead. The meeting was brief. Sentences were exchanged. That was all. Within three or four minutes the stranger returned to his car and Nealey entered the Citroën.

Thinking of his Fiat parked snugly several blocks away, Tom damned himself for an idiot: he couldn't even follow, only watch. He felt vulnerable, though, and testing the door he stood beside, he found it was unlocked. He slid into the front seat, kept his head well down.

Nealey's Citroën passed him, travelling westward. Back to Cap Martin? The other car—an Opel, green in colour—passed close to where Tom sat, and then made a left turn down the avenue that led to the Casino area. At least, thought Tom, I could partly describe that stranger in the green Opel, Nice registration: from a distance, he was about my height but heavier, and broad-shouldered; near at hand, his features were strong, his hair dark. And who the hell was he?

Thoughtfully Tom crossed the street and entered the *Commissariat*.

He was politely received, with just the right touch of official sympathy. They would know more about his brother's unfortunate death by tomorrow. Yes, it did seem as though it possibly might have been a most regrettable accident, a tragic error on someone's part, responsibility still to be allocated. Meanwhile, Monsieur Kelso might consider what arrangements he would desire: cremation or burial here, or perhaps he would prefer transport to the United States and interment there? There were local *agences* who were fully capable of handling such matters. *De rien, monsieur.* But one thing more: he could now take possession of the suitcase that held his brother's belongings, including his wallet, cuff-links, engagement-diary with addresses, wrist-watch, travellers' cheques, keys and key-chain, air-flight reservation for tomorrow to Switzerland, Hotel Post booking in Gstaad—all intact, all carefully listed in triplicate on this official police form of inventory. Be so good as to examine them, and then sign here. *Merci, monsieur. A demain.*

"Until tomorrow," Tom echoed. His voice was flat, unnatural, his movements slow and uncertain. He stood at the doorway, Chuck's case in his hand, hesitating. Something else, he kept telling himself, something else... "Mr. Nealey was here, wasn't he? From Shandon Villa."

"But yes—the Assistant Director. Naturally, he wanted to hear about the results of our investigation. He had the fear that your brother's death might have been suicide. But with your brother's plans for travel tomorrow—" A Gallic shrug indicated suicide was not a likely theory. Then the hint of a tolerant smile covered the next remark: "Perhaps Monsieur Nealey was also afraid of the adverse publicity that Shandon Villa might receive. But he can rely on our discretion. There were two visitors at the villa today, and he was worried about how they might talk. However, he was happy we could provide their names and addresses. He intends to visit them and make a friendly explanation about the necessity for restraint. Shandon Villa, after all, is beginning its meetings next week."

Tom asked bitterly, "Did he not want to view the body?"

A small shocked silence. And then a mild reproof. "Monsieur Nealey wants only to help, in any way he can. He offered to take your brother's suitcase to your house, spare you the trouble."

"But naturally," said Tom, mastering his French, "that was impossible. My signature was required."

"And you yourself were coming here. So Monsieur Nealey left."

I bet he did, thought Tom. He knew better than to meet me here tonight. But at least this proved that the police were efficient: they had removed Chuck's belongings from Shandon before Nealey could examine them, make sure there was nothing to endanger him. What the hell had he expected? Or was it just part of his training that he always must make sure? "Thank you very much," he told the police sergeant, a round-faced middle-aged man with a drooping moustache and kindly brown eyes. "You have been most helpful. Thank you."

"*De rien, monsieur*. And we regret—"

"Yes," said Tom, and left.

He locked Chuck's suitcase safely inside the trunk of the Fiat before stepping into the driver's seat. He switched on the ignition, and then turned it off. For fully ten minutes he sat there, his head bowed, thoughts giving way to grief within the darkness of the car. At last he raised his eyes, looking along the bright street. There were people entering the Casino now. Not many. But enough. He wouldn't be too noticeable.

Pocketing the car keys, he got out, and began walking. Remembering the meeting between Nealey and his contact which he had witnessed tonight, Tom sensed urgency. Nealey's moves had been too quick, too immediate, not to convey a warning. Okay, thought Tom, I'm taking it. He entered the Casino.

17

It was almost eight o'clock. The main hall of the Casino was brightly lit and practically empty. Seven people, all told, and employees at that: a woman, behind a glass-enclosed booth at the far end of the hall beside the cinema; a young usherette, arriving for duty; four croupiers—young, tall, lean, dark-suited—paired off at the two adjacent gaming-tables; a fifth man, similar in dress and manner, on duty at the *Salle Privée*. The dining-room, facing Tony as he took brief inventory—a natural pause after mounting the stairs that led up from the foyer just inside the front entrance to the Casino—was equally lethargic: three tables occupied. And the bar beside him? He turned and entered, dismay rising. Empty too, except for an attendant polishing glasses and a couple of men—one at the bar, the other at a corner table. Two: count them. Tony almost exploded in a laugh.

He halted just inside the doorway, letting his eyes adjust from the hall's brilliance to this small room's imitation moonlight glow. Très chic, très moderne, but mostly disconcerting: it had taken him half a minute at least to see that Georges was the man seated at the bar. And shall we remain aloof, keeping that promised eye on each other, for the benefit of one stranger and a bartender?

The subdued lighting was evenly spread, giving twenty-twenty vision a chance to reassert itself. Tony could soon recognise the man who sat at the corner table and faced the room. He might now be wearing a grey lounge suit instead of this afternoon's work-clothes, but he still had the same fair hair, sharp features, and slightly popeyed look of the electrician, climbing up through the gardens of Shandon Villa at Boris Gorsky's heels. And, thought Tony, he has recognised me. Probably Georges as well.

"Hello there!" he said as he joined the young Frenchman at the bar. "Sorry if I kept you waiting. Had a hard time parking the car."

Georges turned his head to stare in amazement, perhaps in disbelief.

Unperturbed, Tony ordered a Tio Pepe. "Do you want to perch, or shall we lounge? More comfortable over here." He led the way to one of the low tables flanked by four squat armchairs. It provided, as he had hoped, an excellent view of both the bar's doorway and, beyond that, part of the main hall—the most important part as far as Tony was concerned. It lay at the head of the stairs leading from the foyer: arrivals and departures easily noted. "Much better," Tony pronounced, flopping into the chair that faced the bar's entrance—and indicated, with an almost imperceptible nod, the chair close to his left elbow. From there Georges could watch the man in the far corner as well as observe the doorway by a turn of his head. Just as necessary, they could talk at close quarters and yet look natural, no table between them. "Now let's relax and have a couple of drinks before we move in for dinner. There's nothing like sightseeing to exhaust a man. Any ideas for tomorrow? But some place, I beg of you, where we don't have to walk and climb." He rattled on until his sherry arrived, but his voice was dropping gradually until it would reach a level that neither the barman nor Popeye could hear.

Georges caught on to Tony's stratagem quickly enough. But he still hadn't recovered from his first shock. "You're crazy, Tony," was his low-voiced comment. "Here we are, like two sore thumbs, as noticeable as hell."

"We'd be more noticeable if we were sitting apart. Have a look at that man in the corner. He probably saw you passing through the Shandon pool area."

"He and Gorsky—they were together?" Georges asked softly.

"Very much together."

Georges's eyes were grave, his lips tight. Gorsky was a name he knew only too well. The man himself he had seen only once. But there was enough in the Gorsky file to make that face memorable.

"Let's laugh it up a little, shall we? Heard any good stories recently?" That's better, thought Tony as Georges produced a convincing smile. "What did you find down at the beach? Can a boat dock safely there?"

"A rowboat. Not much more. There's only a small jetty. The water is shallow at the shore-edge." As he talked, Georges's eyes had followed a couple coming into the bar—a nice chance to look at the man in the corner. It was a quick but thorough study. "Rocks on either side of the beach. Property boundary, as it were. The beach itself is stony, a romantic but uncomfortable place to swim. The jetty is in shallow water—no good for diving."

So, thought Tony, anything larger than a rowboat would have to lie offshore; and anyone—if Shandon was his target—would use a dinghy to get to the beach. But would Parracini really take all that trouble to get at Shandon? And he couldn't be too much of a sailor; he had been landlocked all his life. Nor did he have enough cash to let him hire a boat and a crew to manage it. And, Tony concluded, I just don't see Parracini rowing all the way around Cap Martin to reach his objective. So he'll have to reach Shandon by car, and that isn't such a simple operation either: too many restrictions on free access. Perhaps he'll give up his whole idea; or perhaps I was wrong—he never had it. Just an unnecessary fear on my part. And yet, his hatred for Shandon must be real enough: he has a large score to even out with Nealey. "Did you reach Brad Gillon in New York?"

"All taken care of. I also got in touch with Brussels via Lyons."

"You did?" Tony was impressed. "So you're all set up? Quick work."

Georges nodded. That morning he had transferred all his special equipment from the *Sea Breeze* to his new room in the Old Town: good and safe communication with Brussels was a first necessity. He eyed two more couples entering the bar. "That's a smasher," he observed of one of the girls.

"Things are looking up all over. Two sore thumbs begin to seem normal. Swelling much reduced."

"I hope that guy in the corner is beginning to believe that too. An odd place to choose. Not much visibility from there."

"My guess is that Popeye isn't here to watch the hall." And thank heaven for that: Parracini could arrive at any moment. A few people had already been drifting towards the cinema.

"Waiting for someone to make contact?"

"And keeping a low profile until he gets the signal. You know, he ought to attend to that thyroid condition before his eyes really bug out."

Georges's laugh was spontaneous. Interesting, he thought, how Tony's attention never drifts far from the hall outside. "Expecting someone?"

"Any minute now. Our friend Jean is going to the movies tonight."

Jean Parracini? Georges's head turned casually towards the hall, as he lit a cigarette. "I don't like it," he said softly. Far too much risk, he thought, and stopped watching the hall. He'd have to keep the same balance as Tony, between looking and not-looking. No staring allowed.

"Oh, he won't be alone. He's bringing Bernard and Brigitte with him—Bill's devoted cook and butler." And devoted they were. Loyal and trustworthy. But the weakness was that they knew little. Only that Bill's household, and Bill's guests whenever they appeared, had to be safeguarded. Parracini was someone who spoke Russian and was learning French: that much was obvious. Parracini was important: that much they had been told. Palladin was a name they had never heard. Few had. "Keep smiling, old boy. We're on camera." More people had drifted into the bar. So far none of the tables near the entrance was occupied, but soon Tony and Georges might be surrounded, and that would make any further exchange of information a very tricky business.

"I still don't like it," Georges insisted. "Why couldn't the damned fool stay at home? He's safe there."

"And getting bored. Wouldn't you be? Besides, he's quite confident he can fool anyone. His appearance has changed. Completely."

"I see—he's trying out the transformation on the moviegoers. But I wish—" Georges checked himself.

"So do I. Perhaps he'll get more sense talked into him tomorrow. Is the boat ready?"

"Everything's repaired. Emil is sleeping on board."

"You've radio contact with him?"

"Of course. Weather reports aren't too good for tomorrow, but improving on—"

"Here they come." Tony's eyes looked away from the three new arrivals in the hall and studied his sherry with disapproval.

Georges registered all three of them: a light-haired man, balding, of medium height; a woman with short red hair, a patterned dress and cardigan; a man, also of medium height, tanned face, thick dark brown hair, a black moustache. Both men wore blue suits, white shirts, black ties. Georges shook his head, finished his drink. "I give up."

"The dark-haired one."

Nothing like his photograph, thought Georges, remembering its details. Nothing. In Genoa, Parracini had been blond, thin on top, with a round fleshy face and a heavy body—corpulent, in fact. "He doesn't even wear glasses." Georges's voice had dropped to a whisper. "Contact lenses?"

"The miracles of modern science," Tony said. "Why don't you slip out, have a closer look at him? See they all get into the movie safely."

"All the way?" Georges suggested.

"Might be an idea to mark their position. We may join them later." And as Georges shot a quick glance at him, Tony said, "Why not? We have to put in an hour and a half until the movie ends. Better there than here, perhaps." Then, very quickly, "Make sure no one is tailing them."

So that's it, thought Georges, already on his feet, excusing himself, moving into the hall. We're here as added protection for Parracini. And for once, Georges didn't think old Tony (nine years older than Georges's thirty) was overworrying. Georges was still slightly shaken by Parracini's self-confidence, even if an outing of the domestic staff from Garavan House would seem to be normal downstairs procedure: cook, butler, chauffeur out on the town for their night off. He caught up with them as they were about to pass the roulette and baccarat tables. (So far, no customers there.) Brigitte was already complaining about the coolness of the air, while the two men, in comfortably warm jackets, discussed the lighting overhead. Parracini seemed totally natural and quite oblivious to those who passed him. He put on a good show, Georges had to admit. Searching for the price of admission, he angled himself near enough to Parracini to have a front view of the new face. Totally unrecognisable. Reassured, Georges made his way just ahead of them into the cinema, felt its cold air strike the back of his neck, and wondered how long Brigitte in her thin dress and skimpy cardigan would last.

* * *

The bar was now almost half full, and a couple of men had taken the table next to Tony. It had to come some time, he thought: when Georges returns (four minutes gone, allow him ten at least to get Parracini & Co. nicely settled), we'll be reduced to discussing Uncle Joe's gall-bladder operation, or the weather, that good old standby. Which reminds me that tomorrow's forecast, according to Georges, is not promising. Let's hope that a rising sea won't distract Parracini too much from our questions—or us from asking the right ones to start unlocking his memory. He must know more about Alexis than he has been able to recall so far. It's all a matter of deep recesses in the mind which have to be explored: we all need that now and again. Yes, I'm convinced that he knows more than he realises. Or am I being too insistent that he can lead us to Rick Nealey through Alexis? No. I don't think so. Why?

What, for instance, would I myself have done if I had been Palladin? On that day in Moscow when I was faced with disaster? When I knew there was no option but escape? My plans would have been long made, ready for such an emergency. What would I have done with the time left me before I could set these plans safely into action? (We *know* from the delay in Palladin's alarm signal to us, that several days had elapsed before it was safe for him to set out for Odessa. He hadn't just received the NATO Memorandum, with Alexis's covering report, and walked out of his KGB office, there and then. He had played it cool, probably sidetracked the report for at least a few days of respite; no sign of panic to arouse suspicion, no precipitous flight.) How would I have used those last three or four days in Moscow?

Of course, it's easy to *say* how I'd have reacted: I am sitting here in a quiet bar, not in my KGB cubbyhole with wary eyes all around me. Still, as Palladin, I'd have done some things automatically—I was a topflight operator, with a built-in sense of what was vital information, and powerful enough to make a try for it. I'd have damned well found out every possible detail about this Alexis in Washington, the man who had ended my career and smashed everything I had built up over the last twelve years. And I'd have brought those details out with me. Not just an educated guess—but hard information, even if it was in small bits and pieces. Every little helps. That's the first rule of the good investigator. And you were that, Palladin.

An educated guess... The phrase rankled in Tony's mind. Alexis was middle-aged, was he? A Washington reporter or columnist? Oh, come on, Palladin, you were one of the best we've ever had as an agent in place. But as Parracini, you're a real pain in my— Tony's thoughts were chopped off. The man entering the bar, looking directly at the corner table without even having to let his vision become accustomed to the understated lights, was Boris Gorsky.

As Popeye rose obediently, payment for his drink already calculated down to the obligatory fifteen per cent tip, Gorsky turned to leave with a sweep of his eyes around the other tables. Tony sat unmoving, totally uninterested, a picture of boredom. He had resisted his first impulse to drop his cigarettes under the table and go looking for them. Too obvious a manoeuvre, enough to solidify Gorsky's suspicions of him. What has he chalked up against me so far? Tony wondered. Someone who always seems to turn up where he isn't wanted? I hope that's all, I hope to God that's all...

Gorsky had left, trailed by Popeye at a short distance. Keeping that formation, they strolled towards the other end of the hall, and soon were out of sight from Tony's vantage point. A new worry lunged at him, gripped his mind. Somehow, some way, they had managed the impossible. Gorsky knew who Parracini really was; he had found Palladin.

How?

A traitor among us?

No. Couldn't be... Bill, Nicole—both were unthinkable. Bill's faithful retainers? Unlikely. Someone closer to home, like Georges or Emil? Totally impossible. Gerard, receiving reports of Operation Parracini in far-off Brussels? Or someone on his staff, a trusted aide? Hell and damnation, Gorsky is turning me into a paranoiac, throwing suspicions around like streamers at a New Year party. Tony signalled to the bar attendant, made a sign for his bill. Pointless now to keep on sitting here. He had to see for himself. His fears might be unfounded: Gorsky could be here on other business than Parracini.

"You didn't drink your sherry," said the attendant. "Perhaps it was too dry for you, sir?" Only appreciated by true connoisseurs, his manner implied.

"I had a sip." And that had been quite enough. "Of both of them," Tony added with a smile.

The man was uncomprehending, counted out Tony's change in silence.

Resist complaining, Tony decided. He wouldn't believe me anyway, that someone had accidentally mixed two sherries together, an Amontillado with a Tio Pepe, and hadn't thought it mattered—both were dry, both light in colour. Who'd notice?

What was more important, thought Tony as he left for the

hall, was to find Georges and alert him, and then keep Gorsky under judicious observation. Now I can be thankful that this is a quiet night in the Casino—no mob-scene to increase our difficulties. Gorsky must have bought some chips: he was one of a small group forming at the opened roulette table. Some distance away Popeye was circulating aimlessly. And Georges, equally nonchalant, was walking back towards the bar.

Tony halted to light a cigarette, let Georges do the approaching. "Gorsky is here."

Georges stood still. "That's big trouble."

"More so if he and Popeye had headed for the movie-house. Where's Parracini?"

"On the aisle, third row from the back, Right-hand side of the theatre as you enter."

"Watch Gorsky. At the roulette table. Can you identify him? He's wearing—"

"I know him. Not all my identifications are made on the strength of photographs," said Georges. Or perhaps it was the sudden increase in worry that had spurred his sharp response.

"Then he knows you." Tony's voice was extra mild.

"Not necessarily. There were at least a hundred journalists milling around Kissinger at that Paris press-conference on the Vietnam peace talks. Gorsky was there, calling himself Zunin, a representative from Tass. He had no reason to be interested in me."

"But you had a reason to be interested in him."

"He was masterminding that West Berlin kidnapping—" Georges forgot Berlin. He was looking past Tony's shoulder. "Someone's just arrived. Very uncertain. But he keeps watching you. Almost six feet, dark hair greying at the temples, rugged features, light tweed jacket."

Kelso? Tony risked a glance behind him and met Tom Kelso's eyes. "Hold the fort," he told Georges. "Don't let Gorsky out of your sight. I'll be back as soon as I can—a matter of minutes."

"Something wrong?"

"I hope not. Something important, though." If it wasn't, Tom wouldn't be here. Not tonight. And he had stayed only long enough to catch Tony's attention. He was already out of the front door into the street, as Tony walked (don't run, show no sign of haste) down the short flight of stairs into the small foyer.

The convergence of avenues and streets around the Casino was placid enough; there was little automobile traffic and less people; bright lights over empty sidewalks, a town dozing off into early sleep. Tom was maintaining his head start: he had crossed over to the English Church, was striding on without one turn of his head to make certain that Tony was still with him. And for his part, Tony was keeping to his side of the avenue—he had no wish to catch up with Tom until he was reasonably sure that no one was interested in their movements. Apparently no one was. Not one loiterer or follower in sight. A short distance beyond the church, Tom stopped at his car and got in. Within seconds, Tony was slipping into the front seat beside him.

"Neat," Tony said. "But I can't drive around and talk. Have to get back—"

"This won't take long. It may not be as important as I think it is. But you ought to hear about it." Tom, without wasting a word, plunged into a brief résumé of what he had seen and heard tonight on his visit to the *Commissariat de Police*. "So," he concluded, "they know where you are both staying in

Menton. The way Nealey went after your addresses was just too purposeful."

"We'll disappoint them. Thanks for the warning, Tom. And for the other details too." Boris Gorsky was driving a green Opel with a Nice plate, was he? "Most useful."

"What did they want with Chuck's suitcase? There's nothing of interest to them inside it, as far as I saw. No letters, no documents. Not even a diary—just an address-book with a section for engagements."

"Have a careful look through that," Tony advised him.

"For what?"

"Anything that catches your eye. And you've got a good one, Tom. I'll call you later, around midnight. If possible."

"Call me as late as you like. I'll be awake."

"And one thing more. When Brad Gillon puts in a call from New York, any hour now—yes, we let him know about Chuck—ask him to start working hard on Katie Collier. The FBI must have made a thorough check on her 'phone bills. Get Brad to find out the calls that were made from her apartment *during the week-ends*."

"Made by Nealey?" Tom asked quickly.

"Always a possibility. Sorry to lay this on you tonight, Tom. Really sorry."

"Don't be. I need something to do. Take care, Tony."

Tony half-smiled. "You know me, old boy," he said as he stepped out of the car and began walking back to the Casino. The deserted streets were still innocent, so he made no detours but concentrated on speed. Sixteen minutes since he had left Georges, whose usual sang-froid must now be simmering with anxiety.

* * *

Georges met him as he reached the hall. "Thank God," he said. "It's all breaking loose. Haven't enough eyes to keep watching everyone. They've left the cinema."

"Parracini and party?"

"Brigitte insisted on leaving. Her complaints about incipient pneumonia were loud and clear. She's walking around the hall, trying to warm up, while Bernard has gone to pick up his car and bring it here to take them all home."

"And Parracini?"

"Walking around too. Damn his eyes."

"Gorsky?"

"Deep in a game of roulette. His friend is playing at the other table."

"Let's move in their direction, By the way, Gorsky has discovered my hotel. And the *Sea Breeze* too. Don't go near her tonight. You've left nothing of your special bag of tricks on board?"

"Nothing but Emil's transceiver—enough to keep contact with my room. I'll alert him when I get back there."

"Do that. Where's Parracini?" Tony couldn't see him. The red-haired Brigitte was now alone, standing still, hugging her cardigan close to her body, looking around her in rising alarm like an abandoned waif.

"He was near the big windows—only a minute ago. With Brigitte." Georges's face was as tense as his voice.

"We'd have seen him leaving," Tony said reassuringly, but his own stomach tightened. Then he relaxed a little. "I spot him." Almost in despair, he added, "I could wring his bloody neck."

Georges had followed the direction of Tony's eyes, looked aghast at the carefree Parracini sauntering around the tables. Roulette seemed to fascinate him. He halted, found a place in the small grouping of onlookers, listened to the croupiers' calls, watched the turn of the wheel with obvious interest.

"Let's join the spectators," Tony suggested. But not too close to Gorsky and keep behind him: nothing noticeable. And as Tony was about to congratulate himself on finding a place where they could see without being observed, Parracini made his move.

He reached Gorsky. Halted. Stood beside him. Seemed absorbed by Gorsky's play. He bent down to drop a few friendly words of advice in Gorsky's ear. There was a brief but amiable exchange between them. All most casual, it seemed, all perfectly natural, the polite smiles included. Gorsky went on playing, concentrating on his winnings. And with a final remark, Parracini turned away, his gaze now sweeping around the spectators. Both Georges and Tony, apparently absorbed in the game like the others who crowded near the table, passed muster. Parracini gave them neither a hard look nor a second glance. He strolled off in search of Brigitte.

There was a long, long silence between Tony and Georges.

At last it ended. Georges said, "I think the roof just fell in."

Tony had no reply. For once he was quite speechless. They began their leisurely walk back towards the other end of the hall.

"A drink?" suggested Georges as they neared the bar.

Tony shook his head. "We'll leave."

"Right now?"

"Right now." Tony led the way downstairs.

18

They came out of the Casino into the cool night air. The streets seemed more deserted than ever, although it was barely half-past nine. Tony halted for a moment, took a deep breath to steady himself. "God," he said, "what a fool I've been."

"We've all been," Georges reminded him. "And you," he added with pained frankness, "least of all." There was I, he thought, reporting back to Gerard earlier this evening, relaying Tony's apparent doubts; and there was Gerard, convinced that Tony might really be going off half-cocked about the Parracini debriefing in Genoa. Gerard's final comment had been acerbic. *Lawton not completely satisfied? Indeed. Or is he too intent on finding a quick solution for his Nealey problem?*

But Tony was in no mood for post-mortems. After that brief pause on the steps of the Casino, he had set a smart pace, cutting along the avenue towards their left, then taking the first road down to the sea. It was as dark and restless as his surge of emotions.

They crossed the front street to the promenade. Is this, wondered Georges, where we cool off? Yet after a brief stretch of salt air and lonely beaches, Tony plunged back into the town once more. Making sure that no one followed, Georges decided: that was obvious. But as well as that? They were still not far from the Casino; had been circling around it, in fact. If no one was interested in them—and Georges, in his own mind, was sure that no one was—then this was the time to take up position within safe view of the Casino's entrance. "We could keep an eye on Gorsky," Georges suggested, breaking the long silence. "We can sit in the car. I parked it not too far—"

Tony brushed that aside. "Not tonight." His emotions had subsided; jumbled thoughts were coming back into order. At least, he thought, we know the worst. We can start from there.

"Let him think he has won?" Even if that gave Gorsky a false sense of security, Georges still didn't like it.

"Why not?" Reappraisal, decided Tony: see how we stand; then act.

"We're missing a first-rate opportunity. We may never have a second chance to find out where he is holed up."

"And risk raising his suspicions still more?"

But Georges persisted, found good reasons to bolster his own impulse. "We didn't add to them tonight. We showed absolutely no interest in him at the Casino. Why shouldn't we have been there? We're tourists. And our visit to Shandon Villa was equally understandable. We haven't given Gorsky any reason to suspect—"

"Then we'll keep him unsuspecting for as long as possible." And that won't be too long, Tony thought. How much did he actually learn about my movements in New York, last

December? Or at New Jersey's Shandon, or in Washington itself? His voice sharpened. "Damn it, Georges, you are a hard man to persuade."

"That makes two of us."

"I'm telling you to forget Gorsky. Meanwhile."

"How can we? He's in charge of this operation."

"Not he. Think back to that scene at the table."

"I see," Georges said with a touch of sarcasm. It strengthened. "That's why Parracini was the one to make contact? Here I am, sir. Reporting for duty. Any new instructions?"

A matter of protocol? Tony repressed a smile. "He had no other choice. Where's your car?"

"Next street," said Georges stiffly, and led the way. But he was thinking back, as Tony had advised. True enough: Parracini had had no other choice than to make the first move: he had come out of the cinema earlier than expected; he hadn't had much time at his disposal—five or six minutes at most—before Brigitte would find him. "He's good," Georges admitted. "He's flexible. Decisive. Isn't fazed by any variant in a set plan. But that doesn't prove he's important enough to outrank Gorsky."

"Which of them had the last word?" Tony didn't wait for a reply, stepped into the car as if to close the argument.

Parracini—yes, Parracini. Administering a final piece of advice? Or instruction? "If this is true—" Georges began, and paused. The idea of Parracini's importance was still too shocking to be easily believable. What have we been protecting—Bill, Nicole, all of us? Keeping him happy, comfortable, worrying our brains out about his safety? Yes, the joke is on us, a very sour joke indeed… Georges got into the driver's seat, sat there, staring at the wheel. We haven't only been fooled: we'll become a laughing-stock when this news gets out. And Gerard, for one, may find his career—a good one, too—suddenly amputated. "If this is true," Georges repeated, but he was less doubtful now, "Nealey is here to run the Shandon Villa operation. Parracini is here—among other things—to supervise Nealey. And Gorsky, Executive Action department, is here to supply protection." Which meant that Shandon Villa must be of far greater importance in future KGB plans than either he or Tony had first guessed. "You know," he admitted frankly, "if you hadn't been so intent on Nealey, we would never have stumbled on all this. It's one hell of a situation."

Tony had been keeping a careful eye on the street, fore and aft. It seemed as safe as those they had passed through in the last ten minutes—no more than twenty people encountered: couples, homeward bound; an occasional singleton, self-absorbed; but no one dodging into a doorway, no one dogging their footsteps. He relaxed now, lit a cigarette, offered one to Georges. "It could be worse."

"That is what appalls me." Georges was remembering his discussion with Tony only that afternoon, about Parracini's future in a cosy career with NATO. "My good God," he said, "what have we escaped?"

A KGB agent in perfect place, thought Tony. "Let's get moving. Take the tunnel, head for the other side of town." I've had enough of this one. "Can you put me up for the night?"

"Of course." Georges manoeuvred the car out of its parking place. "We can always toss a coin to see who sleeps on the floor." His high spirits were returning with the thought of some action. There would be plenty to do before either of them stretched out to sleep. There would be a sense of decision, of accomplishing something important: the good feeling of being in the centre of things. His luck had been in today, and Emil's had been out, stuck as he was on board the *Sea Breeze*. That was the way it went: stretches of boredom, of patient duty. And then—suddenly, like tonight—the big chance. "We'll have to move fast, Tony. And Gerard could be a problem, so paralysed with shock that we could lose two good hours. Parracini has been his pet project, remember. How do you deal with that, I ask you?"

"That," said Tony, "is what I am trying to think about."

It was a gentle reminder to stop talking and leave Tony in peace. Georges grinned, said "Yes, sir," and concentrated on the rear-view mirror. No car was following.

The Casino, the shopping area, the public buildings and private houses all vanished behind them as they entered the tunnel and sped through the hill on which the Old Town stood. This was a short cut, the underpass that linked the two other sections of Menton, west and east. A strange way for a town to grow, thought Georges. First, the mass of medieval houses and churches packed together on a steep spine of rock. Then, centuries later, a spread of people to lower ground, with their houses and markets and churches clustering around the base of the hill on either side. Three towns, actually, with the most ancient of them still functioning—not a historical relic, but a place with a life of its own. Today he had settled in nicely *sous les toits de Menton*, and had imagined that he'd be part of the Old Town for a pleasant week. But now, it was possible he'd be out of there by tomorrow. Parracini had changed all plans.

They swept out of the tunnel, entering on the broad avenue

that followed the shore of Garavan Bay. The Old Town, dominating the harbour, rose up behind them. "The quick way up to my place," Georges said, pointing backwards.

Tony jerked round, but saw only a solid stretch of high-rising tenements.

"It's the street—a flight of steps, really—that lies about half-way along that row of shops and Italian restaurants."

"I'll find it."

"Are you sure? Perhaps we'd better make the climb together."

"Negative. We'll stick to our usual routine. Except that I'll follow you more closely than usual."

"We won't have far to go. My room is on the bottom layer of the Old Town. Lucky it isn't up on the pinnacle. And it faces the Mediterranean. I have a front-row seat to all this." He gestured with his right hand towards the dark in-curve of water edged by the continuous lights of promenade and avenue.

Another night, thought Tony, and I can admire the view. But now—his eyes followed the shoreline ahead of them and reached the new anchorage for yachts and cabin-cruisers. "That marina at the east end of the bay—wonder if it has boats for hire. Nice big boats with powerful engines."

"We've already got a boat. With a good engine."

Not good enough, not for what I'm thinking. "Let's go to your room." There was sudden urgency in Tony's voice. "Make the turn back at the next traffic light. I have to call Bill before we start sending any message."

"All right, all right." Georges took the next turn and headed back to the Old Town, travelling now along the waterfront apartments and hotels that had recently mushroomed on this side of the avenue. "Sorry about all this delay," he said too politely. It wasn't too much, he thought, only six or seven minutes altogether.

"I've been admiring your caution."

"I always take care when I'm approaching my place. It's the only base of operations we've got."

"I am still admiring your caution."

Georges's defensiveness ended in a laugh. He brought the car to a smooth halt, stopping short of the Old Town to leave them still about two hundred yards to cover on foot. The spot he had selected for parking was well calculated, too: the Renault had merged with a dozen cars that were drawn off the avenue, herded near a garden wall of one of the large apartment hotels. "Now for that damned walk," Georges said, eyeing it with distaste.

"I'll give you three minutes, and then follow."

"Remember—it's the first street you reach. Lies between the pizza palace and the beauty salon with yellow curtains. Forty-seven steps up, and you take the street on your right. I'll be waiting."

"Fine."

Georges had one last look around him before he stepped out of the Renault. "I wish this place wasn't so deserted at night. What we need is a good thick crowd for comfort."

"Next time we'll arrange our assignment for July."

Georges eased into a smile, started along the empty sidewalk.

I don't feel too happy about this either, thought Tony. Yet we've taken every precaution. There was some traffic—a few cars, an occasional taxi—but it was all fast moving. No car had drawn aside and parked. And no one was suddenly stepping out of a doorway to follow Georges. Tony's glance flickered to his watch. The three minutes were almost up. Now it was his turn to step on to that lonely sidewalk, singing the off-season blues.

As he approached the Old Town, he had a closer view of the harbour. The mole, its claw-like arm thrown around the anchorage, was well lighted. One or two people walking out there, he noted; and one or two people, land-side, on the promenade. The boats were hidden, but he could see rows and rows of masts, the long and the short, the slender and the thick, and those of the *Sea Breeze* riding peacefully among them. Yes, he thought, the *Sea Breeze* is another thing I don't feel too happy about. Gorsky will not only have her under surveillance, but he will find out that three of us arrived; and now only one is left aboard. He knows I'm at the *Hôtel Alexandre*. But Georges—where? He won't rest until he traces Georges's real address. He can sense its importance: why else did Georges keep it out of the police records? And he can easily discover that the *Sea Breeze* has been taking on supplies—more than necessary for three people who say they are sailing along the coast. And he may do exactly what I was tempted to do, at that marina on the other end of the bay. He may hire a cabin cruiser. Not a pleasing prospect for the *Sea Breeze* when she sails out of harbour tomorrow.

So we cancel our plan? Tony heaved a sigh of regret. It would have been so simple, a neat clean operation: get Parracini aboard the *Sea Breeze*, but instead of cruising—the original idea—sail direct to Nice, coax him on to a plane for Brussels. Using what as the incentive? An interview for that job in NATO Intelligence? Yes, he wouldn't refuse that invitation. So simple. Like all might-have-beens.

What else was there, to take its place? Convey Parracini to

Nice by car? He'd balk, most definitely. A secret meeting with two senior NATO officers on board the cruising *Sea Breeze*—that would seem logical enough: privacy and security combined. But a sudden switch to a car? He'd sense a trap. He'd never go of his own free will. Messy. A drugged man needs a stretcher and bearers to get him on to a plane. I'm no kidnapper, Tony thought, and shook his head.

Even a helicopter—there was a stretch of open ground near the marina at the other end of the bay—wouldn't serve our purpose. We'd need local permission, and how do we get that before eleven tomorrow morning? And again there is the unpleasant problem of carrying an unconscious man—no, Tony told himself sharply, that isn't the way you work. Just think harder, Lawton, will you?

Pizza advertisements, boldly printed and plastered all over a restaurant's window, shouted at him for attention. Beyond it, a small shop with its hair-dryers showing, and curtains that might look yellow by day, but now, under the electric lights, were the colour of porridge. And between the pizza and the porridge was tucked the street—a flight of stairs—that would lead him up into the Old Town. He began climbing.

It was a steep pull, the stone steps made swaybacked by centuries of clattering feet. On either side, no more than two arm-lengths apart, were the gable ends of houses, reaching high, cutting the night sky into a sliver. But the lights on the walls were evenly spaced, and adequate enough to keep a man from breaking a leg. Tony didn't have to fumble for his footing, grope his way. He could concentrate on moving as quickly and silently as possible. There were scattered windows above and around; sounds of muffled voices, of a radio muted behind shutters. And always, at his back, the night breeze that came funnelling up this narrow street from the sea.

Forty-seven steps, and he could turn, breathing heavily, muscles taut, into a slightly broader street. And flatter too, thank heaven. Three boys, chasing one another, jostled a young man and his girl out of a tight embrace. An older man, fisherman type, walked slowly. Tony kept on his way as if he too were *en route* home. He passed Georges leaning against a wall, heard him whisper, "Second entrance on your right, and all the way up."

Tony reached the top landing, sat down on the last step to wait for Georges. If there hadn't been so many neighbours behind the closed doors he had passed, he might have laughed out loud.

19

Georges had already drawn the curtains across his window and pulled the shade over the glass panels of the door that led on to the midget terrace, before he turned on the lights and let Tony enter his room.

It was of medium size and sparsely furnished: a heavy wooden table and two hard chairs, a narrow bed, a chest beside it with a radio on top, a small wardrobe, a scrap of rug. The paintwork was orange, the plaster walls covered with the work of a previous tenant—abstract murals in scarlet and purple. "Cheerful," Tony said, investigating a narrow door to find a tight squeeze of toilet and hand-basin. "And running water, too." There was a definite drip from the small overhead cistern.

"It may not be the Ritz, but it has a better view." Georges took off his jacket, hooked it on a peg at the door.

"And things to tempt the gourmet," said Tony, examining the contents of the wardrobe, which Georges had selected as his pantry.

"I think you could use some of that right now," Georges said. It was his only reference to Tony's inexplicable attack of laughter that had met his cautious arrival on the landing. Thank God, Tony had suppressed it. And there was nothing funny about all this—nothing.

"Business first. Where are your miracle-workers?"

Georges pointed to the radio beside his bed. "That's one. Didn't you have dinner before we met?" And he certainly hadn't had much lunch today, thought Georges worriedly. Hunger makes a man light-headed.

"Not quite."

"It's five past ten—"

"And time to call Emil."

There was nothing light-headed about that voice. Georges opened a drawer, picked out his transceiver, and made the call.

Tony took over. "Emil—this is serious. You may have some curious strangers wandering near the *Sea Breeze* tonight. How's the situation at present?"

"Normal," Emil's placid voice said. "A few people on the mole, one or two on the quay. And three fishermen practically next door, fixing something on their boat—been working hard on it."

"Since when?" Tony asked quickly.

"Since this afternoon."

"Then they're okay. Anyone you've noticed before eight o'clock tonight is probably all right too."

"So that's when the whistle was blown?"

"Around then. And look—if someone tries to board, don't be proud. Yell for those fishermen."

"If they are still here."

"They like a bottle of beer, don't they, after a stretch of work?"

"Invite them on board?"

"Why not? Give them a friendly hail, anyway. Let them know you're around. See you tomorrow."

"Sleepless," Emil said with a laugh.

"Who won't be?" Tony flipped off the connection, looked thoughtfully at the transceiver, balancing it in his hand before he laid it on the table. It was little bigger than a pack of cigarettes.

Georges said, "All right, Tony. I read you. I'll carry it next to my heart from now on. The truth is, I didn't expect any excitement on this assignment." Just a simple little tour of inspection, hadn't that been our idea when we came sailing into Menton this morning? Make certain that all was going well with Parracini? "*Quel con*," was Georges's final comment on that subject, as he fished out a neat object, disguised as a portable phonograph, from under the bed, along with an equally portable machine pretending to be a typewriter. He placed them on the table where he had already set out his versatile radio, some tapes, a pad, and pencils. "Any time," he told Tony, readying typewriter and phonograph for their proper functions. His entire equipment covered less than one-half of the table.

"Compact," said Tony. "The wonders of modern technology." Georges worked on. He was taut and angry and much too solemn. "No more aerials draped out of windows?"

"It runs on batteries." Georges was intent on the final adjustments. "Ready when you are."

"And no sending-keys? I don't even see you looped up in earphones?"

"That's all past tense. Nowadays we—" Georges checked his

reply and saved himself in time. He joined in Tony's smile. His voice eased. "What's the first message? To Gerard, I suppose." He looked at his watch, nodded his approval of the remarkably brief time it had taken to set up the preparations. "First, you run over the various points you want to make, then I can either tape or scramble—"

"First," said Tony, "I think we ought to get in touch with Bill. But by less exotic means." He picked up the telephone and dialled Bill's private number. He had to wait, impatience growing with each unanswered ring. "This call *is* necessary," he reassured Georges, who was watching him in dismay. "We must know where we stand, before we—" Bill's voice interrupted him.

"Already in bed?" Tony asked.

"No, no, I was in the next room watching television with Nicole. Sorry for the delay. Something new to report?"

"Nothing. Just wondering if they all got safely home from the movie."

"Early," Bill told him. "Brigitte couldn't take the air conditioning."

"What about Bernard? Is he around?"

"Playing chess with Parracini downstairs."

"I don't suppose—no, you couldn't."

"Couldn't what?"

"Tell Bernard to slip quietly down to the harbour. But that's impossible now."

"Oh, I don't know about that—"

"I said *quietly*, Bill. We don't want to alarm Parracini—or the others, either. It's nothing much, anyway. Just a feeling I have about the *Sea Breeze*. I don't like having only one man aboard tonight."

"Why?"

"This afternoon—" and keep the Casino and Gorsky out of this—"I saw evidence of the opposition."

Bill went into high alarm. "They're on the track? They've actually uncovered Parracini?"

"No, repeat no!" Just the opposite, Tony would have liked to say. Instead, he led into the question that had impelled him to call Bill. "And don't set Parracini into a panic about them. Shandon Villa is where the action is. Better say nothing to him. Keep his mind at ease—he has a big day ahead of him. When will you tell him that we've decided to have the meeting on board the *Sea Breeze*, and not at your place?"

"Oh, that's already done. Thought it better to break the news tonight, didn't want to spring it on him at the last moment."

"Tonight?"

"Just before dinner. We were having drinks, and—"

"I hope he wasn't unhappy about it."

"Far from it. It took him but a couple of minutes to see our point of view. I emphasised additional security."

So, thought Tony, Parracini needed only a few minutes to decide. No consultation necessary with anyone. He's the man in charge. No doubt left about that.

"Did I act out of turn?" Bill asked, puzzled by Tony's silence.

"Relax, relax. All that's bothering me is the *Sea Breeze*. She could use some of that additional security. If anything goes wrong with her tonight—" Tony left that idea hanging in the air.

Bill said slowly, "If you feel you need some extra support, I can get in touch with a couple of good men."

I knew it, I knew it: Bill wouldn't be here without some back-up, some kind of insurance, Tony thought. "How soon?"

"They're on stand-by notice today. I don't want to call them though, unless it's absolutely necessary. Is it?"

"With the opposition in town?"

"But not in connection with us, you said," Bill reminded him sharply. "What's their business here, do you know?"

"It was Chuck Kelso."

"That has nothing to do with us."

"I know, I know. But I'd still feel more comfortable with a couple of good men around."

"I'll call them." Bill wasn't too enthusiastic. He liked keeping his insurance well covered. "Where do you want them?"

"No need to go aboard—unless, of course, something breaks. Tell them to keep a close eye on the *Sea Breeze*. That's all."

"Okay," Bill was reassured. "We play it cool."

"All of us," Tony emphasised. And, for God's sake, don't disturb Parracini's sweet dreams, he thought as he rang off with a cheerful "See you—early tomorrow."

And that was that.

Georges, sitting with his feet up on the table, looked with undisguised impatience at his watch.

"I agree. It took far too long," Tony conceded. "It was like pulling teeth. But we did learn something important. Parracini was told about our *Sea Breeze* project before he went to the Casino."

"Then Gorsky knows!"

"He knows." Either this room is getting hotter or my blood-pressure is rising, thought Tony. He pulled off his jacket, dropped it on the bed.

Georges swore softly. "That alters everything." He shook his head in commiseration. "Too bad, Tony. It was a good plan."

"It still is. Sail straight to Nice; and then by air to Brussels.

Couldn't be simpler. Why, even the Nice airport is in the perfect spot for us—right at the water's edge." Tony added softly, "We really can't refuse an opportunity like that, now can we?"

"Drop the whole idea, Tony. We can't pull it off. Not now."

Tony said nothing at all.

"Gorsky will hire a cabin cruiser, and keep the *Sea Breeze* well within sight. The moment he sees we aren't having a leisurely cruise, he will send out a general alarm. We'll never get Parracini anywhere near Brussels. We won't even reach Nice—if Gorsky has a boat that can outrun the *Sea Breeze*— the best we can do in our motor sailer is ten knots. And his men will be heavily armed: he does nothing by half-measures. We'll have a couple of handguns, if that." Georges stared at Tony, his thoughts now back with the Gorsky file. "You know, if he couldn't board us, Gorsky would blow us all out of the water, Parracini included. He'd do that rather than let Parracini remain our prisoner. It's not the first time he has killed one of his own—for the sake of security."

Hands in pockets, Tony had been studying the equipment on the table. "Let's begin," he said, pulling the other chair into position opposite Georges. "But I want to know what to expect here. First, you tape my message, and then—"

"A waste of breath," Georges said. "You didn't listen. The plan is out, Tony. We need—"

"I listened. And you gave me a new idea. Always a pleasure working with you, Georges, my boy. Now, where were we?— Oh, yes. First, you tape the message; then you speed it up in transmission—turn it into a screeching background to harmless chit-chat. And at the receiving end, there's a tape-recorder to pick up the screech. Right?"

Georges nodded. *Tony always knows more than he pretends,* he reminded himself in surprise.

"And when the taped screech is played back and slowed down to the original recording speed, it becomes intelligible. Is that how we'll do it?"

"That's one way. But there's a new and quicker variation."

"Equally safe?"

"Safer. The latest in scrambling devices. Produces screeches that can be directly untangled as they arrive at the receiving end from any ordinary conversation."

"Simple and secure. I like that."

"Highly sophisticated and secure."

Tony's smile broadened as he pulled the writing-pad in front of him. "Contact Brussels." He began jotting down what needed to be said.

"Geneva, you mean. Gerard is there this week-end. He's working late in his office in case we have anything further to report. You really worried him this—"

"Brussels," repeated Tony. "Straight to the top, Georges. Where do you think our message will get some real response? Special Service Division? Attention Commander Hartwell?"

"If he can be reached."

"He can be. Did you think I picked his name out of a hat? He's in charge of night duty this week. Sleeps in his office, stalwart fellow. He's American, so we'll jolly him up with a starting signal he'll recognise: *Officer requires assistance.* Next comes *Urgent call for immediate help, highest priority.* And then we follow with this—" Tony pushed the pad over to Georges. "You'll compress it for coded transmission, but don't drop out any words or phrases such as *vital—necessity—threat of attack—officers' lives in extreme jeopardy.*" And that last phrase, thought Tony, might be no exaggeration.

Pencil in hand, Georges was already abbreviating Tony's notes as he read them back. They were concise enough, but slightly more dramatic than Georges himself would have risked. "High-ranking enemy agent under arrest, escorted by four NATO officers, will sail tomorrow, Saturday, on *Sea Breeze* maximum speed ten knots, departing Menton harbour eleven hours, arriving Nice around thirteen hours, weather permitting. Request immediate air transport to Brussels. Warning added: operation now seriously endangered by Soviet agents (Department V—Executive Action) known to be in possession of sailing information. *Sea Breeze* will be followed, intercepted. Real threat of attack. Officers' lives in extreme jeopardy. Require vital support. Necessity for immediate action. Most urgent request for—"

Georges looked up, his pencil poised in mid-air. "For a naval vessel?"

"A very small one."

"But—"

"How many navies does NATO have?"

Georges laughed, finished the job of abbreviation, began coding. "But why navy, at all?" he asked as he completed the message for transmission. "NATO could find us a medium-sized cabin cruiser. There must be hundreds of them all along this coast."

"If Hartwell can arrange for it, I'd settle for that. In fact—" Tony had an additional idea, and smiled—"I'd like both. A cabin cruiser, not too big to dock in Menton harbour beside the *Sea Breeze*, a navy cutter out in the bay, waiting, ready to escort. Tell Hartwell that too. From me."

"You know him?"

"My old and good friend."

"Even so, you're asking too much."

"And making sure we get at least half of what we need." Tony pushed his chair away from the table, stretched his back muscles, and rose. "Sign off with one last nudge: we are here all through the night, awaiting instructions and final arrangements."

"You're as confident as that?" Georges asked. But there was a renewed assurance in his own voice, an added zest when he made contact and could begin transmitting.

Confident? Tony had wondered, walking aimlessly around the room. If hopes were dupes, fears may be liars. Certainly, doubts never won any arguments, and we'll get plenty of that. But I'm damned if Gorsky is going to blow any of us out of the water, and then report that the *Sea Breeze*'s engine must have exploded. Explosion? Another possibility to take into account... But later, Tony decided, deal with that later. Now, there was a message for Gerard to be whipped into shape.

Difficult, this one. Gerard would have no super-sophisticated gadgets in a small room in Geneva: nothing as costly as the newest equipment available in Brussels. It wasn't only security that was the problem. Gerard was a problem in himself. First, there would be shock, disbelief. But once he was convinced, he'd start sending messages to prepare the two officers who were arriving in Nice tomorrow morning. The name of Parracini would be loose in the air, ready to be picked up by monitors. Or even KGB ears—it only needed a dutiful little secretary or a bugged telephone in Gerard's office to blow everything wide open. Gorsky would warn Parracini to clear out, and Parracini would be into Italy tomorrow morning before Bill had poured his first cup of coffee.

So, Tony thought as he sat down on the bed, we talk with Gerard, make him realise we're faced with a major problem, and say nothing about Parracini. Not even a circumlocution like *high-ranking enemy agent*. Nothing. Yet we can't keep Gerard out of this. Tempting, but not possible. How do we warn him?

Tie loosened, belt unbuckled, Tony stretched out on the thin mattress. How? he asked the ceiling.

He felt a tug at his arm and was instantly awake.

Georges was saying, "Time we called Geneva. Sorry to do this, you were sleeping so deeply that I—"

"Just drifting in and out." Tony swung his legs on to the floor. Exhaustion had left him: he felt as clear-eyed and brisk as if he had been asleep for several hours, but his watch told him it was barely twenty minutes since he had stretched out on the bed. "What about Brussels?"

"Completed. Don't worry, they received the message. Now, we wait."

"And what will we get—pie all over our faces?"

We'll get worse than that, thought Georges, if we have miscalculated Gorsky's possible reactions. What if it could be all plain sailing to Nice, and no interference? Hastily he put that thought out of his mind. "By the way, I expanded that reference to Department V—Executive Action. Just a little. A neat insert, I thought. Hope you don't object."

"Too late, anyway. What did you add?"

"Gorsky's file number. Okay?"

"Wish I had thought of it," Tony admitted, walking over to the table, looking at the equipment, wondering if a telephone call using voice code might not be the quickest way to contact Gerard. He noted that Georges hadn't only been busy expanding references, but had found a spare minute to dump a small hunk of boiled ham, some Brie and Chèvre cheeses, along with a loaf of bread and a bottle of wine, on the free end of the table. "Is Gerard as fascinated by Gorsky as you are?"

"More so. And with good reason."

"What, for instance?"

Georges hesitated.

"Come on, come on. This info could help us now."

"Gerard had a Soviet defector from Disinformation three years ago—sequestered him in a safe-house, twenty-four-hour guard. But Gorsky got at him, through one of the kitchen staff. The defector died, and two of our men with him. Food poisoning."

"What was his code name in Gerard's case-book?"

"That's Gerard's private property. It wasn't even listed—"

"All the better. Less chance of its being recognised by outside ears. Our talk with Gerard could be monitored if we use the telephone. You know that."

Georges nodded. For at least a year, Soviet Intelligence had been able to intercept and record telephone calls in all foreign countries, not only between government officials but between private citizens. Computerised scanners could monitor and separate the microwave frequencies. Fixed antennae on the roofs of Soviet embassies were picking up signals between foreign relay stations—even signals beamed to American communication satellites. "They've been using our technology," Georges burst out, suddenly as much American as he was French. "That's how our telephone call to Geneva could be monitored—by Telstar! Ironic, isn't it?"

Tony said thoughtfully, "Now wouldn't it be nice to cause a hiccup or two in those busy little Soviet computers?" He paused. "What was the code name Gerard gave to his dead defector?"

"Hector."

The Trojan hero, dragged around by his heels at the tail-end of Achilles's chariot... "Well," said Tony, "do we use the telephone? Or have you a better idea of how to contact Gerard?"

"Yes. But he will want to talk with you. And that could tie up our transmitter for the next hour." Further explanations requested, counter-suggestions—"No," said Georges, "we've got to keep our lines of communication open with Brussels."

"Then we haven't any choice, have we?"

"We could always use the old-time scrambler for telephone conversations. That might help."

"What would, nowadays? Twinkle, twinkle satellite, shining in the sky so bright, what d'you hear up there tonight?" That at least brought a small smile to Georges's worried face. "All right," Tony went on, "get Gerard on the line. You speak first, soften him up with a few friendly phrases. He likes you." And the sober truth is that neither Gerard nor I have ever liked each other. We are two Englishmen with clashing personalities, which can make for disagreeable sounds. Remember, Tony warned himself as Georges at last handed him the telephone, don't let Gerard's bloody bullheadedness get one rise out of you. Sweetness and light and firm persuasion. And keep it brief.

* * *

And brief it was, four minutes of talk with Tony in control most of the way. For once, Gerard gave little argument: perhaps the initial shock was so great that its tremors lasted through the remainder of the conversation.

Tony plunged right in with, "Bad news about the condominium you are planning to build here. Serious difficulties have developed with the construction plans; a real crisis, in fact, that needs your personal attention. I know you were sending your two architects to consult the builders, but you ought to be here yourself. Why not fly down with them? We'll meet all three of you, and we can go over the blue-prints without delay. I'd suggest an hour earlier than previously arranged—we have a lot to discuss about building specifications. They must be met— and that means you should oversee the necessary changes in the blue-prints. A brief visit should be enough, but your presence is imperative. We need your guiding hand—just to ensure that your special project goes smoothly and agreeably."

"The blue-prints were excellent. They met all building specifications. Who's objecting to them?"

"One of your rivals in real estate. He has an eye on your property. An aggressive type. The Achilles complex, you might call it. Remember Achilles? He was the fellow who killed poor old Hector and dragged his corpse around the walls of Troy."

"I've read my Homer," was Gerard's icy reply.

"And so you have. Stupid of me to forget. Three years ago— was it? Yes, three years ago you used to have a passionate interest in the Trojan heroes."

There was a short but painful silence. "Achilles is actually in—"

"Intolerable, at times," Tony broke in, blotting out any mention of Menton. "I agree. A memorable character, though: not easily dismissed. Stays in mind, doesn't he?"

"Yes," said Gerard. He began to recover. "I'll make arrangements to join you."

"Good. And you'll inform the others about the time of arrival?"

"They won't like it. It means a very early start."

"A proper nuisance," Tony commiserated, and gave Georges, listening-in with an earphone, a slow and solemn wink. He rang off abruptly before any other question about Achilles might come blundering forth.

"Okay?" he asked Georges.

"Not for me," Georges smiled. "Gerard won't like me giving away the name of Hector—or 'three years ago', either."

"How else could we have warned him that Gorsky is here?"

"But not one word about Parracini's true identity? You could have disguised it, meshed it in with your reference to Gerard's special project."

"Sure, I could have said his pet project had changed shape, got twisted, had an ugly face, turned into a monster to haunt his dreams."

"Don't you trust Gerard?" Georges asked bluntly.

"That isn't the point. If I had told him the truth about Parracini, how do you think he would have behaved? Kept quiet? No. He'd now be sending messages, sounding the alarm, putting his department on red alert—other departments, too. He'd have started some action. And coopered ours. Look, I'm hungry." Tony settled himself at the table, checked the St Emilion label. "Not a bad year," he said, and began breaking bread.

* * *

They made a good supper. "It will help keep us awake," Tony suggested, serving a second portion of Brie along with a large slice of Chèvre—the ham already sliced to the bone, the St Emilion at its last glass. There hadn't been much talk during the meal. But even as it ended and Georges lit a cigarette, his silence continued. "My voluble French friend," said Tony, relaxed and expansive, "what's worrying you now?"

"Gerard. Do I meet him at Nice airport tomorrow?"

"You meet all three, and give them the full report as you drive them to the Menton dock. You've got all the facts. I don't need to be there. I'd like to stay near the harbour."

"I wish you had trusted Gerard more. He's no fool."

"Not always."

Georges said sharply, "It *was* a good debriefing in Genoa. Gerard handled Parracini well. Nothing slipshod, I assure you."

"I believe you."

Georges tried some diplomacy. "If it hadn't been for you, Tony, we'd still be accepting Parracini at face value. I know that. He'd even be on his way to a post in Gerard's department. But—"

"But nothing! How could he have been accepted in Genoa? *That's* the first question to ask."

"He came guaranteed all the way. Made his first contact with us in Istanbul. He knew the address of our agent there, gave all the right identification signals. That *was* Palladin who reached Turkey."

Was it? Tony wondered. He said, "How long was he in Istanbul?"

"Several days. Had to get passport and documents, clothes, money—all that."

And in Istanbul, too, he was given the right recognition signals for his next contact in Lesbos, passed on from agent to agent, each giving him the next name to contact, the next signal to use. *Guaranteed all the way*—beginning with our agent in Istanbul who had accepted him as authentic. Tony said slowly, "Didn't any of you in Genoa know him personally? Was there no one who had been in Moscow and could identify him?"

"Palladin was a careful character. Didn't meet foreigners, avoided all contacts with the West. How do you think he stayed safe for twelve years?"

"There must be someone in NATO Intelligence who saw him in Moscow, knew him as Palladin."

"Palladin wasn't his real name. A cautious type, I told you."

"Even so—there must be someone who could have identified him. What about our agents who recruited him twelve years ago?"

"He recruited himself—as his private protest about the renewed campaign against Russian intellectuals. He volunteered, using a Polish journalist to contact a NATO agent who was briefly in Moscow. He wasn't really taken seriously at first, but the information he started sending—using his own methods to get it out to us—was of excellent quality."

"Where's the Polish journalist now?"

"Dead."

"Where's that NATO agent?"

"Retired. In London. He was hospitalised over Christmas— badly smashed up in a traffic accident. So he couldn't attend the debriefing in Genoa."

"Such a convenient and well-timed accident," Tony murmured. "What did they use to run him down—a truck?"

Georges let that pass. "It seemed merely a piece of bad luck at the time," was his only comment. "And now, of course, even if the old boy came out here on his crutches—well, we've seen how Parracini has changed his appearance. Right under our eyes, too. Ironic touch, isn't it?"

Tony had risen and was moving over to the balcony door. "I could wish the irony wasn't always turned against us these days. Time to start dealing out some of it, ourselves. Switch off that light, will you, Georges?" As the room darkened, Tony prepared to step on to the balcony. "Coming?" he asked.

"No, I'll stay here and watch for a radio signal. What's troubling you now? The *Sea Breeze* again?"

Tony closed the door gently behind him. Yes, the *Sea Breeze*. And Palladin's arrival in Istanbul, too. Or had Palladin actually arrived there? He could have been trailed to Odessa—taken into custody and questioned under torture. A substitution wouldn't be too difficult: find a KGB officer who worked in Palladin's department and knew the same files. He only needed to be Palladin's approximate age—and possibly close to his height too, in case someone out in the West recalled that Palladin was of medium size. (Colouring could be faked or changed. Heights were always the give-away.) Facial differences wouldn't matter: it was the impersonator's photograph and general description that would appear on the new Palladin travel documents. Odessa... Yes, that could be the place. There had been a delay there, before the next step had been made to Istanbul. And the man who was to replace Palladin could have increased that delay. He didn't need to make a tortuous journey from Odessa to Istanbul; he could have flown to Turkey direct, at the last moment, giving him that extra time he needed to question Palladin. And Palladin himself? If not dead then, certainly by this time.

Tony stared down at the harbour and its protecting walls. All was silent, all was at peace. Within the giant horseshoe of black water, white hulls floated side by side, gently, easily. Neatly-spaced lights, like hard bright nailheads, studded the edge of land, secured it from the dark bay. The sea was gentle; small ripples, glinting even and constant under the gibbous moon, stretched to the dark rim of the horizon. The stars were brilliant, barely veiled by the thin clouds teased over the night sky. Silent and peaceful, Tony thought again. He gave a long last glance at the *Sea Breeze* before he stepped back into the warm room.

"All quiet out there?" Georges asked, as he switched on all the lights again. "No signal, so far, on my receiver."

"If we have to use the *Sea Breeze* tomorrow—"

"Better wait for Brussels's answer before you start thinking about that."

"Tomorrow," repeated Tony, "we'll have Emil check under the water-line."

"What?"

Tony saw once more the quiet line of boats, all neatly moored, dark waters lapping at their sides. We aren't the only team around with an experienced underwater swimmer, he thought. He said, his smile self-deprecating, "I keep thinking of an explosion set off by remote control. Don't look at me like that, Georges; it was you who gave me the idea to start with. When do you think we might hear from Brussels?"

"It's barely midnight. And the longer we have to wait for an answer, the better. A flat refusal comes back in no time at all."

"Midnight?" Tony asked, suddenly remembering Tom Kelso. "Damnation." He reached for the telephone, dialled from memory. No answer. "Georges, look up the local directory— under Maurice Michel. I must have got the number wrong." But the telephone-book listed the same number he had dialled. He tried again, more slowly. And still there was no answer. He waited for the space of twenty rings before putting down the receiver. "I don't like this," he said.

"They're asleep. Or perhaps they turned the 'phone off."

"Tom said he'd be awake to take my call—whenever it came."

"They may have gone for a late-night stroll."

"I don't like it," Tony said. He held out his hand. "The car keys, Georges." He was pulling on his jacket as he moved towards the door. "Not alone," Georges warned him.

"How else?" Tony pointed to the electronic gear on the table. "You keep your ear on that."

"And if questions come in?"

"We don't budge from our requests. I'll stay in touch with you. Have you a spare transceiver?"

Georges produced it from a drawer, along with a small automatic. "For reassurance," he said with a grin, knowing Tony's objections to firearms.

Tony didn't argue. He slipped the pistol into his belt. With a parting nod, he closed the door carefully behind him.

20

The house lay in darkness. Tom Kelso drew up beside the deep shadow of the orange-trees, stepped out of the Fiat, and opened its trunk for Chuck's suitcase. His earlier emotions, a paralysing mixture of grief and rage, had left him. The visit to the Casino and the brief talk with Tony Lawton had actually been good for him: pain had been cauterised, mind braced. He could look at the facts, as far as he knew them, and see the shape of things that had to be done.

Thea had carried out his final instructions almost too well. Not only had she drawn curtains and closed shutters and locked doors both front and back; she had also bolted them, so that his keys were useless. He returned to the kitchen entrance— the one they generally used, near their parking space—and knocked hard. Perhaps she was asleep upstairs, and he'd have to go round to the side of the house and throw pebbles up at the bedroom window. He knocked again, called her name, had a moment of real fear—his emotions weren't so deadened after all, he admitted—before he heard her voice answering. Fear subsided as quickly as it had risen. As he waited for her to open the door, he looked around him at the sleeping hillside. Down by the nursery, lights glinted cheerfully from the close group of three small cottages where Auguste and his two married sons lived. Lights, too, from the houses scattered up and down the Roquebrune road. And brighter by far was the rising moon, almost full, silvering the open ground, blackening the shadows of trees and bushes. Nothing stirred. Even traffic sounds were thinned and muted. Peaceful and quiet and reassuring. The door opened, and he could take Thea in his arms and hold her.

"Gardenia," he said, kissing her neck. "So you were having a bath. I was beginning to think I'd need a battering-ram to get in here." He lifted Chuck's suitcase across the threshold, closed and locked the door behind him.

Relief spread over Dorothea's face as she heard him sound so normal. She matched her mood to his. "I heard the car, but I had to dry myself and get some clothes on—"

"And that isn't warm enough, either," he told her. She had only a thin wool dressing-gown, belted and neat, over silk pyjamas.

"I'll be all right." And her outfit was practical, chosen, in spite of haste to get downstairs, to let her cook something for Tom's supper. Besides, with all those windows and doors closed—

"Not warm enough," he repeated, "once you've cooled off from your bath." Her face was flushed to a bright rose, her hair was pinned up with damp tendrils curling over her brow and at the nape of her neck, her smile delighted with his concern but totally disbelieving. She was fastening a checkered apron around her waist, getting eggs and parsley out of the refrigerator. "I'm really not hungry, Thea," he said gently. "And I've some work to do."

"No trouble—and no time at all." She glanced at the suitcase in his hand. Was that the work he had mentioned? "I'll have an omelette ready in five minutes. Why don't you wash and have a drink?"

He nodded, dropping the suitcase on a kitchen chair before he went into the pantry and poured himself a single Scotch. That was something, he thought, a gesture of trust—the first time Thea had suggested a drink in the last five or six weeks. He went to wash in the study's small bathroom, took off jacket and tie, replaced them with a sweater, listening to the clank of a pan on the stove and the sound of eggs being beaten. The smell of the omelette cooking in butter, and coffee beginning to percolate, spread through the house. Appetising, he had to admit as he returned to the kitchen. And a normal scene, with Thea at the stove gently shaking the heavy pan, her face intent as she judged the omelette's consistency. Now she was snipping the parsley into its centre, working deftly. Tom put out the mats on the kitchen table, napkins and forks, resisted a quick visit to the pantry for another drink. "I'm hungrier than I thought," he told her as she folded the omelette, prepared to slip it on to a plate. We've stepped back into our own lives, he thought—except for the closed doors and windows, except for the suitcase lying on the chair.

Thea had guessed something of his thoughts. "Must we keep everything locked up tight?" she asked as she joined him at the table, with a triumphant omelette, oval and golden, green-flecked with parsley, firm on the outside—slightly *bavant* within.

"It's cosier," he said, evading the true explanation. "Come

on, darling, share it with me. You must be hungry too."

"Tony's idea, I suppose," she said, discarding the apron, still thinking of closed windows and locked doors. "But isn't he being over-anxious? Poor Tony... I suppose that's his way of life—an obsession with danger." She shook her head in amused disagreement, a lock of hair escaping further over her brow. "We had a telephone call from New York—Brad Gillon—he had just heard." And as Tom dropped his fork and was about to rise, she added quickly, "Brad will call again as soon as he gets home from the office. That should be around eleven o'clock our time. I told him you'd surely be back from Menton by then. It's only half-past nine now. So we can eat in peace. What about a mild Camembert to follow—and some Châteauneuf du Pape? Then fruit and coffee, and you can tell me what happened down in Menton."

"Feed the brute?" Tom asked, but he was actually smiling. He felt better, much better. Nerve-ends were being smoothed down. "I'll start telling you right now." So he began a full account of his visit to the town.

Dorothea listened in silence. As she rose to clear the table, she said, "You must look through Chuck's suitcase tonight? Oh, really—" she frowned angrily as she stacked dishes into the washer—"Tony is impossible." Hadn't he any imagination, any sensitivity? "Why all this rush? Couldn't he have left us alone—"

"I'd like to know myself, just why Rick Nealey wanted to get hold of that suitcase," Tom reminded her. "I must search through it. No way to avoid it, Thea."

"Then let me help," she suggested, glancing worriedly at Tom. He sounded fully in control, but—even with food and wine relaxing him—his face was haggard and drawn as he lifted the suitcase and heaved it on to the table. He opened it, looked down at the neatly-packed contents, and hesitated. Slowly, he picked out a small book and two manila envelopes.

"I'll look through the clothes, if you like. The diary—"

"It isn't a diary. Just addresses and engagements." But there were some pages at the back that were headed *Memoranda*, partly filled by very small writing, close-packed, words abbreviated. "Expenses," was Tom's first judgment. "Chuck always kept a close account of what he spent in restaurants and theatres and—" He stopped short. There were other items, too, and a few notes. "I'll need some time to decipher all this. Let's move into the living-room."

"Decipher? Is it in code?" Dorothea asked as she turned off the kitchen lights, checked the door's lock and bolt. Tom was already carrying the suitcase through the pantry. He had it open again, placed on one of the couches to let her more easily examine the clothes, before she reached him.

"No," he answered, as he took the address-book and envelopes over to the writing-table in the corner of the room. "Not code. Just abbreviations—an old habit of Chuck's. He used to put as much news on a postcard as most people could get into a couple of pages." He sat down, turned on the small light at his elbow, and began reading.

Dorothea looked down at the opened suitcase. She shivered, and then forced herself to start unpacking the dead man's clothes. Unfold, shake, search every pocket, she told herself. It would be a heart-wrenching job. Chuck had crowded a lot into his suitcase, ready for his winter vacation: ski pants and jacket, turtleneck wool sweaters. The only touch of formality was a navy blue blazer, grey flannels, dress loafers, and a white shirt and three ties—for special evenings, presumably. Or perhaps as a concession to Menton, if his stay had lasted a full week-end.

The police, she thought as she unfolded the blazer, had been as expert in packing as Chuck. Everything looked as though it hadn't been touched since he had filled his suitcase to the brim back in New York. Perhaps the police had only made a cursory examination of the clothes, like a Customs officer when nothing roused his suspicions. Why should they bother with clothes, anyway? They were what they seemed: the usual belongings of a young man who had been planning a holiday and not a suicide.

There's nothing here, she decided, finding only a folded handkerchief in one of the blazer's outside pockets. Inside, there was a slit pocket without one bulge showing in the silk lining. Nothing, she thought again, but dutifully searched inside the slit. Her fingers touched something light and thin, and drew out a folded sheet of airmail paper.

She opened it, and found a half page of typing: a letter, dated the twenty-sixth of February, to Paul Krantz, Shandon House, Appleton, NJ. Across its top left-hand corner were the words *Copy to Tom*. And at the bottom of the page, a hurried postscript, in pencil, with today's date—the twenty-eighth of February: "Tom—I'll hand this to you as I leave this evening. Didn't want to discuss it directly until you had time to read, digest, and think it over. The original letter is signed, sealed, ready to mail—if Nealey doesn't accept my first alternative. He began by denying everything this morning, then ended— after we had a bitter argument which I won—by a tentative admission of guilt, saying he needed time to consider, etc., etc. I have given him twenty-four hours to resign from Shandon

Villa. If he does, then I needn't send the letter to Krantz, and you can destroy your copy. If he doesn't, I'll see you before I leave for Gstaad. Any improvements to suggest on what I've written? As ever, Chuck."

"Tom!" Dorothea called across the room. "I've found something. In the blazer pocket. A letter to Shandon House, telling them about the NATO—"

"Mentioning Rick Nealey?" Tom had risen, the address-book and a newspaper clipping in his hand. Quickly he reached her, seized the typed sheet, and scanned it. Yes, there it was, brief and neat in two decisive sentences: Heinrich Nealey was the only person who knew about Chuck's possession of the entire NATO Memorandum; Heinrich Nealey was the only person who had access to the second and third sections of the memorandum, on the night of the twenty-third of November 1974.

As for the rest of the letter, equally concise, it began with Chuck's admission of responsibility for the removal of the memorandum from Shandon House. It ended with Chuck's resignation from the Institute, together with the statement that he had acted out of conscience and with the belief—which he still held—that the American public had the right to know the full contents of the first part of the NATO Memorandum.

Tom read the postscript again. And again. At last he said, "Chuck never had a chance, had he? He didn't even realise that Nealey was a trained foreign agent—probably thought of him as an American who had been sidetracked into treason. Why else—" Tom looked challengingly at Thea—"did Chuck give him twenty-four hours, why delay in sending the letter when he wrote it on Wednesday?"

Because, she thought unhappily, Chuck was hoping he could

avoid mailing the letter. "Perhaps," she said, "he still couldn't believe Rick Nealey had—" quickly she cancelled the word *duped* and found a kinder substitute—"betrayed him. Not until he met Nealey face to face."

"But Chuck *knew*, before he met Nealey, that he had been tricked." Tom gave her the small newspaper clipping. "I found this tucked between two of the memo pages. It's from the *Washington Post*, published last Tuesday. One of those 'now it can be revealed' items."

It was a brief report by one of the more sensational, but accurate, columnists, that the NATO Memorandum, part of which had been published by a prominent newspaper as a public service on the third of December 1974, had been delivered in its entirety to Soviet authorities. A reliable source at the Pentagon admitted that damage to Allied Intelligence agencies had been severe, and "in several cases, disastrous to agents in the field."

"Yes," Tom repeated, "he knew he had been tricked. Brad Gillon had told him, and he didn't want to believe it. And then this appeared on Tuesday." Tom put the newspaper clipping back inside Chuck's address-book. "By Wednesday Chuck was ready to admit he had been duped. Duped. No other word for it. So he wrote the letter to Paul Krantz, changed his travel plans, came to Menton to confront Nealey—" Tom shook his head. "Good God, what a mess poor old Chuck made of everything! And always so sure he was right. Always so confident he could handle—" He broke off, turned away, said, "Chuck was out of his league."

Dorothea began packing the last clothes back into place. "First alternative," she said reflectively. "What did he mean by that? It was in the postscript, remember?"

317

As if I'll ever forget that postscript, Tom thought. Chuck, still vacillating, trying to show he could be tough. And would he have handed me that letter to Krantz if Nealey had come to him this afternoon, accepted his terms? No, possibly not. Chuck would have taken the letter out of the blazer pocket, destroyed it, persuaded himself there was no longer any need to disturb me about it. And our talk together would have been nothing but evasions and reassurances.

"Tom—" Dorothea was saying, her eyes wide with anxiety as they studied his face.

"'If Nealey doesn't accept my first alternative,'" Tom quoted back exactly. "It's a reference to some jottings he made as a memo in his engagement diary. Talking points with Nealey, I suppose. He was nervous—" The telephone rang. "Here, take it," Tom said, giving her the little diary, pointing to the page, and hurrying to answer the call in his study.

Dorothea looked at the few lines of small writing. *Alternatives:* either N. *resigns, removes self from Shandon Villa or any govt. or official posts,* or I *send letter to Krantz at Shandon House, including statements for necessary authorities.*

Chuck was always hoping, Dorothea thought, that his ex-friend Nealey would accept the facts, disappear gracefully, cause no more trouble for anyone. And spare Chuck himself the necessity of resigning, of publicly admitting— Oh, Chuck, she told him in despair, why didn't you go to Paul Krantz as soon as Brad Gillon had talked with you? Why did you believe a newspaper columnist more quickly than a friend of your brother's? Everything would have been over by this time: Nealey dealt with, and you—yes, I know you'd have lost your job, but you'd still be alive.

Tom came back into the room. "That was Brad. Wanted to fly over here and help in any way. But I told him to stay in New York. There's a job for him to do there—Tony's idea, actually—concentrating on Nealey's New York girl-friend and the 'phone calls made from her apartment. Nealey may just have slipped up there. I don't think there's much of a chance, though. He's a wary devil. Still, sometimes they make mistakes. And every little—"

"But haven't we got enough on Rick Nealey now?"

Tom took Chuck's engagement diary from her, folded the letter to Krantz around it, placed them together behind the clock on the mantelpiece. "Your hands feel like ice," he was saying worriedly. "Better get upstairs and put some warm clothes on. Or why not go to bed? I'll join you as soon as Tony calls."

"I couldn't sleep."

"Then find a sweater and I'll light the fire." He began striking matches.

Dorothea moved towards the hall. It would take more than a fire and a warm sweater to get this chill out of her heart, she thought. "But we *do* have proof now, don't we?"

"About Nealey?" Tom watched the first flames curl round the twists of paper, catch the kindling. "We have nothing that Tony and Brad didn't already know. There's no proof that Nealey *is* a KGB agent. Not a shred of hard evidence." He remembered Tony's frustration this afternoon. Now he was swallowing the same bitter brew.

"You mean," said Dorothea, scandalised, angry, "he could get away with all this?"

"Darling, get upstairs and put some sensible clothing on your frozen back."

"It isn't right, it isn't just—"

"It seldom is," said Tom. "Upstairs, Thea!"

When she came down again, dressed in wool pants and heavy sweater, the logs were flaring, two glasses of brandy had been poured, and the room was darkened except for one small table-lamp.

"Where's the suitcase?" she asked.

"In the hall closet." And let's not talk about it, Tom's voice seemed to say. He drew her down beside him on the couch and handed her a brandy. "We'll soon get you warm, my girl. I was beginning to think you had gone to bed after all." He tightened his arm around her shoulders, drawing her close, tried to relax and forget problems and worries in the gentle peace of this green and gold room. But he kept thinking about the information from Brad Gillon which he'd pass on to Tony when his call came through. A small item—and not worth mentioning to Thea, building up her expectations only to have them choked by more disappointment. But the small item was interesting enough to keep his mind harking back to Brad's voice. "And tell Tony that the long job of examining the pages of the memorandum is almost complete. There was a jumble of fingerprints, but the experts have managed to isolate a few examples. They've got a couple—thumb and forefinger, at the top corner of two pages in section three of the memorandum—which they haven't identified as yet." As yet... But the fingerprints could belong to Chuck, and that would land us right back at the beginning. "What delayed you upstairs anyway?" Eleven forty on the mantelpiece clock. Tony's call should be coming through soon.

"I just had to tidy up the bathroom—I left it in such a mess when I heard the car returning."

"You didn't open that damned window to air the place, did you?"

She almost had, and then remembered Tom's warnings and left it closed. The window was one of Solange Michel's brilliant notions. It was placed along the back of the tub, giving a daytime view of the hillside framed by the wisteria outside that climbed up and around to reach the overhang of roof. For modesty's sake, when darkness came and the bathroom lights were on, the heavy silk shower-curtains could be drawn all around the tub, encasing it like a four-poster bed. "Too much trouble," she admitted. To reach the window, she would have had to step into the bath and get all those heavy folds of curtain drawn back. "I thought this wasn't the night to risk a displaced vertebra. When do you expect Tony's call? Do you think he'll have any further news?"

"I don't know." He cut off any speculations and rising hope on that subject by predicting, "Someone's going to break their neck in that tub."

"But it has the most beautiful view. You can sit in it and look out at—"

"Bulldozers and condominiums?"

Solange had never envisioned that. Dorothea laughed, and said, "Poor Solange."

"Poor Maurice. How the hell does he stand all her high-falutin ideas?" It was good to hear that soft laugh, Tom thought: she's relaxed and warm and she'll even sleep tonight, once Tony calls and we get upstairs. (No place for a telephone in any bedroom, had been another of Solange's ardent beliefs.) "But the effect *is* attractive, Tom," Dorothea said, coming to Solange's defence.

321

"Give me comfort, any old—" Tom stopped short, his body stiffening. "What was that?"

Dorothea felt a current of cold air circle around her bare ankles. "That," she said, dropping her voice, "could have been my omelette pan. I left it in the sink and someone has just put his foot in it."

"Coming through the window?"

"It's open. I can feel a draught—"

Tom put a finger across her lips, set down his brandy glass, drew her quietly to her feet. He picked up a poker. "Leave by the terrace, get down to the nursery and waken Auguste. Tell him to call the police."

"Not Tony?"

"Don't know his number. Quick!" He was listening intently as he talked. Yes, a second sound, muffled but stumbling, came from the direction of the kitchen. He pushed her towards the French windows.

"And you?"

"Get the police," he urged.

She pulled aside the long curtains just enough to let her open a window and step outside. A hand came out of the darkness, gripped her shoulder, and threw her back across the threshold. She half-fell, regained her balance, and then—as the man followed her into the room—retreated in panic towards Tom.

The man was saying, "No violence, monsieur. One movement from you, and my men will shoot both of you."

And Tom, half-way to the window, the poker raised, froze in his tracks as he glanced back over his shoulder and saw, at the doorway, two other men with pistols drawn. Dorothea reached him, stood close beside him. He heard her quick intake of breath as she looked in horror at the two men now advancing into the room. Black ski-masks over hair and face, gashes of white skin at eyes and mouth; black coverall suits, tight over lean bodies; black gloves and rubber-soled shoes: completely anonymous, and because of that, more menacing. He caught her hand, gave it a reassuring grip, thought a hundred wild thoughts, and felt the despair of total helplessness.

21

For a long minute, nothing moved. The two black figures in their grotesque masks had halted, paying no attention to Dorothea or Tom. Their white slits of eyes were on the man who had stepped inside the French window. He preferred the shadows. Certainly he wasn't risking one step nearer the light of the table-lamp beside the couch, although his identity was disguised by a nondescript dark coat, a black silk scarf loosely covering his chin and mouth, and a hat that was pulled well down over his brow. About my height, almost six feet, Tom noted; but of heavier build—powerful shoulders. Even the voice, distorted by the scarf, will be hard to recognise again. But he's the boss, there's no doubt about that. Those two others are waiting for their orders. He will make the decisions.

And he did. "Begin!" he was saying in French. "You upstairs." He nodded to the taller of his two subordinates. To the other, "You—this floor!" He drew a revolver from his coat-pocket, folded his arms, kept his aim directed at Tom and Dorothea.

"Chuck's case?" Dorothea asked Tom softly as she turned her head away from the watching man.

"Yes. And don't let him think you understand French."

She murmured, "That will be easy."

"No talking!" the man commanded in French. "Drop that poker. Drop it. At once! Do you hear?"

Tom kept his grip on it, said to Dorothea, "They'll speak more freely if they think we don't understand what they're—"

"Silence!" Again in French. "Or do you want me to let a bullet give you orders?"

Tom paid no attention. "You're doing fine, darling," he told her. And it was true. The initial tremble in her hand was gone. Panic and fear might still be there, but her face showed little sign of them. She stared at the man uncomprehendingly.

He broke into English. "No talking I Drop that poker. At once I'

Tom obeyed, and took Dorothea into his arms, "You've no objection to this?" he asked as a mild distraction from the poker—he had let it fall as near him as he could risk. "My wife hasn't been feeling too—"

"Quiet!"

"May she sit down?" That could get Thea out of range.

"Stay as you are. Both of you!"

So they stayed. Overhead, light footsteps searched through the bedrooms. On the ground floor, light footsteps padded through study and dining-room. Drawers and doors were being opened and shut. But once they have found what they wanted, what then? They will know we've learned too much, he realised. Why the hell didn't I leave everything in the suitcase? Then we could have seemed ignorant; then we could have stayed alive. How will they fake an explanation for our deaths? Something that could be accepted as purely accidental, a tragic occurrence. But what?

The masked figure who had been searching upstairs was the first to return. Nothing and no one, he reported. Only one bedroom in use, along with its adjacent bathroom—an interior one. The rest of the upper floor, unoccupied: drawers and wardrobes empty, no closets. No luggage. No guests. No servants. These two were living here quite alone.

"And so, no interruptions." The man by the window unfolded his arms, slipped his revolver back into his pocket. "Start searching this room. There may be closets behind the wood panelling."

The telephone rang.

"Let it ring!" he yelled, so that even his man still at work in the study could hear his command. "Don't cut the wire. People are living here. You understand?" Then he fell silent, seemed to be listening intently. "No telephone upstairs?" he asked as the ringing ended.

"None."

"All right. Get on with your search." He lifted back the cuff of his coat, studied his watch, compared the time with the clock on the mantelpiece. "Hurry, hurry! And what's this?" he demanded of his second assistant, who had just entered from the study holding a sheaf of papers.

"Tom—your manuscript—" Dorothea said, her voice rising in indignation. "What do they want with—"

Tom silenced her with a kiss on her cheek and a murmur in her ear. "Show them the suitcase. Get into the hall. And up the stairs—"

Her eyes questioned him.

"Lock yourself in the bathroom and—"

The telephone rang again. And kept on ringing, making his whisper inaudible. Had she understood?

Dorothea tightened her hand on Tom's arm. She raised her voice to be heard clearly above the ringing 'phone. "That manuscript is of no interest to you. But if you are looking for something special, then tell me what it is. I'll show you where you can find it." She took several steps away from Tom.

"We shall find it," the man by the window told her, riffling through the pages of Tom's manuscript. "Get back, there!"

Dorothea didn't retreat. "Have you the time to search all through the hidden corners of this old house? It could take you hours."

That's my Thea, Tom thought, smarter than I am. I'd have blurted out "suitcase," and let them realise we knew more about them than was good for us. And there's Thea, wide-eyed and innocent, nudging them into the first move. But hurry, Thea, for God's sake hurry. That guy in the ski-mask who is thumping on the panelling is just about to reach the mantelpiece. And behind that damned clock he'll find everything they are searching for.

The telephone ended its twentieth ring.

"Hours," repeated Dorothea.

The man actually hesitated. He said carefully, "We want the valuables you have stored in a suitcase."

"A suitcase?"

Thea, my darling, we haven't time to waste. Tom eyed the masked man, who was now only six feet away from the mantelpiece.

"Oh," said Thea, seemingly enlightened, "you mean this

suitcase?" And now she was walking rapidly towards the hall.

"Stop!" The manuscript was thrown on to the floor, scattering widely. "You tell us where it is."

"I'll have to show you." Thea walked on. "A difficult closet to find. The owner of this house simply hates doors that look like doors." She was in the hall now. The two masked figures ran after her, caught her arms. "How can I show you—" she began angrily, struggling to free herself.

"Let her go," the master's voice called out, and his two obedient servants released their grip. "Get that suitcase."

Dorothea pointed to the *trompe-l'oeil* panel. Idiots, she thought, they must have passed this closet, never even recognised the baroque symbolism of plumed hats and draped capes and silver-headed canes. "Just press your hand against that section—oh, stupids, where the grease-marks are—and why the hell don't you speak English?" She pressed for them, just enough to let the panel open slightly, and drew back to let them finish the job. The staircase was behind her. She turned and ran.

There was a shout from the living-room. One of the men left the closet, started after her. But she reached the bedroom door, slamming it in his face as she raced for the bathroom. She had its door—heavy, thick, a solid antique of hard oak—locked and bolted before he reached it.

She threw a towel into the bath for sure footing, remembering to turn on the faucets in the hand-basin to cover any screech the curtains might make as she pulled them partly open—just enough to let her unfasten the sliding windows. The cool night air rushed in, and she stood looking down at the top of an acacia tree, yellow blossoms silvered by the moonlight. Behind her, the angry hammering on the door urged her on.

I can't do it, she thought, I can't. But she sat down on the sill, slid one leg over it, and clutched the side of the window-frame. A pause. Then, gingerly, she reached out for the wisteria, slowly slowly until her fingers touched one of its strong ropes. Her hand closed around it, and tugged. It gave a little, then held firm. If a wisteria could tear a roof apart, then surely it can support you, she told herself. And if not—jump for the acacia.

She edged herself along the last few inches of sill, her hand tight on the wisteria. Now her second hand, and her body swinging loose for a wild moment, her legs dangling, shoulders wrenching, and fear screaming silently in her throat. In desperation, she searched for a toe-hold on the gnarled trunk, found it, and released some of her weight from her arms. Hand over hand, feet blindly testing each twist on the spreading vine, she lowered herself through the fronds of tender leaves and their drooping lanterns of mauve flowers.

She didn't fall until the last three feet, when her arms gave out and she dropped with a jolt. I'm sorry, she told the wisteria and its shredded flowers, as she picked herself up from the ground. She tried to steady herself with a few deep breaths, and began running. But her legs were weak, her feet uncertain. Her pace settled into a stumbling walk.

Did she make it? Tom kept wondering. Did Thea make it? He paid no attention to the suitcase, brought triumphantly into the room. He kept watching the hall, the first few stairs that were visible. He kept listening. There was only the distant sound of heavy beating against solid wood. Then it ceased. But there was no scream, only light footsteps running downstairs. The man tried to be nonchalant. "She shut herself into the bathroom. We might as well leave her there."

"No window?"

"None. I told you. So I locked the bedroom door in case she decided to come out." He held up its key.

"Bedroom windows?"

"Too high—a sheer drop down two storeys on to a stone terrace." He pocketed the key and laughed. "A real vixen, who would have thought it?"

"Get on with your job! Search the rest of this room." For nothing except the two envelopes had been found in the suitcase, so far. These were being examined with excessive care, even Chuck's passport, his air-flight tickets, his hotel reservations, a timetable, a letter from a girl in Gstaad. Anything of paper, anything with writing, anything that could conceal between its pages. Two paperbacks were shaken and searched; so were two magazines. The minutes passed; time was a-wasting.

And now, thought Tom as he felt the rising anger of the leader, things are going to turn ugly. Once that suitcase is emptied, they'll start on me. His one way of escape, through the French windows on to the terrace, was still blocked: two men there, one kneeling as he pulled clothes on to the floor, went through pockets, even linings. And the third man, continuing his slow, methodical search of the room, was at the small table near the mantelpiece: it would be next on his list. The kitchen door was locked. So was the front door, seldom used, double-bolted. In any case, a bullet in his back would catch him before he could even reach the hall. The poker—no chance with that against three pistols.

And then, he thought, why not use some direct shock? Anything to throw that son of a bitch off balance?

Tom said, "If you're looking for an engagement book, you'll find it on the mantelpiece. There's a letter there too, which might interest you."

The man looked away from the suitcase at his feet, stared at Tom.

"It's a copy," Tom went on, "and there are four other copies in various hands. Did Rick Nealey actually think he could wipe the slate clean by this little attempt at robbery? He's a fool. And so are you. He's a marked man. He has been under surveillance for the last three months."

The man at the window hadn't moved, hadn't spoken. And then, from the thin black figure now searching the mantelpiece, there came "Here's something." His gloved hands were holding up a small book and a folded sheet of paper for all to see.

The man at the window came to life, moved forward, arm outstretched, eyes on the letter.

Tom made a sudden dive for the poker, swung it sharply against the man's shins, threw it at ski-mask still on his knees by the suitcase, wrenched the window open, and sidestepped on to the terrace. A bullet passed close. He raced for the lemon-trees. As he leaped into their shadows, two men rushed out of the house, revolvers aimed blindly. And then, suddenly, a loud report that echoed over the hillside. That, thought Tom, was no pistol-shot.

He didn't wait to see the effect of it on the terrace, where three men now stood together. He seized that moment of their surprise, and ran for the nearest olive-tree, dodged behind it, waited for another bullet to sing past his shoulders.

But there were no more bullets.

He heard quickening feet, heels slipping in haste over gravel and earth. They were on the driveway, heading down to the road. And the nursery. And Thea?

Tom left the shelter of the olive-tree, began running.

22

Tony Lawton made a high-speed journey through the sleeping town. As he left Menton and passed through the lower spread of Roquebrune, he assessed the time it had taken him to come this far from Georges's hideaway. No, it couldn't have been done faster than this: three breakneck minutes down the stone steps, another three to the car, including the brief drive along the *quai*; less than a minute to zoom through the empty tunnel; three more for the next four kilometres through deserted back streets and abandoned avenues. Making ten, to this point. Plus another two, at full tilt up this little hill, and he'd be arriving at the Michel driveway by eleven or twelve minutes past midnight. Not bad, even if distances were short in this part of the world. And impossible, if there had been any traffic on the road. Bless all these sweet obliging people who tucked themselves into bed by midnight.

There were always afterthoughts, of course. It could be

that the Kelsos had given up the idea that he would call this late, were already deep in sleep—no telephone upstairs, he remembered, and an old house with thick walls and heavy doors. Yes, it could just be that he had come chasing out here on a wild surmise. And yet, whenever he hadn't listened to the alarm-bell that sounded off in his subconscious mind, he had always regretted it. Tonight the alarm had been sharp and clear. Foolish or not, here I come, he thought and eased his speed, with the nursery just ahead, preparing for a sharp left turn into the driveway.

He began the turn, saw a car, a dark solid mass drawn close to the mimosa trees. He swerved back, travelled a hundred yards farther up the road until he could make a left into Auguste's compound—three small houses grouped near the nursery's own entrance. He brought the Renault to a halt right under Auguste's bedroom window.

He hadn't risked a short blast on the horn—no point in giving any warning to that car down at the Michel entrance— but surely the slight screech of brakes, as he pulled up to avoid the truck and the light delivery-van at one side of the yard, must have roused someone around here. It had: a dog barked, and was silenced. To make sure Auguste hadn't turned over and gone back to sleep, Tony got out of the car and scooped up a handful of coarse gravel to toss at the window-pane, knocked on the door, rattled its handle, and started the dog barking again. And again it was silenced. Above him the bedroom curtains parted. A face looked out. Tony stood back to let Auguste have a clear view of him in the moonlight.

The face stared down. Tony waved his arms. The face disappeared. A brief wait, the door opened, and he found himself looking into the double barrels of a shotgun.

"Old friend, don't you know me?"

Auguste stared. Then his arm relaxed. Three years it had been, since Tony used to visit this yard, sit on that bench under the trees, and listen to Auguste's stories about the Resistance. He laid the shotgun against the door, called a few words back over his shoulder, as he stepped outside, his flannel shirt half tucked into trousers, suspenders dangling, boots unlaced. A broad smile creased his weather-tanned cheeks. There was a firm handshake, a warm greeting thumped on Tony's back. But the shrewd face was speculating hard.

Tony wasted no time on explanations. "There's a car stationed inside the Michel driveway. My headlights picked out one man at the wheel. So it isn't two lovebirds having—"

"Hand me that gun, Lucien," Auguste told the boy who stood just within the doorway. "Tell your mother to call the police." He turned back to Tony. "There has been thieving going on. Yes, even here it has started. They come by night, and load up. Plants taken and—"

"No, no—I think the trouble is up at the Michel house."

"Trouble?" Auguste demanded, alert as a hawk, his beak of a nose jutting out, his dark eyes narrowing as if they were ready to swoop on their prey. "Burglars?"

"That's what I'm going to find out."

"Not alone!" Auguste's son had been quick. He returned now with a sweater added to his shirt and a heavy jacket for his father. Auguste drew it on, zipped it to the neck, said, "Now we go together, eh?"

"Could use some help," Tony admitted. "But first—block off the entrance to the Michel driveway."

"With what?"

"The truck."

Auguste considered the idea, didn't like it much. His truck was valuable property.

"I'll drive it," the boy volunteered eagerly.

Lucien must be sixteen now, but he was thin, all his growth going into his height. One of Auguste's older sons, huskier, would be a safer choice. "Better wake one of your brothers—"

"They!" said Lucien scornfully. "They'd sleep through an earthquake."

Recently married, both of them, Tony remembered. Lucien was making the decision for him, anyway. He was already half-way to the truck.

Tony, starting along the nearest path, called back, "Once you park it, get the hell out. And wait here for the police." Lucien looked disappointed, but he waved and climbed into the driver's seat.

"He can handle it," said Auguste, still frowning, as he caught up with Tony and settled into a quick jog.

"There will be no damage to the truck," Tony assured him. "And if there is, I'll pay for it," he added with a grin. He pointed obliquely across the nursery, to its far corner where the flowers ended and the rough ground of the hillside began. "We'll head up there." Near enough to the driveway without actually being in it; and, to be hoped, not noticeable. A quiet approach to the Michel house could be half the battle.

"This way," said Auguste, catching Tony by the arm, guiding him on to another path between the rows of flower-beds and plastic-covered greenhouses. It was a zigzag course, and Tony might have found himself being forced to retrace his steps if

Auguste hadn't been there to lead. The moonlight had become less dependable: cloud cover was beginning to move in from the sea. In another half-hour there would be nothing but deep shadow spreading over the hillside.

And what about Lucien? Tony wondered. The truck had moved out of the yard, and must be running downhill, but so quietly that he couldn't hear it. Had Lucien, the young idiot, put it into neutral? The next thing they'd hear would be a crash against the stone wall at the entrance to the driveway, and they'd have to veer off course to pick up the pieces: one truck, with gears stripped and fenders smashed, and Lucien jammed up against the wheel. But as they reached the end of their lope through the nursery, he heard the loud—but normal—sound of brakes as the truck pulled up; and then dead silence. "He managed it," Tony said, "Lucien actually managed it!"

Auguste only nodded, didn't seem the least astonished. He had halted, his eyes on the hillside. "Someone's out there." He studied the sparse cloud-shadows that blotched the stretch of open ground above them. Scattered boulders and bushes made it difficult to see. Only the Michel house, a dark silhouette, quiet, peaceful, was clearly visible. Auguste crouched low, pulled Tony down beside him, listened intently. "One man. Running."

"Stumbling," Tony whispered back. "He's having a hard time." Then they both saw him slide down on to the surer surface of the driveway, come running—slowly, blindly, too worried about his footing to notice either them or the car down by the gate. Quickly, Tony glanced in its direction. The driver was out, staring at the truck that had blocked his exit; *now* he swung around to face the running man.

"A woman," Tony said, rising to intercept her.

Dorothea... He ran, but she was making one last desperate effort to reach the acacias. And then her head came up as she halted, suddenly aware of the car, of its driver. They stared at each other.

She turned and came stumbling back on to the hillside, into Tony's arms.

She cried out in fear, struck him, struggled to free herself, beat weakly at his face with her fists. He caught her wrists, pulled them down, saying, "It's Tony. Just me—Tony. Dorothea—it's Tony!" Suddenly her rigid body relaxed, sagging against his. He held her tightly, felt her flinch with pain as his hand grasped her shoulder.

Auguste was beside them. "What about him?" He pointed his shotgun towards the car.

Dorothea was saying, her breath coming in painful gasps, "The police—call the police."

"It's done," Tony told her. "How many at the house?"

"Three. All armed. Tom only has a—"

The silence of the night was cut through by a pistol shot. It came from the house.

"Tom—" Dorothea cried out, "Tom—"

"No, no," Tony tried to calm her. "It need not be." But his own heart sank.

"I'll deal with this one," said Auguste, grim-faced, and moved towards the car. Its driver had only hesitated for the fraction of a second after the revolver had been fired. He was already on the run, dodging downhill through the olive-trees, leaping from terrace to terrace. Auguste cursed, could only aim the shotgun blindly into the darkness, and fired. "I scared the rascal off, anyway. Do we go after him?"

"No—up to the house." Tony pushed Dorothea towards the acacias. From there, she'd find a straight path through the nursery. "You get to Augustine. The police will soon be there. Tell them about the burglars."

"Burglars?"

"What else?"

She nodded, partly understanding. "But I want to come with—"

"No. Get off this hillside!" Tony called back to her, already on his way. He was running hard now, keeping to the driveway for the sake of speed. Behind him Auguste's heavy footsteps tried to catch up.

Dorothea hesitated, attempted to follow, gave up after the first slow steps. She turned away, began walking towards the acacias and the abandoned car. Rick Nealey... It had been Nealey whom she had clearly seen in that one terrifying moment when she thought she was trapped after all. But now he had vanished. There was only the dark green car, its door still open, and behind it—strangely—a truck drawn across the entrance to the driveway. From the Roquebrune road she could hear a singsong siren drawing nearer and nearer. They were all too late, she thought, and burst into tears. They scalded her cheeks, searching out the scratches, stinging them, reminding her of the wisteria. The pain in her shoulder suddenly screamed. And for the first time, she became aware of a bruise on her hip, a dull steady ache that sent her limping into the nursery.

All too late, she thought again, all of us.

* * *

Another forty yards, Tony was calculating as he drew out Georges's neat little Beretta from his belt, and we'll be at the lemon-trees; I can take the French windows, Auguste the rear of the house. And at that moment he heard Auguste's warning shout. In front of him, suddenly appearing around the curve of the driveway, came a tight cluster of three dark figures. They halted as abruptly as he did.

Surprise only lasted for one intense moment. Tony dived for the bank of grass beside him, chanced a shot, and missed. The three had already separated, two scattering on to the hillside above the driveway, with Auguste after them. The third man had darted into the row of olive-trees on his right.

Tony picked himself up, ready to follow, and dropped once more as a shot came from behind one of the trees. Only one shot. Perhaps the man was in full flight, didn't want to give away his direction by any more firing. But he was bound to circle around, head for the car, thought Tony. He got up, quickly scanning the darkening terraces that descended, row upon row, towards Cap Martin. The moon was failing him: she had retreated into a swarm of clouds, dimming all chances of seeing the fugitive for at least several minutes. The car, Tony warned himself: that was to be the quick getaway. He began running towards it.

From above him, on the hillside, came the blast of a shotgun. Tony smiled, kept on his way. There were lights now, near the Roquebrune road. And voices. The truck was still there. So was the car, its door wide open. The minute he saw it, he stopped running, his angry eyes searching the terraced slopes of olive-trees that fell towards that heavy dense band of blackness, the thick woods encircling the bottom of this hill.

"Damn it to bloody everlasting hell," Tony said aloud. That car, abandoned—the man had seen it, veered off.

Behind him, on the driveway, there was a slip and a stumble. He whirled round.

"Hey, don't shoot at me!" a voice yelled.

"Tom?"

"Tom."

"Thank God." Tony's head jerked back to the olive-trees.

"Thea?" asked Tom as he slid to a halt beside Tony.

"Okay."

"Okay?"

"Safe." Tony's eyes never left scanning the terraces below him. "One of them is down there. The others took to the hill with Auguste at their heels."

"The two in ski-masks?"

So that's why they looked like a couple of black skeletons. "Yes."

"Then that's the guy we really need," Tom said, pointing towards the terraces. "He was in charge. Gave the instructions, knew what he wanted."

Tony said quickly, "Get down to the gate. Tell the police to put out an alarm, search the woods, check the Cap Martin roads. Two men headed there."

"Two?"

"The driver of the car—ran off—deserted—wouldn't like to be in his—" Tony felt sudden hope; and then major disappointment. No, that had only been a shift of cloud over the moon, a swaying of branches touched by the early-morning breeze. "Get moving, Tom!"

But it's useless, he realised as Tom raced away. Only shadows out there, shadows and twisted trunks that looked like crouching men. You could call it luck, he thought of the armed man's escape, but he's the kind that makes his luck: instant decision, no hesitations. I must have been an inviting target, standing up here on the driveway; but he resisted the impulse to fire, drew no attention to his escape-route, and slipped safely away. As for the other one—the driver—I'd like less and less to be in his shoes. Instead of running, he could have got into his car, gunned it uphill to the house, given them warning. They'd all have scattered, and neither Auguste nor I would have glimpsed them. And we'd have found Tom dead—he had seen them at work, had known what they were after—yes, Tom would have been silenced like Chuck. How the devil did he escape, anyway? Or Thea? These amateurs, Tony reflected, shaking his head in wonder.

He stayed where he was, still watching the wide stretch of terraces. The driver must have reached the woods some time ago; but it was always possible that the armed man—the leader of this little expedition—was still hiding behind a tree-trunk, waiting for all interest to ebb before he risked another step. From the direction of the gate, Tony could hear the truck being moved, and voices raised in urgency. One quick glance reassured him: two policemen had arrived, one of them still listening to Auguste, the other leaving Tom to run back to his Citroën, possibly calling for reinforcements, certainly putting out an alert. At least, Tony decided, some action has been taken, and he went back to watching those damned olive-trees.

Tom and Dorothea limping along with her husband's arm tightly round her waist, came up to join him. In time, he remembered to tuck the Beretta out of sight. "The alarm has gone out," said Tom. "And two more policemen arrived. They've been sent down to the woods—young Lucien is with them to show them the short-cuts. And Auguste caught one of the ski-masks—wounded him in the leg. The other is being chased right now by Auguste's two older sons. So relax, Tony, relax." Then Tom's voice began to race with excitement. "That car down there—it's a green Opel, same registration as the one I saw earlier this evening. I now think the guy who ordered everybody around was the one who was driving it then. Same height, same build. Yes, could be."

Tony stared at him. Colonel Boris Gorsky?

Dorothea said, "But he wasn't the driver tonight. That was Rick Nealey. I saw him clearly—just before he ran."

Tony began to smile. The best piece of news I've heard today, he thought. He said gently, "How did you manage to escape?"

"By way of the wisteria." She tried to laugh, and failed.

"And you?" he asked Tom.

"Oh—I sort of threw him off balance."

Gorsky? "How?"

"First, by telling him where he could find Chuck's letter—he didn't even know one existed."

Nor did I, thought Tony. But there's no time now for explanations.

"It mentioned Nealey?"

"It nailed him. Then I said there were four copies of it, now in other hands, and that Nealey—" Tom paused. "I blew it, Tony. Sorry. But I had to. No other way out."

"Blew what?"

"Told him that Nealey had been under surveillance for the last three months. Slight exaggeration, of course, like these four copies. Still, it worked. And then I caught him with a poker across the shins, and bolted."

Tony's smile broadened. "Threw him off balance? You yanked the rug right out from under his feet. And you settled Nealey's future, too. Both of you." He kissed Dorothea, clapped Tom's shoulder. They looked puzzled, but he'd explain later, another day, another place. He nodded towards the police car that was starting up the driveway. "They'll want a guided tour and a lot of answers from you. But there's really no need for me to hang around, is there? See you later—when we've all had some sleep."

Dorothea had noticed his second quick look at the approaching car. "Auguste has told them all about you."

"All?"

"You just happened to be passing by. You saw a mysterious Opel in the driveway, you wakened Auguste, and the two of you went after the burglars."

"Burglars?" Tom said with amusement.

"And why not? Everybody knows that all Americans are loaded with cash. Think of all the jewels I have hidden away, darling."

She has recovered, thought Tony. He kissed her again, and began moving towards the police car.

"Hey, there—two in a row?" Tom asked with a laugh. Old Tony was going quite emotional tonight. Tom tightened his grip around his wife. "You think Nealey and his friends will be caught?"

The man in the ski-mask, possibly. Gorsky? Improbable. "Nealey will be dealt with," Tony called back over his shoulder. Of that, he was sure. He was still smiling when he reached the police car. "Good morning, officers," he began briskly, and then stared as Auguste, ending a long description of tonight's skirmish, got out to join him.

"That's all," Auguste told them. "Monsieur Lawton could add nothing."

One of the policemen wasn't so sure. "I believe two bullets were fired. Two pistol shots, monsieur?"

"Yes," Tony said, and could only hope the Beretta's small bulk wouldn't show through his jacket. "And two misses."

"You were the target?"

"I thought so."

Auguste broke in with, "Instead of hugging the ground to dodge a couple of bullets, you'd have done better following me. I caught one of them, lost the other. Together we would have captured them both. Now let's go. I'll guide you back through the nursery. Don't want any more feet trampling over my freesias." He looked at the policeman and tilted his head.

Both of the officers smiled. They seemed to know Auguste well. Tony seized the relaxed moment to say, "If you need me, gentlemen, I am staying at the *Alexandre*."

"Your passport?" the younger policeman asked.

"The concierge still has it. I arrived only this morning."

"How long do you expect to stay?"

"Two or three days. I'm on a sailing holiday along the Côte d'Azur."

"Be so good as to notify us when you leave. We may need you to identify anyone we apprehend. Could you recognise the man who shot at you?"

"By height and build only. And that isn't too certain. The moon was clouded—only patches of light."

Auguste said impatiently, "I've told you all that, Louis."

Louis had one last question. "Do you own a revolver, Monsieur Lawton?"

"Yes."

"Let me see it."

"It's in London, actually—in a bedroom table drawer."

Auguste said, "Much good it did you tonight." He grinned for Louis. "And you know where to find me if you need any more information." That raised a small laugh. The two officers saluted informally, and the car drove on.

I hope, Tony thought, that Tom will keep his mouth shut about finding me with a gun in my hand. Yes, he's got enough sense not to complicate life unnecessarily. "That's a smart young man," he told Auguste.

"Both good lads. They know me well. But why did he ask about your pistol?"

"He may have heard the two shots from a distance. One might have seemed louder, heavier, than the other."

"Were they?"

"Yes." Tony unbuttoned his jacket, showed the Beretta briefly. "Belongs to my friend who owns the Renault I am driving."

"And you happened to find the gun in the glove-compartment? You'd have been a fool to leave it there, when you were going out to hunt down trouble. But you could have told Louis—"

"And used up everyone's valuable time? That doesn't catch any of your burglars, Auguste."

"Do you have a gun in London?"

"Of course. I kept strictly to the truth. Always do, with policemen. And with my friends."

They had entered the nursery, walking slowly along the paths, now dark, between the soft fragrances and muted colours of the flower-beds. "Two shots of different calibre," Auguste ruminated, and smiled. "Yes, that Louis is smart. His father was a policeman too, and in the Resistance, fought alongside me against the Nazis. It was on a night like this, just about this time of year, we helped guide a small group of Americans and Canadians—Special Forces, landing ahead of Tassigny's five divisions—right up through the mountains behind Menton. Didn't use the road, of course, kept to the hillsides, rough country, not like this but rough as the devil's backside, all the way to Castellar. Now, that was a real battle. The Germans were deep inside the mountain, quadrilateral fortifications. But we took it. Yes, a real battle. There were twenty American and Canadian graves up at Castellar, and many of ours." Auguste shot a quick glance at Tony. "And now, when I tell my sons about it, they only count the lives that were wasted. Why not wait for the troops to come in, with tanks and artillery? That's what they ask." Auguste shook his head, a mixture of anger and sadness. "But there was no waste. Many of us died, all the rest were wounded, we silenced the German guns. They didn't blow the troops to pieces down on the beach, or coming up the pass. Yes, we won that battle."

"You won that war."

Auguste said nothing more. Then, as they entered the yard, his step became as brisk as his goodbye handshake. "Next time you choose to visit, make it in daylight." A nod of the head, and he was heading for bed.

"I will," Tony promised. "And tell Lucien he did a fine job."

And that reminded Auguste. "If you see him down by the

road," he called back from the doorway, "send him packing up here. He has a full day's work ahead of him tomorrow."

The door closed, and Tony stepped into the Renault. For a moment, his eyes rested on the glove-compartment. It was just possible that the alert was in force, and there could be police checks on all drivers and their cars in this area tonight. He opened the compartment and placed Georges's Beretta inside, everything nicely legal, for the ride to Menton.

Quietly, he started the car, drove out of the yard and down the Roquebrune road, back to the Old Town.

23

The all-night vigil ended at five o'clock when the final message was received from Brussels.

"All set," Georges said, coming over to the bed where Tony had been having one of his periodic cat-naps.

At once Tony was awake and on his feet. "They've agreed?"

"More or less. Some advice, of course. And one alteration."

"What?" Tony shot out.

"Their cabin cruiser is in the fourteen-metre—"

"Forty-six feet, almost? That's something. How many knots?"

"Over thirty."

"That's about thirty-five miles an hour, more than three times the speed of the *Sea Breeze*," said Tony. "So what's the reason for any change in plans?"

"The length and bulk of the *Aurora*."

"I like her name." But Tony was beginning to see the problem.

"She has ample room for our party and her three-man

crew, but that size would be difficult to manoeuvre inside the anchorage. It might be a very delayed departure."

Tony nodded. The harbour was small, and jammed with boats. "So what do they suggest?"

"That we board the *Aurora* where she is now docked—in the *port privé* at the other end of Garavan Bay. It's big, three times as big as the harbour. Can hold eight hundred boats in its private anchorage, another two hundred in the public section. Actually, it's more convenient for us—quicker to reach from Bill's house."

Tony's voice was clipped. "And just how do we persuade Parracini to accept this change?" Our whole plan will end before it begins, he thought, if Parracini's suspicions start being ruffled.

Georges laughed. "That, they said, was for you to work out."

"Very funny." For once, Tony's sense of humour failed him. "And what about that escort?" he asked, bracing himself for more complications.

"Provided."

"We got it?" Tony's surprise changed to delight. Old friend Jimmy Hartwell had really pushed and pulled. "We actually—"

"Yes, you got what you wanted."

The two men looked at each other. "Then let's see what we can do with it," said Tony. Together, smiling broadly, they moved over to the table.

The next half-hour was an organised jumble of big and little things to be done, all of them necessary. While Georges dismantled his equipment and turned it back into innocuous objects, Tony burned the clutter of notes and scraps of paper in a metal basin, after he had memorised some last details—the *Aurora*'s exact position in the *port privé*; the name of Vincent, their chief contact in the crew; radio signals for communication. Coffee was brewed and drunk while they drew up their timetable for this morning. They washed and smartened up, finished the coffee, and went over their schedule once more.

Outside, it was still dark, with only a hint of diffused light spreading from the east. "Time to call Emil," Tony said. "We'll give him a pre-dawn swim."

"You mean you are actually serious about—"

"Better to look foolish than be stupid." Tony pulled out the transceiver and called in the *Sea Breeze*. Emil was awake. A peaceful night—no actual approach made to the boat. Two men had patrolled the mole. They had been quite obvious, making no effort to hide themselves from the *Sea Breeze*. Two of ours?

"Yes, could be. Possibly Bill's men trying to reassure you. And you heard nothing at all? Not even the lapping of the mere?"

Emil, not a literary type, was puzzled but definite. "Nothing."

"All right. Let's take out some insurance. Get into your wet-suit and slip over the side. Examine the hull—keel—rudder—every damn thing under the water-line. How quickly can you do all that? Twenty minutes? Less? Good: get started before the light strengthens. Call us back."

Tony switched off, saw Georges's amused eye studying him. "Need something to do? Then listen to the weather reports." He himself walked restlessly around the room and then went out on to the small balcony for a few breaths of cold dank air. The sky was slowly turning a bleached black, banded with grey at the horizon. The last of night lingered over the lighted harbour. There the *Sea Breeze* nestled cosily with the other boats, all at rest, everything tranquil. Looking down at her, watching for any sign of Emil—nothing to see, Emil was good at his job, as slippery as a seal—Tony was already working out his own immediate problem: Parracini's tender suspicions.

As the grey of the horizon, softly, surely seeped into the sky, like water over a river-bank, Tony returned to the room. "It looks calm enough out there. Some clouds, but nothing threatening. What's the forecast?"

"Bright sun. Cool. And possibly heavy winds from the south-east this afternoon. But we'll be in Nice before then."

"With luck." Tony picked up the telephone and dialled Bill's number—not his private line, just the ordinary one that would ring at his bedside and rouse him from sleep. He kept his call brief, once he had Bill fully awake. "I'll drop in to see you this morning. In half an hour? No, nothing is wrong: everything's fine. I just want to go over your timetable, make sure that it matches ours. Meet me down at the gates, will you? A walk in the garden will be just what I need—to work up an appetite for breakfast. Yes, at the gates. See you."

"Cryptic," said Georges. "Giving nothing away. Just like your call to him last night."

"Had to be."

"Why? Do you think his telephones are bugged? But Bill's no fool. He makes a regular check on them—a matter of routine."

"And on nothing else?"

"The whole place was thoroughly gone over before Bill and Nicole arrived there. Oh, come on, Tony. Parracini must know about Bill's regular checks—he wouldn't risk a bug in a 'phone."

"What about a small listening device in the calendar on Bill's desk—or in the blotter? Or how about a lamp-bulb with sensitive filaments, near every telephone?"

"Very specialised stuff. Where would Parracini get—oh, I see." Georges was conscious of Tony's raised eyebrow. "From his kind friends in Menton? But still... Does Parracini know enough about installing sophisticated devices? That wasn't his line of business."

"It doesn't take much know-how to screw a light-bulb into a socket."

"No, but it takes someone constantly monitoring. Parracini couldn't sit around in his room all day, listening—"

"There could be a monitor installed in a near-by house on the Garavan hillside."

It was a disturbing thought. Georges had no comment.

Tony said, "Look—they must be guarding Parracini as closely as possible. He's too important. And they've had time to arrange all necessary precautions."

Georges nodded. "One thing has been puzzling me. Surely he must have radio contact with Gorsky; so why did he have to meet him? Why even meet Nealey at the market yesterday morning?"

"I've been thinking about that too. There could be two very different reasons why he had to meet either of them. Nealey—because Nealey was handing him something more solid than a verbal message: one of your sophisticated gadgets, perhaps? Gorsky—because Parracini had been moved out of his cosy corner over the garage into a room next to Bernard's and Brigitte's. Perhaps he could only risk a very quick message on his transceiver, giving time and place for a meeting and important instructions. Possible?"

"Very possible." Georges smiled as he added, "How he must have cursed Bill for moving him into the main house. No privacy for anyone these days."

And then all their speculations ended with Emil's signal. Tony answered it.

Emil's usually placid voice was uneven and hurried. Tony listened quietly. "Put it together again, can you? Just as it was. Stow it on deck—some place unnoticeable but reachable. Don't worry, the *Sea Breeze* will be safe as long as she is in harbour. So there's no danger to anyone. I'll join you well before eleven. Get ready to move out by then, Emil. Yes, you and I—we can handle her, can't we?" A laugh that was genuine, a cheerful goodbye, and the exchange was over.

Georges said slowly, "He found something?"

Tony nodded. "It was taped to the starboard side of the hull, near the engines. He detached it, examined it. There was no time-mechanism, just a remote-control device."

"And you told him to put the damned thing together—"

"We can always heave it overboard once we are far enough offshore."

"Now, Tony," Georges began warningly.

"Mustn't keep Bill waiting." Tony looked at his watch, moved towards the door. "All clear here?" Together they gave the room one last quick check.

"All clear." Georges locked the door behind them, and they made their way down the staircase into the narrow street.

The Renault began climbing the twists and turns up the hill above Garavan Bay. It was a heavily wooded area, with a spread of houses and gardens hidden by walls and trees, dark, silent, mysterious in the sombre light between night and day. Bill's place was as secluded as the others on this narrow road, but he was standing outside the gates to make sure Tony could identify it easily. So Georges's arguments were cut short. Why, he had insisted, couldn't he join Emil and Tony on the *Sea Breeze* once he had brought Gerard and the others from Nice, seen them safely aboard the *Aurora*? By that time he would have briefed them thoroughly.

"No," Tony said as they came round one of the sharp turns and saw Bill ahead. "One of us has to stay with Gerard and his travelling companions. We know what's been happening here; we know the arrangements. They don't. That's it, Georges. You've got to stick close—all the way. To Brussels. You're in charge, actually, but don't let Gerard notice it." The Renault drew up. Tony had the door open. "Good luck, old boy. See you next week." He was out, shaking hands with Bill, entering the gates with a last wave towards the car.

Georges drove on uphill to reach the highroad along the crest of Garavan. Tony was right, of course: Gerard would need a lot of extra details to persuade him to follow Tony's plan without adding some variations of his own. Better not say it is Tony's plan, Georges decided, not until we reach Brussels. Better let him think we have been following Commander James Hartwell's instructions right from the beginning. And so to Nice airport. And to a most exacting cross-examination from three razor-blade minds, once they came out of shock. In Tony's words, dicey, very dicey.

He put Tony out of his thoughts, concentrated on what he would say and how best he could tell it.

* * *

"Did my 'phone call waken the household?" Tony asked as Bill closed the gates behind them.

"Left them all sleeping. Who was that in the car with you— Georges? Why didn't he stop off, say hello?"

"He's on his way to the Nice airport."

"Early, isn't he?"

"Wants to make sure he arrives in time."

"He's a bright boy. Easy to work with."

"That's Georges," said Tony. Looking at Bill's handsome and honest face—oh yes, he could be as devious as the best of them, but basically Bill was a straightforward, no-nonsense-about-me type—Tony began thinking back to Georges's remarks. About Parracini and sophisticated bugging devices that he could manage to install without much specialised knowledge. But what had he used to overhear Bill's conversations? Because, Tony reminded himself, not all talk was made over a telephone. Apart from devices in set places, like a desk or a night-table, what the bloody hell did Parracini use to listen to Bill having a private word with Nicole on the terrace, or with Bernard in the garden? Or even to conversations like this one, with Bill now suggesting they'd head for the kitchen and rustle up some breakfast?

"Sounds good," Tony said. The house was about a hundred yards away. Not far enough, he thought unhappily. "Let's walk a little. I need the fresh air. Cooped up most of the night. You've a lot of garden here. How far does it stretch?"

"About five acres. We've kept a flower-bed or two near the terrace and pool, but all this—" Bill pointed to hedges and trees that sheltered elaborately-shaped plots—"we just let go. Too much work for Bernard." Then, as Tony took the nearest brick path, leading away from the villa itself, Bill said, "You didn't haul me out of bed to talk about horticulture. What's your problem?"

At this moment, thought Tony, you are. I've got a rising suspicion that Parracini knew your telephone rang, is now up and around, and listening to every word we say. "Two things," he replied. "The engine trouble we had on the *Sea Breeze*, and the weather."

"Thought you had got the engine fixed."

"We are still working on it. Oh, it's safe enough, unless we run into any strong weather. The latest reports are predicting a possible south-easter by this afternoon. And that's not a pleasing prospect, Bill, with an engine you can't depend on."

"Then the cruise idea is off."

"No. It's too good a security measure to pass up. But the cruise may have to be cut short if the weather prophets are right As soon as the wind freshens too much, we can easily slip into the nearest harbour before anyone starts feeling queasy. Wouldn't want Gerard to be sea-sick, would we?"

"Gerard? Is he coming, too?"

"That's the word this morning. He's got some news for Parracini. A job with NATO—did you hear about it?"

"No."

"Nor I, until Georges cued me in."

"Does Parracini know? If so, why the hell didn't he tell me?"

"Well, it wasn't definite until Gerard pulled some strings and used his powers of persuasion. But it's all set. One caution, Bill: let Gerard break the good news to Parracini. That's Gerard's pet project, you know. He really will be hopping mad if we jump in ahead of him."

"This job for Parracini in NATO—"

"Very hush-hush, very important. That's all I know."

"A bit soon, isn't it?"

"Gerard thinks not. It will depend, of course, on the debriefing during our little cruise. But I'm sure Parracini will be able to help clear up the outstanding questions."

"About what?"

"About whom. Heinrich Nealey. He's been under surveillance for the last three months. We know he worked for nine years in America as Alexis; and one of his last contacts there was a man called Oleg." *Are you listening, Parracini, are you listening?* "It's just possible that Parracini can add to our file on Alexis. And on Oleg, whose real name is Gorsky, Boris Gorsky."

"I don't think Parracini has much to add to his previous debriefing."

"Memory can play tricks—blot out small facts that don't seem important, recall them later by some new association of ideas."

"Where is Gorsky now?"

"Haven't a clue." And that was true, in its way. Gorsky might be on Cap Martin, or in a cottage up on Garavan, or six miles away in Monte Carlo.

"Could he be in contact with Nealey again?"

"If he is, we'll get him."

"Through Nealey?"

"Yes. And we'll pull in several of the smaller fry too—a pretty redhead who's secretary to Maclehose, out at Shandon Villa, and at least three others working around the place. And they are bound to have set up a system of outside contacts. It could be quite a haul."

"Contacts," Bill said slowly. His grey eyes looked sombre, his pleasant features grim, his usual smile—white against a permanently tanned face—vanishing. He smoothed back his longish sun-bleached hair, now ruffled by the breeze, pulled the collar of his suede jacket up around his neck as if he suddenly felt chilled. "You think Nealey is on to us?"

Tony didn't answer. He had been studying Bill closely. Casual dress—no cuff-links, this morning; and no tie for any clip to hold in place. The suede jacket would only be worn at odd moments, so forget the possibility of buttons being wired for sound. No rings. A belt-buckle, yes. And Bill's watch, that old favourite he had worn for years. Or was it? As Bill's wrist came up to smooth down his hair, then adjust his collar, the watch was in clear view.

Bill's worry was growing. "You think this house could be under surveillance?" With his set-up Nealey must have gathered a lot of information—mostly for his own security—about recent rentals, strangers signing long-term leases.

"I'm sure they've been taking a close look at all new arrivals who've set up house in the last two months. That's the reason why you and Parracini are going to meet these NATO Intelligence officers, instead of them coming to visit you here. We'll have them, waiting for you, keeping out of sight. All you and Parracini have to do is get on the boat as quickly and discreetly as possible. And don't be late."

"Sailing when?"

"Didn't I tell you eleven o'clock? So get to the dock half an hour before that, and you step on board by ten thirty-five at latest. Can do?"

"Why not sail as soon as we reach the *Sea Breeze*."

"Better let us make sure that no one at the harbour is too interested in her—or you. Can you lend me your two men to help me keep watch?"

"Sure. You're taking a hell of a lot of trouble for Parracini. Or is it for the NATO guys?"

"See right through me every time, don't you? It's the NATO guys who are my responsibility. And they are some of our top men. Nealey would give an arm and a leg to know their faces and put names to them."

"A high-level meeting, then." That at least pleased Bill.

"Yes. So let's get down to the last details, synchronise watches, and—hey, Bill, yours is running ten minutes slow."

"Can't be. Only got it yesterday." Bill peered at the elaborate watch-face. "Does everything but talk," he said, "or show the time clearly. These damned numerals—" He froze as Tony held out his wrist, let him see his own watch. The two timepieces showed only one second of difference. "What the matter with—"

Quickly Tony put a finger up to his lips for silence, pointed at Bill's watch; then jerked a thumb back in the direction of the house, and tapped an ear. Bill stared back at him. "Needs winding," said Tony. "Or has it stopped altogether?" Tony unbuckled its strap, drew it off Bill's wrist.

"What the hell—"

"Damned annoying," Tony said. "You'd better use your old one." He was feeling the weight of the new piece—it wasn't excessive, seemed perfectly normal.

"Can't," Bill said. "It got smashed up last Sunday."

"How on earth did you manage that?"

"Not me. It was Parracini and Nicole horsing around the

pool. I laid my watch beside my chair while I went for a swim. They knocked the chair over, and the watch ended up under Parracini's heel."

"How much did you pay for this one?"

"It was a present—Nicole went half-shares on the purchase price and Parracini bought it yesterday morning."

"Now that's what I mean by his taking too many chances, wandering around town like that." Tony had his all-purpose knife out, resisted trying to open the back of the watch—it would be tightly sealed anyway—and worked on its winder instead. Anything, he thought, to give Bill an excuse for not wearing it. "Careful, Bill," he said. "You'll break off that key if you—damn it, you have broken it!" Tony snapped it off as he spoke, hurled the watch into a near-by bush with bright purple flowers. "Let's get one of your acres between it and us," he said softly as he drew Bill far up the path. At last he was satisfied, and came to a halt in a one-time rose-garden. "Now we can get down to business."

"You think there was a bug in that watch?" Bill demanded, half-angry, half-bewildered. "Who the hell could have—"

"Parracini. I'll begin with him, and then go on to details about plans. Be prepared for a shock, Bill. But just listen, don't ask questions—we haven't time for that." Tony plunged into the story of Parracini.

"I'll say this for you, Bill," he ended. "You got a grip of yourself more quickly than I did last night. It took me half an hour to calm down."

"I'll let go once he's trapped in Brussels," Bill said through his teeth. "Now, what about your plans?"

"Here's our schedule." Tony gave their timetable, the

Aurora's name and exact location in the marina below this hillside. "Got all that?"

Bill nodded. "We get there by ten twenty-five. No later."

"And sail by ten thirty. Wait until you've got Parracini in the car, on your way to the *port privé*, before you mention the *Aurora*. That will take all your tact, Bill."

"I'll manage. I can tell him I just had a signal from you belaying the *Sea Breeze*, engine acting up again. As for the weather—you took care of that angle. If Parracini was listening, he caught an earful this morning."

"And he is now locked in your bathroom, far enough away from Bernard and Brigitte or Nicole, trying to get a message to Gorsky on his transceiver. About Heinrich Nealey, *requiescat in pace*. And about Parracini's triumph—accepted into NATO. I don't think he will balk at the change from *Sea Breeze* to *Aurora*."

"You baited the hook too well," Bill said as they left the rose-garden, started walking down the series of paths and steps. He frowned at some new problem. "Nicole—when do I tell her?"

"You don't. She's too attached to Parracini."

"To Palladin, you mean. She admired him. He never took a nickel, worked for the West because he believed in us—such as we are," Bill ended abruptly.

"To paraphrase old Winston, democracy may not be perfect, but it's a damned sight better than anything else around."

"Nicole—" Bill was still troubled about her.

"Just leave her in happy ignorance. I'll tell her tonight, once I hear from you in Brussels."

"She wants to come on the cruise too."

"Impossible!" Tony was really startled. "Keep her out of it,

Bill. She stays here. With Brigitte. And *what* about Bernard?"

"He was going down to the harbour with us, so that he could drive the Mercedes back here."

"May I borrow him—and your car? Just briefly. I'll tell him what I want done, myself. And where do I reach your two men by 'phone?"

"I'll call them and pass on your instructions." And then, as Tony raised an eyebrow, Bill reconsidered. "No, I won't. Those damned bugs—I suppose I'll have to leave them in place and not rouse Parracini's suspicions." So he gave Tony the 'phone number and the two names, with the identification password.

"Bless your sweet understanding heart. Won't forget this," Tony said, and he meant it.

"Okay, okay. Any other pointers you need to give me? Then what about some breakfast?"

"I'd better not meet Parracini. He may have noticed me last night among the onlookers at the Casino. If he sees me here with you—" Tony shook his head.

"How are you getting back to town?"

"I'll start walking down the road. You send Bernard after me in that old rattletrap of his, and he can leave me near my hotel."

The bush with the bright purple flowers was coming into sight. "I'll pick that damned watch up and drop it into my desk," said Bill.

"Have you another one?"

"I'll borrow Brigitte's. I don't imagine she has been wired for sound." As they reached the bush, Bill took out his handkerchief and went searching for the watch. Like a lost golf-ball, he thought, and just as elusive. At last he found it and placed it in the centre of his handkerchief, wrapping it up into a thick wad. Then, clutching it tightly inside his fist, he jammed his hand into his jacket pocket and kept it there. There was a smile on his face as they walked on in silence, avoiding the sound of footsteps on the brick path by moving on to a slope of dew-wet grass. But the joke would have to remain untold till he met Tony again: that damned watch actually had stopped.

Tony chose an oblique approach to the gates, using a row of tall thin cypresses to hide him from curious eyes at the house. Have we forgotten something, left anything undone? he wondered as he walked down the road to its next curve. There he sat on a low wall, waited for Bernard's car, and looked at the view. Far below him Garavan Bay stretched from its eastern boundary of russet cliffs, towering over the *port privé*, to the western harbour sheltering under the Old Town. The red sky, sailors' warning, now fading into a reassuring blue puffed with small white clouds, briefly touched the high cliffs and turned them into a wall of flame. The Mediterranean sparkled in the clear pure light, promising the mere landlubbers a perfect day.

"Good morning to you," Bernard called out, and opened the car door.

I hope it is a good morning, Tony thought. He climbed in, and they began the serpentine descent.

24

Rick Nealey's quarters at Shandon Villa consisted of an outer office, handsomely furnished with couch and chairs, where business could be conducted or important guests entertained, and an adjoining bed-sitting-room for private use only. There, one of the closets had been fitted with the necessary equipment to keep him in touch with his own secret world. Its installation had excited and pleased him, gave him a feeling of increased status, a sense of widening power. Until yesterday. Until then everything had been progressing smoothly and well. And now—

He pulled himself free from the twisted blanket, and rose. Dawn was breaking. He hadn't slept, partly because he had spent the night on the couch in his office, partly because of Gorsky's presence in his bed-sitting-room. It had been the only solution to the emergency that had arisen so unexpectedly on that disastrous visit to the Kelsos' house. Shandon Villa had been the nearest refuge. Impossible, said Gorsky, to continue along the shore road to his rented cottage, even if it was only two kilometres farther west. Impossible, Gorsky had repeated, to risk travelling on foot; the police had been called in, the alert was out, the search was on. So Gorsky had taken shelter in Shandon, with Nealey guiding him safely out of view of the two yokels on their guard-duty against jewel-thieves.

He must give me credit for waiting for him on the road below the olive-trees. I watched him scrambling down those terraces, gauged his direction, was there to meet him. Without me, where would he have been? (I didn't have to wait for him—in an emergency, it was each man for himself.) Will Gorsky admit it? No, thought Nealey, he'll blame me for the whole of last night's fiasco. But it was he who was up at that house, not I. Will he blame me for that too?

Nealey, in dressing-gown and slippers, padded silently downstairs. It was too early as yet for the cook and her helper to be working in the kitchen. Some food and hot coffee, and perhaps Gorsky's mood would be mellowed before he had to leave—soon, within another hour, while kitchen staff and Maclehose family were still asleep.

As he started back upstairs with a loaded tray, he remembered those other mornings when, in dressing-gown just like this, he'd get his own breakfast in his snug apartment in Georgetown. A simple life compared to his present one. Suddenly he felt an unexpected nostalgia for the years when he was Alexis, and worked alone. Not actually alone, of course, but he had felt a certain independence: delivery of reports to agents who stayed anonymous; telephone calls that came from voices without faces; meetings arranged and kept in reassuring secrecy. Yes, it had been a useful life, and comfortable. But here, he had been drawn deeper in. He had learned more, been told more. Yesterday, it had excited him, pleased him. Today it roused a strange disquiet.

He re-entered the office, set the tray down on the nearest table. He could hear Gorsky's harsh but muffled tones droning on, as they had done at several intervals through the night, making contact with someone locally. But this time, the someone had as much to say as Gorsky. I'll never know what this is all about, Nealey thought; from now on, Gorsky will tell me little. I am demoted. And why? It was the Kelso incident that made the abrupt change in Gorsky's attitude to me. It had never been a friendly association, but—on Parracini's orders—not inimical either. Until last night. Apart from two single words (one of them, "impossible," used twice, the other, "idiocy," uttered in blistering rage), Gorsky had only opened his mouth to say, "Where do you transmit?" Not one particle of praise for either the neatly-arranged closet or the clever combination-lock that would defeat more than a curious housemaid. Not one word, either, about the Kelso house. What had actually happened up there? Nealey wondered once more. Probably he would never learn. Gorsky was not the type to admit his mistakes. Gorsky... Oleg. The man he had hoped, in Washington, never to meet again. And now, thought Nealey, he is on my back: I can feel his teeth in my neck.

There was complete silence, now, in the bedroom. Nealey hesitated, then knocked on its door and waited for a response. At last it opened and Gorsky, fully dressed, ready to leave, came out. His face was calm, his eyes cold. He looked at the breakfast tray and poured himself a cup of coffee. Nealey, helping himself to bread, butter, and honey, was suddenly aware of sharp scrutiny, and lost his appetite. The silence unnerved him. He didn't even drink his coffee. He blurted out, "There was no other way. The old man shot at me. I had to run."

"Before he shot at you," Gorsky said, not even concealing his contempt.

"After."

"And he missed? Yet he could aim well. He wounded Gómez and handed him over to the police."

"And Feliks?"

"He got away—with much difficulty. He is at the cottage. I have instructed him to leave, remove what he can, destroy the rest."

"But Gómez will give no information—"

"The cottage is no longer possible. You have ended its usefulness."

"I? I'm not to blame for Gómez—"

"If you had dealt with Charles Kelso effectively, there would have been no need for our visit to his brother's house. We could have concentrated on our real mission here, not on a distraction that should never have been allowed to develop."

"How else could I have dealt with Chuck? He threatened me and I persuaded him to postpone action. That gave you time to—"

"Not time enough to examine the suitcase before his body was discovered! You should have stayed here, yesterday afternoon. You should have gone through his belongings while we dealt with him. But no—you had to run off to Eze, provide yourself with an excuse for not taking part in his death. You could even have stood watch, like Gómez. Yes, Gómez. Who is now in the hands of the police. If he can be recognised as one

of the electricians who were working at Shandon yesterday—"
Gorsky's lips tightened as he stared down at Nealey, who sat
with head bent, coffee-cup pushed aside and forgotten, on the
edge of his chair.

Gorsky's recital of mistakes continued. "You told me that
Kelso had threatened you, that he showed you notes for a letter
he was about to write—if you didn't resign. You did not tell me
that the letter was already written."

Nealey roused himself. "It was only drafted, not actually
written."

"No? Here is one copy." Gorsky placed it in front of Nealey.
"There are four others. You do not have copies without an
original. And it is ready to be mailed. Did he tell you to whom
he sent it for safe-keeping?"

"He only warned me he was drafting a letter," Nealey
insisted.

"And you believed that?" Gorsky's scorn ended in a brief
laugh.

"The letter is probably hidden in his apartment," Nealey
suggested quickly.

Gorsky's contempt increased. "I had a thorough search
made there yesterday, as soon as you told me about Kelso's
notes. And no search would have been possible, if there wasn't
a time-lag between here and New York. But your luck stopped
there, Nealey. We found nothing. Nothing!"

"Then perhaps he was bluffing—there was no draft—"

"And therefore no letter ready to be mailed? What a
comforting thought. Idiot! Read that postscript to his brother.
There *is* a letter, now in the hands of someone he trusts—
someone who is waiting for Kelso's instructions whether to

send or destroy it. As soon as he hears of Kelso's death, he will either mail or open the letter. In either case, disastrous for you. Impossible to stay here. You resign today, and leave by tomorrow morning. I will send two men with you, to make sure your journey to Moscow is without incident."

Moscow? Recall. For what? Nealey said, "How can I resign? I am in charge here. The first seminar begins next week. Do you actually mean to sacrifice all my work, all this project? Parracini would never agree with that."

"Parracini has a bigger project in view than even Shandon Villa. If there is a choice between them, he will concentrate on the success of his own mission."

"And what is it that's so important?" Nealey countered. "To throw away our control over Shandon Villa—that's madness! And Parracini couldn't substitute one of his agents to take over my position here. There isn't time. The job will go to my chief assistant, perhaps permanently if he shapes up. And you know I selected him because he is excellent cover—politically a middle-of-the-road liberal who is against extremes, right or left. How far would you get with him?"

Nealey had made a good point, Gorsky conceded. "When does he begin work here?"

"Tomorrow or Monday. He arrives in Menton today."

Gorsky was silent for almost two minutes. "Then we shall arrange it this way. You don't resign: you will ask for a leave of absence, with your assistant taking charge for the next week or so. This will give us time enough to have another candidate ready for your job—someone who has more distinguished qualifications than your assistant. We will push him hard, just as we pushed you—use every bit of influence, pull every string we can find in Washington. And when we are ready to insert him into your slot at Shandon Villa, you can then turn your leave of absence into resignation."

"But how could I ask for any leave at this moment? The first seminar—"

"You have been working too hard, you've done too much. The death of your friend Charles Kelso has caused you great distress—you need two weeks to rest and regain your health."

"Two weeks?" Nealey was scornful. "You'll never be able to install anyone in—"

"Two weeks." Gorsky was adamant. "And if there is a delay in our plans, all you have to do is to request an extension of your sick leave." Gorsky's anger, held at a low simmer, was beginning to boil. "Any excuse, you fool, to prevent your job from being filled. You keep Maclehose expecting your return. Can't you do even that?"

Nealey moistened his dry lips. "What about Anne-Marie, or the others?"

"They will be sent elsewhere."

"But why?"

"Because of NATO Intelligence."

"What?"

Gorsky didn't explain. He continued with the problem of Anne-Marie. "You will reprimand her this morning, for incompetence. You will create a scene. She will leave in anger. And after that you will ask Maclehose for sick leave. A most appropriate request after the performance you have just given."

"You are clearing us all out of Shandon?" Nealey couldn't believe it. "All our work—all our organisation—"

"We take the loss, and wait, and begin all over again. But

carefully. NATO's agents will keep Shandon Villa under close observation for several months."

"It could be a false alarm about NATO Intelligence."

"Their agents are here in Menton. Three came in yesterday, aboard the *Sea Breeze*. One, Emil Baehren, has been identified—he is guarding their boat. Of the two others, only Georges Despinard can be definitely connected with the *Sea Breeze*."

"Yes," Nealey was quick to remind Gorsky, "it was I who found out his name, and the *Sea Breeze* address, at the police-station. And the third agent is Lawton, who is staying at the *Alexandre*? It must be. They were together at Shandon yesterday afternoon."

"It doesn't follow. An agent like Despinard could have used Lawton to arrange a visit to Shandon." It had been Despinard who had prowled around the gardens, not Lawton. "All we know definitely about Lawton is that he is a friend of Thomas Kelso. He is a friend of many journalists—including Despinard."

"But you have your suspicions?"

"I've had them for many months." Gorsky was enigmatic.

"Haven't you acted on them—had him followed, his rooms searched?"

"If we had discovered anything at all," said Gorsky, as if he were talking to a child, "do you think I would only have suspicions?"

Nealey said bitingly, "I've never known a lack of proof to keep you from taking action." And that, he saw by Gorsky's face, had been a mistake. He hurried on. "So we have three low-grade operatives in Menton, sent by NATO on a fool's errand—to protect Parracini."

"And at last two very senior officers arriving today. But the most senior of them all was already here, yesterday. According to one of our best informants, he sent a brief message to Paris requesting dual repairs for the *Sea Breeze*—two more agents, of course—and identified himself by one of his code-names, Uncle Arthur." And that, he thought as he watched Nealey lose his cockiness and revert to being suitably impressed, restores the correct balance between us. No need to spoil the effect by admitting that Uncle Arthur's real name had never been identified—it was only known to four NATO officials in Brussels, and none of them were talking. As for his colleagues, they were ignorant of his rank and importance, accepted him as one of themselves. It had proved, so far, to be the best possible cover. So far... But he was here in Menton. And Lawton was here in Menton, as elusive as ever. And these two had coincided before. Accidentally? There never had been any proof that Lawton and Uncle Arthur were the same man. And yet—

"When two suspicions become one," Gorsky said, watching Nealey's baffled face with a smile, "then I act."

"But if Lawton is a NATO agent—how could he have any interest in Shandon? We've covered our tracks, we've—"

"NATO *is* interested. Because of you. They have been watching you for the last three months, according to Kelso."

"Tom Kelso? What does *he* know? He was bluffing."

"I received further confirmation only half an hour ago—from Parracini. He was trying to reach you here, give you orders to clear out. I took the message. I am now passing his instructions to you."

"Something is wrong," Nealey protested. "No one has been watching me. Not for three months, or three weeks, or three days."

"Are you contradicting Parracini's judgment? Or mine?"

"No, no. But why didn't NATO move in on me as soon as I reached Europe?"

"Have you forgotten that a suspected agent is watched for his contacts, that the net is not drawn around him until a large haul can be made?"

"I know," said Nealey, and didn't conceal his irritation. He was certain he hadn't been followed, either in Washington or in Menton. "But the point is—"

"The point is that you leave here by Monday at latest. For Aix-en-Provence. A natural choice for a man who needs rest and medical treatment. It has thermal baths, many doctors. More importantly for you—crowds and a confusion of streets. Feliks will meet you without any trouble. It can easily be reached from Menton—a two-hour drive. And it is near the Mediterranean."

Ten miles from Marseilles. "You are shipping me out on a freighter?" Nealey tried to conceal his anger.

"If we have to, yes." Gorsky noted Nealey's rigid smile. "But," he added, "we can offer you more comfortable quarters than that. We have a cabin cruiser available." His voice had lost all harshness, had become almost friendly.

Nealey thought over that idea. Yes, once it was time for him to slip out of Aix-en-Provence, it would be easy to travel ten miles to the coast, be picked up at one of its numerous small harbours. NATO agents would concentrate on the Marseilles docks, the obvious place for a man in flight. A cabin cruiser available? "All right. Shall I type out my request for sick leave now? Make sure it suits your—your scenario?"

"Write it by hand."

Nealey sat down at his desk, found paper and pen. Is this a trap of some kind? Or is Aix-en-Provence the trap? If I am under suspicion, the French police could easily detain me there at the request of NATO. "How long will it take you to find my replacement?" he asked, as he dated his note to Maclehose. "Any delay could be dangerous. Extradition is possible, once the Americans receive Chuck Kelso's information. Or have you forgotten that I am supposed to be an American citizen?"

"You will not have long to wait before your replacement is here. A week, perhaps. Not more."

"A week?" He's lying, thought Nealey. He is ensuring my complete obedience by promises. Does he think I will defect? But this time Nealey hid his anger well. He began writing, pleading this and that, exactly as it had been dictated. He signed the letter, handed it over to be read.

Gorsky nodded his approval, and watched Nealey as he sealed the envelope and addressed it. "A week," he emphasised as if he felt reassurance was necessary.

"I begin to think you have my replacement already chosen."

Gorsky concealed his chagrin. "Every important actor must have his understudy."

"You mean there was always a substitute, waiting to—"

"But of course. You could have met with an accident, or needed a serious operation. Such things happen."

Yes, thought Nealey as he stared back at Gorsky, accidents do happen. Thank God that Parracini is in charge. If he weren't here to restrain this man... And once again Nealey felt the same cold fear that had seized him in Washington.

"Get some clothes on," Gorsky told him. "You'll drive me into Menton, leave me at the market. And don't take long to dress. Two minutes." He had switched off the lights and opened the shutters, and was now making a quick check of the terrace and gardens. He was at the office door, his hat in his hand, his coat over his arm, waiting impatiently, by the time Nealey had pulled on trousers, shirt, and sweater, and slipped bare feet into loafers. Less than two minutes, thought Nealey, but Gorsky had no comment. His eyes and ears were intent on the silent house as he hurried downstairs, led the way through the hall, ghostly in the first light of morning.

He did not speak, even when they reached the garage safely—no one in the garden, no one at any window—and entered the car. Only as they left Shandon's gates did Gorsky say, "Hurry! Drive as fast as you can." He threw his coat and hat into the back seat. "Get rid of them," was his final command. Then, slumping low, head kept well down, eyes on his watch, a frown on his face, Gorsky seemed to forget Nealey completely.

Nealey made one last show of independent judgment. He halted the Citroën a couple of blocks from the market. "Too many trucks pulling in, too many farmers opening their stalls," he said briskly. "I'm not going to be caught in a traffic jam. You get out here."

Gorsky had no other choice: to keep the car standing while he argued would only draw attention to them. He got out.

Nealey had a parting word. "You shouldn't be seen with me, anyway. Or have you forgotten I'm under surveillance?" He smiled and drove on, cutting away from the shore, heading back into town. Surveillance, he thought with contempt, just one of Gorsky's lies to keep me in line. No one has been following me. I'd have sensed it, and, to prove he was right, Nealey spent a few extra minutes weaving in and out of streets and avenues, keeping his eye on the rear-view mirror. As he expected, no one was tailing him.

There's only one real danger as far as I'm concerned, and that is Chuck Kelso's letter. How long will extradition take? If I'm faced with that, before Feliks arrives in Aix-en-Provence to—what would be Gorsky's word? Oh yes—to escort me safely to that cabin cruiser (another convenient lie to keep me trusting Gorsky?), then what do I do? What do I do? On sudden impulse, he swung away from the centre of the town, entered the tunnel that led to Garavan Bay. The *Hotel Alexandre* was along there somewhere.

How easy, he thought, it would be to walk into the *Alexandre*, ask for Lawton, and make a pretty little speech: I am not the American citizen, Heinrich Nealey by name, born in Brooklyn, 1941. I am Simas Poska, born in Vilnius, 1940. As a trained agent of the KGB, I adopted the identity of Heinrich Nealey when I "escaped" from the German Democratic Republic in 1963. Since August 1965 I have fulfilled my duties as a Soviet intelligence officer in Washington. In January of this year I came to Menton to continue these duties. I have no connection with the death of Charles Kelso. Murder is not my bag, my dear Mr. Lawton. And so I defect, if you'll guarantee me this and that, etc., etc.

Yes, how easy. But defection is not my bag either. In spite of Comrade Colonel Boris Yevgenovich Gorsky, affectionately called Oleg by his friends—all two of them if that isn't an exaggeration—I am still a capable, intelligent and loyal officer of the KGB.

Nealey reached the *Alexandre*, making a quick U-turn on

to the west-bound avenue, so that he could pass its door. He slowed down. So easy, he thought again, and laughed. Why not throw Gorsky's hat and coat, unwanted relics of last night, right into the hotel garden? Smiling broadly, he put on speed and headed back towards the tunnel underneath the Old Town.

As arranged, Gorsky had met Feliks, waiting in a dilapidated van, near the flower-stalls outside of the market. "The harbour," he told Feliks. "I want to see if the *Monique* has arrived."

"She's here." Feliks wasn't speaking French this morning. That had been part of his disguise for the Kelso assignment last night, like the black coveralls and ski-mask. His thin face was gaunt, and his voice depressed. The capture of Gómez was a real setback. Together they had made a good team. For almost eight years. Who would be his partner on today's job? Some new arrival from the *Monique*, no doubt, who would want his own way or need everything explained twice. Better to work alone, Feliks thought. Yes, a real setback.

"Then I want to verify her exact position." It had taken a generous payment and some rapid arrangements to get a fishing-boat to leave well before dawn, and let the *Monique* slip into its mooring-place.

"I'll take the tunnel," said Feliks. "It's the quickest route."

As they emerged on to the waterfront, Gorsky scanned each pedestrian, each car. "That black Citroën—just ahead of us," he said quickly. "Nealey. What's he doing over here?" The wide avenue that edged Garavan Bay would never lead to Cap Martin.

"Follow him?"

"Yes."

Well ahead of them Nealey made his U-turn, slowed down as he approached the *Alexandre*.

Feliks was roused from his state of gloom. "What *is* he doing?" He too made the turn, drew to the side of the westbound avenue as if he were going to make a delivery. His face was now as sharp and eager as a ferret's.

In bitter disgust, Gorsky said, "The man who knows when he is under surveillance. Just look at him, Feliks. He hasn't even noticed us."

That would be difficult, thought Feliks, hidden as we are by the high sides of this closed van marked ALIMENTATIONS: eggs and butter, that's us. Still, Nealey's mind wasn't on his proper business. "He's stopping!" But as he spoke, the black Citroën picked up speed, began travelling at last in the right direction for Cap Martin.

"Let him go," said Gorsky. Yes, he was thinking, Nealey always runs. In Central Park with Mischa, or last night at the Kelso place—he runs. He saves himself. Always. And now he is about to defect. I know the signs. I can smell them. "Did you manage to salvage our communications equipment from the cottage?" he asked suddenly, and gestured towards the interior of the van. "Guns, ammunition?"

"Everything. All packed in cartons, ready to be set up or stored on the boat. Also, I brought some changes of clothes for us both."

Gorsky nodded his approval. "The *Monique*," he directed Feliks. Then, back to thinking about Nealey, he lapsed into silence.

25

The *Alexandre*, one of the new hotels facing Garavan Bay, was constructed in Siamese-twin style: an apartment house for long-lease tenants had been built directly on to its side, seemingly independent but conveniently linked by their jointly-shared restaurant. For anyone who wanted to approach the hotel discreetly, it was fairly simple to stay unobserved, provided, of course, that he had previously scouted the area and discovered its possibilities.

Tony Lawton had done just that, as soon as he had checked in yesterday morning. Future insurance. It paid off now. Once Bernard had deposited him a good hundred yards away from the *Alexandre* and the KGB agent on guard duty (a minor character, this must be, Tony reflected, but still an annoyance), he walked briskly to the apartment house and nipped into its hall. There were other early strollers, too, out for a pre-breakfast constitutional or the morning newspaper. Gorsky's man, glued to the hotel entrance, paid little attention.

From the apartment-house hall—one elderly lady, with hair curlers wrapped up like a pound of sausages, being pulled by her small white poodle towards the sidewalk—Tony entered the restaurant. (No patrons: croissants and coffee, standard breakfast, only needed a tray and room-service.) Avoiding the kitchen door, he made his way between the rows of tables and entered the small lobby of the *Alexandre*. Empty, at seven in the morning, except for the night clerk still on duty and half asleep. Tony didn't approach the desk or the self-service elevator. He took the stairs, nicely carpeted, silent, and only three flights to his floor. His room key, behind a mezzotint on the wall near his door, was still in place, jammed between the picture frame and its cord.

Tony's room was modern—small, everything built-in as on shipboard, with a stretch of sliding windows opening on to a balcony and a view of the bay. He resisted both, flopped down on one of the narrow beds, "Bliss," he said, feeling his spine stretch, his back-muscles ease. But not yet, he reminded himself, not yet.

First, a call to Bill's two bright boys. They must be, to have chosen their identification routine. No humdrum weather talk from them. He was to ask, "Is Jeff around?" And the answer would come back, "No, he's out looking for Mutt." Yes, thought Tony, I rather like their style. Their names were Saul and Walt—Canadian, British, American? Bill hadn't said: only that there would be no language hang-ups, and thank heaven for that. Tony's instructions would be quickly understood. And then, to make his message authentic, he was to end with Bill's customary sign-off: "No more muffins for tea—make mine jelly doughnuts."

Happy idiots, all three of them; but their touch of light relief was just what he needed to break up this morning's strain and tension. Tony's mind relaxed along with his body. He stopped worrying about the difficulties and dangers of making an open call to two unknown agents. He rose from the bed and dialled their number.

"A return visit to last night's scene," he began, once the formalities of Mutt and Jeff were over. "But this time come as VIPs and pay us a visit. Be our guests. For arrival, manner should be dignified, dress restrained. Perhaps a dark raincoat to cover more normal clothes? The kind of thing that is worn around that area? Can do? A briefcase would look good, too. Ten o'clock prompt. Sea is calm. Breeze is slight. Understood?"

"Understood," said Saul—or Walt. "Anything to add?"

Tony gave them Bill's jelly doughnut routine. It was received with a brief and business-like "Okay."

So that was settled. Next a check with the *Aurora* itself. Vincent, the man to contact there, was very much on duty. Identification went briskly by a series of numbers. Tony's message was equally crisp: Georges arriving at ten, with party of three, all four with identity cards; two men, both known to Georges, entering marina ten twenty-five, boarding ten twenty-eight, sailing ten thirty.

"*D'accord*," said Vincent. "Will transmit sailing-time to escort. "*Bonne chance*."

And that too was settled, thought Tony as he laid aside his transceiver. Any gaps left? There always were, of course, and then you had to improvise quickly and hope for the best. Too bad that he couldn't be down at the marina to make sure Georges and his party had reached it, or to see Bill and Parracini actually board the *Aurora*, watch them all sail safely out to sea.

It would have been a satisfying moment. But impossible, with the time-schedule necessary to keep Parracini from thinking up some demanding questions. Such as: "*Why* are we leaving the house so early? We don't arrive at the harbour until ten thirty; we board the *Sea Breeze* at ten thirty-five. Isn't *that* the arrangement?" Bill had difficulties enough without those queries being raised, intent as he was on getting Parracini into the car before the *Aurora* was even mentioned. Otherwise Parracini would head indoors for the bathroom, nice excuse, to make contact with Gorsky and pass the word that *Sea Breeze* was off and *Aurora* was on, *Aurora, Aurora,* find the *Aurora.* And Gorsky would... Yes, the original time of departure from the house on Garavan Hill had to be kept. And that, Tony told himself, is the reason why you won't wave goodbye to the *Aurora.* Uncle can't be in two places at once.

He ordered the usual *café complet*, began laying out the necessary change of clothes, shaved and showered. Breakfast still hadn't arrived. The hell with it, he thought, and got into bed. He set the alarm for nine o'clock. That would give him an hour and a half for sleep: enough to set him up for the rest of this day. He needed it.

But fifteen minutes later the waiter unlocked the door, brought the breakfast-tray shoulder-high, triumphant delivery, into the room. Tony came awake as the lock turned. "*Scusi!*" said the young Italian, his good-morning smile transfixed as a naked man leapt out of bed with hands raised karate-style. "*Scusi, signore!*" The tray, almost dropped, was laid hastily on the nearest table.

"Just a nightmare, *un incubo*," said Tony, draping a sheet around him. Two francs for a tip, and the boy's nerves were partly restored. At least he managed to get to the door and close it carefully.

The coffee had spilled over the paper tray-cloth. Half a cup was still pourable, croissant and brioche only fit to be eaten with a spoon. He turned away from the unappetising mess, drank the coffee in two gulps, and dropped once more into bed. Just as he stretched back, preparing to drift off, his transceiver on the table beside his pillow gave its insistent buzz. He reached for it, switched on the connection. It was Emil reporting from the *Sea Breeze*. "Something new was added during the early hours. Must have been between four and five, when I was having some shut-eye. There's a cabin cruiser, the *Monique*, not far from us. She has taken the place of a fishing-boat—"

"Your friends—they cleared out to let her—" Tony began in alarm. Good God, he was thinking, what kind of beer-guzzling pals did Emil welcome aboard last night?

"No, no, that was one of the other fishing-boats. My friends are still here, working away. Two of them dropped in for breakfast. I couldn't call you until they left. All is quiet now. But—" Emil hesitated, "but the *Monique* seemed too interested in us. You'd better have a look at her. When do I expect you?"

"Now. Give me twenty minutes."

"No need to rush. As I said, all is quiet."

"Twenty minutes." Tony signed off, grim-faced. The *Monique*—Gorsky's? Could be. A cabin cruiser... And right in the harbour, not waiting out in the bay until the *Sea Breeze* sailed. Which meant the *Monique* could watch all the moves that Tony had planned, instead of relying on observers stationed at the dock, sending out radio reports on the exact number of men arriving at what precise time. Gorsky, if he was on board the *Monique*, would certainly have his binoculars trained on the *Sea Breeze*, and, unlike his observers, even if he had never seen Bill, he knew the difference between Parracini and Bernard. But how, Tony kept wondering as he called for a taxi to arrive in ten minutes at the apartment house next door, how the bloody hell did Gorsky manage to get his damned cabin cruiser into an anchorage that was already jammed full? Money, influence, or sheer luck?

He dressed rapidly: blue jeans, rough navy sweater, an old denim windbreaker that could reverse into a tweed Eisenhower jacket, rubber-soled shoes, a knitted cap pulled down to cover his hair except for the wild fringe he had combed over his brow, eyeglasses with plain glass lenses, a temporary moustache. In the mirror the effect was good—a workaday sailor, with hands in pockets, hunched shoulders, and a slight roll to his walk.

From the false bottom of his bag he selected two hairpieces, one dark brown, one blond, found a dark moustache, and shoved them into the tweed lining's pockets. Transceiver, Gauloise cigarettes, a small box of coarse matches, and he was ready to leave. Again, his room-key was hidden behind the mezzotint; again, he used the staircase, avoided the hotel lobby, and made his way through the dining-room. He reached the front entrance of the apartment-house as the cab drew up. He was inside before the startled driver could even get out of his seat to open the door.

"The *Petit Port*, and double the fare if we reach it in five minutes," Tony said, bending down to tie his shoelace as they passed the *Alexandre*'s entrance. Gorsky still had a man there, leaning against his car's fender. Either Gorsky had agents to spare, and Tony doubted that, or he had become much too interested in Lawton.

He stopped the taxi not far from the harbour's steps. The double fare was paid, and a good tip added. "Meet me here at ten fifteen," he said. "Can you be sure of that? It will be a short journey, but I'll pay well." The driver, an old sailor type himself, looked at the money already in his hand. Ten fifteen, he agreed. Without fail.

Now, thought Tony as he altered his walk to suit his appearance, we'll have a look at the opposition.

"Did you see her?" asked Emil. He had recovered from his attack of astonishment: he hadn't expected Tony to arrive so quickly; he hadn't even recognised him, mixing with the small groups of sailing enthusiasts and fishermen that gathered for the usual talk or early-morning stroll around the harbour area. It wasn't until a seaman detached himself from three other nautical types as they passed the *Sea Breeze* that Emil actually identified the man as Tony.

"Couldn't miss her." The *Monique* was a sleek and classy lady, with good lines and a capable look. She was smaller than Tony had expected, which accounted for the ease with which she had entered the harbour. She lay just four doors away, as a landsman might put it, cheek by jowl with the fishing vessel under repair. (Emil's friends were now having trouble with one of the sails.) Tony had had to pass her to reach the *Sea Breeze*: a bad moment when—like the three sailors to whom he had loosely attached himself on their walk along the wharf—he paused to admire the smooth and shining cabin cruiser. "She is being loaded," Tony said, as he took a mug of coffee from Emil.

"That only started about twenty minutes ago—just after I

called you—with the tall fellow carrying down cartons on to the dock. He got one of the crew to stand guard over them while he went back for more. Didn't want anyone else to touch them, can you beat that?" Emil's good-natured face, round and blunt-featured, was tired and drawn this morning, but his usual cheerful humour had reasserted itself with Tony's arrival. He grinned and shook his head. "Don't know which is funnier— that man carrying those cartons, one at a time, all by himself; or the way you look." He noticed the mug of coffee was already emptied. "Like some breakfast?"

"A lot of breakfast," said Tony and went on brooding about the loading of the *Monique*. At least eight cartons (extra valuable; contents delicate?), four suitcases, three baskets of hastily-packed food supplies. Two men at work on the project: one of them, slow-moving and deliberate, using a makeshift gangplank, was now doing the heavy work, lifting and carrying; the other, still guarding his precious cartons on the dock, stood close beside them and gave out instructions. He had paused to rake Tony's little group with a very sharp look. Just the usual nuisance, he seemed to decide—curious locals without work of their own to do. His glare was enough to sour all their interest, and they moved on. Impatiently he had turned back to the job of loading, without even a second glance at Tony. But Tony had recognised him. The gaunt face, fair hair, prominent eyes now popping with annoyance, belonged to the electrician who had come hurrying up through Shandon Villa's gardens along with Gorsky. "Where's that explosive you found?" Tony asked suddenly.

Emil lowered the heat under the bacon. "I did as you said. Stowed it in a coil of rope. Want to see it?" He left the cabin, returned in a few seconds with a small waterproof bag. "Plastic and detonator inside. What do we do with it? Give it the deep six once we're out of harbour? The sooner we get rid of this surprise package, the happier I'll be. Who made us a present of it, anyway?"

Tony took the lethal little bag, no bigger than the palm of his hand, studying it thoughtfully as he twisted the wire that tied its neck into a tighter knot. Time was passing: he might be too late. He rose, saying, "Won't be long."

Emil stared after him. He was already outside, stepping on to the dock.

He passed the three intervening boats—a sailing craft, a motor launch, a fishing vessel with Emil's friends communicating in hoarse yells—but kept his eyes on the *Monique*'s loading area. The tall thin man was now boarding her along with the last suitcase. Only the three baskets were left, large and bulging with food, obviously of less importance. They could wait until the two men had got their cartons safely stowed away.

Tony halted, lit a Gauloise, let it droop from one corner of his mouth. The two men, each carrying one of those fascinating cartons (electronic equipment?), made their way aft, heading for the rear door of the cabin. They entered. And Tony moved.

He ignored the two baskets that contained perishable items—bread, vegetables, fruit, cheeses. He went for the one that held a clutter of cans and jars, food that wouldn't need immediate unpacking. He tripped heavily against it, giving it a hard shove with his knee. The basket toppled on its side, and at least half of its contents spilled out. He made a grab for it, dropping the small waterproof bag among the lower layers of cans as he set it upright once more.

"*Mon Dieu!*" exclaimed a woman behind him. "Did you hurt yourself?"

A man told him, "They shouldn't leave their stuff lying all over the place. Could have broken your neck."

Three small boys laughed, began picking up cans and jars, tossing them back into the basket. Fine fun. Several other people had gathered near Tony, attracted by the bang and clatter of his little accident. And on the *Monique* the thin fair-haired man, his eyes popping out of his head, had raced forward. He checked his cartons; relaxed a little; shouted at the boys.

It seemed a propitious time to retreat. Tony walked back to the *Sea Breeze*, leaving the makings of an argument behind him. The could-have-broken-your-neck fellow was taking no snash from any luxury cabin cruiser. Popeye retreated to his cartons—a scene was the last thing he wanted—and it was left to his slow-moving comrade to disembark his considerable bulk and pick up the remaining cans and jars.

"Hurt yourself?" Emil asked as Tony entered the cabin, noticing the slight limp. He turned back to the frying-pan, concentrated on breaking a couple of eggs beside the curling bacon.

"Only temporary." Tony rubbed his knee, restored the blood-flow, and was thankful that—so far—he wasn't a candidate for gout.

"What was all the racket about?" Emil glanced around. Tony was pulling off his knitted cap, smoothing his fringe of hair back in proper place, removing jacket and eyeglasses. Then he sat down, looked blandly innocent. There was no sign of the small waterproof bag. "Where's that surprise package?"

"I thought we'd better return it to its rightful owner."

"Sure you got the right man?"

"Yes. He'll be on the *Monique* before she sails." As Emil gave him a hard but worried look, he added, "He has to be. Who else could decide whether or not to press the button and blow the poor old *Sea Breeze* sky-high? He'll be aboard, that's certain. His chief assistant is there now—that lean pop-eyed blond fellow. The two of them left a dead man floating in Shandon's pool yesterday."

"One of ours?"

"No, he wasn't one of anything. Just a danger to their security. So they silenced him."

"Drastic."

"That's what they are, drastic; the special-action boys of Department V."

"The hell they are," Emil said. That changed the picture considerably. He served up the eggs and bacon, filled two mugs with coffee, produced half a loaf of crusty bread.

"Fresh," Tony remarked, cutting off a thick slice. "Been doing some baking?"

"I didn't leave the boat," Emil assured him with an answering grin. "My fishing friends brought it along—their contribution to breakfast. They brought some bits of news, too. Harbour gossip, of course. But they don't like their new neighbour. That fat crew-member who helped with the loading—he's the only one visible—told them to cut out the hammering: people were trying to sleep."

"People?"

"Three in the crew. And a man who came down to have a look at the *Monique*. Then he walked past here, had a good look at the *Sea Breeze* too. Didn't stop, just walked past, then turned and went back to the *Monique*. He boarded her. He's probably still there. Haven't seen him since. Or two of the crew."

"The underwater experts?" Tony suggested. "Well, they had a busy night. Now they are resting from their labours and preparing for the day to come." He noted Emil's expression. "No more qualms about returning unwanted gifts?"

"No," Emil said most definitely.

"After all," said Tony, "it is really up to the button-pusher, isn't it?" A case of holding your fate in your own hands, he thought. "What was this joker like—the one who pretended he wasn't interested in the *Sea Breeze*?"

"About my height, dark hair, handsome. Husky, too. Good shoulders. Carried them straight."

"Wearing what?"

"A dark suit, a black turtle-neck."

"So he didn't have time to change his clothes, just ditched his coat and hat. Yes, I guess we all had a busy night."

Emil's blue eyes questioned him.

"I know," Tony agreed. "I have a lot to fill in for you. And I will. But let's finish with the *Monique* first. Any more particulars on her?"

"Nine-metre class, but deceptive. Her power is high for her size: thirty knots. She sailed from Monte Carlo early this morning. Not her usual crew, but owner's permission granted. All in order. The owner is an oil heiress who jets around."

"One of the liberal chic? Excessively liberal this time."

"Not too much. The *Monique* is only her second-best boat."

"And where did you pick up all that information? Is it pure gossip, or part-way reliable?"

"Well, I took a bet with Paul—one of my fishing friends— that the *Monique* couldn't do more than twenty knots. He said at least twenty-five. So he went along to the harbour-master's office, where his cousin works. And checked. And I paid up."

Tony's eyes gleamed. "Do you think you can interest him in another bet? How long does it take him to hoist the sails? That would block the *Monique*'s view of us nicely. Around ten thirty, I'd say. Or if you can think of something better—anything to distract attention."

"Distract attention from what?"

My God, Tony thought, he knows practically nothing; he's been hugging this boat for the last twenty-four hours, while Georges and I have been chasing around. All he got from us was a cryptic warning, and a very unpleasant swim. "Let's get the facts out," he said. "Turn on the radio, Emil, and we can talk."

Emil smiled. "There are no bugs here, Tony. I've checked. I was only once off the boat last night—to ask my friends over here for a glass of beer."

"Twice," Tony said gently. "You had that underwater trip around the old *Sea Breeze*. But you did a fine job," he added quickly. Emil was twenty-six, and his feelings bruised easily. "Just fine."

"At least there was some action." Emil set down his coffee-mug, and rose. He began a quick but methodical search of the cabin. It was small: could sleep three, seat six, or stand eight. Yes, Tony thought, Gerard wouldn't have enjoyed his conference with Parracini here: much more comfortable for all of them on the *Aurora*. He glanced at his watch. Five past nine. He had about fifty minutes to brief Emil, tell him the important details: Parracini; the original plans for the *Sea Breeze*; the switch to the *Aurora*; the *Sea Breeze* deception beginning at ten o'clock; their own time-schedule. Fifty minutes would be more than ample.

Tony relaxed, poured himself another slug of coffee.

"Nothing," Emil said with relief, finishing his self-appointed task. "Completely clean."

"Sorry to have troubled you, but I've been seeing some dicey examples of electronic magic. Bill's house is a complete trap. As Shandon Villa will be. You know, the opposition even wired Bill for sound—with a watch, no less, that he only takes off to go swimming. Cute?" And then Tony's amusement ended. "Christ—" He stared at Emil. "Does Parracini own a watch like that one?"

For a long moment, Tony sat completely still, completely silent. "I think I've messed things up," he said softly. His voice sharpened. "There *was* a gap, God damn it, and I didn't see it." His face was white and tense. He could hear Bill's patient voice, explaining to Parracini, in the car, about the necessary change from *Sea Breeze* to *Aurora*, perhaps even giving the advanced time of sailing. And every single word would be sent out by Parracini's watch, to be picked up near at hand, and relayed to Gorsky down in the harbour. "God," he said, and closed his eyes.

Whatever this is, it's bad, thought Emil. "What do we do?"

Can't reach Bill to warn him. Can't risk those blasted bugs near every telephone. Can't leave here either, got to brief Emil at once, let him know what to expect. "Do?" Tony asked heavily. "We don't give up. That's certain." And, he told himself, if I see the *Monique* suddenly preparing to leave at ten thirty, I'll ram her right in the harbour, damned if I don't. "All right. Let's talk."

Emil nodded. He decided to turn on the radio anyway, and sat down to listen.

26

At ten o'clock, prompt to the minute, two men came walking down the dock. They kept a steady unhurried pace, making their way politely but firmly through clusters of people, paying little attention to anything except their own grave conversation. They wore navy-blue raincoats. Their shoes were polished, their heads neat and well-brushed, their collars and ties restrained and impeccable. And one of them carried an attaché case.

Lounging at the bow of the *Sea Breeze*, Emil was the first to catch sight of them. He took out his cigarette-case and turned his back on the *Monique* as he spoke two words into it. "Looks good," he told Tony, who was still keeping out of sight in the cabin. He lit a cigarette, took a couple of drags, and only then did he seem to become aware of the two visitors. His nonchalance left him. He flicked the cigarette over the side and went to meet them, jumping on to the dock with—apparently—a smile of welcome. Actually, it was the Mutt and Jeff identification, delivered in a quick murmur, that was amusing Emil. He gave them a small salute, brought his voice back to normal. "Hope you had a pleasant trip. This way, gentlemen." He even steadied them by the elbow as they stepped on deck.

"You're overplaying it, buddy," the taller of the two said. "We aren't as decrepit as all that." He looked about sixty or a little less, grey-haired, slightly stooped, with a white indoor complexion.

"Just the VIP treatment," Emil assured him. "We're being watched."

The other one said nothing, just pursed his pale lips. He was of medium height, putting on weight like his friend, his reddish hair fading with age. He too looked as though he spent most of his time at a desk.

What a pair of elderly ducks, thought Emil; where did Bill find them? And these are the men who patrolled up and down the mole last night, making sure no one boarded the *Sea Breeze*! If that had happened, they might have needed more help than I did. Emil was smiling broadly as he ushered them into the cabin.

"Hi there," said the grey-haired man. "I'm Saul."

"Walt," said the other. "Tony? Emil?"

They shook hands, looked round the small cabin, noted its tightly-drawn curtains. "Who's doing the watching?" Saul asked.

"That cabin cruiser you passed. The *Monique*."

"We saw her arriving just as we were knocking off duty last night. Neat looking piece. So that's our target."

"Rather," said Tony, "we are their target." His study of the two men ended. "Excellent," he told them, "an excellent job.

But you can start stepping out of character."

"What?" asked Walt. "No more VIP treatment? And just as I was beginning to like it." But without wasting a second they shed the raincoats, pulled off the ties, stripped themselves of shirts and neatly-creased trousers. They were now in tight-fitting jeans, coarsely-knitted sweaters (Saul's was navy; Walt's, a dirty white). The wigs were next to go, revealing Saul's hair to be light brown, longish, sun-bleached at the edges, with a loose wave falling over his brow. Walt had black hair, thick and heavy, curling close to his head. From the attaché case, out came one pair of faded espadrilles, one pair of old sneakers, a small jar of cold cream, tissues, a mirror. With lightning speed they went to work on greasing and wiping their faces. The white indoor look vanished, was replaced by their permanent tans. And once the polished shoes were changed for espadrilles and sneakers, the transformation was complete: two young men, not much older than Emil and equally lithe and lean.

Emil's admiring stare was cut short by Tony. "Time to jolly your fishing friends into making a bet," he was told. He left immediately.

Tony studied the two quick-change artists. "Congratulations," he said. Three minutes it had taken them, no more.

"What now?" Saul asked.

"As soon as some diversion starts on board the fishing-boat, you can slip out and stroll back down the dock."

"That all?" Saul didn't hide his disappointment.

"It's plenty. Did you know you were photographed?" Just wish, Tony thought, there had been three of them; still. Gorsky might possibly deduce, when he saw two men, that Gerard had substituted for one of the officers who were originally coming to meet Parracini. Did I mention "three" to Bill when he was wearing that bloody watch? or did I have enough sense to keep my big mouth shut, only talk of Gerard? No time now to start recalling that garden scene—and stop worrying, there's nothing you can do about it, anyway. "You'll drive some guys crazy, back in Moscow, trying to fit names to your faces."

"Who's running their show here?"

"Gorsky."

"Who's Gorsky?" asked Walt.

"A tough customer. He had his underwater experts attach an explosive to the *Sea Breeze* last night. Emil found it." They seemed to know what that must have entailed, for they looked impressed and were no doubt reassessing Emil. Tony continued, "There is something else you could do. Risky, of course; you'll possibly be on camera again. What I've got in mind—"

But Emil had returned. "No need to place a wager," he told Tony. "They've been working on the mainsail, got it hoisted half-way, and it's stuck. Quick," he urged Saul and Walt, "now's your moment."

Walt didn't budge. "What did you have in mind?" he asked Tony.

"At ten thirty, wait at the head of the dock. You'll see me, wearing this checked tweed—" Tony picked up his denim jacket, showed its lining—"accompanying a man, dark hair and moustache, dark suit. Run some interference for us when we pass the *Monique*. Will do?"

They were on their way. "Ten thirty," Saul said as he and Walt stepped on deck. Quickly, they passed Emil, leaning against a rail, watching the fishing-boat with amusement. So far, its sail hadn't come slithering down, exposing the bow of the *Sea Breeze* to curious eyes on board the *Monique*. Emil drew a breath of genuine relief: the two men were now on the dock, with no connection observed between them and the *Sea Breeze*.

Behind him Tony's voice said, "I've got three minutes to catch a cab. See you." And Tony left, too, almost on the heels of Saul and Walt. He was once more wearing his denim jacket, knitted cap, eyeglasses; his walk—when Emil risked another glance at the dock—was a brisk sea-going roll. He caught up with Saul and Walt, passed them, was lost in the thickening crowd.

Definitely thickening, Emil noted. The harbour had come to life. Now there was constant movement on the dock and on the long mole above it. In the anchorage itself, some boats had already left for a cruise, weather permitting; some were being sluiced down and polished; others, with less optimistic owners, were being secured against any afternoon storm. It was the usual Saturday crowd of week-end sailors, wandering around when they weren't on board, interested in anything new and different. There were tourists, too, taking the air, feeding the seagulls while they had their photographs snapped. And the old salts, gathered in two and threes, watching this waste of good bread on birds who knew how to scavenge for themselves, were more convinced than ever that foreigners were crazy.

Emil left his post at the rail. It was ten fifteen. Better get the cabin straightened up, he warned himself. And what do we do with the clothes that Saul and Walt have left strewn around? Sure, stow them away in a spare locker meanwhile; but how and where do we return them? He went inside, shook his head over the wild disorder that met him, and set to work.

* * *

The taxi was waiting, just as arranged. Thankfully Tony got in: at least this was something that hadn't gone wrong. He gave the driver exact instructions that would take him half-way along the bay front, a brief run that would only last four or five minutes. There, at the same red light where he and Georges had stopped last night—good God, was it only last night?—the taxi made its left turn into the westbound avenue. "Just here," Tony said, money ready in his hand as the cab drew up.

He waited until it was bowling back to the Old Town before he moved over to a row of shops, so new that some were still vacant like the apartments above them. This was where he would meet Bernard, just outside the tea-room.

He had let Bernard choose the rendezvous, as they had driven down to the *Alexandre* that morning, to give the quiet unassuming man a touch of needed confidence. Bernard might be Bill's faithful retainer, but he was the last man Tony would have recruited for the job on hand—except that there had been no other choice available. The tea-room with cakes for sale, Bernard had suggested at once. He and Brigitte often went there; Brigitte liked their napoleons, cream inside instead of custard. It had lime-green curtains and pots of cyclamen. Couldn't be missed.

"All right," Tony had said. "Once you drop Bill and Parracini at the boat, at ten twenty-five, start driving like the hammers of hell. And pick me up near your tea-room."

"Not at your hotel?"

"No. At the tea-room. And waste no time, Bernard. This is pretty urgent. And also our own top-secret plan." That had impressed Bernard, even if he was mystified. "Say nothing to Brigitte or Parracini or Nicole. Bill knows I'm making arrangements with you, so there's no need to discuss them with him."

And Bernard, still perplexed but always obliging, had told Tony to rely on him. He'd be at the tea-room as soon as he could. He wouldn't forget Bill's walking-stick. He'd wear a dark suit, as Tony had suggested. And he wouldn't say a thing to anyone.

So, thought Tony, here I am now, looking at green curtains and splashes of cyclamen, waiting for Bernard. I am far enough from the harbour, where Gorsky must have someone stationed as lookout for the arrival of Bill's Mercedes; I am far enough from the *Alexandre* and its weary watchdog. The taxi wasn't followed. I may actually be in the clear, unobserved except by that girl behind the counter arranging her cream-puffs.

He moved away, farther along the row of shops, chose a safer place to loiter unnoticed—a window display of real-estate photographs, desirable properties for sale—but kept a constant eye on the road that led from the marina. Bernard wasn't late. It was Tony, over-anxious about traffic jams and distances to be covered—he kept forgetting how short they were in Menton—who was five minutes early.

But so was Bernard.

In astonishment Tony caught sight of the Mercedes speeding towards him. He had scarcely time to get his moustache peeled off without taking three inches of skin before Bernard was about to reach him. And pass him without recognition. Tony whipped off his glasses and cap, waved, brought the Mercedes to a startled halt. "Well done," he told Bernard. But, he was thinking, I'm glad that none of my friends were around to see that messy encounter: amateur night at the Palladium. I'd never have heard the end of it. And he wondered briefly, as

Bernard followed his instructions and drove on past the tea-room with its roving-eyed girl, if Bernard was able to do what was expected of him without blowing the whole show. "How did it go?"

Bernard burst into a quick and excited story. Bill had made them leave the house early, insisted on driving, said they could be followed, kept watching the rear-view mirror, taken the winding curves of the narrow road like a crazy man. Then, once round a sharp turn, Bill had pulled up short. And there *was* a car following. It came round the curve, saw the Mercedes standing there, avoided it, side-swiped a wall at the edge of the—

Tony caught Bernard's arm, interrupting the flow of words. "We'll stop here." He was drawing off his denim jacket, pulling out a dark brown wig and moustache from a pocket. "We'll change before we reach the harbour, arrive as expected. So—" he told Bernard, applying the moustache for him—"press hard on it. Hold your fingers there. Yes, that's right. And now this wig. Get it well down. Cover your own hair completely."

Bernard, after his first startled moment, was quick enough. His own thin reddish-fair hair vanished. He studied the transformation in the car mirror, took out a comb to arrange his heavy dark waves in place, fingered the moustache once more, and nodded his approval. "It alters a man," he admitted, and smiled.

Tony had pulled on his own wig, changing his medium-cut hair, indeterminate brown, into longish blond locks. "Serious business," he warned. "No more smiles, Bernard. We could be watched every step of the way, from the Mercedes to the *Sea Breeze*. Let's get moving."

They started on the last lap of the journey towards the

harbour. "What did Bill do?" Tony asked, prompting Bernard back into his story. "Did he drive on?"

Yes, that was what he had done. He had driven like a madman, and turned on the radio, and talked through it—about a change in the arrangements.

"And Parracini? How did he take it?"

"At first, angry. Told Bill to turn around, he was going back to the house. And Bill said, 'You don't want to meet Gerard? Because he's not coming near the house. It's no longer safe. You saw that car—it knew where to pick up our trail. What's your choice? Go back? Or go on, as arranged?' So we didn't go back."

"And Parracini?"

"As relieved as I was to arrive at the marina. Six minutes early." Bernard shuddered, remembering the speed with which they had made that wild descent. "We were lucky, I think. But Bill's a good driver—I'll say that for him." He pointed ahead. "I can park there. All right?"

Tony nodded. Yes, he was thinking, Bill is good. If he hadn't remembered Parracini's watch—well, he did: and I didn't.

The Mercedes came to a halt. Bernard's hands were still on the wheel, his grip tightening until white knuckles showed.

A case of stage fright, Tony thought, and at this moment I'm not too certain of my own lines. "Now, all we have to do is walk along a dock," he said reassuringly. "Look at no one, Bernard. No one. Just keep talking to me."

"Am I supposed to be Parracini?" Bernard's doubts were growing. "We'll never manage to—"

"You're his height, and that's the important thing."

"But if you are Bill, then—"

"I know. I'm three inches shorter, but he never was seen around town, was he? I've got his colour of hair and his limp and his cane. So we'll manage. Shoulders back, Bernard, remember the way Parracini walks. And keep to my left side, your face turned towards me and away from the boats. Ready? Here goes." He reached over to the back seat for the walking-stick, gripped it in his right hand, and got out of the car. Bernard had no choice. He got out too. "Left side, Bernard, left side! And you look fine."

As they crossed the avenue to reach the harbour, Bernard asked, "Are we doing this because of Parracini?"

"Yes."

"To distract the KGB?" Bernard's face was grim.

"Yes," said Tony again, and repressed a smile. "Just a little distraction." And a very big bluff. "Now let's talk of other things. What did you think of that Milan-Turin soccer match last week? A near riot, I heard."

And Bernard, who followed every football game on television, had a topic to keep him going on that nerve-racking walk to the *Sea Breeze*. Once he paused in his monologue—almost as they were reaching the *Monique*—to glare at a couple of young men who were about to pass and then, as they came abreast, slackened speed while they argued about some item in the newspaper one of them was opening.

"Face this way!" Tony got out in time. "Watch me!" Bernard remembered. He averted his head from the two men on his left, ignored their newspaper with its pages being turned, spread wide for consultation, and went on talking to Tony.

The *Monique* lay behind them. Tony checked a surge of relief, kept the same steady pace. Brilliant, he thought of the newspaper: Saul and Walt really knew all the tricks of the trade. They had managed to break the *Monique*'s view of Bernard and Tony, just at the crucial moment of passing; and they had made sure, too, that their own faces wouldn't be clearly photographed. Two bent heads, gesticulating arms, a flutter of turning pages: that was all Gorsky would make of them. Yes, brilliant. And essential. For the mainsail on the fishing-boat was no longer of any help: it had been lowered and furled.

Tony looked at Bernard. His shoulders were squared, he held himself tall, and now that the annoyance of two young men trying to crush past him was over, he was even enjoying himself. "Careful," Tony warned. "Just another ten paces to go."

They reached the *Sea Breeze*, entered its tidied cabin. Emil was now at the ship's radio, talking with the harbour-master. He broke off to say, "Got this five minutes ago," as he handed over a coded message. It was from the *Aurora*. It read, "Cargo fully loaded. Sailed on schedule."

Trust Vincent: everything done navy style. Bill and Parracini might arrive six minutes ahead of time, but the *Aurora* sailed exactly as arranged, at ten thiry.

Tony crossed over to one of the starboard windows, gently eased its heavy curtain apart. Beyond the fishing-boat the *Monique* rested quietly. No sign of leaving. He kept watch, waiting for any sudden activity. Nothing. He stayed there, watching and waiting. At last he let the quarter-inch gap of curtain close. He was smiling broadly. "They couldn't follow the *Aurora* now. She's well away."

"We did it!" Emil said, and slapped Bernard on the back.

"Easy, easy, take it easy," Tony said, restraining his laughter and theirs. "Don't forget that an important conference, with four very serious people, is beginning in this cabin. And you are one of them," he told Bernard. "Don't look out the windows. Don't open the door. Keep the curtains closed." He was removing the blond wig, reversing the jacket back to work-worn denim. The cap he would need; glasses and moustache expendable. "Get rid of the fancy dress," he urged Bernard. "Make yourself comfortable."

Bernard peeled off his dark moustache and wig. "Where are we going?"

"For a pleasure cruise."

"I just sit here? Stay inside? What about you?"

"We're the crew," Emil said impatiently. "And we'll be busy on deck until we clear the harbour. We cast off at eleven. Prompt." He turned to Tony: "I checked with the harbour-master about that. No delay, he said: there's another boat pulling out at eleven ten." Emil's grin was wide. "Guess who?"

So Gorsky was giving them a ten-minute start. Mighty generous of him, considering the *Monique* could raise almost thirty-five miles an hour, while the *Sea Breeze*, under power, could manage eleven and a half. Their thirty knots, thought Tony, against our ten: he will be right on our tail from the word go.

"Also," Emil was saying, "I told the harbour-master we probably wouldn't head in here tonight. Possibly returning tomorrow."

"You did, did you?" Tony sounded nettled.

Bernard interrupted them both. "I've got to get back by this afternoon. Brigitte doesn't know where I am. She's expecting me—"

"She'll wait," said Emil brusquely. And to Tony, "I thought it was a good idea. The *Monique* is bound to be listening for any communication between us and the shore." He paused, guessed the reason for Tony's silence. "Of course I didn't mention Nice. Did you think that I was fool enough to steer them in *that* direction?"

Tony relaxed. We're all getting too sharp-set, he thought. "Then it was a very good idea." It would certainly jolt Gorsky: what overnight trip for the *Sea Breeze*, and where? Not according to plan. And why wasn't Parracini's watch functioning? Why was nothing being received right now from the *Sea Breeze* cabin? Yes, Tony answered him, the watch is functioning, but it has been too far away for any monitoring. Far, far away, Gorsky, and getting farther by the minute. "One thing is certain," Tony predicted, "Gorsky won't let us out of his sight."

"And then?" asked Emil, very quietly.

"It depends on Gorsky, doesn't it?"

"He could try to board us—there are five of them, don't forget. Or he could ram us."

"Oh, come on, Emil. Cool it. Worrying is my business, not yours."

Bernard stared at them. "There's still danger?"

"It's only beginning," said Emil.

"Oh," said Bernard. His face brightened. He forgot about Brigitte and cream-cakes for tea. "Well, I'm not going to stay in here doing nothing. How can I help?"

"By staying in here," Tony told him. "Don't look out, don't be seen. That's the most important thing right now."

"And later?"

"Later, we'll call on you. If necessary." Tony checked his watch for the third time, and stepped on to the deck. He passed quickly to the port side of the boat, where the cabin would shield him from the *Monique*'s view. There he could wait for the next two minutes and time to cast off. He would be seen then, of course, no way to avoid it. But with his collar hunched up, and his knitted cap down over his brow, his head bent, his face averted, he might just postpone identification until the right moment. And that wasn't here, at this dock, at three seconds to eleven.

"Okay," he sang out for Emil's benefit, and moved towards the lines. "Let go."

27

Blue sky and white clouds, steady breeze and rippling waves,
it was the Saturday sailors' delight. Small craft dotted Garavan
Bay, everything from rowing-boats with outboard engines to
light yachts under sail. The *Sea Breeze* headed east as though
she were bound for Italy. She was taking it easy, travelling only
at half-speed so that she'd be less than a mile from the harbour
when the *Monique* emerged.

"There she is," said Emil, "and they've seen us."

"Good," said Tony.

The *Monique* skirted the offshore craft, only began to put
on speed as the *Sea Breeze* passed the high promontory of
cliffs that formed the end of the bay, and was lost to her sight.
Temporarily. The *Monique*, under full power, reached the cliffs,
came sweeping round them to enter Italian waters. She found
herself almost faced with the *Sea Breeze*, which had turned and
was now heading back under full power towards Garavan Bay.

Once there, *Sea Breeze* reduced speed and sailed on, past the harbour, past Menton's west bay, rounded Cap Martin and again dropped out of sight.

Again, the *Monique* gave chase, soon reached Cap Martin, only to find herself faced with the *Sea Breeze* as she turned east once more.

And that was the way it went for the next twenty minutes. The *Monique*, baffled and angry, retreated to a less ridiculous position, where—a couple of miles out to sea—she could heave to and watch the *Sea Breeze* from a distance.

"She should have done that in the first place," Emil said. "Whoever is giving the orders isn't much of a sailor. He's more accustomed to tailing his quarry through city streets."

Bernard, dressed in a heavy ill-fitting sweater borrowed from Emil's locker, clung on tightly to the rail and said, "If he isn't much of a sailor, then he's feeling like me." He was cheerful, but pale of face. He averted his eyes from the waves that seemed to him to be growing bigger. It was colder, too.

"Go below," Emil advised. The clouds were moving, the breeze had strengthened into a wind from the south-east. Not too much force as yet, but it was blowing up.

Bernard shook his head, clung on. Bright sun and blue sky should surely mean that there was nothing to worry about. "I like it here." They were far out in Garavan Bay now. He could see the whole of Menton.

Emil's bout of sharp temper, back in the harbour, had left him. It was the waiting that had irritated him, that and the unnecessary ballast they had been forced to carry in the shape of Bernard. Now, he clapped Bernard's shoulder before he moved inside to the radio. The message from the *Aurora* was due any minute.

Tony was at the wheel, and enjoying himself immensely. He had zigzagged across both the bays, sometimes heading out to sea as though he were actually making for the *Monique*. Then, before he got too close to her, he had steered a wide curve back towards land. In a light breeze, this had been simple enough to manoeuvre, but with the wind strengthening—well, thought Tony, it won't be too pleasant for them sitting out there: they'll have to use more power, keep themselves steady, not let the *Monique* get out of control.

Emil called to him, "Still thumbing your nose at Gorsky? He's got the message by this time."

"But we've lost our advantage," Tony reminded him. Back in the harbour, and even for the first five minutes of this erratic voyage, the *Monique* had been unaware that the *Sea Breeze* knew all about her. The *Monique* had been the watcher, the calculator, the chaser. She hadn't realised that she had been watched, calculated against, and then led into a senseless chase. But now Gorsky knew. The *Sea Breeze* was going no place.

"Well, we've given him a couple of real problems. Is there anyone important on board of us? Has he been duped all the way?"

"And," Tony added, "how much has his own security been endangered? That is what really hurts."

"Just a moment!" Emil pressed his left hand against his earphone, noting down the message as he listened. "Received. Over and out," he said at its end. He brought the slip of paper to Tony. "How's that?" he asked with a wide and happy smile.

The *Aurora*'s message was succinct. *Cargo unloaded. Easy transfer made. Already airborne. Instructing escort return full speed Menton. ETA noon. Will cover your position.*

"An escort?" Emil said. "We could use it."

"If it arrives in time. I think we'll make our move right away. In another twenty minutes that sea is going to be rough. And what d'you make of that, Emil?" Tony pointed to a motor-launch, travelling at full speed, sending spray flying high as it cut and bumped over the waves. "It left the harbour eight minutes ago, has been circling widely around us."

Emil picked up his binoculars. "Looks official to me. Harbour police? They don't like the way you handle a boat."

"I doubt if harbour police would be as wild and erratic as that."

"They're crazy," Emil agreed. "But it must be fun too. I'll go on deck, have a clearer look."

"No. Take the helm. Head her straight out." Tony was pulling all the curtains apart, leaving a glass-enclosed cabin. Conference over, he thought with a smile.

"Towards the *Monique*?"

"That's right. Get within hailing distance."

"Too close."

"All right. Within clear sighting distance. That's all Gorsky will need. His binoculars are as good as ours."

"That's still within pistol range."

"In this rising sea? They couldn't hit an elephant."

"They'll have rifles," Emil warned. But Tony was already stepping out on deck, binoculars ready for a quick look at the motor-launch.

Bernard had retreated to the mast, one arm locked around it. His hair blew wildly around his eyes. But there was still a smile, small but determined, to greet Tony. "No, I'm not going inside," Bernard said. "I prefer to be sick out here."

"So do I," Tony told him. "A useful tip. Stay relaxed. Keep

your knees slightly bent. Sway as the boat sways."

"What's that ship? I think it has been following us."

"That brown boat? A motor-launch. And I think you're right."

"It's like a sheep-dog, moving round and round."

And we are the sheep to be herded? Tony raised his glasses. The launch didn't show any official pennant. Two figures, keeping well down. But not clearly visible, with the spray flying over their heads. Was this some reinforcement that Gorsky had ordered up? Or— "I think you're right again," Tony said. "That's our sheep-dog." But who? Those two crazy maniacs? He kept staring at the launch. Its circling became tighter as it drew protectively nearer. Protective, thought Tony, that's the exact word. They are giving us support. He waved both arms.

Emil was bringing the *Sea Breeze* around. And there, across a short stretch of rough water, was the *Monique*. Clear sighting distance, thought Tony: our empty cabin will be easily seen— Gorsky has his glasses trained on it. He pulled off his cap, said to Bernard, "You take it, keep your ears warm. And stay behind the mast." Then he stepped forward to the rail.

He faced into the wind, his hair blown straight back, revealing his face clearly as he confronted the *Monique*. He could almost feel Gorsky's binoculars boring into him. So there goes my cover, he thought: identity established. But there'll be no rough stuff, no rifle bullet between my eyes. Tempting, though, at this moment, when I'm an easy target. Would Gorsky risk it, with that motor-launch watching? I doubt it. Gorsky likes things neat and natural, all evidence concealed.

Suddenly, the *Monique* moved ahead. Rough stuff after all, thought Tony: she's going to ram our bow, witness or no witness. "Hold on!" he yelled at Bernard.

But within seconds the *Monique* had passed clear, leaving the *Sea Breeze* rearing and bucking in the cross-waves from her wake. Tony picked himself up from the deck, held on to a safety line. He was soaked through. So was Bernard, but he was still in place, both arms tight around the mast.

In the motor-launch Saul said to Walt, "Did you see that?" He stared after the *Monique*. "A real bastard, could have clipped them."

"His last word?" suggested Walt. "All right, let's head for the beach. This storm is really building up now."

The *Sea Breeze* had the same idea. "She'll make it," Walt said. "That kind of old tub usually does."

"Old tub? She looks smooth enough."

"But snub nosed."

"Which was lucky for her."

They fell silent, partly because of the rising sea. The *Monique* was still in sight, on a westerly course, under full power, keeping well clear of the land.

"She'll make it, too," Walt said as they entered Garavan Bay. "Pity that tail wind doesn't catch her stern, tip her bows into—" He stopped short, staring, wiping spray out of his eyes.

For at that moment, the *Monique* had exploded. "My God," said Walt.

And then a second explosion, bigger, louder, flashing a ball of flame.

"My God," echoed Saul. "She had ammunition on board." He looked back at the *Sea Breeze*. But she was still ploughing her steady course towards Menton harbour.

28

By Sunday morning, the storm had blown itself out, the bitter wind and chilling air had gone as quickly as they had come. The promenade was no longer an empty stretch of writhing palm-trees lashed by spray, or a target for pebbles picked up from the beach and thrown by angry waves. Once again people were walking and talking, or sitting at outside café-tables. All had returned to normal.

Except Nicole. She was still partly under shock, Tony noted as he entered under the yellow-striped awnings and saw her seated at her usual window-table. Her dark hair was as smooth and gleaming as ever, and her clothes as smart. But her pale face, perfect in its shape, was even whiter, her large brown eyes still larger. There was no smile on her lips. The morning paper had been pushed aside, coffee was untouched, three half-smoked cigarettes lay in the ashtray.

"Are you early or am I late?" Tony asked as he took the chair opposite her.

"I couldn't sleep, couldn't stay in the house. I've been driving around." She tried to smile, and failed. "But thank you for coming, Tony. It is safe to meet here now, isn't it?"

"Well," he said, "the opposition is in slight disarray. Meanwhile. But let's keep our voices down—until my coffee arrives, at least." He covered her hand with his, and pressed it. "Are you all packed? Ready to leave? I've got a car waiting at the garage—"

"First," she said, drew her hand away, "first I must tell you something." She fell silent, not meeting his eyes, until the waitress brought his coffee and left. Then she looked at him, her voice low but determined. "I'm leaving, Tony. Permanently. I am going to send in my resignation."

"There's no need for that," he said quietly.

"I want out."

"Why?"

"Because I've lost confidence. I was of no help to you. I might even have endangered the whole—"

"On the contrary, you helped a great deal."

"Tony, I don't want excuses and I don't want sympathy. I failed you. I failed everyone."

He glanced around the room, empty except for the waiters and counterman, who were having a discussion of their own in this lull before lunchtime. "You helped," he insisted. "You made that house up on Garavan Hill a very pleasant place for him."

Yes, she thought in anguish, Parracini had found it very pleasant indeed, far easier than he had ever expected. "And so he became too sure of himself?" she asked bitterly. "He thought I was a simple-minded idiot, and Bill was an easy-going American, and Bernard and Brigitte were just part of the furniture."

"Well, he's disillusioned about all that now."

"About Bill—yes."

"It all worked out, you know," Tony tried.

"With no help from me."

"You're really determined to ruin my day, aren't you?" Tony asked half-jokingly.

"Sorry. You should be celebrating, instead of—sorry, Tony. At least you got your sleep, I see." He looked a different man, in his well-cut jacket, excellent shirt and tie, from the one who had driven up to the house yesterday along with Bernard, two dishevelled figures in borrowed clothes, incongruous in a Mercedes. He had stayed only long enough to tell her about Parracini.

"Twelve solid hours."

"At the *Alexandre*?"

He shook his head and smiled. He was thinking of the waiter who had been scared witless. It had seemed the easiest solution to have Saul pay his bill and collect his clothes.

"See?" she asked, and sighed unhappily.

"See what?"

"You don't trust me, Tony."

He said nothing to that. What's behind all this? he wondered.

"You could have told me more when we met here on Friday. You could have drawn me into the action. You used to do that. We worked well together, once."

"I hadn't anything to tell you on Friday."

She stared, incredulous. "You mean, you didn't know about—about his real identity?"

"As much as we all knew, you included."

"Then why did you come to Menton?"

"A simple tour of inspection. That was all."

"But you sensed something, didn't you?"

Again he said nothing.

"You thought I liked him too much. You thought—"

"Let's say you were too uncritical of him." Tony's anger was sudden, surprising even him. He regained his calm. "You didn't keep him in check. But what worried me most, on Friday morning, was that he was endangering himself." Tony shook his head over that stupidity. "We were all fooled, at least part of the way. So shut up, will you, darling? You aren't the only one who's hiding a blistered ego under his celebration shirt."

"Except," she said slowly, "I didn't even earn a celebration shirt. Not this time. And so I'm backing out. If this could happen once, it could happen again."

"All you need is some rest and recreation. I'm driving to Paris, a nice slow trip, regular meals, no wet sea, no telephones. Will you join me?" The question was casual, the invitation not.

She smiled, but she shook her head. "You have plenty of girls, Tony. They'll be at every stop along the way on that nice slow trip." The smile vanished, her eyes left his, her voice seemed strangled. "I liked him, Tony." She looked up, then, "I really liked him."

So that's it, thought Tony. She fell in love with Parracini. "And you're still in love—" he began, and stopped, his lips compressed.

Nicole saw his face tighten. She gathered up her handbag and left so swiftly that he was only half-way to his feet as she touched his hand and was gone.

"Nicole—"

She was out on the sidewalk, walking steadfastly away, the skirt of her loose white coat swinging about her red leather boots.

She made the choice, he thought, and sat down again. His coffee tasted bitter. He reached for the abandoned newspaper, if only to stop thinking about Nicole.

Front-page prominence was given to the two explosions yesterday on board a luxury cabin cruiser, and to a lot of wild speculation. The only factual item was that a naval patrol-boat, arriving just after the *Monique* had disintegrated, had searched for survivors, an impossible task, due to the heavy seas prevailing at that time. None had been found.

But on an inside page, tucked away at the bottom of a column, was a small report on a suicide at Shandon Villa. Tony rose, went over to the telephone, searched for some *jetons*, and dialled the Kelsos' number.

It was Dorothea who answered. "Tony—we wondered where you were. Why didn't you call us yesterday?"

"I was pretty well tied up. But what about lunch today?"

"Oh, Tony—we can't possibly. I'm in the middle of packing. We leave tomorrow. Tom is down in Menton now, making all the final arrangements. About Chuck. He's—he's going home too."

"Did you see that Shandon made today's paper?"

"Oh, that! It didn't tell you anything. But I've got the inside story!"

"From whom?"

"Remember that nice young policeman, the one who came up to the house on Friday night to get our statement about the burglary?"

"Louis?"

AGENT IN PLACE

"He came back yesterday to ask more questions."

That was Louis. Definitely.

"He had been down at Shandon Villa—"

"When?" Tony asked, his interest quickening.

"Around breakfast time. Just after Rick Nealey shot himself. Incredible, wasn't it?"

The only thing that had astonished Tony was the quickness of it all. He'd have given Nealey three or four more days, perhaps a week. What had happened that had made Gorsky move so fast?

Dorothea said, "It *was* suicide, Tony. He was found in his bedroom, with the gun in one hand and a letter in the other."

"Typed?"

"No. It was in Nealey's own writing." She laughed as she added, "You really are a very suspicious man, Tony. Nealey had been overworked; and depressed. As I think he should have been."

Tony restrained a sudden attack of sarcasm. Not to Dorothea, not to dear sweet trusting believing Dorothea. Had she forgotten the fakery of Chuck's accident? "Yes," he agreed. "But who else had been wandering in and out of that bedroom?" One of Gorsky's electricians, or the little redhead...

"You don't think it was—" Dorothea began slowly.

"No need to think anything. It's all past tense now."

"Yes," she said. "Yes." Then she roused herself. "Tom's going to be disappointed he missed you. Can you drop in this evening?"

"No, I'm leaving too. I'm on my way, in fact."

"Then we'll see you in Washington. When are you coming to America again?"

419

"Can't say exactly. But we'll meet."

"Yes. We really must have dinner together. And talk." She sounded vague, as if she were already thousands of miles away.

"Better get back to your packing."

She laughed. "You should see the complete chaos around me. Everything seems to have multiplied."

But that was all she had to worry about now: where to put what into which suitcase. "Give Tom my best. How is he?"

"Fine, just fine," she said happily. "Our thanks, Tony. And my love. See you some time." She ended the call.

"Goodbye, beautiful," he said into the silent 'phone. Some time... That was how it went.

He paid the check and moved quickly out of the café, felt a strange depression as he stood there, among brightly-checked tablecloths under a yellow-striped awning. Now the garage, he thought, and a car with luggage in place, ready to go. But he still stood, undecided. Out of habit he scanned the faces that passed him, the cars that were parked along the kerb. And suddenly, just ahead of him, there was a car he recognised. A small red Opel. He began walking.

Nicole hadn't seen him. She was seated at the wheel, her smooth dark head bent, her shoulders drooping, her eyes on her hands lying inert on her lap. She was a girl crying out for help.

Tony opened the car door. She looked up, her cheeks tear-stained, her large eyes despairing. "Move over," he said. And she did.

He got in and started the engine, glancing round at her suitcases piled into the back seat. "Where?"

"I don't know," she said, barely audible. She dried her

cheeks, and tried to laugh at herself. She broke down once more. "Oh, Tony—I thought I'd never see you again."

He wondered, then, if her tears might have been for him, and not for Parracini. For a moment he stared at her. "You don't lose me as easily as that," he told her. His old smile was back, his spirits rising. He edged out into the traffic and headed for the garage.

ABOUT THE AUTHOR

Helen MacInnes, whom the *Sunday Express* called 'the Queen of spy writers', was the author of many distinguished suspense novels.

Born in Scotland, she studied at the University of Glasgow and University College, London, then went to Oxford after her marriage to Gilbert Highet, the eminent critic and educator. In 1937 the Highets went to New York, and except during her husband's war service, Helen MacInnes lived there ever since.

Since her first novel *Above Suspicion* was published in 1941 to immediate success, all her novels have been bestsellers; *The Salzburg Connection* was also a major film.

Helen MacInnes died in September 1985.

THE HARRY HOUDINI MYSTERIES

BY DANIEL STASHOWER

The Dime Museum Murders
The Floating Lady Murder
The Houdini Specter

In turn-of-the-century New York, the Great Houdini's confidence in his own abilities is matched only by the indifference of the paying public. Now the young performer has the opportunity to make a name for himself by attempting the most amazing feats of his fledgling career—solving what seem to be impenetrable crimes. With the reluctant help of his brother Dash, Houdini must unravel murders, debunk frauds and escape from danger that is no illusion...

PRAISE FOR DANIEL STASHOWER

"A romp that cleverly combines history and legend, taking a few liberties with each. Mr. Stashower has done his homework... This is charming...it might have amused Conan Doyle." *The New York Times*

"In his first mystery, Stashower paired Harry Houdini and Sherlock Holmes to marvelous effect."
Chicago Tribune

"Stashower's clever adaptation of the Conan Doyle conventions—Holmes's uncanny powers of observation and of disguise, the scenes and customs of Victorian life—makes it fun to read. Descriptions and explanations of some of Houdini's astonishing magic routines add an extra dimension to this pleasant adventure."
Publishers Weekly

LADY, GO DIE!

BY MICKEY SPILLANE & MAX ALLAN COLLINS

THE LOST MIKE HAMMER NOVEL

Hammer and Velda go on vacation to a small beach town on Long Island after wrapping up the Williams case (*I, the Jury*). Walking romantically along the boardwalk, they witness a brutal beating at the hands of some vicious local cops—Hammer wades in to defend the victim. When a woman turns up naked—and dead—astride the statue of a horse in the small-town city park, how she wound up this unlikely Lady Godiva is just one of the mysteries Hammer feels compelled to solve...

COMPLEX 90

BY MICKEY SPILLANE & MAX ALLAN COLLINS

THE LOST MIKE HAMMER NOVEL

Hammer accompanies a conservative politician to Moscow on a fact-finding mission. While there, he is arrested by the KGB on a bogus charge, and imprisoned; but he quickly escapes, creating an international incident by getting into a firefight with Russian agents.

On his stateside return, the government is none too happy with Mr. Hammer. Russia is insisting upon his return to stand charges, and various government agencies are following him. A question dogs our hero: why him? Why does Russia want him back, and why (as evidence increasingly indicates) was he singled out to accompany the senator to Russia in the first place?

KING OF THE WEEDS

BY MICKEY SPILLANE & MAX ALLAN COLLINS

THE PENULTIMATE MIKE HAMMER NOVEL

As his old friend Captain Pat Chambers of Homicide approaches retirement, Hammer finds himself up against a clever serial killer targeting only cops.

A killer Chambers had put away many years ago is suddenly freed on new, apparently indisputable evidence, and Hammer wonders if, somehow, this seemingly placid, very odd old man might be engineering cop killings that all seem to be either accidental or by natural causes.

At the same time Hammer and Velda are dealing with the fallout—some of it mob, some of it federal government—over the $89 billion dollar cache the detective is (rightly) suspected of finding not long ago...